P R A ... R N

ALA BEST FICTION FOR YOUNG ADULTS
2014 TAYSHAS READING LIST SELECTION
ALA *BOOKLIST* EDITORS' CHOICE
BULLETIN BLUE RIBBON BOOK

"Sprawling, messy, vulgar, sexy, irreverent, violent, bighearted, harrowing. These are just a few of the many adjectives about to be hurled in the direction of this roaring freight train of a debut. In telling the tale of a tumultuous decadelong antagonism between two boys destined to fulfill their ying/yang fate, Hassan constructs three of the most vividly alive characters in recent YA fiction. A travelogue of the subsequent ten years of parties, drugs, sex, and secrets may sound exhausting, but Hassan writes with such fire and drills down so deep that it's difficult to believe these characters are fictional—this would read fast even at twice the length. Gutsily conceived, written, and edited, this is, quite simply, a great American novel."

—ALA *Booklist* (starred review)

"The story Crash tells is deeply disturbing in its searingly accurate portrait of boys in contemporary society; Crash's voice is insistently authentic, documenting the life of an upper-middle-class, medicated teen reared in a world where values are determined by media standards of appearance and privilege. His relationship with his father, in particular, offers a chilling indictment on the failures of intergenerational communication and masculine values. A must-read for teens and adults alike who want to understand the lack of empathy that permeates contemporary culture; it offers no answers, but the mirror it does present may be chilling enough to awaken readers to the costs of not getting it right."

—*BCCB* (starred review)

"*Crash and Burn* is more than just a coming-of-age story. Dealing with the expectations of heroism, ADD, broken families, and just getting by during adolescence, this story is not only timely but a necessary read. Hassan lifts the veil of what we as a society want to believe teenagers are doing from what they actually are."

—Teenreads.com

"Michael Hassan has written a darkly funny story about a school shooting. I didn't know it was possible but I knew it was brave. Thankfully, he pulls it off."

—Ned Vizzini, author of *It's Kind of a Funny Story*

"Hassan effectively conveys the numbing influence of drugs and alcohol on Steven's life and the messy social relationships of young adulthood, with a tone that blends ennui with an undercurrent of aggression."

—*Publishers Weekly*

"The protagonist is a restless antihero whose maturation and self-realization occur in (often amusing) spurts of self-awareness. . . . Crash's spontaneity is engaging and entertaining."

—*SLJ*

CRASH AND BURN

BY MICHAEL HASSAN

Balzer + Bray

An Imprint of HarperCollins*Publishers*

Balzer + Bray is an imprint of HarperCollins Publishers.

Crash and Burn
Copyright © 2013 by Michael Hassan
www.epicreads.com

Library of Congress Cataloging-in-Publication Data
Hassan, Michael.
    Crash and Burn / by Michael Hassan. — 1st ed.
        p.   cm.
    Summary: Steven "Crash" Crashinsky relates his sordid ten-year relationship with
David "Burn" Burnett, the boy he stopped from taking their high school hostage at
gunpoint.
    ISBN 978-0-06-211291-0 (pbk.)
    [1. Interpersonal relations—Fiction. 2. Emotional problems—Fiction.
3. Violence—Fiction. 4. High schools—Fiction. 5. Schools—Fiction.] I. Title.
PZ7.H2778Cr 2013   2012004280
[Fic]—dc23   CIP
                                                                          AC

Typography by Ray Shappell
14 15 16 17 18 CG/RRDH 10 9 8 7 6 5 4 3 2 1
❖
First paperback edition, 2014

FOR HENRY AND LENA

PROLOGUE

I'm not gonna lie to you.

I'm not exactly the hero that everyone says I am.

Sure, you may have read about me in *People* or in some other magazine that had my picture on the cover: me and Medusa staring out at the ocean, like we're deep in thought, me standing, Medusa sitting good-dog style, both of us poised on a jetty by the ocean, waves pounding. What no one can tell is that my sister Jamie was off camera, holding a box of dog treats, or that I'm being totally soaked.

I'm all Hollywood now.

Which is totally fine with me since I start college in a few months, at a school in the Northeast that wouldn't otherwise have even looked at my application, given that I didn't exactly have spectacular SAT scores, and my GPA, let's face it, sucked big-time. Only six months ago I couldn't get a third-rate college to accept me, even with Newman's incredibly well written essay, and then, surprise surprise, after April 21, a bunch of the first-tier schools that I applied to actually started recruiting me.

The one that I chose (correction: my parents helped me choose) promised they are going to give me the athlete treatment even though I'm no great athlete, which means that I will have a tutor and all kinds of other privileges not meant for ordinary kids, not even the other LD kids.

Get this: They even gave me what is essentially a free ride (heavy-duty scholarship money, to all you people who don't have kids trying to get into colleges, and oh yeah, for you same people, LD stands for "Learning Disabled").

As to being LD, no big, as pretty much one quarter of my graduating class at Meadows High can claim to be one or more version of this label. For example, there's ADD and ADHD and dyslexia and bipolar disorder and a bunch of other syndromes and of course MC, which was Mr. Connelly's label for any kid with learning disabilities (as in "mentally challenged"). More on Connelly later, of course, except to say that he took pride in creating nicknames for those freshman kids who had the misfortune of getting him for English. He didn't, however, create mine.

Kids have been calling me "Crash" since first grade. He wasn't about to change that. More on that later too.

But first this . . .

My name is Steven Crashinsky, and I have attention deficit hyperactivity disorder, ADHD to you. This is the story of how I saved Meadows High. . . .

Scratch that.

Actually I'd rather begin this way:

My name is Steven Crashinsky, and I saved over a thousand people one Monday in the middle of April when a kid named David Burnett went psycho and held the entire school hostage, taking over the faculty lounge at Meadows High armed with assault weapons and high-powered explosives.

You probably already know this if you've read the newspapers in the last two months or bothered to watch the news (if you haven't, Google me now and my name will come up like two hundred thousand times).

Of course, me saving the entire faculty and student body at Meadows didn't exactly happen the way it was described in news reports. There is another part of the story, a secret that only I know. Until now.

OK, scratch that too.

Here's the thing:

I have this book agent, Sally Levine, who's a major milf even though she's probably, like, forty. She got me this book deal of major-league proportions. All because of what she calls "the secret."

The Secret, as it turns out, was also the name of another book. I know this because when I suggested it as the title of *my* book, Sally told me that it wasn't a good idea, being as there already was a bestseller by that name about something entirely different.

Whatever.

The secret, at least *my* secret, is about the words David Burnett whispered to me that afternoon, which ended the siege at Meadows High School, the words that have plagued me since April 21. Since then, whenever anyone asked what it was that David said to me when it all went down, I always answer, "That's between me and David Burnett."

Actually, I didn't mean for it to be a secret. I just didn't want to talk about it at the time. And then Sally ended up making such a big thing out of it, which brings me back to how I got a book deal in the first place.

Since the newspaper reporters wanted to know the secret, and the television reporters wanted to know, and everyone else I met wanted to know, Sally, being good at what she does, found a way to make sure that I would be well compensated for revealing the now-famous secret.

In fact, she developed an entire strategy around it and was able to get me onto all those morning TV talk shows where I did so well that she felt that she could not only get me a book deal, but she could possibly also get me endorsements and stuff. Point being, those interviews were cake, basically because I got to say the same thing over and over again, always ending with some reporter asking about the secret and me answering, "That's between me and David Burnett." Mostly nodding and making sure I looked good on camera, with my practiced look of concern, heroism, and of course, my mysterious Crash smile at the very end, the combination of which was designed to pretty much guarantee me an unlimited supply of tail.

Not that I need any help in that area, no complaints from me, but if I should ever need it, no doubt being a hero and having a book out will most definitely close the deal.

So not only did Sally manage to get a bunch of publishers interested, one of them agreed that I can say virtually anything I want in this book, because she pitched it as the raw truth kind of story, which means, get this: In my contract (seriously), I have a paragraph that says that I have final approval over everything that's printed, which means that if I write it and I want it in, the publisher can't cut it.

Still, she has this vision that the book should be something that high school English teachers would be able to encourage their students to read. So she told me, "Steven, while it doesn't have to be completely sanitized, it should be, let's call it, a 'PG work,' using the movie analogy."

She said this to me during a meeting at my lawyer's office (actually my father's lawyer), this big huge bald guy in an Armani suit who sat behind his huge desk the whole time, taking notes while Sally went on and on, with me sitting forward on this deep leather couch to avoid sinking in, all wired up, thinking about all of the books I have had to read since ninth grade: *To Kill a Mockingbird*, *Kon-Tiki*, *All Quiet on the Western Front*, ugh, *The Grapes of Wrath*, whatever.

And then it hits me for the first time that other kids will actually be reading my book, possibly alongside those so-called classics. That is assuming, of course, that I can actually write it.

Except, of course, what no one is talking about is how the fuck am I actually going to write a book?

Trying to put that thought out of my mind, what I tell her is "I don't think I could do it as a PG version. What about an 'R,' as in kids under seventeen will have to get their mom's permission to buy the book?" (Even though I know kids under seventeen do not need their parents' permission to read anything.)

Just so she's clear, I remind her, no way can certain words be avoided, not if I'm going to tell the story the way it happened. And even though I know she knows what I'm talking about, she still asks:

"What kind of language do you feel is necessary?"

Me: "Like 'fuck.'" (Thinking I'm probably ruining my chance to be like the *Moby Dick* guy, whose books have been taught for forever, but fuck it.)

Sally: "Can it be avoided? Or at least used sparingly?"

Me (thinking about it): "Uh-uh. Ever see *Superbad*?"

From the looks of things, *Superbad* meant nothing to her.

Sally: "Well, can you refrain from vulgarity in any great doses? Use euphemisms if possible? Substitute suggestive words for the vulgar ones?"

Me: "I can try" (knowing there is no way I can try, not if I'm going to tell the real story).

Her. "Good. That's all we can ask."

Me: "So we're good on 'fuck' then?"

Sally shoots me the *enough is enough* look, which, if you have ADHD, you've seen this look more than a few times in your life. So this is nothing new for me.

Now my lawyer gets his turn.

He motions for me to approach his desk, where there are four copies of the book contract laid out side by side by side by side. He hands me a pen, and I pick up one of the contracts and thumb through it. Like no chance in hell was I actually going to read it, but I did want to see the money part in writing. And sure enough, there it was, this big huge number underlined and then spelled out. All because Sally made the secret such a big-time thing.

Thank you, Sally Levine.

The lawyer points out where to sign, and that's when I notice my father's signature on each of the four copies.

Four days earlier, my father reluctantly cosigned another contract, one for a new BMW, part of our deal. Except as he was signing for the car, he made it superclear: He does not approve.

But then again, Jacob Crashinsky has not approved of anything I've done since I was born. Since he does not live with us anymore as my parents got divorced years ago—because of me, or so he claimed (more on that later)—I don't give a shit what he thinks, as he no longer controls my life on a daily basis. And surprisingly, even though he now lives with a young, very beautiful new wife, who has saved my life more than a few times, he hasn't chilled out even one bit since he was living with us.

Point being, on his way out of the BMW dealership, he reminded me that he will be in charge of the funds I get from the book deal, and that he'll be investing the money with the full expectation that I will have to return most, if not all of it, because, like with every other project that I've ever started, he has zero expectations about my ability to complete the task.

That, of course, makes me one thousand percent motivated, just to prove him wrong. Not for the money, not for the fame, not for the guaranteed tail . . . just so I get to wave a manuscript in his face with a big fuck-you smile.

Can't wait, is what I'm thinking as I start signing the contracts. And then the lawyer holds me off for a second.

"Steven, just to confirm," he tells me, "what you are agreeing to produce is an absolutely truthful account of everything that went on in your life, including the events that led up to the siege on 4/21."

I nod. No big. But this is clearly not good enough for him.

"What is essential here is accuracy," he goes on. "What that means is, you *must* avoid writing anything that you cannot verify. Do you understand what libel is?"

Me: "Sure." (No idea, actually.)

Him (knowing I'm bluffing): "It's writing something negative that is not true about another party, something that injures that party's reputation. If you libel Mr. Burnett or anyone else, they can sue you. So as long as you tell the absolute, verifiable truth, there will not be a problem. But just so there's no mistake, if you say something derogatory and it proves false, Mr. Burnett can not only sue you, he can sue the publisher, and he can sue your father, who is signing on your behalf." He says this like it's supposed to scare me.

It almost makes me laugh. But no problem. I don't need to make anything up. The truth is weird enough.

OK, so the meeting goes on and they talk about some other terms in the contract and then about timing, and Sally reminds me again that I will need to finish the draft by the end of the summer, before I start college. And then she talks and talks about the structure of the book and what should be in and what shouldn't and my mind drifts off (no surprise there, ADHD, remember?) and the lawyer is Clear and Sally is Clear and I am Clear: We all have our jobs to do.

Sounds easy enough, except as I leave the office, I start thinking about actually writing this thing, and how I probably should have listened better.

Whatever.

I have the entire summer to figure it out.

CHAPTER ONE

THE CLUB CREW

So me and Newman are smoking in my new car, in the lot across the street from the nature preserve, where pretty much everyone goes to bake, and Newman asks me how's it going with the book and I have to tell him:

"Not."

He takes a long hit on the bowl, hacking up a lung as he passes it back. I snort a major hit, thick smoke out my nose and mouth at the same time.

Excellent weed. Good start-of-the-summer weed. Smooth, herbal tasting, not resiny or rough, but I cough another hacking lung cough anyway. I am feeling it before the smoke even leaves my lungs. Not that I'm a lightweight or anything. I can go hit for hit with you on the fattest blunt you've ever rolled, no flinching. Even when your eyes roll back, I'll be in for a few more hits.

This stuff, however, is superdank.

"What do you mean, *not*?" Newman going for another hit. The BMW is pretty much filled with smoke by now.

It's strange for me and Newman to be smoking by ourselves. Typically, there's at least four of us, sometimes five, sometimes the entire Club Crew, as in me, Newman, Pete, Evan, Bosco, Kenny, and Bobby, in any combination, core members of the Club, which is what we've called ourselves since freshman year. The "Crew" part came later, since Bobby started wearing only J.Crew shirts, which we all thought was totally gay until we all started wearing J.Crew clothes too, since his sister was working there, which of course got us the name Club Crew since we kind of matched, which of course made us all look totally gay, which was what everyone said, and which was nothing but a joke, but it stuck for us.

Point is, we tend to hang together most nights as we have in the past, when we're not hanging with other groups or partying with the Herd Girls at Kelly's or some other house.

And whenever we hang together, of course, we smoke weed together.

Mostly every night. And mostly we start in the lot across the street from the nature preserve. No one ever bothers us there, even though pretty much everybody knows that if there are cars parked by the nature preserve after sundown, some kids are baking there.

"What do you mean, *not*?" Newman is asking again. "It's been two weeks."

"Yeah, tell me about it."

Alex Newman is one of the top five smartest kids I have ever met. He's not just school smart, which he also is, since he never got anything less than an A– in any class, but he's also a super-creative genius, which separates him from the other smartest kids I know. David Burnett, for example, was always an off-the-charts genius, but he was also off-the-charts crazy, so you couldn't count him. Christina is pretty much the smartest book-smart girl I know, but she's kind of hard to understand sometimes, even though she is mad talented. Kenny is brilliant, half Chinese and all, but Newman, with his creativity and his understanding of real-life shit, totally has them all beat, if you ask me. Facts, weird stuff, languages, whatever, he knows all this shit cold (OK, Burnett probably more in this area, I will concede this).

Plus, Newman can do one thing that none of the others can do, as in, on the spot, he can make up a perfect story, totally spontaneously, and then turn it into a screenplay in like a single day.

No one would argue the point about him being a creative genius.

So it makes sense that he wants to write and direct movies, which everyone believes he'll end up doing. Not only that, he is going to NYU film school to learn how to do it. Not only NYU, but Tisch School of the Arts. Like a hundred thousand people apply to this program every year, and like a hundred get in. Newman could have gotten into any college he wanted to. Like, Harvard material, which is where his parents wanted him to go and which he actually got into.

Newman, however, had his own ideas. And so, Tisch.

With him being the most creative kid I know, I figured he would be the best guy to go to for advice. He was away in California for the beginning of the summer, so this is the first time I have seen him since graduation.

Another hit for each of us.

"What the fuck have you been doing all this time, Crash?" Now Newman is starting to sound like Sally, who emails me asking for an update, like, every day. And every day I tell her I'm working on it.

But I'm not.

I'm playing *Grand Theft Auto* on PS3, or *Guitar Hero* or *Rock Band* or some other game. Or I'm hanging with the Club Crew down at Pinky's or going down to Rye Playland or baking by the nature preserve. Or partying with kids from some other Westchester town who heard about me or saw me on TV. Thing is, with all these things I'm doing, I am not writing. Not a word since the book contract was signed.

"Why the fuck not?" asks Newman.

So I confess, "Why the fuck not is because I have no fucking clue how to write a book."

There it is, out in the open. I am in *way* over my head,

thinking will I have to give the Beamer back when they find out I can't do this, plus pay back the rest of the money. And worst of all, admit to Jacob Crashinsky that his son is a failure, no surprise there.

Fuckme.

My cell buzzes. I look at the number: Bosco. Probably looking to score some free weed. Bosco is always looking to score some free weed. I don't answer it.

Newman takes another hit. "You are *fucked*," he says. "You'll never get it done in time." Then he coughs a spitcough, bright yellow lung butter, mostly out the window but not completely. I would not tolerate that from any other friend, but Newman is Newman.

One other thing about Newman: Besides being brilliant, he is absolutely realistic about everything, so when he says I'm not going to get it done, he is probably right, which, tell you the truth, scares me a little more.

I wait for his next words of wisdom.

. . . And wait.

He is playing around with the satellite radio, blasting the Foo Fighters. Switches to some eighties heavy metal, which is practically all Newman ever listens to these days. Adjusting the balance, the treble, then upping the bass until the car is pumping.

Now he can think. I have watched his mind work for four years now. I know his thinking face.

"Have you even tried?" he says, still deep in thought.

I tell him, "I sit there with my MacBook, for, like, at least three hours every day." True, but mostly with a DVD in it, or iTunes, looking for music, movies, or otherwise checking out porn. C'mon, Alex, I am thinking to myself, watching him think. Come up with *something*.

Thing is, he's working on his own screenplay of the siege at Meadows High School. It starts, he tells me, with a shot of the elementary school, camera following down the main hall, panning down the stairs to the basement, all spooky and dark, then into the janitor's office, where the door opens, then closes, and we see two eight-year-old boys, a mountain of toilet paper rolls, books, and newspapers between them. One kid fat and sloppy, the other thin and wiry. You can tell right away that the fat kid is in control. Fat boy grabs a small bottle off the shelf, pours it on to the paper mountain, then takes a lighter and works it through the pile until the entire thing ignites. Thin boy, looking startled, slinks back, just as . . . the door opens, and a tall, authoritative male figure walks in. Freeze-frame. Titles under the boys, "How David Burnett Got His Nickname."

It is genius, way better than I can do.

My cell phone buzzes again, this time a text message. Again from Bosco, asking where we are and whether we're gonna meet him.

I text him back.

Not now.

"So you think I should start all the way back in grade school?" I ask, which had never occurred to me, because I was mostly thinking that the whole book was just going to be about the days that led up to me saving the school, which is what I tell Newman, who says:

"Dude, you can't make it just about the siege. It's got to be about your relationship with David from the beginning, the story from an insider's perspective. Otherwise it's going to be the same as all the news stories that were already printed. That's what I'm doing for the screenplay. For me, it's about two kids who are oddly alike and yet completely different. I even thought about telling the same story from both perspectives. Flash to Crash, flash to Burn. Get it?"

"Sure, I get it," I tell him, although I have no idea what he's talking about. Not only that, but I wonder what he meant by "oddly alike," given that there is no part of me that is like David Burnett. Newman is, to tell you the truth, pissing me off.

He continues. "You should exploit the parallels: both of you guys having your issues with school, you know, your fathers, the Thanksgiving thing, his mom and your mom were friendly, everything, you know, with Roxanne, then there's basketball and poker and Christina and Massachusetts and the wedding. You have a ton of things to write about. Make them each a chapter. Write about all of that. You admitted that there were times when you two were friends."

"Not really. . . ." He is further pissing me off.

Newman shoots me a look like I'm missing the point, which I probably am.

My cell phone buzzes again. This time it's Pete texting,

> **Where's Newman? You got trees?**

I am now feeling the full effects of the weed, and I'm starting not to care so much about the whole book thing, so I text back,

> **With Newman now, meet us at Pinky's**
> **When?**
> **15**
> **You talk to Bosco?**
> **Not yet.**
> **He's going crazy.**
> **So?**
> **So who's got the shit?**

Now I'm completely annoyed, because they all know I have the shit. The way it's been going down all summer is Bosco relying on me for weed to always get him high, not working or contributing at all, then complaining that it's shwag and smoking it anyways, saying he can get better, but never having the money, then one by one, the rest of the Club hitting me up for my stash, all counting on the fact that I have book money to fund them getting fucked up.

We get to Pinky's. Once an amusement park for kids, now a burger palace/ice cream and coffee store, a combination Johnny Rockets, Starbucks, and Dairy Queen, which is perfect for two things: hanging when there's nowhere else to go, and eating like an animal when you're high. Perfect because of its gigantic parking lot where the rides used to be, a parking lot where hardly any adults ever park. Perfect also because for some reason the cops never come around or bother anyone as long as everyone sticks to the Pinky's Rule, which is, never get high or drunk in the parking lot itself. Pretty much we all stick to that rule, being as we are all high or wasted by the time we get there.

I spot Kenny's Explorer immediately and we pull up beside it, me trying to figure out who is in the car. They are clearly violating the Pinky's Rule because the inside of the car is clouded in smoke. Kenny and Evan and Bobby and Bobby's girlfriend, Ashley, who is in the backseat with Bobby. She has been coming along with him too often for my taste. Not that she's all that bad, just that she's real quiet, which makes Bobby quiet, which is annoying because Bobby was never quiet before. Plus she's a little weird, if you ask me.

Me to Newman: "Doesn't he go anywhere without her?"

Newman: "She's kind of like his Yoko." Which to me is a cool reference, because Bobby is a musician, probably the best guitarist in our school. And from what I've heard, he started bringing her around during every practice with his band. And even though I have no proof, I heard he wrote a song about her.

Newman: "Can't *wait* to hear his new song." So I guess the rumors are true.

The Explorer's windows roll down. Kenny sticks his head out and says, "Yo, Crash, where the fuck is Bosco?" But I'm already getting a text from Bosco that says, "where the fuck r u?" Which means either he was stupid or didn't see us, because I told him where we were going. So before I text back "Pinky's" I see him walking over with Pete and two guys I never saw before, which means that they are probably there to mooch off me. Now I am even more pissed off, because Bosco, no doubt, has promised to share my stuff with people I don't even fucking know.

So now I'm sitting in a booth with the P Burger Special with fries smothered in cheese sauce, ketchup on the side, and it is fucking awesome, awesome enough to make me forget how pissed off I am. Newman is across from me, has his own version of the munchies with a Diet Coke and a V Burger, which is the veggie version of my real meal, as Newman is now some kind of vegetarian and has not eaten any animals since the beginning of senior year.

Bosco and the others decided to wait outside, being as they already ate and they are there mainly because they are waiting for my weed. Fuck them, they can wait.

"I've been thinking how I would approach this book thing. . . ." Newman is scrunching his eyes with his fingers, either really stoned or *really* thinking.

"You want some milk shake?" I ask him. He waves me off, still scrunching. I keep forgetting that he's the kind of vegetarian that won't even have milk. I mean, like, nothing that has anything to do with animals. No shit, since September, I don't think I've seen him eat anything that I would eat.

Bosco's coming in now. I knew he couldn't wait until after my burger.

"So, Crash . . ." Bosco leans over the table, practically dribbling into my fries.

Newman now begins to recite out loud:

"Bosco is a skinny kid, lanky, almost gawky, which makes him look taller than he actually is. Curly haired, freckled with acne, he sometimes looks in the mirror and wonders if a girl is ever going to love him or touch him where it matters. Maybe one day, but definitely not this summer, and definitely not Amanda Jenkins."

"What the fuck?" yells Bosco, though I totally get it. Now either I'm really thinking clearly or I'm really, really stoned, because I am thinking on Newman's level for a minute, which I can sometimes do when I'm superhigh, as in see into other people's minds. And what I'm seeing amazes me, because at that moment I know, *I totally know*, that Newman can, if he wants, dictate my book from start to finish without blinking, without missing a beat.

I mean, his description of Bosco was a better Bosco than Bosco was himself. I immediately know two things: (1) his screenplay is going to be way better than my book, and (2) he doesn't care about his screenplay, because he is trying to teach me how to do it on my own. I wouldn't even have thought to describe Bosco in my book before that very moment.

"Why did you have to bring up Amanda?" Bosco literally snaps at him, like he doesn't know that everyone knows he loves her and he's got no shot with her. No way, not ever.

"Give us a minute," Newman tells him, and Bosco, being majorly offended, is already on his way out anyways.

My mind is suddenly spinning with the possibility that I could, if I continued to think like Newman, actually bang out a book in a few weeks.

"Like I said, I've been thinking about how I would approach this if I was you. All you have to do is dictate stuff right into a voice recorder and then have it typed up. It will definitely be better than you think," he says, shedding absolutely no light on my problem. "Thing is, you need to write about everything, every day, no matter what. Start a journal and put everything in there, absolutely everything you can think of into it, stuff like your thoughts, what's going on in your life now, whatever you can remember from back in the day. This stuff . . ." He motions around the room to what is going on in Pinky's at that very moment.

"Pinky's? I'm not putting Pinky's in my book," I say, not getting it at first, but then sort of getting it.

He continues in his Newman way, not even hearing me, being all consumed with his thoughts. "Then, when you have enough stuff, just give the whole thing to your agent. Let her worry about it. I mean, you can definitely do this, Steven, I *know* what you are capable of when you get your mind going on something. No one knows better than I do. Plus you happen to write really well. Did you forget what you learned? I don't think so. Why don't you start by just going grade by grade, building up to the day you saved the school. You can absolutely describe what you felt that day. Hour by hour—we've done that before. Use that total-recall thing you can do when you're high."

He's right. I still remember every minute of that day, from the moment that I passed Burn on the steps of the school when he was going in and I was coming out to the exact conversation I had with Jamie when she called me on my cell after I went back to sleep that morning, wasted from the night before and determined not to show up for any classes. After all, it was our unofficial Senior Skip Day.

Maybe it's just being in Newman's presence, or maybe it's the weed, but I'm actually beginning to believe I can do it. I can write a whole book. Starting from that very moment in Pinky's and working my way backward.

I can do this. No doubt in my mind. All I have to do is to approach this thing the way I do everything else:

Superhigh.

HOW BURN BECAME BURN

William McAllister Elementary School.

The oldest building in the neighborhood. I remember the smell more than anything else. That and the fact that it was supposed to be haunted. I think William McAllister was some kind of general in the Revolutionary War, at least that's what I remember hearing, but I couldn't prove this having searched the internet and having not come up with his name.

Anyways, when we started there, the older kids told us that General McAllister's spirit still lingered in the lunchroom and always made strange noises throughout that building. Point was, you definitely didn't want to go down those halls by yourself. Not ever. Pete once claimed to see a woman walking on air when he was on his way to the nurse's office.

And the principal, this super-old guy, Principal Seidman, looked pretty much like a goblin, all pasty and hunched over. Sometimes he showed up in the middle of class and just stood around with his hands clasped together in front of his belt, watching us through these really thick glasses.

He had this saying, which he would blurt out all the time. He would look at one of us (mostly me) and say, "A word to the wise is worth two of the eyes."

What the fuck was that supposed to mean anyways?

He's dead now, so there's no way of finding out.

He knew me by name because I was always getting into trouble. Sometimes he would stop me during recess in the playground and say, "Steven, a word to the wise . . ."

"Yeah, I know, Principal Seidman . . . ," I would say, trying to get away from him. "Two of the eyes." I was probably running too fast or throwing a ball too hard or teasing some girl badly enough to make her cry or something. Like I said, I was used to getting yelled at. So I didn't expect him to call me over with any other kind of question.

But on this one particular fall day, he did.

"See that boy over there?" he asked, squatting to get down to my size. I remember looking past my teacher, Mrs. Henderson, beyond the swing sets and the jungle gym, to where Seidman was pointing, to the very farthest corner of the playground, where this superfat kid clung to the fence, his hands clawed to the chain links like he was planning an escape.

"His mom dropped him off this morning. They just moved into town. From Chicago."

He said "Chicago" like it was supposed to mean something to me, like it was as important as "two of the eyes." I didn't know whether "Chicago" was a city or a state. Or a country, for that matter. And so I wondered if the kid even spoke English.

"His name is David Burnett. His mom said that he's shy. I would like you to talk to him, maybe introduce him around."

I looked into Principal Seidman's thick eyeglasses, trying to figure him out.

"Why me?"

"Because all the kids seem to like you, Steven," he answered, surprising me.

"Go away," said the fat kid when I finally got over to him. He was fatter up close, and he had a funny way of talking, almost like he was an adult trapped in a kid's body. An adult with a really funny lisp. No wonder he was trying to escape.

"Do you play soccer?" was all I could think of to say.

"No. I do not *fucking* play soccer. Do you think I'd be this fat if I played *fucking* soccer?"

"What about baseball?" I asked. "Pacelli plays baseball and he's kind of fat."

"No, you fucking moron. I don't play sports of any kind. I have anxiety." He turned his attention back to the fence, never actually having let go.

I wondered if anxiety was a disease that kept you from playing ball. I think I confused it with asthma. I must have, because I was thinking that he probably carried an inhaler. Like Chris Anders, he had one and so did, I think, Jessica. But Chris played ball, so maybe it wasn't asthma, except that whenever Chris played, his mom would stand over him and always ask was he OK?

"I have ADD," I announced, almost proudly, having been recently diagnosed with this disorder. The way it was explained to me at the time, there was a medical reason that I was unable to concentrate, and I had just started taking some kind of medication that would make it easier to listen in school.

"That's not actually a sickness," he answered, like he was some kind of authority. "That's just another way of saying that you're stupid."

"Is not," I answered. "I'm on medicine for it and everything."

"Well, my cousin has ADD, and he's, like, fucking retarded," the fat kid spat back. "My sister makes fun of him all the time and he doesn't even know."

I wondered if his sister was another fat kid suffering from some other kind of disease that I never heard of before. At least I had heard of ADD. Like five kids in my grade told me that they had ADD even before I found out that I had it.

"What about video games? I have Sega." I tried changing the subject, not because I wanted to talk to the fat kid anymore, but because I noticed that Seidman was still watching us.

Except the kid had turned his attention back to the fence and apparently decided to ignore me. OK, I was thinking, I did my best. Most of my friends were already kicking the soccer ball around and recess was short, so I was pretty much done with the fat kid.

I was about to walk away when he said, "Sega sucks."

"Does not," I said, even though I knew it wasn't the best gaming system out. Truth was, all I ever dreamed about at that time was getting a PlayStation, which was like three hundred dollars, and my father said no way, not until I learned to listen better. As it was, he threatened to take my Sega away at least once a week, whenever he thought I wasn't trying hard enough or whenever my sister Lindsey complained to him about something I did. I already knew that my father held out little hope that the medicine was going to cure me. As far as he was concerned, I was as stupid as the fat kid was saying I was.

"Besides, I'm getting a PlayStation," I told him, even though this wasn't true. Still, I had a feeling . . .

"PlayStation sucks too."

"Does not."

"Does so. Compared to Nintendo 64, it does."

Nintendo 64 had been out for, like, maybe two months and was really hard to get. I played it in some stores and kids were just starting to bring it home. It kicked ass. And was maybe the best system ever, with *Donkey Kong* and *Mario* and everything, and I would have begged for it.

Except for one thing.

The one thing was: PlayStation had a new game that was, in fact, the best game ever, a game that I would become closely identified with.

The game in question had come out a few months before and was about a red-and-brown, two-legged dog-thing that kept running and running and running and running, jumping over ditches, spinning around turtles, popping on them, sending them hurling into space, and then running while being chased by humongous boulders and having to jump over pits, while spinning through crates and breaking things, never stopping, except to get an oingaboinga and otherwise stop and you're dead.

Everything in the game mirrored exactly how I felt every single day of my life, while teachers and others tried so hard to sit me down and keep me still, even though I was spinning; while they were giving me my ADD medicine to try and stop my constant need to move, and to stop me from trying to break free from my chair and the room and the school. Letters on the chalkboard, words in a book, and all I could think of, all I could keep feeling, was *get out*.

Get outside.

When is school over?

When oh when is recess?

When oh when oh when do I get to go to Pete's house and play the game again?

It got so bad for me that I sometimes skipped baseball in order to get to Pete's, because he was the only one who had the game. And no one played the game like me.

Because I was him and he was me.

I was Crash Bandicoot. And I hated Doctor Neo Cortex even more than I hated sitting in the chair in school every day, waiting and waiting, practically sweating, while Mrs. Henderson talked on and on and on and on about science and history and math and language and writing and English.

People reminded me often enough that my nickname was Crash even before the game came out.

Whatever.

What I remember is, from the time I first played it, the name "Crash" took on a new significance for me. Because I could sit absolutely still for hours and hours with a controller in my hands and Crash on the screen; because I could solve every puzzle that frazzled Crash and the rest of my friends;

because I could collect every life and find every secret and never have to stop or worry about feeling like I missed something important.

And being that my name, Steven Crashinsky, had "Crash" in it, I pretty much believed that the universe had created the game just for me; that somewhere out there, they knew, *they totally knew*. Given my name and my constant craving for movement, how could it have been otherwise? It was secret proof to me, a cosmic validation that I was capable of anything if I was able to concentrate, no matter what my father or my sister or anyone else said about me, including the fat kid clawing at the fence. I was a genius in my own way. It didn't matter whether anyone ever noticed.

"Whatever" is what I said to the fat kid, ready to move on. The soccer ball called.

"So you acknowledge, then, that Nintendo is a superior system?" asked the fat kid in a voice to match his odd use of words.

Being a secret genius in my own way, I recognized that, for some odd reason, it seemed superimportant to this kid to be smarter than me. I almost always know whether a kid is truly smarter than me. So I knew right away, the fat kid was definitely smarter than me.

But I also knew that he would never hit a three-point shot, or kick a game-winning goal, or catch a football crossing over into the end zone, no matter how old he got. So I pretty much summed him up as a smart loser kid. Besides, I sensed that, even though he was smarter than me, there was something off about him. Really off.

"Maybe," I answered about the Nintendo/PlayStation issue. "Except . . . except Nintendo doesn't have Crash Bandicoot" is what I told him in my moment of triumph.

"Shit," said the fat kid. "I will acknowledge that Crash is an awesome game . . . ," he added, his voice drifting off as he said it. And I knew that I had defeated my enemy, conquered the big boss of level seven, and was ready for the next round. Except I also knew that this kid was not the kind of kid who was destined to be my friend. So we were done.

And just in time, Pete passed the soccer ball to me, actually probably at the fat kid, but I intercepted and then cut left and cut right around everyone else on the field, and all alone, I angled toward the goal and kicked a perfect center goal kick, right past Evan, who was diving for the ball. He never had a chance.

It would be a long time before I won another argument with David Burnett.

Anyways, a few months later, it was Christmas.

For the Crashinskys, as in Jamie, Lindsey, my mom and dad, and me, Christmas also meant Hanukkah, given that my father is a nonpracticing Jew and my mom is a superstitious Catholic. Anyways, under the Christmas tree/Hanukkah bush, there was a present from my father's sister, Aunt Randi, which was twice as big as any size box that she had ever given me before. And I knew, *I totally knew* even before she handed the present to me with a wet-cheek kiss: PlayStation.

You would think I'd be happy. But instead, I was totally panicked. Because my father had still not let up on the "No new toys until you do better in school" rule, which he was adamant about, because even with my new medication, I was, according to him, still not "applying myself" in school and still being lazy and distracted. I already knew that my mom wasn't going to stand up to him, as she had secretly given me the new Sonic game a few days earlier. Sonic, of course, was, in my mind, the single greatest video-game hero ever, until Crash, and the reason I was able to survive in school until PlayStation.

So I was physically rattled as I tore open the menorah-patterned wrapping paper to get to my aunt's present.

The system.

And out spilled the game. My very own *Crash Bandicoot*, no more begging Pete to get to his basement. There it was.

And there *he* was, my father, standing over me, shaking his head in a way that clearly said "no."

He waited until the system was completely unwrapped, then grabbed it from my hands and handed it back to his sister.

"I thought we talked about this," he said, practically barking at her.

"It's Hanukkah," she yelled back at him, grabbing it and trying to hand it back to me again. "Give the kid a break."

Now they were both holding my PlayStation, just above my head, with me under it, cross-legged, afraid that if I moved even the slightest bit, the game would be gone forever.

One quick yank and he was in sole possession.

Now he focused his attention on me. "Do you really think that you've earned this?" he said with a sneer.

I dared not answer.

"He doesn't have to earn everything," his sister told him. "That's what the holidays are all about, Mr. Scrooge."

"Stay out of this, Randi," he commanded. "The child has to learn."

I could feel the game slipping away with every word from him. Because I had five, maybe six seconds left before I totally lost it on him, as I usually did. And I could feel it coming on, taking control of me.

"Steven," said Aunt Randi, "will you try harder?"

"Yes" was all I could manage.

"There," she said.

Maybe my level of control swayed him, since it was so unusual, or maybe it was the Christmas/Hanukkah spirit or something, because my father, for no reason at all, dropped the PlayStation into my lap.

"It's either this one or the other," he said. And at first, I had not a clue what he meant, except that he wanted me to choose and it seemed like he was testing me again, like he was always testing me in some way, and if I got this wrong, I would lose everything. So my mind raced. If "this" is PlayStation, "the other" must be Sega. That had to be what he meant.

"This" was all I said.

I was up most of the time between Christmas and New Year's, beating level after level. I was magic. I was fast. Faster than anything I was capable of before, body tilting to keep up with the controller, to keep up with the levels. Standing, twisting, ducking down, all with my fingers constantly moving, even faster than I moved on the soccer field. No shit. I *actually became*, with no part of me not believing this, Crash Bandicoot.

"Heard you got PlayStation," David Burnett said to me the first morning back at school after winter break.

He was in Mrs. Bender's class, in the room next to me, so the only time I ran into him was either lunch or recess. By then, he and I had a weird kind of relationship. For one, our mothers met each other at some parent-teacher conference and seemed to strike up a friendship of some sort. His mom was a superstitious Jew, his father a nonpracticing Catholic, so we had, in a way, the religious/nonreligious thing in common. And apparently our fathers were in the same kind of business and occasionally took the train into Manhattan together. Plus, we both had sisters who were two years older than us, as in me with Lindsey and him with Roxanne, although they apparently did not like each other very much.

Point is, by then, I didn't think that he was all that bizarre, except rumor had it that he was a supergenius, always showing off his superknowledge, like, every day in class and challenging

Mrs. Bender all the time. Even finding mistakes in the tests she gave and correcting her.

Plus he was always coming up with strange ideas.

Once on the playground, I was wearing gloves, and he asked if I knew where mittens came from, and then he told me "mats" and laughed like it was funny and told me he was writing a book.

Another time, he asked about Christina Haines, who was this kiss-ass who always had her hand up in class, for, like, practically every question, and he told me that he heard that she liked me and that he thought that she had a very nice voice, of all things.

Another time, during lunch, he told me that he was building a rocket that would go backward in time for a science project.

He seemed to be making a few friends, but for some reason would never participate in after-school activities or even take the bus with the rest of us, and always waited for his mom to pick him up after school. Also, apparently his parents were pressuring mine for a family get-together or a group trip on a random Sunday. My mother seemed interested, but my father, typically, was preoccupied with work or something.

Then, one morning right before the break, his sister literally rammed into me on the bus line, even though I had never actually talked to her before.

"Crash Ban-di-cute, Crash Ban-di-cute" is what she chanted as she purposely bumped me, almost knocking me over. She had these pigtail braids and reminded me of Wednesday from *The Addams Family* movie. And she kept staring at me like she was trying to verify something that her brother told her. "Are you really Crash Bandicute? Or do they just call you that because your real last name is so horrible?"

It never occurred to me before how horrible-sounding my last name was. Not until I heard her pronounce it superslowly, like she was talking to a handicapped person or a foreigner.

"KRAH . . . SHIN . . . SKEEEEEEEE?" Contorting her face as she overpronounced the syllables.

Then I thought about what David had told me about her when we first met, about how she made fun of their cousin all the time and he never knew. Was she doing that to me?

"When are you going to come over to our house to play with David? *Puleeze* come over to our house to play with David," she repeated, but then sped off in the direction of a honking Audi. And there was David in the backseat, looking suitably miserable.

Now, seeing him after the break, he didn't look miserable at all. He was all loud and everything, yelling at kids in the hall and laughing for, like, no reason. The first thing I thought of was that I was probably going to have to go to the Burnetts' house for some kind of playdate. My mom had mentioned it a few times in passing, like it was no big deal. But I was not prepared to do that, as he just didn't seem like any fun, not the kind of fun that I was used to. And I couldn't help but wonder whether his sister would be there and whether she would try to knock me down again or find other ways to torment me.

"Heard you had to give up Sega," he announced loudly, more to other kids in the hall than to me.

"I could get it back," I announced with equal loudness but no conviction whatsoever.

"Heard your dad said that you can't play the game on school days."

Yeah, all I had to do was do better in school. And "apply myself," whatever that meant. This was the way my father interpreted my promise to Aunt Randi, when he informed me the night before the break ended that there would be no PlayStation on weekdays. "Until further notice," whatever that meant. I did not take the news well. I had been on my best behavior, at least I thought I was, and no way should I have been punished for no reason whatsoever. But, whatever. How did David Burnett know all of this, anyways?

"You can play at my house, if you want," he informed me, his way of telling me that he got PlayStation too. "How far did you get?"

"The High Road," I told him, referencing my last save point, which I calculated to be like 75 percent done. "No cheats." He had to be impressed.

"Well, I already beat it, so you can start anywhere, if you want," he said in triumph.

"You beat it?" No one I knew had actually beat the entire game at that point. I was going to be the first, assuming that I could get my game back at some point.

"In a few days. Of course, in fairness to you, I don't actually sleep, so my days are longer than yours."

A week later, my mom told me that she heard that David was being disruptive in class and that Mrs. Burnett had to go down to the school and meet with Principal Seidman.

When I saw David the next day, he bumped me, just like his sister, and said, "School sucks."

I pretty much repeated his words. "Yeah, school sucks."

I had lost my right to play the game that past weekend because I didn't do well on my vocab test. So yeah, school sucked. Home sucked too.

"If I could make it better, so you wouldn't have to go back, would you want to help?"

"Yeah, OK." Which is what I usually say when I don't understand the question, or if I'm not sure whether there was even a question at all.

"No, I mean it, Crash. No more school. Forever." He looked deadly serious when he said this.

"Sounds pretty good to me" was all I could think of, which

it did, not that it was a real possibility or anything. At least not in my mind.

One morning, a week after that, as me and Evan and Pete were heading into McAllister, I heard his voice from behind me, and turned and saw him and Roxanne getting out of their Audi. He was racing toward me. She was holding her books, just staring in my direction with that same look she gave me the day she rammed into me. My friends abandoned me, seeing as Burnett was coming. Both were in Mrs. Bender's class with him, and both had told me that he was totally out of control.

"Crash, I got it to work," he said. "Just like we planned. Remember, you promised to help. You can't back out now. Just think of it, no more school."

Which is how I ended up in the janitor's office that afternoon.

Actually, you might need a few more details. It was lunch period. I was eating at my table, and David came over again and whispered to me that I absolutely had to follow him since I promised to help, that he had built the most amazing thing, and no, of course I couldn't invite anyone else, it was a secret that he would only share with me. I was the only one he could trust; I was the only one who hated school the way he hated school. I was the only one who understood.

So like the idiot that I could sometimes be, I snuck out of the lunchroom with him and headed down the corridor, heart pounding, hoping that the ghost of General William McAllister had not followed us to intercept us and take us to the poltergeist dimension.

We reached the basement stairs, and he motioned for me to go down. At first I said no way, but he was convincing. No, more than convincing, he was *determined* and bubbling over with energy. And I was overwhelmed with curiosity. And he just kept talking, sounding increasingly persuasive with every step down the stairs.

Then down into the dark, humid basement and down the hall, with the air heavy with the scent of mildew and dirt, a smell that absolutely lingers in my nostrils even as I write this.

The McAllister smell.

Then he motioned to a door that read JANITOR'S OFFICE.

"Dave, I don't think this is such a good idea."

And as soon as I stepped into the room and saw the mountain of newspaper and torn-up schoolbooks in the middle of the floor, I finally figured out that something was catastrophically wrong.

"David?" I stopped, wondering what I had been expecting in the first place. And wanting to turn back.

He stepped behind me and closed the door, grabbing a bottle off the shelf.

"Remember how I told you I was building a rocket that would go back in time? Well, I figured out how to make one that would destroy the school."

I saw, for the first time, fireworks, cleverly woven into the pile of papers. He noticed that I noticed.

"I got a package from my uncle. He bought them in North Carolina where they're legal, all kinds." He was circling his pile, examining it. Then, opening the bottle carefully, he started sprinkling liquid onto the papers and the books.

"This is my invention," he boasted, holding up the bottle. "Rocket fuel. Out of stuff I found in my garage." He continued sprinkling, getting closer to me. "Guaranteed to close the school down." He started moving superquickly around the pile. "Just like we wanted."

I shook my head adamantly. "David, this is a bad idea. A real bad idea," I told him.

"Don't be such a baby, Crash."

"Kids could get hurt." I tried to reason with him.

"Only the stupid kids," he said, preoccupied with his plan, but then looking at me like it was clear in his mind at that minute that I was one of the stupid kids.

He moved toward me, and I stepped back toward the janitor's desk in the corner and managed to separate myself from him by the mound of papers. Problem was, I was against the wall, and he was blocking the doorway. Then, in another instant, he took out this lighter, and he was flicking it again and again, thumbing the top until he got a flame that was the size of his own fingers. He moved his hand to the pile.

I shrank back as the flame made contact with the paper.

And then the fire, in a *whooooosh*, as everything went up.

By the way, all of this took, like, less than two seconds, so when you're reading this, picture it in slow motion, then play it back in your mind, only speed it up. Get the picture?

I checked the doorway, thought I could make it, but then the fireworks started going off. And this massive mound of popping flames blocked the door from where I was standing. David Burnett was on the other side. He would be able to get out, but I would not. Not easily. Not safely.

Except I started to think like this was the game and I was really Crash. I could run left, but there were rockets firing left. I could run right—bombs were going off right, but there was room. Except when the next bomb went off, the fire exploded higher, to the ceiling, spreading farther to the right.

So left would be easier, safer. But there was also David Burnett. He was standing to the left on the other side of the mound, and he was huge and fat and solid, and he looked like he didn't want me leaving for some odd reason. If I hit him, I would bounce back into the flames. Game over.

Or maybe I could jump the pile, hope to get over it, and another jump out the door. There were places the fire didn't extend to at that very second. This might have been my only hope.

Except . . . The room was quickly beginning to fill up with smoke, and it was quickly getting dark in there. Another second passed, and I could hardly even see David Burnett. Another bunch of rockets went off. I was still Crash Bandicoot, but my health meter was dipping down to dangerous levels.

And then . . .

The door flung open, and there was Principal Seidman staring at us. And Dave Burnett quickly pocketed his lighter, like nothing was going on at all, except that Principal Seidman was not a stupid man, and he figured it out right away that we were in a dangerous predicament.

"WHAT ARE YOU BOYS DOING IN HERE?"

Meeting Darth Vader could not have been worse. Except I realized after my first thought that Principal Seidman was actually Obi-Wan in this picture and Burnett was Vader.

"Help" was all I was able to say, mostly cough, at this point.

And then Principal Seidman was gone, but then was back with a long red fire extinguisher, spraying the pile down, and Burnett tried to leave but Seidman wouldn't let him.

"David Burnett is trying to burn the school down," I blurted out, no shame in telling on him, although Seidman probably couldn't hear me over the explosive sounds of the fireworks.

Seidman continued to spray foam at the mound until the fire was finally out, which took a while, because the fire had gotten pretty large by that point. Moving very quickly for an old guy. Kind of like Yoda, now that I think of it.

In that instant, I ran around the pile toward the door, thinking that I would keep going forever, out of the room, out of the basement, out of school, and out of town.

Except Seidman caught me with one hand, still restraining Burnett with the other.

"WHAT DID YOU BOYS DO?"

"It wasn't me," I said, struggling to get free. "It was David Burn . . ."

"DO YOU REALIZE HOW DANGEROUS THIS IS?"

"It wasn't me." I screamed and struggled.

And David Burnett said absolutely nothing. Just smiled. A weird spooky smile.

Seidman looked at me, then he looked at Burnett. And he seemed to understand everything in a single instant.

"WAIT OUTSIDE, MR. CRASHINSKY," he said to me in the Darth Vader voice.

I slipped around him and ran. Not just out the door, but down the hall and up the stairs and back to the safety of my class and Mrs. Henderson. On my way out, I heard Burnett talking calmly to Seidman.

"Call him Crash," I heard him say. "Everyone else does."

CHAPTER THREE

HOW THE PRESCRIPTIONS ALMOST KILLED ME

"What the hell is wrong with you?"

I was sitting at the dinner table, trying to eat my chicken nuggets, picking at the broccoli, having to listen to my father go off on me again. I wasn't much in the mood for eating anyways. Those days I either ate a lot or not at all, depending on the dosage of medication that I was on. Also, being that those particular nuggets were frozen-food nuggets and not the McDonald's or Burger King ones, I didn't much care if I didn't eat.

Especially with my father hate-staring at me constantly from the other side of the table.

I did notice that he wasn't eating either. He was, however, on his third Scotch. His favorite bottle within arm's reach, on the serving table, so he could get to it easy in an emergency.

"I already told you. It wasn't my fault."

"Then why am I going to the principal's office tomorrow morning?" Wiping his mouth, which he didn't have to do since he didn't eat. "I had to cancel a very important meeting."

I didn't actually know exactly what my father did for a living at that time, being that every time he explained it, he used words I didn't understand. From what I could tell, other people trusted him with their money, but he wasn't a banker, and it had something to do with hedges and fun, but nothing ever sounded fun about it.

Whatever it was, he was good enough at it to afford to build a customized house, which was huge by normal standards but average for the Westchester neighborhood we lived in. So I didn't actually know that it was huge.

"You don't need to go," I told him, looking at my mother for help. She was also looking at me, but not with the same hate-stare that I was used to from my father. She had her own look, which was like maybe she was going to cry at the very next word if I didn't say exactly the right thing.

Funny thing about my parents was, he always said these horrible things about me and it never bothered me. But when she looked at me like that, with her lips so tight on her face, I hated myself and actually believed that there was something wrong with me. I had made a promise to myself a million times by then that I would be better for her sake.

Of course, I had no clue how I was going to do that.

"I didn't *do* anything," I practically screamed.

"Then how, exactly, how did you end up in the janitor's office?"

Welcome to another dinner at the Crashinsky house, never mind that this was an unusually bad one.

It was always something. As I may have mentioned, this wasn't the first discussion that would end with both my parents going to visit Seidman the next day. So I pretty much knew how it was going to go down.

My sisters were the real victims during these dinners. By then, Lindsey mostly had nothing to do with me. Occasionally she was nice to me, mostly not, being as she blamed me for making my father all pissed off all the time. She typically ate fast, without looking at anyone, and bolted to her room the second she could.

This night was to be no different in that respect.

"May I please be excused?" she said, rolling her eyes. She was *always* rolling her eyes. That was a typical Lindsey move.

Jamie, two years younger than me, four years younger than Lindsey, idolized me and would cry virtually every time I had a fight with one of my parents, which meant that she was crying by the end of almost every dinner.

"Take Jamie with you," my mother told Lindsey. That was not a good sign. They tried their best to shield Jamie from everything that I did, apparently worried that my behavior was somehow contagious.

My sisters were gone; their half-eaten plates remained.

I tried my best to eat. My father did not try at all. His plate was completely untouched.

Another sip from his drink. That meant he was trying to control himself. It was going to be a long night with constant questions.

"Answer me. If you didn't do anything, what were you doing in the janitor's office?"

"I already told you."

"Tell me again."

"David Burnett said that he wanted to show me something."

"And so you just went with him to the basement of the school? You had to know that you were not allowed to go there."

"He said that he had a surprise for me."

"If David Burnett told you to jump off the roof, would you do it?"

"What are you *talking* about?"

"I'm talking about you, Steven. When are you going to learn to follow the rules?" His voice was getting louder and angrier.

"I didn't *do* anything wrong." My voice got louder and angrier.

"Wasn't it wrong to be in the janitor's office in the first place?"

"Yes, but . . ."

"And are you saying that you didn't help David build the bonfire?"

"I already said I didn't have anything to do with that!" I was screaming. "Mom. Tell him. Principal Seidman told you it wasn't me." I looked over to my mom for support. Her lip was quivering. She was not going to get between us this time.

"You could have been killed," my father said.

"It wasn't me!" I yelled. "How many times do I have to tell you, David Burnett tried to murder me."

In the hours after the fire, I had come to that realization. I mean, he was this supergenius kid, so he had to know that I would be stuck in that room when the fire spread. Being as he planned everything out perfectly, from his own personal rocket fuel to the mound of papers stuffed with fireworks, there was absolutely no way that he would have lit the stack with me cornered behind it unless he was trying to kill me. Plus there was a look about him at that instant that was beyond insane, at least that's how it felt to me, and say what you will about psychic ability, some things you just know. So even if my logic was faulty, I knew from another part of me that the second Burnett had put the flame to the mountain of paper, it wasn't just about burning down the school. He wanted me dead.

And no matter what I said to anyone, they dismissed this concept, like I was making it up. Because to them, Burnett wasn't out to get me, it was about the fire. And "we" could have burned the school down. That's what mattered. This from Principal Seidman, who called me into his office to tell me that he had called my parents; then also from my mom on the way home.

So if my teacher didn't believe me and the principal didn't believe me and my mom didn't believe me, I wasn't about to convince my father. He was already busy thinking about the punishment phase of our conversation. I could tell from his scrunched-up-forehead look.

"No more PlayStation until summer," he said now, gloating. "Do you understand?"

I looked at my mom, pleadingly. I had just gotten it back again.

The pain of being without Crash Bandicoot was almost as intense as my fear of David Burnett. This could *not* be happening.

Except my mom's lips were now in full tremble. She knew all too well what that punishment was going to mean. It was not going to be a quiet night. Lindsey had to study for a test. Jamie wouldn't be able to sleep.

"No, you can't take it away!" Now it was me, with the tight lips, fighting tears. I probably screamed this.

"Too late."

I thought I saw him smile, just a little, which really, really pissed me off. Still, I tried to remain calm, even though my body was rapidly heating up, as it sometimes did whenever I got frustrated or angry.

"No video games. And no TV. At all. For the rest of the year." And now, after all this, he started to eat. And took another sip of his precious Scotch. Case closed.

Next thing I know, the chicken nuggets are off my plate and bouncing off his face and his chest. Swear to god, I do *not* remember actually throwing them. I *do* remember the screaming fit and the crying (I'll admit this), first me, then my mother, then hearing Lindsey slamming her door and saying that she hated her whole entire family. Oh yeah, and I also remember being dragged up to my room, half carried, half pulled, and flung onto my bed, pretty much with the same force as the chicken nuggets were flung.

My father was way stronger than he looked.

I also remember banging on the door until my fists felt pulverized and screaming about PlayStation over and over again.

And falling asleep on the floor.

"Thanks a lot," David Burnett said to me, when he finally showed up at school again. "Do you know how much trouble *you* got me in?"

It was a week later. No one knew what happened to him after the fire incident. Rumors had spread that he had been transferred to another school. And of course, word was out by then that he had tried to burn down the school—and that I had tried to help him.

Kids started calling him Burn, instead of Burnett, in his absence. With a little help from me, as I kind of made up a song about him, to the tune of the *Barney* "I Love You" song, which I sang to Pete and Evan and they sang to everyone else, a song that practically everyone thought was superfunny.

> *Dave BURNett. Dave BURNett.*
> *Have you burned the school down yet?*

Well, practically everybody, except that kiss-ass Christina Haines, who told me that it was cruel to make fun of a kid who had problems, not knowing that I was the one who made it up in the first place.

Point was, most kids who knew me knew I didn't have anything to do with the fire, but even my best friends, as in Pete and Evan and Kenny, didn't believe me when I told them that Burnett had tried to kill me.

In the meantime, my parents met with Principal Seidman, and while they were assured that, in fact, I had nothing to do with the bonfire, they also talked about my academic issues and my recent diagnosis as having ADHD, not just ADD, the H being for hyperactivity, another important component that apparently kept me from listening. While I previously had been on a small dose of Ritalin to see if it would slow me down, now the school was officially recommending that my parents have me more fully tested and better medicated. Which meant another round of doctors and questions about whether I could concentrate, even though I thought was doing well enough, which was why my mother was reluctant to put me on the strong stuff earlier.

Now, a week later, I had already visited the pediatrician and had an appointment with some psychologist guy who wanted me to see some other doctors.

So when Burnett tried to tell me that it was "all my fault," I was just about ready to totally kick his ass. Which I would have done, except that my father warned me not to associate with David in any way, which meant not even talking to him.

"I didn't get you into any trouble," I said, trying not to talk to him, but talking to him anyways as I spiraled a football back to Pete. It was cold, and my fingers were feeling like ice. I rubbed them for warmth.

Burnett, however, was not even wearing a jacket.

"You told Seidman," he sneered. "That's why he showed up. He ruined everything."

"If 'everything' means you not killing me and not burning down the entire school, then yeah. And if I knew what you were trying to do, I would've told him. But I didn't tell him. I didn't even see him."

Him: "Then how'd he know?"

Me: "How am I supposed to know?"

Him: "Fucking liar."

Me: "Whatever."

Pete threw the ball back to me and it stung my hands, like it was a rock.

Him: "Everyone's calling me Burn now. Because of you."

Me: "Not my fault."

Him: "Is too. You made up that song about me."

I had to wonder how he found out, as I only sang it to Evan and Pete and they were the ones who made such a big deal about it.

Me: "Whatever."

Throwing it back. No point in arguing.

Him: "I have to take a new medication. Because of you."

Me: "Whatever."

It occurred to me that I was probably going to have to take a new medication. Because of him.

Him: "It's making me dizzy and sometimes I can't eat without vomiting. Because of you."

Me (you guessed it): "Whatever."

Him: "So I decided. When they told me that I had to come back to this fucked-up place. I decided that you have to die. And one day, I am going to kill you."

Me: "You already tried to kill me. Remember?"

Why did I even have to remind him of this? Why was I even talking to him?

Him: "Believe me, Crash. If I wanted to kill you then, you would already be dead."

Me: "Whatever."

OK, you're probably thinking I didn't sound all that concerned. Well, that's because I acted that way in front of Burnett. But, I'm not going to lie, if any other kid had said that to me, I would have laughed it off. Kids say stupid things all the time and you let it go, or you fight over it. Either way, by the next day, you were best friends again and throwing the football or kicking the soccer ball around, no problem.

But not so with Burn.

His words plagued me. Worse. Tortured me.

Because I knew that David Burnett meant every word with all his heart. And I also knew that he was smart enough to somehow come up with a way to do it.

In the weeks that followed, I couldn't sleep, couldn't eat, and most definitely could not concentrate on anything at school, even though Burn was not in my class and even though I mostly didn't see him. I couldn't tell my parents about his latest threat because they had already warned me not to talk to him. I couldn't tell my teachers because they couldn't be trusted not to somehow get me into deeper trouble with him by telling his mom. I couldn't tell my friends because they would make fun of me for taking Burnett seriously. Plus it would definitely get back to him. I couldn't tell Lindsey, who never listened to me. I couldn't tell Jamie, who wouldn't understand.

So by the time I met with the psychological doctor for my next appointment, I was a jittery mess. He talked to me for a while and then separately to my mom.

And then, inexplicably, upped the dose of Ritalin again, this time with some other medication.

Which only made things worse, because after a few weeks, still thinking about how Burn was going to kill me, my heart started racing and I always felt dizzy. I had stopped eating completely. And the only time I felt tired enough to sleep was when I had a headache so bad I couldn't even see straight.

And I didn't know if it was the medications or the threat of being killed by Burn, with him coming at me when I least expected it. Maybe with a knife or another weapon. Maybe poisoning my lunch. I racked my brain trying to think how he was going to do it, which only made my heart race faster and my dizziness more intense. I couldn't think of anything else. Because I totally knew that since he was some kind of supergenius, he was thinking about ways that I couldn't think of, ways that I wouldn't be able to even imagine.

It got so bad that my parents must have noticed, because they gave me back my PlayStation. But I couldn't even concentrate on the game, or any other video game for that matter. Plus I was afraid of running during recess, during baseball, during soccer for fear that my heart would explode in my chest.

Which it felt like it was going to do practically all day, every day.

And my mom called the doctor, who claimed that I was over-reacting to the drugs and that it was a matter of time before my body adjusted to it.

And even though she was concerned, she didn't take me off them, so I continued to take them.

Until the day I fainted during school.

And then they still had to wean me off.

So it took, like, a week before I started feeling like Crash again. And all that time, my father, in his infinite wisdom, accused me of faking it because he knew I didn't want to take the medication in the first place.

And then he wondered why I didn't want to act all happy and sing him happy birthday with the rest of my family. Yeah right, happy birthday, Dad.

Anyways, it was spring, and I was pretty much back to normal, back in the schoolyard, and Burnett came over to our group and asked to be included in our game.

And me being a lefty and him being a lefty, someone said that he should borrow my glove, as we were on different teams, and of course, he didn't have one of his own (what kind of kid doesn't have his own glove?).

I was literally shaking when he approached me. Was there a way for him to do something with my glove that would kill me? Sneak a poison into it that would eat away my hands or paralyze me? By then he had become, for me, a diabolical and sinister evil genius along the lines of Doctor Neo Cortex.

So we played. And I watched him with my glove. And every inning he was out there, I never took my eyes off him, even as I was striking out inning after inning. On easy pitches, with Pete yelling at me, "What is wrong with you?"

At the end of each inning, Burn would toss my glove to me, and I would examine it for the most insignificant changes. I even made Bosco try it on, just in case.

Then, after the game, he came all the way over. His team won, thanks to me striking out, going 0 for 4, and he handed me the glove and said:

"I got a copy of *Star Fox* for Nintendo 64. And *GoldenEye*. They're awesome. Do you want to come over and play?"

CHAPTER FOUR

ANOTHER NIGHT OF PARTYING WITH JUNGLE JUICE AND WEED

It was a week after the night at Pinky's. We were back at the nature preserve, hiking to our special place deep in the woods, which had become a nightly ritual. Long ago we had built a campground between two giant boulders, where we could hide our stash and hang without anyone ever finding us. The perfect setup, with a circle of rocks that we had moved together and makeshift wooden benches that Newman and Kenny built out of half-rotted trees. There was even an overhang so we could party there on rainy Sundays when everyone's parents were home and there was nowhere safe to go.

On this particular night it was me, Newman, Kenny, Bosco, and Evan. Also this Spanish guy, Ruiz, who used to work at Target with Bosco.

Kenny passed a bottle of a sports drink, which was actually his now-famous jungle juice, consisting of any fruit juice he could find plus a whole lot of supercheap vodka.

I felt like I could celebrate, having just written my first chapters, so I took an extra-long swig and passed to Newman, who, for some odd reason, rejected, and passed to Evan, who swigged and screeched, "Sweeeeeeet!"

Evan almost always said some version of "sweet," like, over a hundred times a day.

I flinched, not from the drink, which was completely smooth, but from hearing Evan's mantra.

"Sweeeeeeet" was really, *really* getting on my nerves.

"It's Urova," Kenny said, acting all scientist-y, referring to a brand of vodka that was low-rent, kid-friendly engine fuel, didn't burn a hole in your pocket, but possibly would to your stomach.

"No way," said Evan and Ruiz together. More from Evan: "Dude, this is smooth shit. Doesn't even smell. Like, not at all."

"I filtered it," Kenny said smugly. "I borrowed one of those water filters from Pete. We did a taste test against his parents' Ketel One. Just as smooth. We made, like, gallons." He lifted the lid of a cooler that he carried with him, exposing six huge sports drink bottles.

Ruiz took a turn. "Fuckyeah." Then he downed the rest of the third or fourth bottle and laughed. "You are a fucking genius," he told Kenny.

Kenny *was* a fucking genius, which we all knew. And this was not the first time that he presented us with another invention that revolutionized our way of getting trashed. A year ago, we were at Pete's house, and Kenny showed up with a contraption that he had built himself, claiming that he got the directions off the internet. It was, in fact, a homemade vaporizer, guaranteed to deliver the most THC possible with every inhale without spending like $500 on the real thing. So like his current cocktail, you didn't need to buy primo shit but could use shwag, and it would be just as effective as Cali medicinal.

No question he was right; that vaporizer fucked us up bigtime. Got beyond high, to superhigh, so fucking torched we couldn't move. And Evan, swear to god, freaked out, said he could hear his heartbeat and then didn't, which made him think he was dead. In fact, the vaporizer ended up freaking almost everybody out except me and Newman, so we stopped using it.

Turned out that Kenny gave it away, to, of all people, David Burnett.

So sitting there in our usual spot, taking another swig of jungle juice, it hit me that Kenny and Burn had a lot in common.

Like the math team and chess and the constant A's in their AP courses. Like Kenny, Burn was always working on inventing something, not to mention developing the complicated devices that he set the day of the siege. I made a note to interview Kenny about what he remembered. But now was not the time.

Newman finally started drinking even though he was supposed to be our designated driver, which didn't matter much anyways because Newman driving drunk was better than most kids driving sober, which made him our designated drunk driver. He was laughing about something with Ruiz, who was pretty excited since he was going to one of our parties for the first time tonight, which would officially make him part of Club Crew.

He was chill. Quit his job at Target after hanging with us and started working at a clothing store where he was constantly picking up girls. Almost every time he showed up to hang, he had some new girl with him, each hotter than the last, and he knew it, high-fived us behind their backs, shared stories of his conquests. Plus he always brought his own weed and had no problem smoking us down, as in sharing (no wonder Bosco liked him so much). Plus, after meeting us, he started making fun of Bosco at every opportunity, which was what we all tended to do.

So he was most definitely chill.

I was thinking about Kelly's party, and I wondered whether any of the Herd Girls would be hooking up with him that night.

I climbed into the front seat of Newman's father's Range Rover, and, passing a blunt to me, Newman finally asked me how it was going with the book. This time, I was all over it. In fact, all night I was preoccupied with what to write next, and I knew he would help me.

I told him how things returned to normal for most kids after the fire, including Burn. Normal for everyone except me. Burn's parents ended up going out for dinner a few times with my parents, which didn't make sense to me, because my dad was one hundred percent crystal clear that I should have nothing to do with David, but my mom was, like, constantly on the phone with Mrs. Burnett. According to her, David was back to fine on his meds, not that that was going to change anything in my mind.

And, being as Burn's father was one of the coaches for Little League, Evan and a few of the other kids who were on his team would sometimes end up at the Burnetts' house, enticed by Burn's increasingly large collection of the latest video games. Even Lindsey was there a few times on homework dates, although she always came home complaining about how she didn't like Roxanne at all.

Still, whenever Burn invited me or whenever any of the other kids asked whether I was going, I always had an excuse. And even though the other kids thought Burn was super-weird, they would end up there, being as Burn had the largest house in the neighborhood, with a superhuge pool, a tennis court, and a rec room with maybe the first flat-screen TV in the neighborhood.

I never got to see any of those things. Truth is, I was still out-of-my-mind panicked, and increasingly certain that the invites were all part of a calculated plan to get me to go to his house where something terrible would happen to me. So I remained absorbed in my terror.

But that was only for one spring.

Because that summer, I started going to sleepaway camp.

And Burn's family moved away.

Which made me feel pretty stupid, since I wasted most of that summer in a panic zone, wondering what Burn had planned for me when I returned to school.

And then he was gone. Totally, completely, and permanently gone forever. As in moved-back-to-Chicago gone.

So that fall I was set free, and my mind stopped spinning, and I started to do better in school. And I even got along better, at least temporarily, with my dad, who started talking to me like he didn't hate me for a while. Of course, that didn't last, because school got harder for me, and I was still out of control at home, bouncing off the walls when I had to study for tests. Or fighting with Lindsey or getting into trouble at some after-school event or religious class that I didn't want to go to in the first place. Or getting yelled at on the baseball field because my dad decided to assistant coach and benched me during the final innings of more than one game for no apparent reason. Which, of course, caused me to lose my temper, more than once. What was the point of having a father who coached if he always benched you anyways?

Which, of course, ended up in public displays of mutual hatred, which, of course, turned my dad against me again. He was constantly ragging on me about my room, or my school-work, or my lack of sportsmanship, or leaving shit in the den, and always with his own mantra, which was:

"What the hell is wrong with you?"

And then it was seventh grade, the fall of 2002, and we (me and Pete and Evan) were at the mall to see *Jackass: The Movie* with Pete's brother. And there, on line for candy, right in front of us, was a tall kid who I didn't recognize until he turned to us, started talking, and singled me out among my friends, and, in a deep, almost manly voice for a kid, said, "Yo, Crash. Are you still alive?"

Newman swerved around a possum in the road and brought my attention back to the drive, which I guessed he was doing OK with, though I was pretty wasted.

"Start there," Newman said.

Evan was asleep in the backseat, and Kenny was playing with his new iPhone, probably investigating the next great invention to get us fucked up. I turned back toward Newman, feeling dizzy, and all I could see was the empty bottle of jungle juice in my lap. I wasn't feeling so hot.

"That should be the opening for your next chapter," Newman continued.

"I guess," realizing that I must've been thinking out loud, even though I had no idea I was actually talking.

I tried to question him but instead belched up a vomitburp. Not a good sign.

Kenny from the back: "Youwananotherhitdude?" as the smell of weed hit my nostrils

"Notgonnamakeit," I said, not sure if Newman understood me.

Newman, being Newman, figured it out immediately. He pulled over, and I flung the door open.

Just in time.

I was feeling better by the time we got to Kelly's house, back in form again thanks to a pure old-fashioned Gatorade (as in the alcohol-free version) and a pack of gum.

Kelly's parents were in Europe, just like always, and her older sister was gone. Pretty much everyone from our town was already there, so we had to park like ten blocks away. All for the better; the walk was helping me clear my head.

Pete greeted us at the door with two redcupfuls of mix. Someone else's version of jungle juice; this one tasted of Red Bull and Crystal Light.

"Yo, ma' brothers, time to get fucked up," he says, handing us the redcups.

Newman chugged a cupful down in one gulp, tossing the

empty back to Pete. He remains completely indestructible. I had no choice but to follow. Ice cold, cherry, and deadly strong. It occurred to me to just pass on it, but I couldn't disappoint. I had my own rep to live up to.

"Christina's been asking for you, dude," Pete says, ushering us through the house. "She's in the back, by the pool." He stopped at the table for another drink, as did Newman. I had no choice but to take another as well.

"It's crazy back there, and she's pretty wasted," Pete added. Then, as he handed us our refills, he was already focused on the next people to enter the house. Two of the hotter junior girls were trailing behind Bosco and Ruiz, and the juniors were not seeing Bosco at all, as they were looking overly interested in Ruiz, who had changed out of his dirty LET'S GO METS T-shirt and was now dressed all South Beach: clean-shaven, hair slicked back, gold chain, halfway open Boss shirt.

"Look at Tony Fucking Montana," says Pete.

Me and Newman are looking at each other. We don't have to say it, but both of us are thinking, When did he have time to shower? Where did he get clothes to change into?

I'm in my Abercrombie tee and a pair of Diesel jeans, as always, every night out, which is fine since I am pretty comfortable about looking good, which I definitely do well. Way better than the rest of the guys in the Club Crew. I need to keep looking sharp, not just for me, but for them, as they usually count on me to get with the friends of the girls I hook up with.

And so I was thinking I was looking pretty good now.

But not, apparently, as good as Ruiz. I know I am going to have to keep him away from Christina, especially with her being wasted and all and me so close to tapping her, which I definitely plan to do this summer.

"Looks like there's a *new* celeb in town," Newman said, and I understood that he was referencing my dwindling fame.

It was mad crowded around the pool. Blunts were being passed around, and cans of Keystone with some bottles of Corona mixed in littered the lawn. Most of the faces were familiar, though I did spot a few that I didn't recognize. Newman was talking a lot, which he always did when he drank, and he was going on about how everyone had their own celebrity, in the sense that there were one or two characteristics that differentiated each kid from every other kid. I was trying to listen but kept getting distracted, because there were so many people around and Christina was absolutely nowhere in sight.

"Yo, dawg." A hand reaches out toward me. Brian Hill.

"Wrestler," Newman whispers. "He's defined by it. Scholarship and all." I understood that Newman was doing this for my benefit, because he knows it's hard for me to describe people when I write. His point is that you don't have to say much. Say "wrestler," and you think of a thick guy, solid neck. That's all you need.

He goes on as we walk around the pool:

J.D.: Supernerd. No street sense whatsoever. He will believe anything. He will be a professor of physics and never get married.

Robby Michelson: Two words—panic attacks.

Akheel: If Apu had a son . . . (the only one of the three Indian guys I know who actually sounds like he's Indian).

Hartman: Multiple DUIs, sloppy belly to prove his love for keggers. Got kicked off the football team.

Tommy Leeds: *Guitar Hero.* Need I say more?

Pat: A die-hard Patriots fan, New England above all. Not surprisingly, he is headed to Boston University.

Then there's the group of super-straights. They will have, like, one beer, walk around for, like, forty-five minutes, talking mostly to each other, and then they head home by themselves. Mostly guys, like Scott Ginsberg, Richie Krane, Neil Blei (the super-straight girls almost never show up to our parties).

Madelaine Brancato: Was once everybody's mom. Super-responsible. But of course, thanks to me, as some people say—and I'm not gonna lie, they're probably right—now the superslut of our graduating class.

Gerry Earnshaw: The official gay guy of our grade. There are others, but Gerry was king queen, being as we all knew he was gay from, like, the McAllister days. He is, of course, hanging with the hotgirls. He thinks that he is, in his own way, one of them.

Which brings us to "Cheerleader City," a cluster of the school's hottest girls—all of whom are dating college guys. A few are there with them, and they all have Coronas with limes, like our normal cheap brew is not good enough for them. The cheerleaders never hung with any of us, as they were previously committed to the Prime Time Players, which is what the football guys have called themselves since ninth grade. Will, Terry, James, Tyler, Danny Greenberg—they're OK, I guess. We will occasionally hang with a few of them, especially when one of us has a new supply of weed, or if we need guys for b-ball after school or in the summers.

Then the next group, the outsiders:

Nicole Weinstein: Pierced eyebrow. Pierced tongue. Pierced navel. *Pierced eyebrow.* That says more than any other piercings. Oh yeah, do I need to mention jet-black hair? She used to be the straightest kid in middle school until she started hanging with Roxanne's friends and trying to imitate her in every way possible, but always missing the actual point about Roxanne.

Mark Duncan: "Sandler" is what we call him, not because he looks like Adam Sandler, but because he has seen every single Sandler movie from the *Airheads* days on. If you name a year— say, 1999—he can tell you what Sandler movie was out (this includes all of the Rob Schneider movies, as Adam Sandler had a small part in each of them). Duncan sometimes hung with the Club Crew when we let him. Most times, he was superquiet.

Franklin Hawkings: *World of Warcraft*—need I say more?

Caitlin Lewis: Newman whispered "one word" and I got it straight out. The word was "iPod." You never saw her without it. Even tonight, she was plugged in. She brought the iPod not only to listen to music, even though there was music playing by the pool, but because she (and many other people at school, including me) firmly believed that her iPod could predict the future. It was one of the megamemory old-fashioned iPods, like 160 gigs, and it was all LimeWired up with everything she could download.

Sometimes at parties, when we were tripping balls, we would circle around her, and she would switch it to shuffle, and we would ask her questions, one at a time, then wait for the song to respond.

Marisa said that she once asked it what college she would go to, and the song that came up was something by a group called Kansas. And guess what? She's going to some school in, guess where? Kansas. OK, not conclusive in my mind, as I am usually skeptical of everything. But this thing was scary accurate, no question, better than the Magic Eight Ball.

Also, no one will forget about the party that we had one Saturday night some weeks before 4/21 when someone (I think it was Kelly) asked about what was going on with Burnett, who had taken to showing up to school only occasionally and then always hidden under a massive hooded sweatshirt. And the song that came up was "School's Out" by Alice Cooper. We thought it was weird enough that the selection had the word "school" in it. But then, the day after 4/21, we fucking totally *knew*.

When you think about it, you have to wonder, what were the chances? Out of like twelve thousand songs. She didn't even know she had that song. Spooky, huh?

My own iPod Touch sucks at this. I have tried time and time again to get it to give me answers to questions with no luck at all, but I only have like 500 songs. Pete has thousands of songs on his and could do no better.

We cross the bridge over the pool (did I mention that Kelly has an awesome house?) and get to the Herd, which is what they call themselves. The girls in the Herd mostly hang with us and include Annie Russo, Natalie, Marisa, Sarah, and of course Kelly. I look beyond them to the area around the pool house, where a bunch of people are hanging, searching for Christina.

"Crash. Alex, what happened to you guys? You're *sooooo* late." Annie puts her arm around mine. She once gave me head when we were both drunk. Then, after, she said it was a mistake, and it would never happen again, but she always acts likes it's a possibility for another time.

Kelly says that her friends from camp are up for the weekend from New Jersey, and Newman is all smiles as she points them out, because he knows, like I know, that New Jersey girls are *easy*. Trashy, but easy.

The drinks and the weed are definitely hitting, and I'm feeling pretty good again, because if Christina was not going to leave with me, I know it has to be a lock for some head from one of the NJ girls. After all, I'm still celeb material to them. It's becoming clear to me that my star power is dwindling in my hometown, but it is apparently untarnished with girls everywhere else.

That is, of course, unless they catch notice of Ruiz first. Which makes me think, Where is Christina anyways?

And then there is Newman again, as we pass the drama group, and he whispers in my ear, "Christina Haines," nodding that I should turn around. Then, from him: "One word."

I run through the possibilities in my mind and come across

a few choices. "Smart." No, not good enough. She's more than smart—what she is, is "accomplished," being in the National Honor Society and being part of some sort of special volunteer program and winning some kind of special town award. "Athletic." No, not that either, although she was captain of the girls' field hockey team, plus a scholarship swimmer, plus tennis. "Political," because she organized the High Schoolers for Obama campaign before any of us had even heard of him, and also her work with some orphans in, like, Nicaragua or Guatemala or somewhere starting a food and clothing drive. "Talented." She had all kinds of training, art, music, as in she played the piano and sung (sang? I forgot which word . . .).

"Star," says Newman, not waiting any longer for a response from me. In addition to all the rest, she was in, like, every school production, playing mostly leads. She had done other performances, musicals, throughout Westchester. Went to summer camp for actors. Appeared in an actual off-Broadway play. Plus she was the only kid in town (other than me, of course) ever to be on television, in a sitcom that didn't last for more than a few weeks and she didn't have a major part. But still. Plus she has a true presence, a glow that makes her look prettier than she actually is, which isn't to say that she isn't hot, which she definitely is.

So as we finally cross over to where she's hanging with her group, I recognize that in Newman's mind, "star" is probably as close as you can get in one word.

"Steven. You are so *late.* Are you high again?" She kisses me with full-on lips against lips, glossy wet, and a taste like beer and flowers. Warm and cool at the same time. I am now fairly certain that I will not be going off with any Jersey girls tonight, even though I am also certain that Christina, like always, will tease me and not get me off. Still, maybe on this night, at this party. I am already thinking about the ways this could happen.

"Well, *are* you?" And she sounds, like she always sounds, like she is on stage and reciting lines perfectly, like some character from another time.

"Well, *you* are definitely wasted," I tell her.

"So are you." Lots of touches with her hand, on my chest and arms. Now, in closer, so I can smell the beer and flowers again. I definitely want to experience another one of those kisses. She is, I keep telling myself, not the hottest girl at the party. No doubt I could do better physically, get way hotter. Annie Russo, for example, is probably hotter, has a better body. I look at Annie, then back at Christina. Annie, all made up like a model. Christina, almost no makeup at all, looks like she doesn't care how she looks. Still, Annie moves like she's stuck up and desperate at the same time, and Christina moves like she is a dancer and music is always playing for her.

But Annie is looking at me, like, why have I been paying so much attention to Christina this entire summer? Only a week before, Annie commented to me that me and Christina had never had anything in common, since she wasn't a member of the Herd and since we never really spent any time together, not in McAllister (other than the one grade when she was in my class), not in middle school (except for one particular night), not in high school. And I'm not going to lie, I never thought too much about her on my own before junior year. Never paid that much attention to her, except for when she was in plays and shit and then only because of Burnett. And then, of course, there was that Massachusetts thing.

Which was my answer to Newman, who had already disappeared into the crowd. I was pretty sure that he was headed in the direction of the Jersey girls.

One word to describe Christina: "Burnett."

After all, David was obsessed with her ever since he saw her play Maria in the middle school production of *West Side Story*.

Everybody knew about his obsession, because he told every person he talked to: kids, teachers, parents, Christina, Christina's friends, the janitors, even the waitresses at Pinky's. So this was certainly no secret.

In fact, he once sent her a DVD of *Beauty and the Beast* with a note that said, "Love, the Beast." Plus the whole "destiny" thing, like, during sophomore year, he kept telling people that they were destined to be together forever.

So Annie had it all wrong that me and Christina had nothing in common. We were both, in our own ways, terrorized by David Burnett for a good portion of our lives.

Now, standing there with her close up breathing into me, all I could think was that it was a good thing that Burn was safely locked away. Because if he saw me with her and the way she was looking at me, he would try to kill me all over again if he could.

"How far did you get since last Thursday?"

Last Thursday we were at another party, at Natalie's house, and Christina and her drama group friends were there for a while. We got to talking, and I told her, actually lied to her then, that I was making progress with my book.

"Doing good." I found myself saying as little as possible to her, figuring the more I say, the less opportunity I might have to get with her.

"Did you get to my part yet?"

"Getting there soon," I told her, even though I was nowhere near the point at which she first factored into the story.

"When are you going to let me read it?"

"Soon, I guess." I didn't really want her to read anything that I wrote.

"Alex said he thought it would be a good idea if you, you know, interviewed me."

I knew what Newman was up to with that line. Winging for me, no doubt. I stood there for a long second (maybe like a minute) thinking, Am I actually nervous with a girl I've known, well *kind* of known, virtually my whole life? And never actually thought was *all that*?

"You look hot tonight" is what I said to break the silence, which was definitely off my game, but definitely going for it. Fuck, if it didn't work, there was always the Jersey girls.

"So do you," she says, and leans in and does another perfect lip-kiss, this time pressing her body against mine. Then she moves backward slowly, and I'm feeling hypnotized, dizzy. And way buzzed now.

"Dude, Duncan brought shrooms."

Suddenly, Evan gets between us, like he has no clue as to what's going on. "We're shrooming. Are you in?" He opens his hands and shows that he already got some. "Sweeeeeeeeeeeettt," he says, popping a bunch into his mouth and walking off.

"I *hate* when he says that," Christina whispers. So we have another thing in common.

And then we are crowded with people around us: the Crew, the Herd, the Drama Group, even Prime Time, talking, mingling, laughing, like it was a coordinated attack to keep me and Christina apart, and it feels like I already dropped a shroom, as if somehow Burnett has orchestrated the disconnect.

Even Evan notices. "Good thing Burn isn't here to see you two together."

Richie Krane adds, "Remember, dawg, he's not actually in prison. Just a psych ward upstate. Everyone knows he's gonna escape one day."

"Plus he's probably got his spies," says *World of Warcraft* Franklin, sounding very much like he could be one of Burn's spies. Rumor had it that Franklin had been iChatting with Burn, from wherever he was. No one wanted to ask whether it was true, probably for fear that it was.

Tyler starts telling everyone to leave me the fuck alone about Burn, and I realize that here, in this last summer of our high school careers, everyone is hanging together because of me and because of what I managed to do on 4/21, as in save everyone's life. That feels pretty good.

Except, I also know that Richie Krane is right about Burn escaping.

"Fuck Burn," says Bobby. He has Duncan's shroom bag and is handing out pieces all around and then yelling "Candyman," distracting us all from thinking about Burn (except maybe not me with that reference—if he says it three times, will Burn show up?).

Now I am faced with a dilemma, as in (1) my rep pretty much requires that I take some shrooms, since I am known not to turn down any chance to get fucked up, and (2) Christina is equally known for not getting high. Plus, she told me at the last party that she kind of resents that I do when I'm with her.

So I'm thinking about Morpheus from *The Matrix*: "This is your last chance. After this, there is no turning back. You take the blue pill: the story ends, you wake up in your bed and believe whatever you want to believe. You take the red pill: you stay in Wonderland and I show you how deep the rabbit hole goes."

For me, I am wondering, which one is the red pill, Christina or the shrooms?

I pass on the bag, not so much to impress Christina (which is partially true), but because now I am thinking about Burn escaping from wherever he is and it is freaking me a little, and the last thing you wanna do is do shrooms if you're freaking.

Me rejecting the bag did not go unnoticed, both by Christina (who smiled at me), and by the rest of the group, which was getting increasingly larger.

"What's up with that?" Bosco, on my left, takes his share,

passes it back to me. I move it across to Tyler; let the Prime Timers get lit. Tyler takes this as a challenge, coming from me, with me knowing that Tyler won't take it.

"I will if you will," he tells me, grabbing a few.

Dare.

Fuckme. Now, I am all in. I'm about to say "I will if Christina will," but I know this is a real bad idea. I am going to just have to man up on this one. So I reach into the bag, not looking at her, and take the last few; if Tyler can handle it, no problem by me.

We munch them down at the same time.

Christina walks away. Or starts to, because the commotion is not done. Crazy Madelaine is pushing her way in through the crowd, looking heavier than I remembered. Coming right at me. Wobbling toward me, actually, as she was *wasted*, more wasted than she was ever known for being. Of course, she was not known for being wasted at all until after we went out during sophomore year, so everyone pretty much blamed me for the fact that she went from superprude to superslut, as I said before. Thing is, I did kind of like her at one point, even though I admitted it to absolutely nobody, so in my mind, blaming me seemed kind of unfair. But whatever. We had not talked at all since we stopped going out (well, since the last time we ended up going out).

So this was not going to be good, her coming at me.

"FUCK you, Steven Crashinsky."

I thought she was going to vomit on me or something. As it turned out, I would have been better off. "FUCK you so much for ruining my life, Mr. Goddamned Hero of the School."

She was coming closer.

". . . and fuck everybody who stopped talking to me, all because you were done with me, and because you and your Crew boys are so fucking immature that you discard girls after you have sex with them."

OK, this actually made me feel good for a moment, because I had never publicly told anyone that I popped her cherry, which as it turned out I didn't actually do anyways.

"You made me drink and you made me smoke and you made me kiss girls, all because I liked you and I would have done anything you asked. So fuck you for taking advantage of that."

Gothy Nicole was behind her now, looking angry (and making me think about Roxanne), and also Nancy Deacon, and I wondered whether there was going to be a bitch stampede over me.

Now Nancy: "What do you have to say for yourself, Mr. Hero?"

I did notice Christina walking away.

What I *was* going to say was that I was younger then, which was true, but that didn't matter, as the Club Crew kind of did that to girls, as did Prime Time, whenever we were done with them.

And I'm not going to lie, I did kind of take advantage of Maddy, knowing that she liked me since, like, McAllister days. And I did go out with her just to use her, and my boys did stop talking to her after I stopped going out with her. But that's just what we do.

Plus it was way more complicated than that and Maddy knew it and I knew it and that was all that mattered to me. So if she really wanted to have a go at me, then there were a few things I could get into.

Except I didn't have to get into any of them for two reasons.

The first reason was, her face was starting to bloat, and I could tell she was getting ready to go, so I stepped back. And she vomited at me. But not on me, because, like my namesake, the ever-ready Bandicoot, I remain quick on my feet, avoiding all obstacles and death traps.

Which left the pool behind me, which is where she vomited.

Now Kelly was going to be pissed at me forever.

And the second reason?

Someone said the magic word, and we all prepared to scatter.

The magic scatter word at any party was, of course, "cops."

And so we separated, some sneaking into the pool house, others running into the woods through the backyards of other houses. Already in Crash Bandicoot mode, I bolted and didn't stop until I got to Newman's car, ten blocks away.

Then I threw up again.

HOW THE PANTHERS GOT THEIR SPOTS

"Yo, Crash. Are you still alive?"

I was twelve years old, in seventh grade, when *Jackass: The Movie* came to town. By then, almost everyone in town called me "Crash." Even though at that point, the video game character meant nothing to me. I had moved on, beyond Crash Bandicoot and PlayStation.

All the way to PlayStation 2.

And MTV.

And *Jackass*.

And my new hero, Steve-O. Sure, there was Johnny Knoxville and Bam and Ryan and Wee Man and the others. And of course, Johnny got all the attention. But if you really knew crazy like I did, you'd recognize immediately that there was something entirely different about Steve-O. Those other guys did incredible stunts and you couldn't help but be shocked into laughter.

But mostly, with Steve-O, you just watched in awe.

Because Steve-O actually should have died.

I don't mean once. I mean like *every* single time you saw Steve-O, he really should have died. Over and over and over again.

But he didn't. And if he survived, so could we. And I was as good at playing Jackass as any kid could be.

I rode shopping carts down the two hundred steps from the front entrance to the town hall. I tried to feed a psychotic pit bull a Slim Jim, with the Slim Jim in my mouth. The dog was on the other side of a fence, but still would have been able to reach more than just my lips if he wanted to tear off my face. I had my friends attach different size fishhooks around my neck in the most painful necklace ever made. No shit, I have the proof; there are videos of the stunts we did.

I did it all. I was creative; I was awesome; I was completely and totally fearless. Well, completely and totally fearless until I heard the words "Yo, Crash. Are you still alive?" while standing on the popcorn line the Saturday of opening weekend.

Pete's brother got us the tickets and waited with us. I had enough money from my mom to buy him refreshments, which my mom suggested that I do to thank him for the ride. So all I was thinking about in the moments before I saw him was what was Pete's brother going to want and how long it would take and would we get really good seats.

And then this tall kid singled me out among my friends and spoke to me in an almost manly voice for a kid, which sounded oddly familiar. Staring at him, I had this feeling that time and space converged and then stood completely still, a feeling that I have never since been able to duplicate without weed or shrooms. Except for once, during the siege, and that was a different matter entirely.

Only this first experience was not a pleasant feeling at all.

Because as soon as it clicked in who I was talking to, I was no longer Steve-O, fearless and immortal. I was immediately back in the panic zone again.

This simply could not be.

What I said was "You're in Chicago." I said this not as a question, but a demand, like just saying it would somehow magically transport him halfway across the country where he belonged, with his new life, far, far away from mine.

"It appears not." He stepped back, closer to us.

Pete recognized him too and said, "No way."

"Way," he said. "Chicago was history ago. We moved back, actually to Long Island."

"So why are you here?" I demanded to know.

"We're moving back here again. In with my aunt."

I remembered that his aunt lived in our town, in this huge house off Main Street, the one with the porch that surrounded the whole house. My mom had to go there once to pick up some kind of makeup thing, and being as it was after school, I had to go with her. I remembered Burn's aunt as a fat lady who smelled like urine. So, as I remembered, did her entire house.

"Why?" I asked. For me, this wasn't just "why," it was more like "no," like "go back to wherever you were," "don't be real, be some kind of nightmare dream," which is what I felt like I was in.

"My father was dusted in the towers," he said.

I had no clue what he was talking about. And then his sister, Roxanne, came over, yelling "Oh my frickin' god, it's little Crash. Do they still call you that?" I couldn't tell whether she was genuinely happy to see me or secretly making fun of me. If not for the hurdles between us, I think she would have barreled into me like she did when I was younger. Seeing her again, I felt like I was back in McAllister and that somehow everything between the moment that they left town and the very instant before seeing them was all some kind of illusion.

"You got so *cuuuuuuuuute*," she squealed, adding to my feeling of being in elementary school with no time having passed.

And there, wobbling out of the women's room, was their fat Aunt Peesmell, looking exactly as I remembered her.

So there it was.

Of course, I couldn't concentrate on the movie at all (except for the scenes with Steve-O, which, as always, were over-the-top great). I remember sitting there, in a sweat, thinking about whether Burnett remembered that he wanted to kill me.

Maybe he had forgotten. Or gotten over it.

Maybe he was different now.

Then, after the movie, he came over to us again and told us that he had Xbox, and did we want to come over to his aunt's place. And Roxanne said, "When are you going to come to my aunt's house to play with David? *Puleeze* come over to play with David," sounding very much the same as she had sounded when we were in McAllister and totally different at the same time. Different because her voice was deeper, more grown up, and she now had breasts and all, which she totally caught me staring at, although I didn't intend to stare. I remembered that she was Lindsey's age, but she looked older, more mature than Lindsey. And she did have kind of a cute face for someone who kind of looked like Burn. Kind of a mix between Burn and Christina Ricci.

Pete's brother drove us home, and I lay in bed all night, wondering whether I would ever sleep again.

And then it was Monday, and I didn't see Burn in school, though I checked in every class to see where he could have been assigned. And when class after class was Burn-free, I decided that it had to have been a hallucination after all.

Except.

Except that Burn was standing there. Between me and my bus. And oddly, I was completely by myself, which was rare for me, since I was almost always with some of my friends.

And he was walking over to me. I remember needing to take the worst shit ever and hoping I made it home in time as my stomach was increasingly tightening every second throughout the day. Now I was in trouble.

"Did you think we were done with each other?" he said, getting up close to me.

"Well, yeah."

"Don't you know, Crash, that we are like Voldemort and Harry Potter? We are dependent on each other." The look in his eyes left no doubt as to which of us was which. It was not lost on me that Voldemort will not rest until Harry is dead.

I could feel the shit liquefying in my intestines. I had to use every muscle in my body to keep things from flowing out. I clamped down with my arms and even my teeth. He must've noticed that something was wrong, because he backed off, and I looked beyond his shoulders.

My bus was leaving. Without me. I was unable to move.

Fuckme. How was I going to get home? How was I going to get to a bathroom? And how long did I have to live?

From behind us a car horn was honking.

"That's my mom," he said, walking backward. "See you tomorrow."

Me, still not moving.

And him, apparently noticing that there were no buses left, "Do you want a ride?" all nice and everything. Did he forget that he had just threatened my life again?

Then his mom pulled up and said "Get in" to both of us, and I really had no choice, because even if he was going to kill me, it was probably, like, days, weeks, months away, and in my condition I was not going to otherwise last for the rest of the afternoon.

So this is how my mom and Burn's mom became friends again.

Mrs. Burnett calls my mom on her cell phone on the way home to tell her that she has me, and I have to give her the directions, which of course means that Burn now knows exactly where I live. Then Mrs. Burnett pulls into my driveway and I thank her very much and fly, literally, fly out the door, bulldozing past my mom, who is coming out of the house at the same time, and I am hitting her with my backpack, nearly knocking her over and flinging it into the closet, then bounding up the stairs to the hall bathroom and just making it, instantly exploding into the first restful moment for me since Burn showed up at the movie theater three days before.

Then I come out of the bathroom, breathe for the first time all day, and Mrs. Burnett is in the kitchen, sitting across the kitchen island from my mom. They are having coffee together and talking like old friends, which is so far from the universe that I wanted to live in that I practically scream, but before I can scream, my mom says, "David is in your room, honey," and I rush up the stairs faster than I've ever moved before. And . . .

Burn is sitting on my bed, controller in hand, playing *Jak and Daxter* on my PlayStation 2. All of my other video games are laid out on the floor, my closet flung open and ransacked-looking.

"Your games suck, dude" is what he said. "How do you not have *Final Fantasy*? Xbox is so much better. How could you not have *Halo*?" Then he looked at me looking at my room, now in total disarray, and seeing I was pissed off, he added, "Don't you have any porn?"

And I watched him play my games for like an hour until my mom called up to us to come down, and then I followed him down to the living room. And as he was leaving, in front of his mother and my mother, he said to me, "Sorry for getting you into trouble in elementary school, dude. I had some really big problems then. I'm on much better meds now."

And he extended his hand out to me, all gentlemanly.

I looked at his mom and my mom and wondered if he was apologizing now, then what was up with the Harry Potter/Voldemort line from earlier in the day.

"He's a troubled child" is what my mother said that night as we were sitting in front of the television. As usual, we were watching some Nickelodeon show, being as Jamie was a true Nick addict. She came home after school every day, sat on the family room floor with her homework, and never actually took her eyes off the screen.

Me and Lindsey would sit on the couch when we were younger, each of us on a separate side since Lindsey refused to get any closer to me, and keeping our ritualistic distance, we watched the classic shows together—*Doug, Ren & Stimpy, Angry Beavers, Rocko's Modern Life, Hey Arnold!, Real Monsters, Catdog,* and, of course *Rugrats.* But always like three, maybe four in a row and we were done.

Not Jamie.

She knew most of those shows, the ones that were still on, but supplemented those by also watching *The Wild Thornberrys, Rocket Power, Oh Yeah!, The Fairly OddParents, Pinky and the Brain, Invader Zim,* and, of course, *SpongeBob* (which OK, I never missed either). Plus, *All That, Keenan & Kel, Sabrina, the Teenage Witch,* and anything else on Nick. And Nick at Nite. She switched channels only for *Full House,* which she watched with total rapture, reciting every word from every character simultaneously with the actors. (I tried to get her to do this in front of my friends, but without the actual shows, she could remember nothing.) She had recently started cheating on Nick whenever *Lizzie McGuire* or *Kim Possible* came on, but mostly switched back and forth during these shows, out of loyalty to Nick. Which, of course, would be the one word to sum up Jamie.

Loyalty.

She was mostly a B student (as compared to my C's and C minuses), which made my parents crazy, because Lindsey was all straight A's and they thought Jamie was as smart as Lindsey.

But Jamie didn't care about stuff like schoolwork or sports or friends or anything else. If she liked something, she pretty much stuck with it, without questioning it, and dedicated herself to it, whatever it was, pretty much to the exclusion of everything else. And the one thing she loved more than anything else was Nickelodeon.

My father tried to keep her from her shows, first encouraging her not to watch, thinking all the time that she would do better at school without TV (which she didn't; actually, when she did her homework without the TV, her grades went *down*). And when that didn't work, he tried bribing her with other things, but there was nothing else she wanted except Nick shows.

More than once, my father attempted to threaten her, saying, "Do you want to end up like your brother?"

Which, of course, wasn't a threat to her, since I could do no wrong in her eyes, even when I continued to tease her, fight with her, trip her, knock her down, barrel into her, or use her for one of my Jackass stunts. Nothing I could do to her would make her love me less (the exact opposite of Lindsey, who I had given up on and who hardly ever talked to me).

So as Jamie folded her math homework into her notebook and *The Jimmy Neutron Show* was about to start, my mother started talking about her conversation with Mrs. Burnett, how her son has been on different medications his whole life to control his bipolar disorder and his anxiety and depression, and that he never had many friends wherever they went, and how, to make it even more difficult for him, his father's job required that they had to move frequently.

In fact, my mother said, according to Mrs. Burnett, David told her that he still considered me to be his best friend, even though he hadn't seen me in like four years.

"She said that you were the only kid who made him feel comfortable here."

And I responded, "Did you remind her that he tried to kill me when I wouldn't help him burn down McAllister?"

"Yeah, well, he had this thing about fire and explosions when he was young," she said, and it was almost like she was making excuses for him. "But his mother said that he's over it now."

"I just don't get why he's back" is what I told her.

I was totally unprepared for her response. In my twelve-year-old mind, there weren't too many possibilities. The Burnetts had only lived in our town for a short period, and Burn always said it was a sinkhole, not only for him, but for his family. He actually said that no one in his family liked our town at all. And he definitely didn't like anyone here, including me. So why not stay in Chicago? Even Long Island could've been better.

"His father died" was what she said. "He was killed on nine-eleven. He was in the World Trade Center. North Tower. *How horrible.*" My mother actually shuddered, looked like she was really thinking about how horrible it was. At that time, I didn't understand the concept of irony well enough to realize how ironic it was that Burn's father died from the very thing that fascinated Burn most. As in explosions.

"So he really needs a friend, Steven."

As she was talking, Lindsey came down from her room, all high-schooled up in her makeup, with her attitude, head-tilt, glanced at the TV (like she was expecting something other than Nick), shuddered (which she did like once an hour), and made a face of cartoon disapproval at our choice with her official eye roll (she was officially out of Nickzone). She said something about needing money for some after-school activity to my mom, and my mom was all, your father will be home within the hour, ask him, which of course would not be a problem for Lindsey, her being his favorite and everything. In fact, it seemed to me that those two only talked to each other and never to any of us (actually, he only seemed to talk to my mom about answers to questions from her or questions he had to have answered, not like "how was your day, dear").

"In fact," said my mother, more to Lindsey than to me, "the

whole family seems to need a few good friends. They are going through a very difficult period."

"Who?" Lindsey with her sarcasm.

"The Burnetts. Mrs. Burnett, David, and the girl . . . Roxanne."

There goes the eye roll again. "Uugggh. She's like el wierdo. I saw her today. She sits next to me in English and talks all the time."

Jamie, not missing a beat, matching Lindsey's sarcasm, "Thankfully, they don't have a kid my age."

You had to love Jamie.

"I invited them over for Thanksgiving," my mother responded.

Lindsey and I actually made eye contact on that one, one of the few times we bonded. Disaster was certain.

"Dad's gonna *love* that," said Jamie, never taking her eyes off *Jimmy Neutron.* Even as she said it, Lindsey and I knew exactly what she meant. When it came down to it, Jamie was more insightful than Lindsey and me combined.

As I said, you had to love Jamie.

"Jamie's right," Lindsey added, ever the lawyer. "Dad's going to hit the roof when he finds out that you are encouraging Steven to spend time with the fire boy." Another eye roll from her, and she turned as if ready to go back to her room, but she wasn't done yet. "C'mon, Mom, he's even more out of control than Steven."

Apparently any bonding time between us was over. Thanks, Lindsey.

About to leave, she turned back to my mom to add, "You should know better," sounding very much like my dad; her condescending tone was a perfect match.

That was my cue to go to my room. My dad was going to be home soon enough, and I retreated whenever I could to avoid contact with him. I would open my homework and get it started; actually the truth was Jak and Daxter were waiting for me on the PlayStation, just where Burn had left them.

The next day in school, Burn found me in the lunchroom with my friends.

"My mom thinks your mom is very stressed out" is what he said. And I wondered, like, what kind of thing is that for one kid to say to another kid? I didn't know how to respond. Of course, I didn't have to, because he started talking again, and it was like we were back in McAllister and the fire incident and the subsequent death threats were an illusion.

"And if my mom thinks your mom is stressed, then she must really be stressed, because my mom is as stressed out as a person can be."

I didn't think that my mom was stressed, until that moment. But his line got me thinking, as in, why was my mom stressed at all? She didn't work; all she did was basically get us up for school, then to after-school activities, and feed us, plus she had people to clean the house and make sure to put away everything that I left out before my father got home and had a fit about it. Plus Isabel stayed with us whenever my mom went on vacation with my dad or her friends. Isabel, of course, was our au pair when we were younger (at least until she quit because of me not being in control, but that's another story). So why exactly did Burn's mom think my mom was stressed?

Pete got involved. "Dude, all moms are stressed. It's how they are."

Kenny agreed, which surprised us, as his mom was Chinese and she certainly seemed different from the rest of our moms. More calm, definitely. But then again, Kenny never, ever talked back to her.

This was the deepest conversation we had ever had. And we

all seemed to be done with it. But Burn hadn't finished. "My mom thinks your mom could really use a friend. She even invited us to Thanksgiving at your house. So hopefully you will have *Final Fantasy* by then."

"My mom only invited you on account of your father dying in the Twin Towers" is how it came out when I said it.

Burn stared hatefully at me. As soon as I said it, I knew it was the wrong thing to say, but what was up with him and my mom? Still, all of the other kids at the lunch table shifted uncomfortably.

"Your mom invited us *before* she found out that my father was an innocent victim of the government's secret plan to engage in Bush and Cheney's personal war against the Muslims."

Now Pete jumped in, our resident political know-it-all (this was before Newman came to town). Pete was saying that Burn was out of his mind, that there was no American conspiracy surrounding the destruction of the World Trade Center (and I instantly remembered Burn's earlier statement to me—"my father was dusted in the towers"—and finally understood what he meant). Pete said 9/11 was the consequence of the United States not being able to control Islamist extremists, thanks to the Clinton administration, and that ever since 9/11 everything had changed, thanks to President Bush's quick actions.

Now Burn was fully in gear and argued back, "Oh yeah, where the fuck is Bin Laden? And how come no one has been able to capture him? Perhaps because we're not supposed to capture him?"

To be honest, I knew almost nothing about 9/11. Neither did most of my other friends. Exactly one kid at my school, who none of my friends knew, lost an uncle. Otherwise we were untouched by the event. None of us were all that big into current events in the first place, unless it was about Britney, Paris, Eminem, or some movie guy.

We were all too busy singing songs like "It's Getting Hot in Here." According to Mark Duncan, the Adam Sandler expert, the movie of the year was *Mr. Deeds*, even though some of my other friends would have considered *Spider-Man* or *Star Wars Episode II: Attack of the Clones* or the first Harry Potter or even the third Austin Powers to be far better movies. For Pete, it was a horror movie called *Cabin Fever*. For me, as I said, it was *Jackass: The Movie*.

So yeah, the World Trade Center being destroyed was fucked up, but when all was said and done, it made not one bit of difference to us.

Other than Burn. And something always seemed to matter to Burn anyways.

Still, his father *had* been dusted.

"I'm sorry that it was your father instead of mine" is what I told him, all sincere. "He was a really good coach and all." I remembered that Burn had a very close relationship with his dad, who wasn't the asshole that mine was. Point being, my comment was not so much about Burn's father living, but more about getting rid of mine. However, as it turned out, Burn was apparently deeply moved by my offer to substitute my father for his. He took it as a tribute to his dad and as the ultimate gesture of friendship, which apparently made up for the fact that I was his mortal enemy.

And after that he started doing things for me.

Like homework, for one thing. Not only giving me the answers, but explaining the concepts in a way that made me actually understand what was going on. Like getting me out of trouble with my mom for almost getting caught in a Jackass stunt that involved Lindsey, though she didn't know it. Like getting me rides home with his mom so I didn't have to take the bus, once asking me whether I knew if Christina Haines liked him. I told him how should I know, I haven't talked to Christina

Haines since, like, third grade.

He was also proving to be the supergenius that everyone said he was, getting perfect scores on standardized tests and acing his courses, breezing through the work and correcting teachers whenever they said something that he considered to be inaccurate, knowing all these minute details about virtually everything, like he was constantly preparing for a test that only he knew he was taking.

He went to the mall with us on a few Saturdays, came to the school pre-Halloween party as George Bush and stayed in character the whole night, and had playdates with like half the kids in the grade. He seemed comfortable around my friends (as comfortable as Burn ever was, at least), with the exception of Pete, who just didn't like him and avoided him whenever he could.

Plus, going from a kid who kind of sucked at sports, Burnett was now a decent basketball player. So good, in fact, that he was tapped to try out for the Panthers, the middle school traveling basketball team. Actually, everyone was allowed to try out, but apparently Burn's mom got a call from Coach Rhinehart that he was as good as in.

It was days before tryouts, and I was practicing in the gym after school with Evan and Mark Duncan and a few other kids when Burn walked in and all of a sudden barreled into me, knocking me off my feet, taking my breath away.

By then I had enough practice with falls and sudden impacts to keep my wits about me, so I rolled, turned, and scrambled away from him. "What the fuck, David?" It occurred to me then that he was back to the David Burnett who wanted to kill me, because there was a flash of a look in his eyes that I remembered seeing before, during the McAllister days, but it was gone a second later. Plus by now I was a proven survivor. Thank you, Steve-O.

"You shoot like shit." He threw the ball to me, all back to normal.

"Fuck you." I threw it back, and he turned, pivoted, and sank a three-pointer, nothing but net, then followed the ball, got the rebound, and laid it in again and again, finally tossing it back to me.

"Now you," he challenged. "Go ahead. Three in a row."

I chucked. Nothing but wall. He rebounded, second try. This time I hit the backboard, nowhere near the basket. He tossed me the ball again. Third time, nothing better. No big deal. I was streaky, could hit like ten in a row one day, then none the next.

"You're taking the shot on the way down. As you run. Try it again on the way up. And arc your arm." He demonstrated.

So I slowed down and did it. Just like he said. And three in a row. Like I said, streaky.

He trotted out of the gym, satisfied.

I was equally streaky during tryouts; could steal the ball from any kid, could defend the box and pass to anyone, but could not for the life of me hit the basket on the attempts they gave me. Coach Rhinehart, taking constant notes, had one of his assistants hand me the ball and asked me to shoot. So I stood at the foul line and, just like Burn said, moved up, not down, and extended my arc and dropped three in a row.

Then went zero for seven.

When it was reported back to me, the reason that I did not make the team was that I had talent and speed, but lacked control (story of my life . . .).

Coach Rhinehart told my mom that maybe it was because I was on the young side and a little "rough around the edges," but I should keep trying because there was always next year.

Which is how my mother described the call she got from Rhinehart earlier that night.

My father described it differently: "I heard you didn't make the team because you are too immature. You remain a disappointment" were his actual words.

I think he was baiting me to see if I would lose my temper, as always, so he could start a fight with me and make it out to be my fault, a pattern that I had come to expect. But I didn't lose it, not that night. I didn't much feel like fighting, and, not going to lie, I might have cried if I had to talk to him. So instead I went to my room, hearing my parents argue, as my mother did not appreciate my father's negativity. She seemed to be getting increasingly irritated whenever she talked to him. Before I got to my bedroom, there was Lindsey, sticking her head out of her bedroom door, and she sneered her Lindsey sneer, telling me it was all my fault that they were fighting again. Fuck you too, Lindsey Crashinsky.

What my mom didn't tell me, what she may not have known, was that I was on the reserve list, actually next up if any of the twelve players dropped out. One of the assistant coaches stopped me in the schoolyard the next morning to tell me that he thought that I did pretty well and that I should keep practicing. "You never know, Steven."

Thing is, I already knew the roster, having IMed with my friends all night, so I was already aware of who was in and who was out by the next morning. There were a few surprises: specifically two kids, Leeds and Hartman, who shouldn't have made it over me. My friends expressed as much outrage as you could put into an instant message.

Didn't matter. Done was done. Or so I thought.

Later that day, during lunch, Burn stopped by our table in the cafeteria on his way to sit with the rest of the newly formed basketball team. When he saw me, he said, "Don't worry, Crash, not all of the Panthers have their spots yet," which is the way Burn sometimes talked. And which would have made no sense to me, except this was the second time in a day that I was hearing some potential reason to hope. Plus, I did have the element of magic on my side, historically. So I took the comments in and said nothing.

Pete, however, had been continuing to make it clear to the rest of us that it was either him or Burn. We were going to have to choose. With every day that passed, he seemed to start an argument with Burn, usually over nothing. Simple, stupid things. Burn claimed that he never needed sleep, and Pete argued that it was a medical necessity. Burn and Pete went at it over football stats, music, cars; whatever one brought up, the other objected to. We were basically getting used to the two of them constantly bickering.

So when Pete heard Burn basically promise me a place on the Panthers, he immediately started in, as usual. What Pete said was "Burnett, you jerk-off, panthers don't have spots."

Burn was, all of a sudden, in Pete's face, saying, "You fucking cretin, the term 'panther' comes from *Panthera*, which includes the lion, the tiger, the jaguar, and the leopard. The black panther on your fucking jersey is just one variation of the species. . . ."

Now Pete was up and backing away from Burn, who continued to attack, pinning Pete against the wall and continuing, "And panthers are not necessarily black. They can be tan or even *spotted*."

He was spitting the word "spotted," still holding Pete.

"Consider, for example, the Florida panther—not the hockey team, but the endangered species. There are only like eighty left, and many of them are *spotted*." Then he was getting louder and louder, keeping the pressure on Pete with his forearm against Pete's neck. Pete struggled to free himself, but Burn just continued.

"And even if you considered only the black panther, then you must have forgotten that black panthers, especially when born, are *spotted*, and many panthers' coats contain multiple pigments, black against blacker, so they remain *spotted* throughout their lives."

He then let go of Pete and walked back to the lunch table. By then, the entire crowd in the lunchroom was watching him. Pin-drop quiet, I don't have to tell you. That's when I saw it: the exact look Burn gave me when he lit the fire.

And while the others who thought that Burn was actually going to hurt Pete were relieved to see him walk away, I was preparing myself for the worst. Especially since it all went down so quickly that none of us could react, and I didn't know what to expect next.

And, as if on cue, as Burn was on his way to the basketball table, Pete, being Pete, wasn't about to let Burn have the last word, and so he yelled out something like "What do *you* know?" which seemed innocent enough. But I guess that was all the fuel Burn needed, because he suddenly turned back and pounced on Pete again.

"Can you name one of the things that distinguishes *Panthera* from other cats?" Pinning Pete against the wall again.

Pete was under pressure to answer. Or, possibly, die.

This time I was better prepared and was able to get up, behind Burn. I moved toward them cautiously. I had Pete's back and would not let him get hurt, at least not without getting hurt myself, which I was guessing was probably going to be the case, because I realized that Burn was beyond wired, in full psycho mode, and at that particular moment I fully believed that no one could have brought him down if they tried.

Still, I had Pete's back if it came to it.

"Well? Answer me! What distinguishes *Panthera* from other cats?" Burn howled.

"I don't know," squealed Pete.

"Their ability to *ROAR*," Burn yelled, roaring full blast, then laughing and releasing Pete as if it was all just a big joke, which it may have been. Who could tell, given Burn's very strange sense of humor?

I looked at him and he looked back at me, and the look I saw before was gone. He was totally and completely back to being new Burn, the good one.

And of course, joke or not, by then Mr. Campbell, the principal of middle school, was behind me, along with half the teachers, motioning for Burn to go with them with two words—"Mr. Burnett"—and a hand signal.

"What?" Burn said. "Nothing happened."

The male teachers surrounded him. One put a hand on his shoulder, and he shrugged it off, twisting violently.

"NOTHING FUCKING HAPPENED!" he roared again, but more like a very loud whisper this time.

He did not fight, he did not resist. Instead he very respectfully and cooperatively followed the teachers out of the cafeteria.

And then he was gone. Not in school for the rest of the day. Not in practice with the rest of the team. And that night, while I was watching *SpongeBob* with Jamie, the phone rang. My mom got it, gave it to me.

Coach Rhinehart.

I was on the team.

Next practice was Monday.

CHAPTER SIX

HOW THANKSGIVING GOT RUINED, PART I: ANOTHER DAY AT THE OFFICE

After Burn was removed from the cafeteria, he simply disappeared. He wasn't in any of his classes the rest of that day and didn't show up at school the following day or the day after that. No one said anything or knew what happened to him. But we all figured that he was in some kind of trouble.

Which, as I said, made no sense at all, not really, because he hadn't actually done anything wrong. OK, he argued with Pete, may have gone too far and may have been too loud, but the two of them never actually fought, so it wasn't like he had done anything different than any other kid would do, in a way. Maybe he was a little more intense, but that was just Burn being Burn.

Tommy Leeds had come from a New York City school before he got to ours, and he said that Burn's outburst would not even have been noticed in the school he went to. There were, he said, actual knives and weapons taken away from kids, and they had metal detectors on the doors and bars on the windows.

So Burn yelling about panther spots was really No Big Deal.

The funny thing was, barely a month after I had lost sleep over the fact that Burn was back, I was actually concerned about what happened to him. My mom tried reaching Mrs. Burnett all week and was told by Aunt Peesmell that she was out of town.

Over the weekend, I periodically checked my AIM account to see if he signed on. Burn was always signed in, as he almost always was on his computer when he wasn't in school. Not this weekend, however. Not once in all the times I checked.

The following Monday, I got to my first basketball practice and realized that my spot on the Panthers was actually the spot that had originally belonged to Burn (duh . . .).

Coach Rhinehart went through the roster to get acquainted with us. Burn's name was not on the list. It was like he had never actually come back to town at all. Or like we were in some kind of science fiction movie, with one of us going missing and the others either not noticing or all pretending not to notice.

Except for Pete, who bragged about the fact that he got Burn suspended. In his mind this was a good thing because, according to Pete, Burn was a "motherfucking time bomb, waiting to explode." Thing is, no one disagreed with him at the time, including me, not after recognizing the look in his eyes that I had seen before.

As for school, and lunches at the cafeteria, it was real quiet for the first couple of days after the blow-up, but then it pretty much went back to normal, with kids yelling at each other and arguing over sports, TV shows, video games, and whatever girls argued about amongst themselves. When Burn's name came up, it was never actually about him, but all about what happened to him.

Then it was the beginning of Thanksgiving week, and we were off from school starting that Monday. Which would have been great, except that my mom and Lindsey had gone to Maine to see my aunt on Saturday. They weren't going to be home until the following day, and for some odd reason, my father decided to take me and Jamie into work, as he still didn't "feel comfortable" leaving me alone in the house for extended periods of time, which was absolutely ridiculous as my mom almost always left me in the house for extended periods of time.

I had been to my father's office a few times when I was younger, but never for more than a few hours, and every time

I went, it totally sucked. Superquiet, with all these people in cubicles, and all these TV monitors turned on to the same channel, none of them with anything interesting on them. And my father in his office, on the phone—actually on his headset—pacing back and forth, yelling at people, pointing for me to sit down, get up, keep quiet, don't touch that, or gesturing about something that I had to do and me having to pretend that I knew what he wanted when I had no clue.

So that Monday morning when he woke me, I had this bad feeling.

Jamie was already dressed, and I was apparently already late. She had her schoolbooks with her; I guess my dad expected me to bring mine, even though I had no actual homework to do. So I threw my Game Boy Advance and some Pokémon games into my backpack for extra coverage when it got superboring, which it was no doubt going to be.

Jamie had already eaten breakfast; I was too late. My father was already agitated about me not being ready and wouldn't let me get anything to eat.

Then the long car ride, with him listening to some boring guy on the radio talk about the stock market and periodically yelling at me to keep it down, which meant lowering the Pokémon music on the Game Boy.

Then, as we got out of the car in the parking garage, he turned to look at me for the first time that day, noticing that I was in jeans and sneakers and giving me the usual look of disgrace, and all he said was "Try not to embarrass me today."

And I stared back at him, not saying, but hearing in my head, the very words that I had repeated to myself so many times by then, which were "Fuck you, Jacob," which made me feel good, because the one thing my father hated, more than anything else, was being called Jacob, having unofficially changed his name to Jack, and so he was Jack to everyone except his mother and his sister, Randi.

After introducing me and Jamie to the people he worked with, even though we had probably met them before, he quickly ushered us into his private office, with a look like he was going to kill us if we said anything wrong.

Then us sitting on the couch across from his desk, watching him talk on the phone until we were bored.

. . . and me nudging Jamie and Jamie nudging me back,

. . . then another nudge for each of us,

. . . then a push,

and then a full-on slap on the head, first me, then Jamie,

then . . .

"*Enough*, Steven," Jacob said in a deeper voice than he used at home. "Do I really need to separate you two at this point?"

Now Jamie starts crying. So Jacob gets all fatherly to her and comes across the desk, sits between us with his back to me, and tells her that everything's fine, not to cry, even touching her face. I'm behind her, and when I see she stops crying, I start making my dad faces, mimicking him, which makes her laugh, and now my dad turns to me, grabs me by the arm so tightly I can practically feel his fingers touching my actual bone, and he whispers in a very controlled voice, so that even Jamie can't hear him:

"I *will* hurt you, if that's what you want."

"I didn't *do* anything." Me, defiant.

"You never *do* anything."

"Lemme go."

"Do you understand me, Steven?" he hissed, his grip tightening. "This is your last chance to behave. If you can't control yourself, things will have to change. Am I clear?"

"Yeah, right." I yanked my arm back the instant that he eased his grip.

"There are special schools for children who can't control themselves. Boarding schools where we can send you, schools where they teach you how to behave properly."

"I didn't *do* anything," I said, not believing him at all.

He stood up and one-finger motioned for me to follow him. As he crossed around his desk, he motioned for me to sit in his chair. When I did, he reached down and opened one of the desk drawers, pulling out a huge folder, dropping it onto the top of the desk. "Open it."

I sat in his chair, looking up at him, hate in my eyes, not touching his precious folder. *Fuck you, Jacob,* was all I heard in my brain.

"*Open* it."

I flipped open the file folder and stared at a brochure for a school in Vermont, with pictures of kids older looking than me in military uniforms. There were handwritten notes scribbled across the front of the brochure. I recognized my father's hand-writing.

"That one takes kids your age" was all he said. "Not all of them do."

I flipped to the next brochure. Another school, this one in Pennsylvania, also with my father's notes on it. Then another, and another after that, all with boys my age standing stick straight at attention. Serious-looking kids.

I started to believe, and believe me, it was not a good feeling.

"You can't make me go" is what I said defiantly.

"Of course I can," he answered matter-of-factly. "If I decide that you are going, then trust me, you will go." He snatched the folder away and placed it back in his drawer.

Jamie was suddenly on high alert; apparently she had been listening to everything from her seat on the couch.

"Daddy, you can't send Steven away." She was out of her seat and about to start crying again. "Youcan'tyoucan't."

Now his focus was on her again, not because she was in full cry, which she was, but because she was getting loud enough that other people in his office were likely to hear her. Immediately he transformed back into "caring dad," whole different expression, going quickly over to her and putting out her flames. "Steven's not going anywhere, princess. We're just talking."

His arm around her now, going full-on sitcom dad, a role I rarely saw him play. He sat down beside her. "Why don't you do your homework?" he told her. "Steven and I are going to take a walk."

"Where?" Now just sniffles, but still with suspicious eyes.

"To get him something to eat. He never had breakfast. Did you think I forgot?" He wiped Jamie's tears away, making sure she was back in full control. "Do you want anything? A bagel? A muffin?" Her eyes lit up at the mention of a muffin. She was always a sucker for a good muffin.

I looked at the office door. While he was distracted, I was busying myself with possibilities. In my Crash Bandicoot mind I judged the distance from the chair behind his desk, and I realized that I could hop over the desk, step right between the chairs, fake right, go left, bolt out of his office, around the mazes of cubicles, and through the glass doors to the elevators or stairs.

He turned, looked at me.

Quick. Think!

Elevators or stairs? Stairs or elevators? Stairs. He would never follow. Down the thirty-two flights, into the lobby, into the street, into a cab, give the driver all the money in my pocket, like seventeen dollars, and say "Drive," until the seventeen was all ticked out on the meter and then figure out where to go from there.

Which I might as well do, I thought. Because in the instant I opened that folder in my father's desk, I knew, *I totally knew,* that there was no place like home anymore. So fuck you, Jacob, for making me feel that way.

It seemed as if he was reading my mind, because he immediately got up from Jamie's side, turned to me, and instinctively blocked the door, reminding me more than a little of Burn the day he tried to set me on fire.

"Still hungry?" he says (not asks) with a nod, his face totally back to being "angry dad" again; "sitcom dad" is most definitely gone.

I follow him out, not looking at Jamie. Whatever was going to happen, I did not want it to happen in front of my little sister.

Then we're out in the hallway.

"Marcie, order up a couple of muffins and bagels, butter and cream cheese on the side," he barks at his secretary as we walk down the hall, his arm planted heavily around my shoulder, evidently to keep me from going anywhere. "And a large cappuccino."

He steers me into the conference room and closes the door. I can see out the window at the buildings across the street from his office. I can see people moving around in that office, congregating in a bunch of cubicles like bees and I wonder how they can stand it being cooped up all day in these cages. I hear a siren going off on the street below, and I wonder whether someone was hit by a car and how far a hospital is from where we are.

"You actually have your friend David to thank," he tells me.

I wasn't going to look at him, but now I have to. I'm thinking, what does Burn have to do with my father being such an asshole?

And then he explains how my mom's been in touch with Burn's mom and how Mrs. Burnett explained to my mom that the administrators at my school suggested that Burn might be better suited for a different kind of learning environment. They were, my father told me, concerned that David's aggressive behavior would escalate like it did when he attended McAllister and apparently like it did when he was in another school in Chicago. So, basically, what I am figuring out is that Burn got kicked out of our middle school and will now be going to a special school.

And, my father continued, the problem was that Burn kept having adverse reactions to the medications he was on, which the school knew, which was why they were watching him so carefully, and which was why they chose to act so quickly. According to my father, those medications were apparently keeping him from sleeping and making him increasingly aggressive and manic, so now he was in a better place, both emotionally and physically, in this boarding school in Massachusetts.

Which, Jacob explains, got him thinking about how difficult it has been for me in school, with different medicines not working on me, and wouldn't I be better off in a place where there would be one-on-one learning, where no one would judge me for not getting A's, and wouldn't I be able to do better if I were in a special program where I could actually excel at something for a change? And then he drops this line, which I totally didn't see coming, like he was the good guy in all this:

"I'm trying to save your life, Steven, and now is the time to do it."

And I realize that all the while that my father is talking to me, he has returned to his "sitcom dad" concerned expression, like all he cares about is me doing good, and maybe in his mind, he actually believes it. And all I'm thinking about is, this guy really thinks I'm fucking retarded. Really . . . how could anyone do well with a father who thinks you're a fucking retard and wants to put you in a school with real retards?

And besides, he tells me, now the sitcom dad face totally

gone again, I need to learn how to control my anger and my frustration when I don't get my way, and he lists the number of things around the house that are broken, some of which were my fault, OK, but some of which I had nothing to do with but I got blamed for anyways.

And I'm still thinking, fuck you Jacob, fuck you Jacob, fuck you Jacob, while he's going on about my lack of maturity and while most of the schools don't recommend midyear entrants, the one in Vermont, the one in the first brochure, actually encourages them.

And Marcie comes in with a tray: muffins, bagels with butter and cream cheese, two bottles of Nesquik, and a Starbucks cup.

And my blood is now boiling, which he probably knew was going to happen when he closed the conference room door, so he is as surprised to see her as I am.

Seeing how our eyes are locked together, Marcie just puts the tray down and bolts, eager to leave us by ourselves.

And I'm about to burst and hit him with the tray of food, the Starbucks, the bagels, everything, and it takes practically all I've got, trying with all my might to control the anger, when he says, "However, I've agreed with your mom to give you one more chance to shape up."

About now, my hands are literally shaking with the force of wanting to see him screaming from a lapful of hot Starbucks and the equal force of having to control myself or lose my last chance to stay home, at least for now.

And then there is a painfully loud screech outside, so I rush to the window and look down below. There must have been some kind of accident in the street; everyone is honking their horns and that's all I can hear.

I have noticed that one of my ADHD symptoms is this total aversion to loud unexpected noises. They throw me off my game, get into my insides, and freaking unnerve me. I have gotten used to this over the years and manage to counteract that feeling most of the time, but loud sounds still disturb me. I just don't like them. I mean, I'm OK with totally loud music or fireworks or movie explosions, it's the surprise factor that shakes me to my core.

Apparently it wasn't just me, though, not this time, because the people in the next building are all staring out the window and for a split second I think they are staring at me, but then there was this truck accident that they were actually looking at, down in the street beneath us.

"Do you understand me, Steven?"

I had, incredibly, forgotten about Jacob Crashinsky.

I tell him yes, thinking many things at the same time:

Not only did the sound of the accident drain the anger from me, just like loud, unexpected noises tended to do . . .

In some superhero sort of a way, I might have either caused the accident through telekinetic energy, with my uncontrolled anger exploding into the universe and causing the cars to collide . . .

Or otherwise the magic was working for me again, as it had on many other occasions.

OK, even if you don't believe in magic, consider that if not for the accident, it was highly likely that I would have hit Jacob in the face with hot Starbucks, sending him into a scalding fury of horror-movie proportions, which would have most definitely led to me being sent straightaway to that school in Vermont or some other school where I probably would have stayed, which, now that I think of it, might have resulted in something different going down on 4/21, like maybe people getting killed.

So yeah, magic.

I also figure out pretty quickly that the man standing across from me, calling himself my father, the guy who is supposed to make me feel secure and protected, was determined to send me away, and that he was not doing it now only because of my mom, as she wouldn't want to break up the family, no matter what. But as strong-willed as she was, she was unfortunately no match for him.

So given my inability to control myself, and given his impeccable track record of getting whatever he wanted, I also knew at that moment that I had a very limited time before something else happened that would give him an excuse to get me out of his house. For good.

I was going to need a plan. Not just an idea, or a concept, but a full-blown, foolproof plan that would put me in control and allow me to stay put in my house and not have to go off to some faraway school where they wear hats and stand at attention all day.

Which of course takes us to Thanksgiving.

CHAPTER SEVEN

HOW THANKSGIVING GOT RUINED, PART II: HOW BURN LITERALLY SAVED MY LIFE

OK, this chapter was originally called "How Thanksgiving Got Ruined," being as I didn't originally plan to write about how my father was planning to ship me off to boarding school. But then I started thinking about everything that happened on Thanksgiving Day that year, and I realized that it would make no sense if you didn't already know how high the stakes were for me.

Keep in mind:

One thing wrong. Just one. Anything at all. And I was out of the house, out of the family, out of middle school, off the basketball team, far from my hometown, gone from my friends, shipped off to some foreign state where I would become one of those kids in a crew cut saluting the flag whose photograph would be in the next brochure that some other kid in some other state would find on his dresser one afternoon after school as a warning for him to shape up.

You get the picture?

If so, then you can imagine the stress I was under. Not only on the drive home from my father's office, but then back at home. Everything was just-another-day-normal for everyone else in my family, but for me: *one false move* and I was gone.

And here's the thing: I had *no idea* what it could be, because there was no way I could predict what could trigger my father's decision—reason being, virtually every day I got yelled at for virtually everything that I did. Clothes on the floor. Plate left out. Empty cup in the family room. Not cleaning up. Leaving the TV on. Not taking out the garbage. Bike on the lawn. Fighting with Jamie. Even talking to Lindsey.

And to make matters worse, it was entirely possible that I might have done something in the past week or month that Jacob would find out about now, and if so it would count as a "now" thing, even though the thing that I did wrong I did way before getting the warning.

What I realized when we got home was this, simply put:

My house was a fucking minefield.

I had no choice. I had to escape. So I called Pete and worked it out to sleep over at his house. Then the next day, I stayed at Kenny's, and the day after that, at Evan's. My mom called me every day to find out when I was coming home, like nothing was wrong.

How could she not know?

And during the entire time that I stayed out, I thought constantly about my father's threat, and I thought about her, my own mom, not coming to my rescue, and I was starting not to like her, not that I hated her like I hated Jacob, but the question that had to be asked was: How come my own mom didn't have my back?

And lying in bed, not actually a bed, but an air mattress in Kenny's room, I had to wonder whether my father could have been right. Would I be better off in a school where they could teach me the way that my mind wanted to learn? Maybe it wouldn't be so bad. After all, I had no problems going away to camp for the summer; maybe this would be more like that than a military school.

But what if they were thinking of sending me to the school that Burn was sent away to? Would they do that? An immediate panic set in, and the rest of the night was lost to it.

And when night became morning and Kenny was still snoring away, I thought: Would anyone from my family actually even miss me?

My final answer before falling to sleep: Jamie.

Nobody but Jamie. But then again, she would be too busy with *SpongeBob*, *Rugrats*, and *Boy Meets World* marathons to worry about me.

As for my friends, they would be upset at first, but then they would be too busy playing *SOCOM* or some other video game and would hardly even notice I was gone.

And of course, Lindsey would be happy. At least the house would be quiet so she could study. So that brought me back to Jamie, because other than her, I was essentially a kid without a home or family. She was, somehow, my only hope. Plus, more importantly, way more importantly, she needed me. She wasn't capable of dealing with Jacob on her own. Without me there, he would have to turn his attention to her, and soon enough she would be banned from television or some other punishment that felt to him like he was saving her.

When my mother picked me up at Evan's on Thanksgiving morning, she did all the talking, in her typical momlike way, rambling to no one in particular:

"Your father took Jamie into Manhattan to see the Macy's parade—remember how good the view is from his office? Lindsey didn't want to go, and I'm cooking—we're having the Burnetts, and your aunt Randi, and two families from your father's office. I've been cooking all morning . . . You know how you like stuffing? Well, this year, I wasn't going to make it, then Elaine . . . Mrs. Burnett said she would take care of it and that she would bring a few pies, pumpkin and apple. Do you think we should stop for Häagen-Dazs? Or Ben and Jerry's? Serita is coming at four to help out, but I *will* need your help before everyone gets here. Do you think you can handle getting the chairs out of the garage? Your father's not going to want to do it. They should be home by three, which should give me time; the turkey's been in the oven since seven and it's unusually big, so I'm not sure how long to leave it. We're not having sweet potatoes, do you think anyone will notice?"

"I dunno."

Why wasn't she talking about the boarding school? Why wasn't she telling me that I didn't have to go?

I wasn't going to bring it up first. I wasn't going to even talk at all. I didn't have the strength. I was so completely tired.

Except. What was this about the Burnetts coming over? I figured that after the incident at school, we were done with them. So I asked, "Burn, I mean David. He's still coming?"

"Yes, honey. After all, I did invite them. Months ago. Elaine is going through such a hard time, with her husband being gone, and then that boy, something's not right about him, with his bipolar disorder and his other issues. You will be nice to him, won't you? And Lindsey says that his sister's not much better. Weird, that's what Lindsey says about her. Lindsey thinks she has a tattoo, and, according to Elaine, she hasn't made many friends since they came back to town. I did tell you that David was transferred to a school in Massachusetts that specializes in kids with emotional issues, didn't I?"

"Roxanne" is what I said.

"What, honey?" She was distracted from driving, which she always did extraordinarily badly.

"Burn's . . . David's sister, Roxanne," I said. "Actually she's OK." I was thinking about Roxanne and the few times I ran into her since the Burnetts moved back. She said the vilest things every time I saw her, yelling, screaming my full name at me, like it was a curse:

"CRA SHIN SKEEEEEEEEEEEEEEEE!"

Not just to me. She was vile to virtually everyone, with absolutely no care where she was or who heard her.

She was so loud.

And almost everything she said was funny, so funny that you had to laugh, especially when she was making fun of her brother. Or my sister. Lindsey hated her, which gave her street cred as far as I was concerned. She would definitely make Thanksgiving more interesting. I pictured her doing her fake sneeze at the dinner table, sneezing out my last name, just like she did in the mall once when she bumped into me and my friends.

"CRA CRA CRA SHINSKEEEEE," into her sleeve, all blinking with mock allergies. Over and over again. You couldn't help but laugh. OK, you had to be there.

Jacob wasn't going to like that at all.

Then it hit me.

Jacob.

DAVID.

ONE THING.

I was immediately exhausted again. Fuckme.

"I just didn't know Dave was coming . . . ," I said, realizing that Burn could be a major problem for me.

"What's the problem?" My mom sensed my panic, but then her cell phone rang and she was turning left (one of her worst driving abilities) and answering at the same time (another thing that she didn't do well at all while driving). And when she hung up, it was all "Look, Steven, I know he's got issues, but it *is* Thanksgiving and they have nowhere else to go. It's the right thing to do."

My mom continued driving, playing with her cell phone again.

I'm watching a jogger on the side of the road, being very afraid.

"Your dad is helping them out," she said, pulling into our driveway. "Investing for them, doing what he does . . ."

"Mom," I ventured as she was getting out of the car.

"What?"

"Never mind."

"Fine, Steven. Help me with the packages. Are you feeling all right? You aren't coming down with anything, are you? You look run-down. I never should have allowed you to have three sleepovers in a row." She leans over to feel my head with her lips, checking for temperature.

The seed was planted.

I told her that I wasn't feeling well at all, that maybe I was getting sick, maybe I needed to rest. So I went to my room and lay down just for a minute, and tell you the truth, I actually wasn't feeling too great at that point. Next thing I know, Burn is standing over me, looking down at me.

"Yo, Crash, you still alive?" nudging me into consciousness.

I sat up immediately and stared at him. I hadn't seen him since that day in the cafeteria, and something was different. I couldn't put my finger on it, but he had a different look, like he was less likely to suddenly go into a rage, like maybe he was finally at peace with who he was.

"How's it going?" I mumbled, concerned. Not for him, but for me.

"You look like shit. . . ." He sits on my bed, next to me as I get up.

"What happened to you?" I ask.

"I'd rather not talk about it," he tells me, dismissively.

"Well, you're gonna have to. Because my dad is threatening to send me away to a school like the one you're going to."

"Trust me. No way will your parents be sending you to the school that I'm going to."

I couldn't help but wonder why he was so convinced.

"Did you get any new games?" he asks, inspecting my collection.

By now I am up, across the room, closing the door. "Maybe you don't get it, but my dad is planning to send me away. Like, forever."

"You need a plan," he said, and while he couldn't have known, all I had been thinking about for the past three days was coming up with a plan. Pete couldn't help me, Evan didn't seem to understand, and Kenny came up with really stupid ideas that would more than likely get me kicked out of my house than keep me there. So it was refreshing to hear from someone who, at least, got the point. Someone who was, in spite of everything else, brilliant.

"Yeah, I need a plan" is what I echoed.

He busied himself with the *Grand Theft Auto III* box, opening it, not finding the disc, then searching, not looking at me, but talking. "Know this, Crashinsky" (sounding more than a little like his sister), "by the time they tell you that they are sending you somewhere, the process is pretty far along. They have probably talked to schools; my guess is they already chose the one that they think is appropriate for you." I was nodding, and listening to him like I was Luke Skywalker and he was Yoda, as he bounced around my room still searching for the game.

"My mom was apparently prepared when she got a call from your school," he said. "They said I was a potential threat to other kids, which at first didn't make any sense to me because I didn't do anything. But then it hit me that there was this incident in my school in Chicago which, OK, was attributable to me. . . ."

He found the game disc, wiped it on his jeans, and placed it in the game console. I wanted to know what the Chicago incident was but couldn't ask.

"I will acknowledge that in addition to Chicago, there might have been a few other things that they claim justify an evaluation of me as 'high risk,' whatever that means. They even brought up the McAllister thing. Isn't that crazy? We were, like, eight."

He set up the game as he talked.

"Also, the kids in Chicago were total asswipes. At least here there are a few cool kids. How's the basketball team doing?"

"OK," I answered reluctantly, not wanting him to know that I had his spot, afraid that he would get pissed off.

"So you got my spot then?" He laughed. "Better you than that cretin Bosco. He can't play for shit. So I guess you owe me one." He started from my saved point in the game, but I didn't want to tell him that I didn't want him to play. After all, I owed him one.

"And of course, you will be forever in my debt if I can develop a scheme to keep you out of boarding school. Trust me, you *do not* want to go away, especially in the middle of the year. It has *not* been easy. Especially the school they picked for me. By the way, are you aware that your father has been advising my mom, and that it was because of his 'financial acumen,' as my mom called it, that she was able to afford to send me away? In fact, I understand that she consulted him at length before determining that I had to go away, and that he was instrumental in her decision to send me. So I will be sure to thank him for that."

He played and I watched, mostly in silence. But then, I had to ask:

"What's it like? The school?"

"Think Harry Potter, Hogwarts . . . *from hell.* Without Ron and Hermione, well, actually, that's not true, imagine Ron and Hermione are there, only they are certifiably *insane.* There's almost no sense of reality in the student population, and the instructors are essentially prison guards—are you familiar with the SS?"

I was not. "Are you able to learn better?"

He shook his head, like he couldn't believe my question. "Crashinsky, don't you get it? Don't you know anything about me? I've already learned everything I'm ever going to learn in any school. That's part of my problem. I'm way beyond their elementary textbooks and into an entirely other dimension of thought and learning. And they want to replace that ability with a computer chip that responds to basic rules without questioning them."

He paused the game.

"I see things in a way that they don't, and they don't get it," he said. "Doesn't that sound familiar?"

"Why should it?"

"Because we share that in common, don't we? C'mon, you do it too. I've seen you do it. Actually, my sister was the one who pointed it out to me. You see things that even I don't see."

"Your sister?" Was he saying that I was some sort of genius too? Because deep down, I understood what he was saying. I did, in fact, have the ability to see things in an entirely different way from my friends and my family, in a way that I could not verbalize and certainly couldn't use on any schoolwork, but there was something I could access that I knew that people around me weren't able to touch.

I nodded, not knowing how this was going to keep me from going to hell-school and not knowing whether Burn was actually making any sense. He was either mad crazy or the smartest kid ever, and I was feeling a whole lot smarter listening to him. Either way, it was good to have an ally.

"What does any of this have to do with going away to school?"

"Do you know what 'axiom of choice' means?" He was starting to sound like he did that day in the cafeteria, but without the edge of violence. "Of course you don't. Axiom of choice is the ability of a mathematician to choose the elements of a set without determining which is correct. I'm oversimplifying it, but the point is that each of us has the ability to choose what he wants to learn, and in the end it all works out. And here's the thing—" He turned to me, handed me the controller, finally giving me a turn, and said, "Everything you can imagine, everything you can think of, everything that makes up our society and our current state of consciousness, every single fact, conjecture, speculation, and thought is actually, for the first time in our collective existence, in one place."

"Huh?" Me, not getting his point at all.

"On the internet," he said smugly. "Just think what that means."

He was way beyond me at that moment.

Then, from the hallway: "Steven, David, come down please."

I immediately obeyed (remember the predicament I was in: one thing out of line).

David grabbed the controller back, shooed me away, and returned to the game, not caring to listen.

I went down to the living room.

"Carsh Insky." Roxanne in a miniskirt thing, multicolored leggings, her hair jet black. Tight, tight belly shirt accentuated her body and revealed that she had pierced her belly button; definitely not Thanksgiving attire. My father was going have a field day.

"Rox Anne."

"You are soooo cute. I wish you were my brother." She gave me a pat on the head, turned to Lindsey, and said, "Do you want to trade?"

Lindsey had the usual look of disgust and dismissal on her face. It was the same expression that my father generally used whenever he talked to me.

"Oddly, no," she said, shaking her head and doing her eye roll, and I knew that was a major dis of Burn and me at the same time. It was actually pretty funny. For Lindsey.

Roxanne stared back at her, and I realized for the first time that she was no happier being at our house than Lindsey was at the thought of having her over.

"Your mistake then," she told Lindsey, "because if you picked my brother, you'd only have to see him on holidays. He's in boarding school."

"So will . . ." Lindsey started to answer, but stopped herself. She knew. She *fucking* knew!

I was now staring at Lindsey with mind-reading intensity. I could feel my body warming with tension. If she knew, then everyone else knew, and I certainly would not put it beyond Lindsey to try and push my buttons to make it happen.

"Where's David?" said Roxanne's mother, and that's when I noticed the others.

Actually, what I noticed first was this model, standing in the middle of our living room, sipping champagne. This dark-haired woman in black heels and a slender black dress with an expensive-looking necklace. This perfectly shaped goddess who lit up the room with a glow that was normally reserved for celebrities. Then I saw these two girl kids beside her. She was one hundred percent milf. The milfyest milf in history.

I immediately thought of Burn, sitting upstairs with *Grand Theft Auto*. When Burn saw her, he was going to go absolutely *crazy*. This was a guarantee, because among all of the kids in my grade, Burn was easily the biggest horndog. When he wasn't searching the internet for "axiom of choice," whatever that was, he was surfing for porn, and since he hardly slept, he knew every major porn site. He told me this during basketball tryouts. He even said, if he didn't make the team, it would be OK, as it would give him more time for porn.

So this milf was in trouble, because no way was Burn going to be able to eat without staring at her the whole time.

"Where's David?" Roxanne's mother asked again.

"I'll get him," I said.

* * *

Back in my room:

"Dave," I told him. "You gotta come down. There's a major-league milf in my living room."

Dave immediately went from undistractible to totally interested. "What's she like?"

"I dunno, hot."

"No, describe her."

"Why? All you have to do is come down."

"First tell me exactly what makes her so hot. Is she blond?"

"No, actually she has dark hair."

"Big tits?"

"Kind of." I was out of my league with these questions. All I knew was "hot." "Really, Dave, you are gonna have to see . . ."

What we didn't see was Jacob standing in the doorway, listening to us. He walked in. He closed the door behind him.

And smiled.

It was not a happy smile. My father rarely had a happy smile. In fact, I only heard him actually laugh out loud like once, and over some political guy on TV. He never laughed at like *Seinfeld* or *Family Guy* or anything really funny, he just nodded, like he got the joke.

So seeing my father smile was not a good thing.

"Listen to me, you little assholes," he said in a controlled whisper. "I have people from my company here, and the last thing I need is for either of you to make a mockery out of this holiday. Do you understand?"

Burn fake-smiled back. "This holiday is already a mockery. Its very purpose is to express gratitude for the harvest. Well, excuse me, sir, if I don't express *my* gratitude as my father was incinerated in the World Trade Center and my mother has drugged me and sent me off to a school filled with psychotics, thanks to your advice. Consequently, there is no harvest for me."

Fuckme, is what I thought.

That's when Jacob turned to me. "Steven, this is on you. If he's out of line, I'll consider it your fault."

Double fuckme.

He was gone in an instant, having nothing left to say.

And I was now in full panic mode.

And Burn was all smiles. "We got him just where we want him." He laughed. "Now let's go meet the milf."

Turns out she wasn't a milf, as she was neither a mother nor even a wife, but just a superhot woman who worked in my father's office. The kids I noticed earlier belonged to another family from my father's office. The milf was there with a stocky ex–football player type. Maybe he was in shape once, but not anymore, and he seemed as serious as my father and also, I thought, a whole lot older than the woman.

I wondered why I hadn't seen her during my office visit earlier in the week. I would definitely have noticed.

"OK, Crashinsky," Burn whispered to me. "First off, you were correct in your assessment of 'hot,' as this woman is absolutely and perfectly stunning."

He went to the couch and sat down. I followed him closely, overwhelmed by my father's threat.

"Secondly," he continued, "see the guy she's with? These people do not belong together." We watched her interact with her friend/husband/date, whatever he was. She was sampling some hors d'oeuvres. Burn was doing his overthinking thing, examining the two of them like they were on TV.

"Cut it out." Me, whispering.

Then the other couple, apparently the owners of twin-looking five-year-old girls, joined the goddess and the guy, and the four of them were talking like they knew each other. Jamie, having to take a break from *Rugrats*, was distracting the girls, playing with them and giggling. Roxanne was standing in the corner, just standing and looking at the woman. I didn't see Lindsey.

"You know what she is, Crash? She is porno pretty. Lookit, even Roxanne is mesmerized."

Roxanne did seem mesmerized.

"Is your sister, like, gay?"

"I don't think so," he said. "She's just . . . Roxanne."

The ex-football guy goes into the dining room. More hors d'oeuvres, and then my father goes over to the goddess and hands her another glass of champagne, which she takes super-gracefully. She throws her long hair back and laughs, with her free hand gently touching her neck. I'm thinking that she is movie-star hot. Angelina Jolie hot, if you ask me.

"Dude. Your father is way into her."

"What are you *talking* about?" My father could not be way into anything except being superior to everyone, with the possible exception of Lindsey.

"Look at the way he is looking at her. And the way she is looking at him."

The two of them are talking, which doesn't seem so strange to me, given that Jacob invited her and all. She is saying something that Jacob seems real interested in, and Burn is right, he is paying her way more attention than he does my mom. But, OK, even he has to notice that she is superhot, and then she is laughing and then, holy shit, he is laughing with her. Actually laughing so I can hear it.

He turns, looks at us looking at him, and we make eye contact. His laughter is gone. He moves toward the kitchen, away from her, but as he does, she gently glides her hand across his arm, just for a second.

"Did you *see* that?" Burn is now leaning into me, head to head. "Houston, we have a problem."

"What's Houston?"

"Forget it," he said. "I'm going to touch her. See how she reacts."

I grabbed his arm, much the same way that my father grabbed mine a few days earlier. *"Pleeeze,"* I begged him. "I don't want to go to boarding school."

"Don't worry. I know what I'm doing."

He maneuvered around the table, getting hors d'oeuvres and pretending not to notice the Woman. In the meantime, Roxanne comes over and sits with me.

"You like me, don't you, Crashinsky?"

I thought momentarily about what Burn said that his sister said about me. I wondered whether she actually meant it, or if I was being set up by the two of them.

"Well, you're definitely a whole lot nicer than Lindsey," I said, not sure how she meant "like."

"Do you think she's pretty?" Roxanne asked me, nodding in the direction of the Woman.

I nod. "I guess." Because no denying it, the Woman was an incredibly beautiful woman.

"Do you think I'm pretty?" She tugged down on her shirt, which tightened around her chest and made her boobs stick out more. And, of course, made it more difficult to look at her face. But, yeah, I kind of thought that under all the strange makeup she wore and the spiked hair, that facewise Roxanne was kind of pretty in her own way, prettier certainly than Lindsey was. Except, she also kind of looked like her brother.

"I guess" is what I said, only because I had to say something.

"Did you ever make out with a girl, Crashinsky?"

Now I'm thinking, this is the craziest family ever.

I am stuttering, because, no, actually I never did make out with a girl, and I didn't think any other twelve-year-old I knew did, but I wasn't about to tell her that. Shit, I didn't even know what making out was exactly, but I couldn't tell her that either.

"Want me to teach you?"

Now Burn, with a plate full of goods, starts walking back to us, which for my account could not be soon enough, and then, true to his word, he twists to the right and starts talking with the Woman. Standing next to her, he actually looks a lot older than he is.

"What's he doing?" I ask Roxanne.

"My brother," she answered, "is a strange bird. A very, very strange bird. So do you? Wanna make out?"

Burn is holding his plate and offering it to the Woman, and she actually takes an hors d'oeuvre. Then, while talking, he puts his hand on her arm, trying, I think, to copy what she did with my dad.

And she gracefully retracts her arm but accepts another thing from his plate. As she does, he turns to me, smiling, like he just scored the winning basket of a big game. Then they really get to talking, like she's interested in what he has to say, and next thing I know, he's leading her over to the couch and she puts her hand out to me.

"Hello, Steefen. My name is Felicia," she says in this weird accent, pronouncing her own name in a bunch of syllables so it comes out Fileeeseeya. "Davit tellz me you are interistet in learnink more about vat your father does atvirk, for a livink."

David offers her the loveseat beside the couch and she eases herself into it, crossing her legs like a model. All the time, Roxanne is watching her real closely.

"Feleeseeya is from Slovakia," David tells us, and I'm wondering is this a joke, because I never heard of this country before, but I'm used to not knowing certain things, so I go with it. "She manages accounts at your father's company."

She is even prettier up close.

"Eeesenchewally, we are a privit fun dat invests piples

money in vedyous tings, just like a bink, but wit a deefferent feelosofee."

Yeah, that pretty much cleared it up for me.

I nod. Roxanne nods.

David asks questions, detailed questions about the types of investments and how do they pick the companies that they invest in, and how a hedge works, and Lindsey walks over now to try to listen, but the conversation is above even her head, and then Jacob sees us all talking and flies over in a controlled panic, which I recognize, but no one else does. He has this stride that looks normal but is actually really rushed, so he's over to us real fast. Only to find Felicia explaining how to minimize exposure to risks while still allowing your assets to grow.

"Jack, dese cheeldrin shoot com to de offees."

"I was just there," I volunteer.

"And you did note introtuuce us?" she says accusingly at my father.

"It was Monday." They both shake their head, like Monday meant something.

"Dinner." My mom sticks her head in from the other room.

We only eat in the dining room like three or four times a year, and mostly it's a room that I never go into. It's very long and very formal and dark, with lots of stuff in there that if I even touched gently would break into a billion pieces. We have this huge table, big enough to accommodate all of us, which meant every kid, even the tiny twins, could sit at the adult table, which as you probably know is not normal, because with virtually every single holiday that I have spent at other people's houses, the kids are in one room, the adults in another.

Had that been the case on this night, my guess is I would have ended up going to the school in Vermont, or some other boarding school in some other state, and *that* pretty much would have been *that*.

But we were all in the same room.

"Odd group," my aunt Randi whispered to me. It was a tight fit. There were, and I counted, fifteen of us, clustered around trays of every imaginable Thanksgiving food that I have ever seen except sweet potatoes.

Down at the far end of the table was my father, with Felicia on one side and Office Worker One to her right. Felicia's guy-friend was directly across from her, on the other side of my father. And right next him was Burn, as he pushed his way into the next available seat. So I immediately had to grab the one next to him, knowing that I was going to have to control him if necessary, squeezing into my chair as my aunt sat on my other side, followed by Roxanne and then Lindsey. Across from me was Office Worker One's wife. And next to her, their kids, and Jamie, who is still playing with the girls, then an open seat, apparently for Mrs. Burnett, and another blank for my mom.

My mother came in and started suggesting moves, but Burn started dumping stuff on his plate and drinking from the glass, so he wasn't about to move. Apparently my mom conferred with Mrs. Burnett and they decided to leave things the way there were.

Again, had she insisted on putting the kids on one side of the room and the adults on the other, which would have been a pretty normal thing to do, I probably would have ended up in Vermont. Or even if she'd had the balls to tell Burn to move to accommodate the other guests: Vermont.

But not on this night.

"How are you doing, kiddo?" my aunt asked me. I wondered what she knew. My father didn't talk to her much, so I guessed she had not been told of his plans to essentially kick me out of the family. "I got you a present. It should be in my bag, if I haven't forgotten it. Remind me after dinner."

"Thanks," I said, distracted.

"Is he still giving you a hard time?" she asked, motioning to my dad.

"Yeah." As I'm saying this, I feel my lip weaken and I get a little choked up.

She notices. "He can be a real scumbag," she says with a sneer.

I turn to her. She is OK looking, but not at all noticeable in a room that also has Felicia in it, and I wonder if she'll ever get married. I think she thinks she no longer can. Whenever she gets involved with someone, it never lasts. I once heard her tell my father that the reason that she could not have a successful relationship was because of him and how hard he was on people. As far as I knew, she is pretty much the only person who ever stood up to him and actually makes him back down.

Randi notices I'm upset, and she pokes me in the ribs. "Hey, kid. It's Thanksgiving—don't be a downer. I'll talk to the guy. I'll straighten everything out."

"That's not going to help."

And my mom comes into the room with even more food, and they are trying to fit it between the plates.

And Roxanne announces that she is going to observe Thanksgiving by becoming a vegetarian because it's inhuman to celebrate the death of other animals, and then she takes a huge dollop of stuffing and drops it onto her plate.

And Lindsey waits until Roxanne tastes it, then laughs and tells her that there's sausage in the stuffing, which she should have known because her mother made it.

And Jamie, not knowing that Lindsey is trying to goad Roxanne, innocently announces that the gravy is filled with turkey juice, just as Roxanne is pouring some onto the stuffing.

And Roxanne backs slightly away from the table, and my aunt Randi whispers to me, "Fire and ice." And I'm not sure which she thinks is which except I am rooting for Roxanne, who I know from my few experiences with her is not going to drop it, and I wonder if I could actually have made out with her or if she was just messing with me.

And all this time, Burn is asking Felicia questions, like what's it like growing up in Slovakia and how'd she learn English and what made her come to the U.S. She seemed to enjoy talking to him, and my father seemed to be encouraging it. Seemed like he was in a supergood mood for him until Lindsey and Roxanne started to bicker, and then he took control of the room, giving a speech about the importance of family and sharing a holiday with others, and I'm thinking if family is so important to him, why is he trying so hard to get rid of me?

And then we are all up and circulating the table, taking spoonfuls from plate after plate. And I could see that something is up with Roxanne, and my aunt notices also, because they work out to switch seats so that Roxanne is now sitting next to me with her plate of stuffing and vegetables.

"Your aunt is a very smart woman, Crashinsky" is what she whispers to me. "Besides, I like it better here," she says, talking to me but staring at Felicia, who is still talking to her brother.

Then we are eating and people are all talking at the same time. And now my father is talking to Burn and seems to have the patience for him that he never had for me.

Jamie asks the twins whether they know "It's Getting Hot in Here," and they are singing it together, knowing all the lyrics, but not knowing it's about sex. I don't think that Jamie knows either, except for the "take off all your clothes" part.

And Burn asks Felicia what kind of music she likes. She talks about how she was trained on the piano and the violin, so classical, some jazz, and of course club music.

And Aunt Randi asks Roxanne on one side and Lindsey on

the other how high school is, being as they are both freshmen, and Lindsey says she loves it, but Roxanne doesn't answer.

And Burn asks Felicia what she likes to read, and she talks about historical fiction, rattling off the names of books I've never heard of.

And my mom asks how's the turkey, because she got the recipe on the Food Network and it's different, which everybody agrees is pretty good, except for Roxanne who whispers to me how she's not really a vegetarian, but just wanted to piss off her mom for sitting her next to Lindsey, and I say "Better you than me."

And Roxanne laughs hugely, which makes me forget all about the *one thing wrong* problem for the first time since my father forced me to look at the brochures in his office.

And then Mrs. Burnett says that everything is perfect and that she and her family wanted to thank mine again for having them.

And my mom, ever the gracious host, thanks her back.

And Office Worker One thanks my mom and dad, and says he is thankful for his own wife and kids.

And then Burn thanks my mom too and then turns to Felicia and asks her:

When did she start sleeping with my dad.

And there is an instant of total silence.

No one is eating. No one is moving.

But then the twins start singing again: "It's getting hot in here. . . ."

And Jacob Crashinsky erupts like a volcano, screaming at Burn, but that doesn't stop Burn from pursuing his line of questioning.

"How long have you two been involved in a relationship? Anyone watching the two of you would notice these things. Does Mrs. Crashinsky know?"

Now Felicia is leaving the table, out of the house in a storm, but the guy with her is still just looking at my father. So they go off to another room. And Office Worker One apparently goes after Felicia, and the twins are crying, screaming, and so, for some reason, is Jamie.

And my mom leaves the room.

And Roxanne whispers to me, "Well, now your father's truly fucked."

Now Mrs. Burnett is all over Burn, smacking him across the head, and they are out of the house, Roxanne following after them, leaving me and my sisters and my aunt and the crying twins with their mom as the only ones left at the table.

And Jamie is still crying, and I don't know whether it's from my dad screaming or because of what she heard.

Now Aunt Randi is up, gently taking Jamie by the hand and suggesting that she and Lindsey go with her to their bedrooms, and then she tells me that maybe I should do the same thing.

So I go to my room and I am really freaked out. Because if I had any shot of staying in my house, Burn has just completely eliminated any possibility, and I'm thinking that maybe I should start packing now. Maybe not even wait, maybe bike over to Pete's and stay there for the night.

How freaked out am I? I am in my room with my door closed, staring at my computer screen, and I am crying—that's how freaked out. And even with my door closed, all I hear is a lot of doors slamming and cars driving off, then quiet for a while, but I decide not to leave my room.

And then I hear my father's voice, but I can't make out what he is saying.

But then his voice is totally drowned out by my mom's voice, and she is screaming: "I want you out of here. I want you out of here. I WANT YOU OUT OF HERE!"

And I try to calm down, so I turn on the television, trying

to block out the screaming. I'm not going to lie to you, the two of them have had screaming matches before, but in the past, almost always, it was about me. And now it wasn't, and you know what? That actually felt pretty good. And I stopped freaking out.

Then the door slamming again.

And then quiet. And me still staring at the computer screen in a daze until the AIM bell rings.

It's Burn with an instant message:

Revenge is sweet.

And I immediately write back:

You just fucked me.

Thinking about how maybe that was his plan all along.

And almost immediately after I hit send, another message comes back.

Don't be a cretin, Crash. I just saved your life.

CHAPTER EIGHT

WEDNESDAY AT THE WESTCHESTER

I had been writing for like a week, feeling pretty proud of myself for getting the whole Thanksgiving scene down accurately, and it was generally going real good when I got this friend request on Facebook from this girl Nadine. So I check out all her friends, mostly high school girls, but I don't know any of them. So of course I accept anyways, and it's this girl from White Plains and we start IMing.

> **ru the Steven Crashinsky from TV, the one who saved the school?**
>
> yes
>
> **the hero?**
>
> I guess.
>
> **me and my friend Jodi want to meet you**

She gives me Jodi's full name and I friend her, and Jodi is mad hot. And also in like every picture she's holding a drink.

> **where?**
>
> **How's the Westchester?**

Which is a humongous mall not too far from my house. Not ideal for an immediate hookup, but being as I didn't want to take a chance of scaring them off, I figured it would be as good a place as any to start off with.

> **brb**

I am on the phone immediately, calling Newman, who I know is at work but will bail as I soon as he hears the news. He has been looking to ditch work and hang out because we hadn't seen each other since the night at Kelly's, who got into deep shit resulting from Maddy vomiting in her pool.

To my surprise, pretty much no one blamed me for what happened. No one except maybe Christina, who I didn't hear a word from even though I texted her like five times. Also, I expected that I would see her pop up on my Facebook wall or at least IM me a few times when I was on as we usually did every day, but that wasn't happening. And being as it wasn't, I had to guess that she was pretty much a blown opportunity. I didn't feel all that good about it, given our history, but hey, I tried my best, and it was still summer and the Westchester girls would definitely make me forget about screwing it up with Christina. Plus, there were bound to be other parties; she would be there and I would approach her then and try to fix things. I'm much better in person anyways.

Also, as I said, the kids in my neighborhood were starting to take the hero thing for granted, so it was good to have someone remember in a good way.

Only Newman wasn't answering his cell. I might need backup. Back to Nadine:

how many friends can you bring?

just me and Jodi

I look through her Facebook photos. Like three hundred. I come across a picture of two girls kissing as I scroll through her pics. I flash my mouse control over the picture and the tagged names pop up.

What about Claudia?

u no Claudia?

saw her tagged in your pics

Claudia is oh so wacky

is that bad?

I mean, wacked out.

That seems like a plus to me.

So?

So I'll call her.

And we set it for six P.M., which gives me like six hours to get some of my boys together and figure out the plan.

Then I get an unexpected call.

It's Jacob, and he wants me to drive into the city with Jamie because he is supposed to spend time with her, and I tell him I'm busy, which does not go over well. But truth is I don't care. I tell him I'm writing, and to take it up with my agent, knowing that Sally will tell him that she actually got a bunch of chapters from me by email, thinking that should quiet him down. So I hang up quickly. I don't want him to know I'm taking the day off.

Then he calls me again, this time using the more father-stern voice to tell me that it wasn't a request, it was a requirement. And if I want my weekly money (which he puts onto my card from his online account), then I better take a break and drive my sister. And I ask him, does he want me to stop, knowing that the book is due soon? And he says cut the crap, Steven, you can take a few hours off. And I tell him, no, I can't, I'm, like, in the middle of an important part. I hang up again, knowing that he doesn't believe me one bit. And knowing that we are not done and that he will be calling again.

And sure enough, the phone rings, only this time, it's Newman. He got my message about the girls from White Plains and will most definitely bail on work, so we are most definitely on. We talk over the list of candidates, as in which of the Club Crew should join us. We both agree that Pete has to come if he is around, as Pete has had virtually no hookups this summer and is counting on me to provide, based on my hero status, and has been severely disappointed in me as I have been focusing all my attention on Christina. Plus, Pete, better than Evan or Bobby, can wing for us, not that I need it with new girls. And besides I have my Beamer.

Except, as Newman reminds me, this is Westchester; virtually everyone's got a BMW in Westchester.

So I'm IMing back to this girl, "six is good," but my cell phone buzzes, another call and, thinking it's my dad, I ignore. And then the home phone rings. I know this trick all too well.

I am not caring; I am not going to the city.

And Jamie comes in. "It's for you," she says as I wave her off. "It's Felicia."

Felicia, it turns out, is . . . she's the only reason that me and Jacob are still talking at all, and since Jacob is now my business manager (did I have a choice?) and investment adviser (again, what choice?), as well as being my dad (again, no choice), I *do* have to deal with him. And since neither of us can deal and since we both love Felicia, whenever it breaks down between us, it's Felicia to the rescue.

I take the phone.

"Cresh," she says (I told her from the beginning that my friends called me that, well not exactly that, but "Crash," and being as she wanted an informal relationship with me, she had to call me that too). "Cresh, I fookedup."

In the five years since that Thanksgiving dinner, her accent hasn't really changed. Everything else, however, is a different story.

Brief history: There was a lot more yelling between my parents in the days after Thanksgiving. Between the holidays that year, you did *not* want to be at my house at all, trust me on this. Then, around Hanukkah/Christmas, there was this family discussion, all of us sitting in the dining room (ironically, the scene of the original crime) with my father telling us, "You should know your parents still love each other, but neither of us is happy anymore, and happiness is very important, more important than living together and fighting all the time" (which wasn't actually the case, since they hardly talked). Then my mom, "Your father will be taking an apartment in Manhattan."

And the three of us said nothing.

I expected Jamie to cry, but she just stared beyond them, like there was an invisible TV on the opposite wall.

I expected Lindsey to ask all kinds of questions, which she didn't, so I figure she must have been briefed before the official family meeting.

As for me, it seemed like a good thing. I only had one question and couldn't just ask it, but I also couldn't *not* ask it, so I tried to be patient. I was more than patient ever since my father told me he was going to send me away, and so I had to know: What about boarding school?

Actually I had another equally pressing question: How did Burn figure out about my dad and the Woman?

The first question was answered right after the family meeting, when my father put his hand on my shoulder and walked me into the living room.

As to the second question, it turns out that Burn may not have been as perceptive as I gave him credit for, because I later found out that my mom had been confiding to his mom that things were bad, that she never believed that his increasingly late hours at work were completely work related. Plus she apparently had caught him cheating before, which she apparently forgave on a one-time basis only. So my guess is that Burn must have overheard his mom talking to my mom and figured that if a woman like Felicia was offering, then no way could a man like Jack Crashinsky resist, especially given his prior misconduct.

In the weeks after Christmas, in one of his random IM updates from boarding school, Burn told me as much, as in, according to his mom, no way was Caroline Crashinsky out to forgive and forget again, not this time, not with things being as bad as they were, not with my father making it intolerable to live in the same house.

But, oh yeah, back to question one and the father-son chat in the living room, away from the other family members, with him telling me that now I was my mother's problem, not his, and it was up to her to decide whether or not I should stay at home or go to school somewhere else, that he was officially giving up on me, and also not to expect him to continue to support me until I learned to shape up and respect him and the things he stood for. Which I didn't actually understand, I mean, what exactly did he "stand for"—mentally abusing his kids and manwhoring on his wife?

And, again, he's telling me all this with his arm around my shoulder, like he's my Little League coach and we're talking about getting the last batter in the last inning out. Then he released his hand, moved toward the window, and said:

"I hope you understand that this is all your fault. Your mother and I would never have started fighting if you had learned the proper respect."

And I was not about to take it: "Was it my fault that you decided to fuck some ho and Mom found out?" (Thank you Eminem and Snoop for teaching me the right words to say.)

He came at me.

"You spoiled little bastard." His hot breath, right in my face, spitwords hitting me with the spray and all. "Don't expect anything from me. Ever!"

I pretty much didn't expect anything from him before, so *that* wasn't much of a threat.

Also, since Jacob had pretty much been out of the house most of the time anyways, given that he worked in the city, took the early train in and then the late train home most days (increasingly later trains), we were used to him not being around, so it didn't feel like it was going to be much of a change.

After he moved out, Jamie went back to Nickelodeon, Lindsey went back to being a supercunt to me, and my mom was the same exact mom she was before, overly concerned about every small thing.

And for the first time in my life, I went to sleep at night without worrying that something I did during the day would trigger a screaming match the following morning.

It actually felt good to be home, something I had never experienced before. I started having friends come to my house instead of escaping to theirs. I started to believe in my ability to produce magic when it was absolutely necessary to do so. After all, in spite of my father's threats to get rid of me, he was the one living in exile.

And he came over every other weekend for visitation, but he was drastically different. He would pull into the driveway to pick us up, honking the horn, and my mom would remind me that I had to go, so I did, along with my sisters. We usually went to movies, or he took us all to the Westchester Mall for lunch and shopping, sometimes with my aunt Randi, sometimes not, and there were times when he secretly agreed to drop me off with one of my friends instead of actually spending time with me, which suited me just fine.

So it wasn't until the summer of that year that we found out that Felicia had moved in with him. Which I didn't get at all, her being supermodel hot and him being, well . . . Jacob. Since then, I have asked her more than a few times what she sees in him, and she reminds me that she sees things in me that others may not, so maybe my father has some redeeming qualities that I may have overlooked.

She is, and has always been, the only adult who understood that I had the ability to produce magic. She wasn't at all surprised when I told her that I could. In fact, she even admitted, on the promise that I would never tell anyone else, she has some magic in her too. She stares at me sometimes like she knows something about me, something that even I don't know, but we never talk about it. Point is, she gets me.

"Cresh, I totally fookedup."

I know as she says this, before she says anything else, that I will now be driving Jamie into Manhattan. I know this because there is nothing that I would not do for this woman, being as she was always there for me. So I don't actually need to hear the rest of what she's going to say.

"I mate plans wees your seester and was goink to tek the tren to Wide Plens." (It takes a minute for me to think . . . White Plains.) "But I just now gut home from deecee."

I'm not sure how this translates to me driving into the city. But I am already gone.

"And we have tickets to Gris. On Brotway." Finally, the pay-off. "The mateenay."

OK, is what I tell her, wondering what a mateenay could be.

"Do you vant to calm wid us? I'm sure your father ken git another tiket."

I tell her that Broadway shows are not my thing. What the hell is Gris?

I also tell her I'm on my way.

Jamie is dressed and ready even before I am off the phone. She is holding her overnight bag for a sleepover. She is also literally holding the answer to my question, the soundtrack for the show *Grease*.

"No way we're listening to that on the way in," I tell her.

"Please, Steven. I wanna know the music."

"Isn't it on your iPod?"

"Oh yeah."

Newman comes along for the drive. We will be going straight to the mall and meeting Pete there. We talk in code, as Jamie is with us and we don't want her to know our evil plans, but she is busy singing over the music, white earbuds in her ears, and doesn't hear us anyways.

Drop-off time, like over an hour later, bad traffic, in front of my dad's building. I have Jamie call, not wanting to talk to Jacob, and Felicia tells her that we should park and come up. Instinct tells me no, but like I said, I cannot refuse her anything. Also Newman is hot to see what she looks like these days.

He is not disappointed. Slinky black dress, bright red lipstick, like she's made up for a club night out even though they are only going to a show. I'm thinking that I have never actually seen her in, like, sweats; in fact, I've never even seen her dress like a regular girl.

She gives me a squeeze and a kiss, which no doubt makes Newman wish, at least for a second, that he was me.

"Steven, you're late, as usual." The Voice from the other room. Good old Jacob, never changes.

"Jack, liff the boy alone," Felicia yells back. Then to me, "What he mins is thenkew for drivink Jemmie." Then, back at him, "Isn't dat right, Jack?"

Now emerges Jacob, looking younger than ever. And shiny. I'm thinking, is my dad actually getting work done? I know this look from some of the moms in our neighborhood. Botox. He is dressed typical Jacob, casual version: boots, jeans, sports jacket, hair slicked back.

"Thank you, Steven." He holds his hand out military style. I'm overwhelmed by all the affection (not). He knows that the only reason I'm there is Felicia, and I tell him so.

"Thank her."

"Boyz," Felicia says. "Rilly, you two."

We both actually smile at her, breaking our own concentration on hating each other. "Progress," brought to you by Felicia Crashinsky. She went from an unusually long name with lots of consonants stuck together—multiple Zs and Cs—to an equally vulgar last name (thank you, Roxanne, for pointing that out to me), when she finally married my father last year.

My father then greets Newman more warmly—"Good to see you again, Alex"—like maybe he's going to offer Newman a drink, then talking it up about Newman's choice of film school and what it's like to be going to a college in the city. Then he turns his attention to me, and here comes the talk, which we both knew was coming the second that I agreed to come up.

"You are overdrawn again." He is referring to my debit card. I am, admittedly, not that good at money.

"Gas," I tell him. "It's like five dollars a gallon."

"I can't keep putting money in your account to cover you," he says. "You're spending way too much for a kid your age." Then, suspiciously, he adds, "What are you doing with the money?"

"Everything is superexpensive, Mr. Crashinsky." Newman to the rescue. Newman knows that I cannot conserve any cash, ever, and that I'm always out, no matter how much I get. According to my mom, it is just another symptom of my ADHD. Well, OK then, all is forgiven, part of my disease.

"Besides, it's my money," I tell him defiantly.

"Don't!" One word from Jacob; he's beginning to turn red. Time to go. We have plans at the mall, and we're going to cruise the city first.

Felicia gives me another hug and I feel her hand on my back pocket as she whispers, "For degaz."

Another kiss on the cheek and we are out of there.

* * *

On the way down, I count the cash. $300. I am thinking, how do I even thank her?

"Wow," Newman says, shaking his head. "Motherfucking wow. Wowweeeeee!" he screams in the confines of the elevator. "Did you see that body? Did you see what she was wearing? Dude, your father must have made a deal with the devil."

"What do you mean?" I am only half listening, still thinking of her.

"Pot of gold at the end of the fucking rainbow, is what I mean. Face it, no matter what you think of the guy, you gotta give it to him. Your father is living the great American dream." Newman has it all analyzed. "Made enough money to trade up from ordinary family to a trophy wife. Apartment in the city, summer in the Hamptons. Give it a year, you will have a new half brother or half sister. Mark my words, dude. Mr. Crashinsky is a master. I bow to him." Newman is suddenly twirling a blunt, the first of many we will be smoking before this day is done.

I am now thinking about my potential new siblings. Newman had a point.

I add to it. "And, having already fucked up one family, he can probably learn from his mistakes and create a really good one. Or at least with a new family to concentrate on, he'll have less time to fuck us up." I was also thinking about Felicia with a kid, and her having a kid with my father would definitely mean that she would be around for a while. Which was just fine with me. I have previously imagined that she would wake up one morning and question her existence as she turned to watch my very humorless father snoring away, as he did when he lived with us. In this vision, I always pictured her in the next scene, at the airport, holding tickets and looking for the next flight back to whatever Slovakia she is from.

Now I have another image. It would serve him right to get like an autistic baby or some kind of real retard, karma for the way he treated me growing up. I think this and immediately try to freeze out my thoughts. After all, because of my ability with magic, what if my wish turns out to be true? I have, in the past, had these random thoughts that turned out to be real.

Sometimes being in my mind, you have to be really fucking careful.

Plus, I wouldn't wish it on Felicia.

Newman taps my shoulder. He has taken his first hit of the evening.

I do the same, a little uncomfortable about walking the NYC streets with a lit blunt. Newman brushes me off. He is going to be living there soon; better get some practice.

We end up getting to the mall late. Pete is already there, which we knew from the text messages he was sending, and his first report was not good. We also knew already that the girls were nasty. He was providing the details:

> Nadine = fugly, just fugly
>
> Jodi = fat + bad skin
>
> Claudia = butterface; big Ts tho

Which is OK with me, as I already put in for Claudia, based on those Facebook pics.

We spot them sitting at a table in the food court. Pete did not do them justice. Two of them were not just fugly, they, as in Nadine and Jodi, were heinous, nothing like their Facebook pics. But I thought Claudia was way cuter than Pete gave her credit for.

They get up to greet me like I'm Brad Fucking Pitt, and I instantly remember again how great it is to be a hero. Sometimes a random person will nod at me like they know me, not realizing that they just recognized me from TV. I have, on occasion, signed autographs. Tonight I am planning to get even more familiar.

Newman tells them that we are carrying, plus he produces two "bottled waters," and we pour some Kennyjuice into their Diet Cokes, which, for girls who have probably been warned not to take anything from strangers, does not seem to be a problem. They drink and laugh and Nadine is all over me, but I am focused on Claudia, who, I'm thinking, Pete is totally wrong about. Not only is she kind of pretty, she also has a sexiness to her. Pete, the most discriminating of us, would call her porky, but she wears her roundness well, as far as I'm concerned. She's got this Latina vibe that makes her way hotter than the average girl. What does Pete know anyways? I have definitely questioned his taste in the past.

So we go out into the parking lot and light up, and the girls all want pictures with me, so I accommodate, posing with my hand held out in a sideways V, pursed lips, the same pose like I am in all my pictures. Then Pete gets into a discussion with Nadine, and I have my chance with Claudia, and next thing I know we are hooking up outside and so we move it to the BMW . . .

And I get her to go down on me.

She was *unbelievably* good at it. This girl had absolute technique. Plus she moved her entire body the whole time, like she was into it even more than I was, even though, tell you the truth, I wasn't doing anything for her at all.

I could not stop laughing when she was done. I was laughing so hard that she started laughing too, even though she had no idea what we were laughing about, which kept me laughing even harder. I realized that I hadn't actually laughed uncontrollably with a girl, not like that, since Burn's sister made me laugh back in high school. Immediately I knew that I was going to have to see this girl again, no matter what. If for nothing else, to see if she was really this much fun, or whether it was just the weed and the night.

We stop laughing when my cell phone rings.

Christina. Fuck. It's almost like she knows. I think this for an instant before I realize that she can't possibly know. Plus she stopped calling me, so there is no reason for me to feel guilty, which I do not feel anyways.

Plus I am not in the mood for a serious conversation. I let it ring.

"Aren't you going to answer?" Something about Claudia has changed for me, and she has become even more attractive.

Still, I better answer.

"Hi, Steven." She sounds so serious. I look over at Claudia, who looks like she is ready to laugh again. No seriousness in this one. "Are you there, Steven?"

"Me? Yeah."

"So. Hi."

"Yeah, hi." Again, I am never completely on my game with Christina.

"So I was thinking. I haven't seen *The Dark Knight* yet and pretty much everyone else has."

"Yeah, I saw it." Then, realizing what she was actually saying, I stopped myself, not wanting to miss out on the opportunity. "Yeah, I would definitely see it again. Look, can I call you back?"

"Tonight?"

"Yeah, in like an hour."

"No, I mean the movie. Tonight? It's at the IMAX."

"Can't. I'm not home now," I tell her. "What about tomorrow?" I look over; Claudia is losing interest. I don't want her to leave.

"Can't tomorrow."

"Friday?"

"Yeah, OK."

Then she hangs up, leaving me to figure out what exactly was going on in her mind. My last image of her was her walking away in disgust and me almost getting vomited on.

Oh well. I chalk it up to the residue of the magic, which I always seem to get an extra dose of from Felicia (or which, she claims, I have in me in the first place).

"Is that your girlfriend?"

"It's . . . complicated."

"Whatever she can do for you, I can do it better."

"Yep" is all I say. As in, yep, I will definitely be seeing this girl again.

We exchange cell numbers. I double-check that it's correct by calling her, so she answers while still in my car. She likes this, and she starts laughing again. This girl certainly laughs a lot. As for me, I want to be absolutely certain that I get to see her again.

I drop her off by her friends. Newman gets back into the car, takes a look at me, and laughs, knowing I got a hero's welcome, which is what he calls it. It got me to thinking that Burn had his own code word for it, as in the "Ultimate Kiss."

CHAPTER NINE

HOW BURN GOT HIS FIRST KISS

In the months after Jacob moved out, my mom went from being this stressed-out housewife to this supercharged business woman/working mom, constantly in a rush, constantly in control, as she adjusted to her new life. She filed for divorce almost immediately, not that any of us thought for a second that there would be any kind of reconciliation, not after what happened. The other thing that Caroline Crashinsky did immediately was revert to her maiden name and go back to being Caroline Prescott. She also started working out like a fiend at the gym in the same strip mall as the real estate office where she worked. So in a few months, my mom, already considered a milf in her own right, was getting even more milfy (this according to my friends, as I would not have recognized this on my own). Maybe because she felt she needed to show my father that she could survive without him, or maybe she was just as happy as I was that he was gone. Who could tell?

Point was, she didn't seem to mind the whole divorce thing one bit.

They had their separate lawyers and almost never talked, except through Lindsey, which only made Lindsey feel more important, especially since she was essentially in charge of all of our visitation plans, having the most frequent direct access to Jacob. As for Lindsey, apparently her war with Roxanne had escalated as word got out about all of the explicit details of the Thanksgiving Day fiasco. Lindsey figured Roxanne was the source, as who else could it be? The only other potential source, David, had gone back to his school for emotional misfits and was out of touch. I wondered whether Roxanne would have done that—not that I would have blamed her—and I hoped that I would get a chance to talk to her again, just so I could tell her it was just fine with me. But, being as we went to different schools, I never actually got the chance. Besides, although I couldn't admit it to Lindsey, it might have even come from me, for all I know, since I didn't exactly keep it a secret from my friends.

I heard very little about Burn for the rest of seventh grade. After a few random emails between Thanksgiving and Christmas, there was radio silence from him. And while my mom still talked to Mrs. Burnett, the conversations were apparently kept to a minimum, as my mom was fully preoccupied with her new life. The one thing I remember overhearing was that Burn was still having a problem with medications, and they were constantly experimenting with new treatments for him, but nothing mattered because no matter what they did, he continued going through his lifelong pattern of being either Too Up or Too Down, which was the way me and my friends often described him throughout high school.

For me, there was baseball and going to kids' bar mitzvahs almost every weekend and school, which was going OK, except for math and Spanish, which I totally sucked at, and of course, just living life without Jacob, which was, not gonna lie, fucking fantastic.

Then, sometime in June, as if no time had elapsed, I get an IM from Burn with a one-line message: "How big are your father's balls?" which I stupidly took literally and wondered what he knew about Jacob's manhood, until he explained that he meant that any man who brings the girl he's fucking home to his wife had to be out of touch and totally self-absorbed, especially if he thought he could get away with it.

He asked me how's it going, and I told him that I saw Jacob every second or third weekend and that it wasn't so bad, even though there were still fights (like every time). Then Burn asked me when was I going to officially thank him for saving my life, being as I didn't have to go to boarding school and he had heard that my father moved out for good.

I found it funny that the kid who actually tried to kill me when I was younger, in fact, turned out to be the only person to come to my rescue when it really mattered. I guess at that moment I had decided to finally forgive him for what happened when we were kids.

I asked him how's it going, and he told me that school was still hell—no, worse than hell—and they kept trying to fix him and make him fit in, which wasn't going to happen because they didn't understand that genius was not a disease, or at least a disease for which there was a cure.

I asked if he was coming home for the summer, and he said that coming home was not an option that was open to him, as his mother made arrangements to keep him there. What were my plans? he asked.

And of course before I could answer, he was gone, leaving me with one line, which was actually the title of an Evanescence song.

"Bring me to life."

And I realized that, forgiveness or not, it was still a supreme relief to know that he wasn't going to be back in town.

So seventh grade ended, and summer was about to begin, which meant that I would be going away to camp, which in the past was a great thing when I could escape for a few weeks from the fury of Jacob. Only this summer, with Jacob gone, I wanted to be home for the summer baseball league. Most of my friends were going to be playing in it, and they needed a shortstop, which was pretty much me or Feinblum, and Feinblum was going away all summer. So I worked out a compromise with my mom to go to camp in August, not July.

And so it was in July, on a Sunday night, after a rainy weekend of movies, one after another—*Pirates of the Caribbean* (the first one), *Terminator 3,* and then *Finding Nemo* (again)—with Jamie, that I heard from Burn again:

How HOT is Felicia, dude? Heard your dad moved in with her.

Which was how I got the news that Felicia was still in the picture.

I asked how he knew and, get this, he said that he knew because there was a photo of the two of them at some New York party that he found on the internet. He directed me to the site, and sure enough there were a bunch of images of the two of them at some sort of benefit thing, the kind of reception that Jacob would ordinarily have required my mom to attend with him.

And there she was again, looking model hot, even hotter than I remembered, which of course made my father look like a celebrity, but that didn't mean that they were necessarily together as a couple—after all, she worked with him, and I said so to Burn and his answer was, "Trust me, dude" followed by "Bring me to life" and he was gone again.

It wasn't until just before school started up again that I found out that Burn was telling the truth about my father and his girlfriend. I got this phone call. Actually Jamie handed me the phone while I was in the middle of playing the new *Tomb Raider,* telling me it's for me and yeah, yeah, had to be Jacob doing his call before the weekend. Only not this time.

"Steefen, this is Felicia. We met before. Your father and I vood like your company dis veekent."

And so my first time out with her, with them, was surprisingly normal: more movies, and me having to sit through *Legally Blonde 2* with Lindsey, Jamie, and Felicia, and then shopping, where I noticed that most people were staring at her like she was some kind of royalty.

Like in the restaurant where we went for lunch, with waiters stopping by almost constantly to refill our water glasses, or the boutique she took us to, where everyone knew her by name and treated her more like a friend than a customer. She had this informal way about her, casually touching people all the time, like she had known them forever, and bursting into laughter with a comfortable confidence that you had to notice. I instantly liked her, almost as much as I disliked my father. She quickly won over Jamie as well, but Lindsey remained cautiously suspicious.

A few days later, my final year in middle school began, and I was feeling optimistic that I was going to do OK for a change. I just felt it, like this was the year it was all going to click in for me.

It wasn't just me. Jamie, for some reason, was also in this great mood all the time. It got even better for us that fall because one particular afternoon just after school started, my mom, feeling guilty about not being around all the time as work got increasingly busy, decided that she wasn't paying enough attention to Jamie's needs. So after many years of us begging even though the answer was always no, my mom finally relented and decided to get the family (mostly Jamie) a dog, a chocolate lab named Medea, which Lindsey thought was a great name, so me and Jamie decided we had to change it immediately and I came up with "Medusa," which was close enough for her to respond like it was always her name.

The deal was that Jamie had the first line of responsibility for the dog, which my mom thought would get her away from the TV for a while, but which also meant that Jamie had to be the one to feed her and take her for walks before and after school, although it was up to Lindsey and me to do it at night.

So Jamie couldn't be happier. She was all about Beyoncé, singing "Crazy in Love," going around the house, gyrating, "Got me in love, so crazy right now," like, constantly. She was all about the "Naughty Girl" song. And "Baby Boy," so yeah, Beyoncé was big in our house that year.

And I aced my first math test. Not so good in English.

Halloween came and went. School got harder. Nothing clicked at all. Not in math, not in English, not in science. In fact, things were clicking less and less. I got a tutor. Jacob paid, and reminded me of that every time he called the house.

Thanksgiving that year was, get this, at Jacob's apartment in the city, with Felicia doing the hostess thing. Apparently my father got us in the custody contract thing for this particular holiday, which made me wonder why he would even ask for it, given the negative association and all.

I was on my best behavior. My aunt Randi was there, with a loser-guy who seemed like a science teacher or something. He had, like, not a full beard, but this scraggly growth in clumps on his chin and cheeks. He smelled like burned wood, like right out of the fireplace. What was that about?

Felicia looked totally knockout hot (no surprise there) in a black dress with pearls, which seemed to be her more or less constant look.

After dinner (no altercations this time), she played the piano, this classical piece where her hands moved practically faster than you could watch them. And she asked me for a request, any song. Thinking of Burn, I said "Bring Me to Life," thinking no way could she do it.

Only she played it perfectly. With her head down, like a rock and roller, she turned the piano into this loud rock orchestra. Even Lindsey was speechless at the performance.

Later that night, we were hanging with her in the TV room and she handed us all presents: clothes for my sisters and a new digital camera for me. We took pictures together, including one with her squeezing me playfully, which I thought I would send to Burnett if he ever IMed me again.

She suggested that I use the camera to take pictures of my girlfriends. I said I didn't have any girlfriends, and Jamie laughed and blurted that she heard that a bunch of girls in school thought I was hot. Felicia actually got Lindsey to acknowledge that a few girls in her grade kind of thought I was cute. And then she absolutely insisted that Lindsey spill the names of the girls who were interested in me, so Lindsey reluctantly mentioned two of her friends, girls who were at our house all the time and constantly made fun of me. In fact, these girls were relentlessly teasing me about being stupid, so I didn't think they liked me at all. But according to Lindsey, they said I was not only cute but "really, really cute." And Felicia asked for more names and got another one from Jamie and then, according to Lindsey, "that horrible Roxanne Burnett."

And I wanted to ask how she knew, being as I knew that she and Roxanne were sworn enemies, but of course I couldn't exactly act interested. And besides, Felicia noticeably flinched at the name Burnett, so no point in belaboring that particular subject.

Then Felicia said something that stayed with me all through high school and in a way saved me when I sucked at other things. She sat beside me and leaned on me against my hair, even though my hair was all spiky and gelled with BedHead, and she touched the spikes gently and said to my sisters:

"You know, gils, never underestimate your brother. He has talents are not easily definable. Besides, he is absolutely ator-able. He will never haf a problem vit vimen." This, with a kiss on my forehead as Jamie took the picture.

I still have this picture on my bedpost to this day. I have

to admit that I did look kind of hot in that shot. I will be taking it to college with me. And, OK, I kind of knew all the time that girls liked me before, but ever since that point I was totally armed with a different kind of mojo, given that, like, the hottest woman in the known universe thought I was cool.

Which of course is how we get to Burn and his first kiss.

My last year in middle school was not an easy one academically speaking. I had just about decided to give up on learning. My grades continued to plummet, even with a tutor, and my mom decided that I was going to have to go through more testing to see why I wasn't learning.

It was increasingly difficult to sit and read when you knew for sure that no matter how hard you tried to get it, you could think all the facts are in your head, and then the test comes and you know that you knew more than say Bosco, but then he gets like a C+ and you get a C−.

And everybody knew Bosco was an idiot. So what did that make me?

I continued to laugh it off, but mostly it sucked. So I didn't think it was such a bad idea, my mom trying to find another doctor who could help me study. Except she got busier at the real estate office, which meant less time around the house, which meant no way was I going to do my homework when no one was standing over me requiring it to be done.

So winter became spring and pretty much the back end of eighth grade was devoted to video games, not learning, baseball, playing with Medusa, and internet porn. And while some teachers expressed little hope for me, by some form of magic I managed to do just well enough to get through the school year, although in my mind, the only reason to go to school at all was to see my friends.

And then there was this party at Stephanie Coogan's house

in early May that changed things for most of us. Changed things because we (as in me, Evan, and Pete) got to see real breasts for the first time (this by accident, so I won't reveal the circumstances); and also, there was alcohol there, and most of us got wasted for the first time, and also got to see weed up close for the first time, although none of us actually sampled it back then.

Also I got to actually make out with Stephanie's sister Hailey, who was a year older than us and did it on a dare from her friends (whatever it takes . . .).

Also April Walker apparently . . . (And I hesitate to write this since I didn't see it myself, but since it figures into what happens next, has to be said.) April Walker apparently gave two kids BJs.

April was this gawky girl who, sometime during eighth grade, was beginning to not be so gawky anymore, and just as people were starting to notice the change in the way she looked, she was starting to be a little "out there." She was always out there on account of having some kind of learning disability, but up until eighth grade, she was, let's just say, not very popular (as in most people didn't even know her name), and then suddenly, there was a buzz, as in, did you see April, did you see what she was wearing?

And now, she apparently chose Stephanie's party to change her image.

Problem was, word got out. Which meant that like every parent in town was doing the twilight bark the next day until virtually every adult heard about the party at the Coogans' house.

My mother called me into her room, one hand still holding the phone, and asked, was I there at Stephanie's house? (She didn't know since I slept over at Pete's that night.) What did I see? (I wasn't about to tell her about the actual naked breasts.) And was I involved in any drinking or sexual activity? Of course, I told her hell no (even though I probably drank the most of my friends and actually got a make-out kiss). And surprisingly, she dropped the entire conversation after that, apparently because my name didn't come up during her phone call.

As to the making-out, it was no big thing as Hailey basically just did it to me for like ten seconds when I ran into her alone in her kitchen, and by the time I knew what was going on, it was over. Still, it totally left me spinning with new possibilities. So much so that the day after the party, all I was pretty much thinking was, how was I going to even talk to Hailey again, since she was older and not even in my school. I couldn't call her, couldn't IM her, couldn't ask Lindsey, who was, in fact, a year older than Hailey, so I had to put it out of my head, or tried to, but it was difficult because the story about the party and April's antics was superbig news, and even the principal got involved and decided to have a meeting with parents to talk about what they called "adolescent experimentation."

Which happened on a Thursday. All of the parents, including my mom, went to the meeting and came back with questionnaires and pamphlets for us to read (right, as if every kid was going to stop being a kid because of some kind of magic brochure, ha). My mom tried to sit me down to talk about this, but a few eye rolls later, she gave up, saying that she knew that she had to "choose her battles" with me.

Yeah, whatever. By then, most of the time when we argued, my mom gave up, saying that she had to choose her battles.

Then the next night, a Friday night, was some kind of big basketball event at the high school. I wanted to go since I was hoping to be on the high school team, even though my game was struggling in middle school and I didn't have many minutes of playing time during actual games.

It was a warm night, like summer, so we were outside, and a few of Lindsey's friends came over, saying that they heard I was a good kisser and did I want to try it with them. So we went around to the side of the school and I hooked up with two of them, each for not long, one of which tasted like cigarettes.

Lindsey found out on Saturday. "Stay away from my friends" was all she said to me.

But her friends were always at the house and apparently wanted to practice kissing with me, so I worked out an arrangement that they could if I could, you know, get to second base. And most said no, but one said OK.

So a few weeks later, I was on the baseball field, another game. Actually, it was the fourth inning against the Red Sox, and after pitching the first three, I was benched, so I left the dugout and wandered over to the Porta-Pottys, and guess who shows up?

No, not Burn . . . Actually, technically, a Burnett though, as in Roxanne.

"Heard you're a frickin' make-out machine, Kirshunsky." Another intentional mispronunciation, which I found entirely entertaining. I wondered whether she ever did this to Lindsey.

She looked unusually out there, even for Roxanne. She had dyed a blue streak in her hair, and she was dressed in all goth clothes and Converse sneakers.

"I guess."

"Cool sunglasses. What are you, a pitcher or a catcher?" She laughed, like she was finding herself funny, which she usually was.

"Sometimes," as in baseball, I was both.

"Oooooh," she said, "that's hot." And of course, I didn't know what was so hot about it.

"You promised I would be your first," she continued. "And now I find out about Hailey Coogan."

"She told you?"

"We *are* in the same high school." Which wasn't an actual

answer. "Are you any good at it?"

"OK, I guess."

She stepped in toward me and, with a graceful sweep of her hand, knocked my baseball cap off and pulled me close to her, with her hands around my back. Then she opened her mouth into mine and pulled me closer, so I could feel the warmth of her entire body. And the curves, all of them. With her tongue practically dancing in my mouth at the same time.

And then letting go.

"Forget it. Hailey is a much better kisser," she said, wiping saliva off her face. "You might want to practice some more before I catch you again." She laughed.

I couldn't figure out what to say. I was spinning from the closeness and my body's intense desire to continue what we had been doing. This was an entirely different version of making out than I was used to.

And then she added, "David's coming back next week. He's going to be really pissed off when he finds out that you kissed me." She reached down, swooped up my cap, and tugged it down over my eyes. "Just kidding, Crishansky." And then she was gone and it was just me and the Porta-Pottys. Spinning.

What was up with that family?

More importantly, when my head finally cleared, I had to wonder, what was up with Burn coming back? Was she kidding about that? Or about telling him about the kiss?

After that experience, making out with Lindsey's friends was pretty much pointless to me. Although I still kind of liked it, all I thought about during was the way Roxanne moved and whatever her tongue did when she did it.

Anyways, about Burn, I got to find out two weeks later, when Pete's mom drove me home after baseball. New car in the driveway, a Prius. I eyed it suspiciously, thinking that I overheard my mom talking to Lindsey the night before about her having a date with some guy.

I didn't expect it to be Mrs. Burnett, sitting at the kitchen counter with my mom. I hadn't seen her in a long time. She looked different, weird. Short, wavy hair, overly made up, like she was the one with the date. Skinny and fat at the same time.

"David's up in your room," my mom said. "I hope you don't mind."

"Heard you made out with my sister," he said while playing the Indiana Jones game. He looked even older than he did the last time I saw him. Hard core. Short hair, like a marine. He had clearly been working out, was jacked, like, too jacked.

On the screen, Indy was involved in some puzzle that I hadn't made it to yet, beyond my saved points. Burn was always ruining my saved points.

"Not exactly made out," I answered him, "as she kind of attacked me."

"Either way, if it happens again, I will kill you." This without missing a beat, without looking up from the screen, as Indy swung from vine to vine across treacherous terrain.

By that point, I was used to him telling me that he was going to kill me, and it hardly got my attention this time. However, I wondered which Burn I was dealing with: Too Up? Too Down?

"Don't worry. It won't happen again," I said, although I knew that, given the opportunity, I could not possibly resist, even considering Burn's death threats.

"Just kidding, Crash. If I had to kill all of the guys Roxanne's made out with, I would need an M-sixteen," referencing one of the assault guns that he would later obtain, although neither of us could have possibly guessed that at the time.

"One other thing," he said. Indy now, strafing along a ledge high above the earth, climbing higher still. "I have to make out with one of your sisters."

"Take Lindsey," I said without missing a beat.

"Yeah, right," he said, still playing. "No, seriously. If not one of your sisters, then one of your girlfriends. Seriously. Roxanne told me you are, like, superpopular with older girls."

"Where have you been?" I tried changing the subject.

"You don't want to know."

"How long are you here for?"

"For good. I'm going to Meadows next year with you," he said, referring to our high school.

"How come?" I must not have sounded happy. I was thinking that the Burn on my bed was closer to the Burn in elementary school than to the seemingly normal guy who returned for a short while in middle school, only to turn crazy in the lunchroom a few weeks later.

"You seem disappointed," he said, still playing. He always fucking *knew*. You had to be careful with every word you said to him, and every single gesture, because he could read something into everything.

"Just surprised is all." Which was mostly true. "I didn't think you were coming back."

"Moms ran out of money," he said. "Still waiting for World Trade Center distributions. Plus I am, apparently, certifiably sane now. Point is, I *am* back. And you still owe me big-time for saving you from the life I have had for the past two years. Plus you made out with my sister. What kind of guy would do that to a friend? And I don't want to go to high school with people thinking I haven't made out. So you owe me."

I looked at this jacked monster on my bed, calling me his friend, and wondered would I have looked like that if Jacob had sent me to military school. I didn't respond to him, and he took my silence as a yes, because he said, "Good. We start tomorrow night. There's the play and the party. Do you think kids remember me?"

The middle school production of *West Side Story* was scheduled to open in the middle school auditorium the following night, and there was supposed to be an after-party in the school gym, supervised, of course, given the town's new awareness of the "adolescent experimentation" going on in my grade. Virtually everyone was going to be there, which meant that Burn would be an obvious attraction for people who hadn't seen him since he was escorted out of school, almost two years ago now, a not necessarily positive attraction.

So I quickly figured out that he was counting on me to be his wingman, and a way for him to be accepted by the kids in our grade. My mind flashed back to elementary school, to the kid clutching the fence and Principal Seidman telling me to go over and talk to him. This time, though, I was obsessed with trying to get some girls in my grade to hook up, as this had become an addiction for me after my intoxicating experience with Burn's sister, driving my desire to find someone else who could duplicate that experience. No question, he would interfere with my plans. But then again, he did save my life, as he reminded me over and over again. So I owed him.

"My mom agreed to drive us," he said.

"I was going with a couple of the guys."

"Not according to your mom," he said. "You have to take Jamie."

Thing is, I wasn't actually planning to stay for the entire play, since none of my good friends were in it, just get there, stay until the lights went down, and duck out until the after-party. And while we had Jamie with us, that wasn't going to be an obstacle, because when Mrs. Burnett dropped us all off at the school, I immediately took care of my obligations by finding some of Jamie's few friends in the crowd and suggesting that she sit with them. She didn't seem unhappy about it, and I felt I did my job well, because I noticed a random mom sitting with those other girls, which meant they had supervision.

Well covered, I turned to Burn, who was following me around like a shadow, and said, "Let's bail." He said no, we have to stay. Then I spotted a bunch of guys in a cluster, including Leeds, Feinblum, Evan, Kenny, and Mark Duncan. They all nodded at Burn—how's it going—him nodding back, no one looking him in the eyes. Then they looked at me, with a "what's *he* doing here?" look. I figured I should have warned them, but also figured that if I had, they would have bailed on me.

Duncan said he was depressed because there were no good movies coming out for the entire summer, which pretty much meant no Adam Sandler movies since that was all he liked. Feinblum said that he had just seen *Shrek 2,* and Kenny said he had to take his sister to see *Mean Girls*, because all of the girls in middle school were all about *Mean Girls* and she hadn't seen it yet, and I said that Jamie already saw it and ever since she had been walking around the house talking like one of the Plastics, memorizing entire speeches from the movie, and Feinblum said which one did she imitate, and I said the stupid one and he said Karen.

Burn just stood behind me, looking out of place.

Then Pete came over and right away started staring down Burn, and I totally forgot about the possibility that things were over between them.

"How's it going, Dave?" Pete said, no letup on the hate stare, no fist extended for the obligatory fist bump.

Burn smiled back. "Learn anything new about panthers since I last saw you?" Totally nonthreatening. This wasn't much of an apology, but it made us all laugh and things were going to be fine, at least for the moment.

We argued, do we stay, or do we go and come back for the after party?

I can admit now that we all secretly wanted to stay, but, being boys, we couldn't admit it to ourselves or to each other.

So the play starts, and we are all sitting together when Jamie shows up in my row and wants to sit with me. Only there's no extra seat so we find a way to share, which means me pushing against Burn on one side, her pushing against Pete on the other, which is OK for her since she likes Pete, but notsomuch for me having to touch Burn.

The lights dim, and the orchestra kicks off playing.

And the Jets come out and there's Richie Krane (forgot he was in it) and a few other kids and Gerry Earnshaw (this was way before his official "I'm gay" announcement, like there was any doubt) and the rest of the Jets, coming out onto the stage, snapping their fingers. And the orchestra is playing along and it all sounds pretty professional to me as they walk across the stage snapping, where on the other side is Ed Wexler, playing Bernardo, looking more gay than menacing.

And this goes on for a while, and Gerry now has to get his buddy Tony (played by equally gay Billy Cobb), and now Billy is just singing for like hours and I whisper to Jamie, "Shoot me, please," but Jamie is into it and so apparently is Burn, as I look over at him and his eyes are wide open and so is his mouth.

And next scene is Annie Russo playing Anita arguing with Maria. Maria is played by Christina Haines, the kiss-ass from McAllister, and she looks great, but all I can think about is Annie Russo, who is looking freshly sexy in an adult way.

So the next scene is this big dance scene and like every kid who ever wanted to be in drama is now on the stage at the same time, and it goes on and on, and my ADHD is starting to kick in, because my leg starts vibrating and I need to get up, and without thinking about it, I keep kicking the chair in front of me and Jamie asks me to stop.

So does the lady in front of us.

And then suddenly all of the dancers move back behind a screen, except for Christina and Billy, and she steps forward toward the front of the stage. The lights are only on her, and without saying a word she has stopped even me from squirming.

She was no longer Christina to me. She had actually morphed into Maria, the Puerto Rican girl, and she was staring at Billy like he wasn't Billy and like she recognized him but didn't know him at all.

And beside me, there was a noise, a snorting noise coming from Burn. Like a bull sound was what I thought. What the fuck was up with him?

The play goes on and Burn is still snorting. Bunch of talking, then rooftops, and Annie Russo moving like a stripper with her boobs practically popping out.

Go, Annie. I am into this song. And looking at Annie in a whole new light.

Now comes Billy, prancing around the stage yelling, "Maria, Maria," well, you know, and now Christina comes out, and she's got this gleam that you could see in the audience, all the way to the back end of the auditorium, and then the two of them get closer and closer and Billy doesn't seem so gay anymore because he and Christina are suddenly in each other's arms, singing "Tonight, Tonight" together like magic, real magic, in perfect harmony.

And Christina's voice is so absolutely incredible that songs should be made just for it, songs that are sung so loudly and clearly that it would break mirrors with its absolute brilliance.

So brilliant that it practically stopped time.

And then I noticed Burn.

Burn was sitting there, completely and utterly captivated

by Christina's unquestioned brilliance, just like the rest of us. Except he was crying.

Not just crying. Weeping.

Get it? Absolutely weeping. Out loud. OK, some of the adults were getting a little teary-eyed, and the kids, but no one moved. It was absolutely quiet, not a sound.

Except for Burn's snort and his absolute weeping.

They almost stopped the show from the sound, except that everyone in the audience started clapping, not just clapping, but standing and clapping and stomping and whistling. So they finally did stop the show until we all stopped and they started up again.

First talking:

"Te adoro, Tony."

"Te adoro, Maria."

And then, real quiet. And back to singing:

Tonight

Toooooooniiiiiggggghhhhhhhhhhhtt.

Intermission.

People are standing and clapping as the curtain comes down and the lights go up.

And Burn has his face buried in his hands, still uncontrollably weeping, folded into his chair like a newborn. Sunken into it.

I was, tell you the truth, more than a little freaked out by the sight of this. I have not seen a boy cry since, like, fifth grade, when Bosco lost it on the mound after giving up like nine runs in an inning. So I have no clue what I'm supposed to do, like, was I responsible for him?

When did he become my pet?

I look at Jamie, Jamie looks at me, and I can tell from her eyes she's not in. It's not going to be her problem; it's all on me.

Do I get a parent over to see this?

I look at Pete and the others. They are moving out into the far aisle, looking at me like they are not in, not their problem either.

I'm about to use my cell phone and call my mom when Burn looks up at me, all cried out, like everything is instantly back to normal, and says, "She understands what it means to be human."

Yeah, Burn, I am thinking, she understands everything, all right, whatever that means.

"She's the one, Crash," he says. "You've got to make this happen."

I immediately reflect on the conversation in my room. If I could set him up with Christina, then I would owe him nothing else, which means freedom for me, nothing he could hold over my head, as we would be squared away even after making out with his sister.

Except that from what I remembered, Christina didn't exactly like me very much, given that I kind of publicly nick-named her a kiss-ass and all.

"Not doing it, Dave" is what I told him. "She hates me."

But then, I notice April Walker coming up the aisle, and it was obvious to me that she too has been moved to tears as she is clutching a handful of tissues and wiping her face. And I imme-diately remember how Felicia told my sisters that I had special talents, and while she didn't say what those were, I understood that one of those talents is knowing when the universe presents me with an opportunity. And there, in the middle school audi-torium, it was clear to me that the universe was up to its usual tricks, because, if April and Burn hit it off and he got what April has become famous for giving, then I'm guaranteed off the hook with him, like, forever.

I move into the aisle, blocking her path. "April, that was really good, huh?"

"It just got me, Steven, you know?"

"It got my friend too. Do you remember Dave Burnett?" I point over to Burn, who had this glazed-over look. "He used to go to school here." It was obvious that she didn't know him, which meant that she also didn't know *about* him either. Thank you, universe.

"He was totally moved to tears," I told her. "Just like you. Did you hear him crying?"

She reached out and extended her hand to him. "That was you? Yes. Hi, I'm April. It made me so sad to hear you crying" is what she said.

He reached up, took her hand. And, get this, they walk up the aisle together, talking. A few minutes later, the lights go down, Jamie comes back and the curtain goes up, and we wait for Burn but he doesn't return.

Finally, darkness.

After a while, Jamie takes his seat and I finally have some room.

And the rest of the play goes on fine, until the very end where Christina/Maria is on her knees, singing another song that absolutely rattles the audience.

"There's a place for us. Somewhere, a place for us."

And again, in the middle of the song, this time coming from the back of the auditorium, you could hear someone snorting and weeping, Burn going off again.

Maria/Christina looked up, stunned for an instant, and went back to it.

I was thinking: Yeah, it was touching and all when Tony died, but get over it, Burn.

Burn wasn't at the after-party. My mom picked up Jamie, as planned, and thanked me for taking care of her. Jamie thanked me too, which was nice, family stuff. And then I searched the gym for him. He was gone and so was April. Meanwhile, everyone was clapping like crazy when the cast came out into the gym, one by one, until only Christina was left to come through the doors. And like a bride, carrying flowers in both arms, she made this great entrance, like this wasn't just middle school, it was opening night on Broadway.

There was food, snacks, and drinks, no alcohol, but you still felt that you were in a special place and that something spectacular happened onstage that night. Later, after the group was thinning out, some kids started dancing, and so I did too, when Annie Russo asked.

And then I bumped into Christina, who stopped me after my dance with Annie.

"Thanks a lot, Steven," she said, extrasarcastic. "Your friend almost ruined the entire night with those sounds."

"He's not my friend," I told her.

"He was with you. Everyone told me."

"Yeah, well he was and he wasn't. It was David Burnett, you know, from McAllister days, and he came with me, but he wasn't, you know, *with* me. He lives here again." Me, trying to justify, then switching gears. "Still, you were pretty good. I mean, Burn wasn't the only one crying from your voice," I told her. "You should be on *American Idol* or something."

"Yeah, thanks." She was now distracted by someone, about to leave, but I stopped her.

"No, really," I continued, "you were beyond amazing."

"You mean, amazing for a kiss-ass?" So there it was, just in case I thought she had forgotten. "People still call me that."

"Not after tonight," I told her. "People will call you a star after tonight."

This totally stopped her in her tracks and completely disarmed her. I knew this because her body shifted from defensive to relaxed and her face glowed with the compliment.

And I saw the possibility of the universe presenting another opportunity, even if it was a long shot.

"Hey, you wanna hook up?"

Now she was standing in place, with this terrific smile, and I figured no way did she hear what I said. She shook her head like I was completely crazy, which I was, but given all the attention I had been getting from older girls, I was pretty full of myself. Since I had set out to accomplish a goal, what better way to do it than with the celebrity of the moment?

Still, she wouldn't stop shaking her head in disapproval.

So imagine my surprise when she said, "Yeah, sure."

CHAPTER TEN

CHRISTINA AND THE DARK NIGHT

Friday, two days after my experience with Claudia at the Westchester Mall, I am on my way to New Roc City with Christina to see *The Dark Knight*, like everything is totally normal again. Christina is going on in that dramagirl way of talking, which is pretty much constantly, about Maddy and how she was just doing what Maddy does, as in looking for someone else to put it on instead of taking responsibility for herself, about having some self-respect as a girl, and then about preparing for college, was I nervous yet, because she was getting nervous, and how many more weeks did we have, was I counting.

And my phone buzzes, another text from Claudia. She has been texting me ever since we hooked up. At first I was anxious to talk to her, but now, two days later, my patience was being stretched by the constant flow of texts and voice mails. So I stopped responding. Maybe *she* should have some self-respect and wait until I call her.

I flick open my phone, just to make sure it's not someone important. It's from Claudia.

Have you seen the picture yet?

I'm wondering how she could possibly know that I'm going to the movies. Is she stalking me and will she somehow show up when I'm on line at the IMAX?

I single-hand text her back while driving, Christina watching me with adult eyes that make it clear that she doesn't approve of texting and driving. No surprise there.

What picture?

u no. The one.

"The road, Steven" is what Christina says, and I realize that I am swerving into the oncoming lane and I also realize that it's not the smartest thing texting a girl you just hooked up with in front of a girl you're trying to hook up with. So I flip my phone closed and ditch it in the back pocket of my jeans.

And Christina doesn't miss a beat because she goes on and I try to listen, and now she's talking about Heath Ledger and how good an actor he was and how sad it was that he died and I'm wondering what am I even doing with her. If I had asked Annie Russo out, she would have been looking all flashy, and definitely into smoking and drinking and not complaining about a few innocent text messages. Also, we might not even make it into the movies, which was OK, with me having seen *The Dark Knight* like five times already, no big.

"So you *never* ever smoked weed?" I instinctively touch my stash, hidden inside the sunglasses case in the side pocket of the car door.

"Steven, we already talked about this," she says, like I'm supposed to remember. The answer is once, she didn't like it.

"Maybe you should try it again, for the movie?"

"Steven, you already know the answer." More than a little annoyed.

"OK, OK, no weed" is what I say, relenting.

I'm thinking of something else to say, planning to get to Burn, which is what we always end up talking about. But nothing is coming out. The dreaded silence. She's done; I'm tapped. Even the BMW is too quiet. There was never any silence with Annie Russo. Or the Westchester Mall girl, Claudia. At least so far. My cell buzzed again through the fabric of my jeans. I fought the urge to find out who was texting me.

How much longer to the movie theater? And how I am going to see *The Dark Knight* without blazing?

Then . . .

"Do you think David Burnett is right? About the three of us having this cosmic connection and all?" she asked me, like, out of nowhere. Whenever she referred to him, it was always by his full name. I wondered whether she did this to my name as well whenever she spoke about me to someone else.

"Do I need to remind you that Burn had a theory about pretty much everything?" I told her, and she actually laughed. "But he never told me that one."

"David Burnett said that you and he were connected and that he and I were connected so it made sense to him that you and I were connected."

This felt more like an SAT question to me than something that someone would actually say. I was still trying to figure out the first part of the equation. Burn had said that before, about a connection between me and him, but Burn said a lot of truly crazy things, so I never thought about it in any legitimate way. Also, he described our relationship, as I recall, in a very Harry Potter way—as in Harry and Lord Voldemort—one must die so that the other could live.

"Look, as far as I'm concerned, any connection was all in Burn's mind," I told her. "Plus, no way are you connected to Burn. Just because he stalked you throughout high school doesn't make it a cosmic connection."

"I don't know," she answered. "Remember, he and I did go out for a while during sophomore year, and he was perfectly normal then. And when he wasn't stalking me, he did, on occasion, actually teach me a few things. Things that no one else could have taught me."

I made a mental note that I would have to interview her for the book, that she would have insights that I might have missed.

"I don't see how that connects you to him or that you and I are somehow connected. Are you saying that we are?" More importantly, I wondered, if she thinks we are connected, then do my odds increase with respect to getting with her?

"Well, I *did* have the biggest crush on you in elementary school. Like insanely big. You were kind of my first love until you started calling me names. And then, after my first performance of *West Side Story* in middle school, you were there for me."

OK, I did find it strange that she would bring up the *West Side Story* thing, almost immediately after I had written about it, as she had no way of knowing this. I didn't think that me getting to make out with her counted as "there for her," but I wasn't about to tell her that, given what the potential stakes were. I also didn't want to tell her that I didn't have any real recollection of her for a long time after we were in McAllister together, and I certainly had no idea that she was drawing hearts in her notebooks with my name filled in next to hers.

"Still, we had pretty much nothing to do with each other in high school, or even middle school except for a while after you were in that play."

"And yet you were there for me whenever Burn got out-of-line crazy."

"It was just that one time, really." I was referring to an incident in our junior year.

"I'm not just talking about Massachusetts. Even before, I heard that you were always defending me whenever he talked about me."

"That doesn't mean we're connected."

"OK." She tried to reason with me. "Why are you here now? I don't believe that you came along just because you think I'm going to hook up with you. You know that's not me, Steven. I'm *not* going to just have sex with you."

I turned off the highway, dismayed at this latest piece of information, even though part of me already knew this. I definitely should have called Annie Russo. Or spent the night with my boys.

The movie theater was in my sights now. This was getting out of hand. Now I had only one choice left: I had to reel her in, show her my pimp hand. That's what you had to do whenever a girl got all about herself and wanted to suck you in.

"Maybe I just want to interview you on Burnett for the book. Or maybe you're here because you're finally giving me the opportunity to hook up when no one else is around." Point for me.

"You can interview me over the phone. And as for hooking up, you haven't. Tried. Not all summer. And we've been alone more than a few times. And I have given you more than one opportunity. To try. And from what I know, you're not shy." Point for her.

"Just waiting for the right time." My point again.

I pulled into a spot in the parking lot.

"When is the right time? Is it right here, right now? Should we just *do it*?" She looked into my eyes with this. It had me thinking, yeah, quite possibly, as it would not be the first time this week that I had hooked up in a parking lot. But looking back into her eyes, I knew this was not going to be the correct answer. Even as she moved closer to me.

"C'mon, Steven, is that all you really want?" Now pressing against me, kissing my neck and moving her arms around my shoulders. "Well, then, go ahead."

Only it didn't serve to get me off at all, but somehow made me feel exactly the opposite way, as in claustrophobic. I mean, I am used to aggressive girls, which to me is usually a good thing. Except the ones that I'm talking about were usually either drunk or stoned or both, and sloppy and sexy.

"What's the matter, Steven?" she said. "You look nervous." Now squeezing me tighter. Then she lifted my hand up and placed it on her left boob, clamping down on my hand hard enough to lock it against her. "Here, does that make you happy? Isn't this why you abandoned your friends on a Friday night? Or could it be that maybe you want to actually explore what we have?"

I pushed her back, held my hands up to stop her. "OK, I get it" is what I said, but what I was thinking was that she was lucky I wasn't drunk or high, because if I had been, I would have *had* to do something. But being as I was stone cold sober, I realized that this girl was looking for it in a different way.

"You get what?" she asked.

"That it's different with you." This surprised me as much as it surprised her when I said it.

She backed off. "OK then, can we please see the movie?"

So we're sitting together, passing the popcorn, waiting for the movie to start, and I'm thinking about Burn again. Point was, after the night of the play, Burn was, at least for a time, eternally in my debt, as he claimed, because I was responsible for him getting his one true wish to come true, as he not only got to make out with April Walker, but then he got what he called the Ultimate Kiss, becoming the first kid I knew to get head before high school. Even still, he was upset with me when he found out that Christina and I had hooked up, but said he couldn't be angry because he also believed beyond a doubt that if it wasn't for me, he never would have met Christina, which of course made no sense with them being in the same school and all, but whatever.

So just as the movie begins, I tell her, yeah, maybe Burn, being Burn, and knowing that he did see things more deeply than, like, anyone, maybe there was some kind of connection.

And with this, she leans into me and kisses me gently on the mouth. It felt like honest-to-god magic until the guy in the row behind us kicked our chairs and said:

"Watch the fucking movie, you two."

Only I couldn't watch because my mind was spinning like it does when I overdo bong hits, only this time it's spinning with questions—as in, what am I doing with this girl and why do I feel so good when I'm with her and what does she mean by connected and how good did that one boob feel for the ten seconds that she let me touch it and how experienced exactly was she and what if I screwed this up because, let's face it, I have never actually had a girlfriend, unless you count Roxanne, but you can't count Roxanne because that was an entirely different thing than everything else in the world, but then so is this, in its own way, an entirely different thing. And now that we kissed, should I try for it again, and how far should I go next time? Not in the parking lot of course, since she already made it clear that parking lots were not her thing, and as for actual sex, did she say before that she wasn't going to have sex with me at all or just not have sex with me for now? And if it's the second one, what did I have to do to get to the next level?

All this while the Joker was doing his best to baffle Batman.

And all the time that I'm thinking about her and about Burn, my cell keeps vibrating in my pocket. While I'm tempted to take it out and find out who it is that is trying to reach me, I know if I answer it, the guy behind me is going to crap out a kitten.

Afterward, we are walking back to the car, and both of us go for our cells. Mine is loaded with messages and calls. This was probably the single longest time I have ever gone without answering my cell, and it felt pretty good not to be tied to it, but now I have hell to pay and have to sift through lines and lines of text messages. One after another from Claudia, all about the picture, did I see it yet? And sorry, it wasn't her fault.

And then Newman.

It's all over.

I text back.

whats all over?

And Kenny. And Evan. And even Bosco.

r u OK, man?

Even Lindsey, and Lindsey never ever calls or texts me.

Where r u? Call Dad. Now.

Christina is going through her own messages, but looking at me like I'm a serial killer or something.

Buzz back from Newman.

U R all over the news.

"I think you better take me home" is what Christina is saying, as I'm calling Newman and getting a call from him at the same time. I pick up Newman, and then Jacob is buzzing in, so I reluctantly pick him up instead.

"You've gone too far."

"I have?"

"Where are you now? How soon can you get here?"

"Here? Where?"

"My apartment. I've been waiting for you to call back all night. Have you talked to anyone?"

"Like who?"

"Like the press."

Now my gears are spinning. With all the earlier talk about connections, I figure out pretty quickly that Burn has probably escaped from wherever they are keeping him and probably he is coming after me because he somehow knows that me being with Christina is inevitable. I am instantly in panic mode. Reaching total panic as I start driving, almost sideswiping another car as I absentmindedly zip through the parking lot.

Wait a minute. What did Jacob— *I* went too far?

"I haven't talked to the press. I haven't talked to anyone," I tell him. "Why would I talk to the press?"

163

"Good. Get over here now. Before you make this any worse. And call me when you are in the neighborhood. You are not to talk to anyone, do you understand? You call me first. I'll tell you where to park, and I will have you escorted up. Do you understand me, Steven? Please confirm that you understand."

I hated when he said that, which was like every time we talked. In this case, how could I possibly understand? Understand what? "Sure" is what I tell him, as always, just to shut him up. I had, at that moment, no intention whatsoever of going to his apartment.

He hangs up and Newman has been on hold all along.

"Alex, what the fuck is going on?"

I'm stopped at the light now.

Christina pushes her iPhone at me. And there on her display is a crystal clear photograph of me with my arms around Claudia and one of the other Westchester Mall girls, with me holding up a perfectly rolled blunt, the smoke billowing up from it, and the girls' faces have been fuzzed out so you can't make out who they are. But you can most definitely tell who I am.

It takes me a minute to get to the caption: "Hero to Zero." I scroll down and read the next sentences, none of which are all that flattering, to say the least, me with the blunt and my famous Crash smile, flashing a horizontal V peace-sign formation with my right hand.

Back to my phone. "I'm looking at it now. What's the big deal, Alex?"

"The big deal is that drug use is illegal, and they have you in a photo with a blunt dangling from your mouth, dude. Where are you?"

"At the movies with Christina."

"Take me home, Steven," she says again, loud enough so I can't hear Newman. I pull over to the side of the road, letting other cars pass me. Why was she upset? What difference did it make? Was it me, or was the whole world out of whack on this? I never said I didn't smoke weed, so what was the big deal?

"Alex, I'll call you back," I told him. Then, turning to her, I said the most absolutely brilliant thing I could have possibly said, or at least I thought it was brilliant.

"Come with me to my father's apartment." Me thinking, if I had a girl there, a remarkably responsible one, then Jacob would have to control his temper. I was thinking, this was my insurance, in case Felicia wasn't there, and even if she was. I was thinking mostly about me, but here's what I came out with:

"Come with me. This could be very good for you."

"Good for me?" she responded with a shocked look. "How do you figure that a picture of you getting high with some lame girls translates to being good for me? Are you out of your fucking mind?"

OK, it took me a couple of seconds to get over Christina actually cursing. Not because of the language itself, but because she made the word "fucking" actually sound musical. I kind of wanted to hear her do it again. I also didn't want her to go home. I was pretty sure if she did, I wouldn't hear from her again.

"If there's press, then you get your picture in the papers," I rambled, realizing that the idea played out a whole lot better in my head than it sounded when I tried to explain it. "And your name."

"Yeah, associated with a druggie."

"It's just weed. *Everybody* smokes weed."

"Steven, who are those girls?"

"Just some randoms that we met earlier in the week, based on me being a hero and all."

"And you want to know why I'm not having sex with you," she said matter-of-factly. "Isn't it evident?"

"I did not hook up with those girls," I said, so convincingly that even I believed it. Thank you, President Clinton.

"Why should I believe you?" she said, and I realized that, for some reason, it mattered to her, which meant that if I got the answers right, maybe I could still get with her before the end of the summer.

"You already said you weren't having sex with me, so there's no reason for me to lie," I lied, wondering, as I said it, if it made any sense at all.

"You always get your way, don't you," she said, and I knew that she wasn't buying, but she was calming down. Point was, whether I was incredible at persuading people or had some great instinctive talent to relax them, I did almost always get my way, part of my magic, which made this entire catastrophe seem like no big whatsoever. I just wasn't seeing how this was a problem. Well, except for having to deal with Jacob, which was where she could be supremely helpful.

"Take me home, Steven." And despite all my magic, we were back to square one.

I started to drive.

Then stopped.

"Please come with me, Christina. Not because it's good for you or anything. Because the absolute truth is, I really need you," I told her, surprising myself with my own honesty.

An hour later, we are on our way into the lobby of my father's building and yes, there is a TV crew outside in the street and, sure enough, they stop me as I head into the building with Christina. She walks ahead, pretends not to know me. I hear questions being asked and a microphone is thrust at me, but almost instantly, the doorman to my father's building whisks me inside.

"WHAT THE HELL IS WRONG WITH YOU?"

There is nothing quite like hearing Jacob's voice to bring you back to reality. I am sitting on the couch, across from Christina, who is adjusting her skirt and, just for a second, I think I see all the way up. Sorry, Christina.

"What part of 'call me when you get close' did you not understand?" He sits on the coffee table between us, quickly glances at Christina dismissively, like he's sure she's just another airhead girl, which she must be, in his mind, if she's with me.

"Where's Felicia?" I ask, not willing to go through this with him unless I have backup.

"Inside." He sneers. "She has to be up early tomorrow. If she misses her flight back to Prague, it's on you. As it is, I was supposed to go with her, and now I will be here doing damage control. Do you understand? So this is definitely on you, Steven. Own this, for once."

"It's always on me, Dad."

"It *is* always on you, Steven."

"In your opinion . . ." I'm in his face. He's in my face.

"In *my* opinion, it was a dark night in hell when you were born."

Yep, here we go again. The dark night in hell routine that I used to get when he lived with us. That's right, Jacob, remind me again that I'm not like the other kids, remind me that I don't listen, don't sit up straight, don't learn, don't clean up after myself, don't dress the way I should, don't do my homework, don't work, don't respect authority, don't care about rules, don't turn my music down, don't try to see things your way, don't take care of myself or my sisters, don't stop disappointing him, don't stop embarrassing him . . .

Point is, no matter what I do, he will always believe that I'm just lazy and pampered and that there's nothing whatsoever wrong with me, as in my learning disability. According to him, I have used my diagnosis all my life as an excuse not to work hard, not to excel in a way that he believed that I should be capable of.

I have to wonder if he's at least partly correct. If his assessment is right, then I'm probably smarter than I think.

"Excuse me, Mr. Crashinsky . . ." A timid voice from behind him. "Did you forget that your son is a hero? If it wasn't for your son, I might not be here today."

Jacob moves to the left. My eyes meet Christina's and, with my eyes, I tell her this: *Thank you, Christina, for being here, because as mean and nasty as he sounds, this is nothing compared to what it would be like if you weren't here with me.*

And her eyes shoot back: *You are covered, dude.* It took a lot out of me to admit that I needed her, but she instantly responded to it, like total forgiveness, nothing else mattered.

And all this between us is shot to hell in a heartbeat, because Jacob snaps his head back to her. "KEEP OUT OF THIS" is what he tells her.

I take a long, slow breath.

Wheewwwwww. Blow the air out of my mouth.

Slowly.

Years ago some therapist taught me to do this in order to control my sometimes out-of-control anger. Anger that I have been mostly in control of ever since Jacob moved out, but anger that is deep and quick and sometimes just below the surface. I am angry enough now to leave or worse, because maybe it's time to show him that he can't treat me like a child anymore. I'm about to get up when Christina shoots me another look, like it's all right with her. If I didn't see that look, I possibly could have hit him hard enough to knock him out.

"I don't need this," I announce. Another breath. I'm thinking that I am not getting through this one without Felicia. Where is she?

"Listen to me very carefully." He turns back to me, more controlled. "You and your indiscretions will hurt my business, because if clients believe that I can't control my own son, they will lose confidence in me. These are not easy times, Steven. I can't afford for you to continue to be a loaded cannon. So here's what's going to happen. You are sleeping here tonight. A limo will be by in a few minutes to collect your friend and send her back to wherever she's going."

"Princeton," I yell out. "She's going to Princeton, Dad. My friend is going to a school that didn't even accept you."

I saw his hand come up and I was thinking, good, hit me. I will definitely hit you back, Jacob, and you *will* go down. Instead, he turns to Christina, tells her congratulations, and I'm sorry for yelling at you earlier, I was wrong, but there is a line in the sand and my son has just crossed it.

Looks like Princeton quiets him down. Yes, Dad, I have friends in high places too.

Then, back to me. "I assume she's not going to Princeton tonight. So there will be a car to take her home. Tomorrow morning you will wake up at seven. By eight we will be having breakfast with a woman named Olivia, from a PR firm I work with, who will strategize with us on the presentation to the media. Most likely she will issue a statement from you apologizing for your irresponsible behavior. By nine we will consult with my attorneys to prevent charges from being brought against you for whatever crimes you may have committed, and by ten we will be on the phone with your publisher to convince them not to invoke the morals clause in your agreement and not to request a reimbursement of the advance. We might have a shot; they seem to be moderately satisfied with the chapters that you have produced so far, so we might be able to salvage that relationship. But any endorsement deals will be gone, and I was close to negotiating one."

Christina perked up at the sound of an endorsement deal that I apparently lost without even knowing about it. Me on a box of cereal, or sneakers, or whatever, not going to happen. All because I got high. Thank you, Afroman, you warned me.

"Then, by noon, we will get you out of town, to a rehab program, where you can stay until you finish your commitment to deliver the rest of the book, and hopefully you can start school on time."

I shrugged my shoulders. "No way I'm going to rehab, Jacob. I'm not fucking twelve anymore."

"You will do what I tell you to do."

"No way am I going to rehab for smoking weed."

"Get over it. It is long overdue. Time for you to grow the fuck up."

"Fuck you, Jacob."

I'm on my feet. He is on his feet.

This one is going the full distance.

"Fuck you, Steven. You spoiled, irresponsible brat."

"I fucking hate your fucking guts, motherfucker."

"You *will* learn respect."

We are *totally* in each others' grills now. I am using everything I have to control my anger, but I am losing it. The heat is rising from my collar, sweat dripping down from my armpits. I am going through meltdown.

I have seconds . . .

"Stop it! Boat ov you."

An entirely different Felicia than I have ever seen before was standing on the far side of the living room. No makeup, barefoot, wild hair pressed back in a headband, she was dressed in an oversized Mickey Mouse T-shirt and nothing else. She was holding a plastic bag in her hands, which I couldn't make out, but I wasn't actually focused on it, because the woman looked so remarkably different from any time that I had seen her in the past that she just didn't appear to be the same person as the hot model who walked into my living room a few years earlier. This version of Felicia was equally enchanting, but in an entirely natural way. She looked like a kid, but also like a woman in her thirties at the same time, if that was possible.

"Allo, Cresh," she said as she approached me, glazing my cheek with a soft kiss.

Without her high heels, she was actually smaller than me, and sexy in a way that I had never experienced before. I looked down at Christina, preparing to introduce her, and also doing a quick mental comparison. While Christina looked as hot, in her own way, as a girl my age could look, she was nevertheless completely outclassed by my stepmom, who needed absolutely nothing to make her more beautiful or more perfect.

Felicia crossed between us, and I noticed the plastic bag again, which oddly didn't surprise me, as there had been another time in my life when she gifted me with something in a plastic bag that changed things for me forever. So now I was very much in anticipation mode as she dropped this particular plastic bag on the coffee table.

I looked down at it, looked up at her, looked at my father, then looked at Christina.

No one said another word.

I sat down on the couch, picked up the bag, and could see through it to Christina, who was watching me. I glanced back at Felicia. No contest, even without a stitch of makeup.

I was hit by a spark of true love, like a lightning bolt, and the object of my deepest, most profound affection was neither the woman beside me nor the girl across from me.

Because inside the bag was the purest, dankest weed that I had ever seen in my life.

I opened the bag and sniffed gently, wafting in the almost minty skunk-smell that instantly intoxicated me.

Now, I know weed. I can tell blindfolded, just by one sniff, the aromatic scent of sour diesel and the difference between white widow and purple haze. But this stuff, with its complex combination of musky fragrances, defied recognition. It had no name, was so unique that it astounded me with its perfection. This stuff was magic weed.

"Maybe you shoot join your son in rehab, Jack," she said. "Work it out—I need to sleep."

Then she was gone. I reached into the bag and grabbed a nugg, feeling the resin stick to my fingers, leaving a trail like a slug on the pavement during a hot summer night.

"Put that down," Jacob said weakly, but there was no point, because I was holding my father's weed, and there was nothing, absolutely nothing, he could do to stop me. All the anger drained out of me, and as I stared at the magnificent specimen, I realized that I had been wrong all this time.

It wasn't Burn who saved me from this man. It was Felicia all along. Just by showing up at my house that Thanksgiving, as if by magic, and then again and again, all the other times and now, she had saved my life again.

If there was such a thing as a soul mate, then mine was a thirty-three-year-old Slovakian woman who never stopped being beautiful.

Sorry, Christina, if you thought it was you.

CHAPTER ELEVEN

HOW ME AND BURN (AND THE REST OF US) ADJUSTED TO MEADOWS

"I can already see that we have a *special* class."

These were the first words I heard as a student at Meadows High School.

Staring out the window at a perfect September morning, I tried as hard as I could to listen to Mr. Connelly tell us about what to expect for the semester in freshman English.

I was two weeks into some new ADHD medication (for me at least), as in Adderall, and my mom was hopeful that I would finally be able to focus on my work.

After two weeks, I felt absolutely no different.

Except that I wasn't sleeping at all.

Just in time for high school, I was officially labeled a 504 kid, which is some kind of special plan that is apparently designed for learning-disabled kids, which also meant that I was entitled to special accommodations to help me study and take tests, but which also meant that I had to go to a special class with other 504 kids, who, I already knew, were the biggest losers in middle school and bound to be worse off in high school. I don't have to tell you that this caused more than one major fight in my house, with me telling my mom no way was I going to that class with those losers and her getting Jacob on the phone (which she almost never did), who told me that I had better respect my mother (like he was the fucking voice of God) and buckle down (or buckle up, whatever).

Plus, I was supposed to see this lady doctor once every three weeks to check on the medication levels in my system and talk about how I was feeling.

Which left me pretty much thinking that high school was going to be nothing but a four-year suckfest.

And, as if to prove my point, this angry-looking middle-aged bony dude with the pointiest nose I had ever seen was telling us that nothing that we did in middle school was going to prepare us for his class, which was going to prepare us for everything else in high school and college, and if we took it seriously enough, every other high school class was going to be a breeze by comparison.

So I was actually trying my hardest to listen.

"Our curriculum will include reading the following books and other literature," he said. "*To Kill a Mockingbird*, *Lord of the Flies*, *Of Mice and Men*, *The Old Man and the Sea*, and two books chosen by you for your own personal project. In addition, you can expect to read *The Crucible*, and for those of you who have no previous experience with William Shakespeare, you are in for a treat as we will be reading *Romeo and Juliet* and watching several movies based on Shakespeare's plays. You will also be keeping a weekly diary to enhance your ability to express yourselves, and we will, of course, be writing short stories, one a month. Also poetry, writing and reciting, and, finally, we will create a class project. Be prepared to spend at least two to three hours a day on our assignments. There will not be time to catch up if you miss a class or ignore these assignments. Any questions?"

I looked around the room.

Other kids, swear to god, were taking notes, and I was still thinking about what happened to summer, and what was I supposed to be writing down, because it didn't seem to me that he was saying anything worth writing.

Also, it seemed to me that almost every kid in that class was like supersmart genius material: Kenny, Sarah, Evan,

Madelaine Brancato, Mark Duncan, John Kramer, and sitting in the back, David Burnett, next to this new kid, someone I had never seen before.

There had to be some mistake, putting me into this mix. There had to be some kind of easier English class where the not-so-smart kids were.

Then I spotted Bosco and thought maybe it wasn't going to be so bad.

But then the new kid raises his hand and asks whether the structure of the curriculum was intended to incorporate some kind of unified theme, because it seemed to him that many of the book titles had animal references.

Some people laughed at this. I, of course, did not get the joke, not even remembering what the book titles were in the first place. But Burn turned to him, looking like the new kid had out-Burned him, and gave him this congratulatory look, like, good one, dude.

I was fucked.

Fucked for two reasons actually. One, no way was I going to do as good as these kids in this class. Two, no matter what kind of ADHD medication I was on, no way was I going to be able to read all of those books. All my life, I hated books, didn't matter what kind. Textbooks, stories, comics, whatever, they were all the same to me. I felt like I was in prison every single time I was forced to read. So clearly I didn't understand how other kids actually got pleasure out of it (like Lindsey, who could stay in her room for hours just reading while me and Jamie watched virtually everything there was on TV with Medusa curled up on the couch next to us).

Also, wasn't that the whole point of movies? So you didn't have to read? I wondered how many of the books that Connelly listed were made into movies. I wondered a lot of things while Connelly was busy calling out the names on the class list quickly one after another, except that he stopped when he got to Burn, who looked all clean and polished, sitting up with perfect posture while the rest of us slumped over our desks. I was thinking that maybe he had gotten taller over the summer, or maybe he was used to sitting at attention from his days in that school that he went to. Whatever. My mom told me that he was adjusting very well to his life back at home, although I hadn't seen him since the night of the play.

"Aren't you Roxanne's brother?" Connelly asked, and I wondered whether that was a good thing or a bad thing.

"Yes, sir." Burn sounding real formal. According to my mom, he was spending most of his time at April Walker's house and they were virtually inseparable. Mrs. Burnett assured her that David was absolutely ready to tackle the challenges of Meadows. From what my mom had told me, Mrs. Burnett was now having issues with Roxanne, but I couldn't get her to tell me what they were.

"She's an interesting character, I must say," Connelly remarked. I wasn't sure whether he meant it in a good way or a bad way.

"You're the brother with the problems, I assume," Connelly then added, and you could see by Burn's face that this comment did not sit well with him.

"No, sir," Burn shot back. "I'm the other brother."

He was so confident sounding and so sincere about it that I had to wonder if, in fact, the Burnett family actually had another child I didn't know about. Call me stupid. Sometimes I'm a little unsure of comments like that, especially when teachers are involved.

Connelly shot him back a look. "Aren't you the one they call Burn? The one who comes to us from the Clinton School? The school for emotionally disturbed kids? Aren't you the one who tried to set McAllister Elementary on fire?"

So now he was pegged. The rest of the class laughed nervously as some of them remembered the incident. How did this guy know? That was like ancient history. No one ever even talked about that anymore.

"Old news," Burn said. "I've moved on to other things."

I had to wonder what "other things" Burn had in mind when he said that. Connelly did not ask. He went back to the roster.

"Sarah Cohen." Which caused Sarah to raise her hand high enough so everyone could see that she had developed a brand-new set of breasts over the summer. Everyone was staring at them in awe. Everyone except Burn, who seemed, at least to me, to be still seething over Connelly's remarks.

"Steven Crashinsky."

I reluctantly raised my hand. I already knew that Lindsey had Connelly as a teacher. She called him the toughest teacher she ever had, one of the few teachers she had hated. Enough, in fact, to actually feel some level of sympathy for me in getting him.

"Brother of Lindsey Crashinsky," he said matter-of-factly. "You can relax, Mr. Crashinsky. I see that you are 504. No one here will be expecting you to be the student that Lindsey was. Lightning doesn't often strike twice, and I really don't expect much of a spark from you. That is, unless you and Mr. Burnett decide to once again display your pyrotechnical abilities."

I saw some kids writing down that word. I figured that he was talking about the McAllister fire, which, again, I was not actually involved in, except as a potential victim, and I was about to tell him, to set the record straight, but he had already moved on.

"So this class is special indeed, because I have the dubious honor of having Crash and Burn in the same class. How fortunate for me," he said to more nervous laughter.

"Mark Duncan?"

After hearing how Connelly totally skewered me and Burn,

Mark looked really scared about having to raise his hand. I wondered what he had to hide.

It was immediately clear to me that this guy Connelly was going to be one major asshole.

It wasn't just me thinking this.

In the hall, after class, kids were coming over to me, saying how everybody knew that Connelly was a dick and that he had no right to talk about me like I was a retard. Burn walked by, gave me a nod, like we were in it together. I nodded back, uncomfortably, knowing that we might be targets, but for entirely different reasons. I was going to ask him how he was doing, but he cruised past me, over to where April Walker was standing with a bunch of kids I had never seen before.

"That guy's fucked up, eh?" the new kid offered, sticking out his hand on our way to the next class. I was thinking that he must be from like Canada or something because of the way he talked, but he said "Boston" in an unusual accent. Then he said, "I'm Alex. Everyone calls me Newman."

He seemed like a nice-enough kid.

"I'm going to call the principal first thing tomorrow," my mom said when I told her what happened. Actually, what I said was:

"Mom, you absolutely *have* to get me out of Connelly's class."

I told her what he said to me and Burn and she was beyond upset. She immediately went for the phone and called Burn's mom. Right away, she started in with Mrs. Burnett, in her irate-mom voice. Can you believe what this teacher said and how inappropriate and how did he expect to instill confidence in children when he is insulting and embarrassing them and shouldn't the principal know what's going on, even Lindsey complained about him, and she didn't expect this to be an easy year for me, but to hear this on the first day . . .

And on she went as I headed for my room, thinking about school and how much I hated it. Math, science, health, gym, and history went much better, at least the first day, but I already knew that my notes were not going to be good enough to figure out what I had to do for homework in any class.

I set up a PlayStation game, one of the *Final Fantasy* games, and tried to play.

I was tired and wired at the same time, focused and yet unable to concentrate. I didn't know if it was me or the Adderall, which other kids were swearing by. And this school thing was definitely on my nerves, because it was light-years until the last day of class, and I wasn't seeing the light at the end of the tunnel, not one bit, because all I was seeing in my mind was Connelly's pointy-nosed face smirking at us, actually mostly smirking at me, and I knew, I fucking *knew* that he was going to be trouble, big trouble.

Not only him. I couldn't shake this feeling of doom that I was experiencing, this instinctive knowing that something was going to go majorly wrong. What made matters worse was the fact that whenever I had these feelings, I was always right, and for some reason I was getting them more often on this new medicine.

My mom came up after her call with Burn's mom.

"Don't worry, honey. You will not have to stay in that monster's class."

She was gone, but the bad feeling was not.

And, as it turned out, I did have to stay in his class. So did Burn.

We ended up meeting in Principal Singh's office two mornings later, with our moms being all kinds of agitated, talking over Principal Singh's voice as he unsuccessfully tried to calm them down. Burn was sitting superupright in his chair, and I was on the cluttered green couch, wishing I was anywhere else.

And then Connelly walks in, puts his hand on Burn's shoulder, which I can see is making Burn superuncomfortable, and then Connelly apologizes for his comments, both to our moms and then to us directly, assuring us that he did not intend to be mean-spirited, and he understood why were upset, we had the right to be upset. He had crossed the line, he acknowledged, and he promised us it wouldn't happen again, and then he politely bowed forward and dismissed himself, closing the door behind him, leaving the four of us with Principal Singh, who asked that we give Connelly another chance. When Mrs. Burnett asked why should we, Singh read a letter to us, holding it close to his face, like he had an eye problem or something:

"A few words in support of Mr. Connelly," it started. "He may be a difficult man who appears to lack compassion, but I can honestly say that I learned more in his class than in any other class that I have had at Meadows."

Imagine our surprise when he handed us the letter.

It was signed by Roxanne Burnett.

On our way back to class, as I walked with Burn, neither of us said anything until I asked what was up with his sister. He said that he had made the mistake of siding with his mom on certain Roxanne issues and that pissed her off and that he was sorry that I was collateral damage in his family battles, but you don't cross Roxanne and expect it not to come back and bite you in the ass. I kind of knew what he was talking about from my limited experience with her, but I hadn't done anything to her. I was going to ask him what could have pissed her off so much, but we were already at his classroom and I was late for pre-algebra, but then before he went in, he grabbed my arm to stop me, and I figured he was going to apologize for me getting stuck with Connelly and all. Instead, what he said was:

"Are you still seeing Christina Haines?" Which of course I

wasn't, as I didn't actually spend any time with her after the night of the play, so I told him that there was nothing going on with me and Christina. He said he was happy to hear that, because he liked her, as in really, really liked her, so I asked him, wasn't he all about April?

"She's fun, but she's not long-term, Crash," he said. "Guess how many BJs I got this summer?"

I shrugged, in one way not caring, but in another way kind of pissed that he was getting them and I was not, as I no longer seemed to be making any connections with girls, which trickled down to no contact whatsoever by the end of the summer, for some odd reason.

"Go ahead, Crash, guess."

"I don't know. Like twenty-four?"

"Exactly twenty-four. How the fuck did you know?" He had this all-screwed-up look, paranoid, like I had somehow peeked into his mind, which I could sometimes do with other kids, thanks to the Adderall. After his initial shock, he recovered enough to ask, "What do you think the record is for a freshman?"

I said I didn't know, and he went on about how it was all because of me that he had all these new friends and did I want to go over to April's that weekend because she was having some camp friends over. Then he asked about Christina Haines again and all I knew was that I was going to get hell for getting in so late to pre-algebra even with a pass from the principal's office.

Burn never mentioned the party at April's after that, and I wondered if she had decided that having me over was a bad idea or something. Point was, as the month progressed, I was more and more off my game. By the end of September, I was behind in everything. I was beginning to think the Adderall was making me worse, because I was having those bad feelings all the time, but other kids in the 504 program were constantly telling me how great it was.

Caroline Prescott went to school to advocate for me and ended up hiring a tutor, who showed up just once, then made some excuse not to show up again, and I was feeling like a totally lost cause.

Then my mom has this superbrilliant idea (she's the only one in the world who could think of this): have Lindsey tutor me. She tells us this like it's going to make both of us happy, and both of us look at each other and know, just know, that it's not going to work. I mean, Lindsey was getting a little mellower by then, being a junior and all and way more into boys and her friends than school for the first time, so now she wasn't on 24/7 bitch patrol, and while she didn't actually act like she liked me, she seemed, for the first time in our lives, indifferent to my existence. Don't get me wrong, I wasn't feeling the love. Just not the hate.

I didn't know at the time, but this was around the point in junior year when Lindsey discovered weed, which, while she never became a stoner, she *did* seem to like, as it took the edge off her. Regardless, no way was Lindsey going to be able to handle me.

But give her credit, she tried for a few weeks. Coming home every day after school, going through my backpack, extracting the sand-crusted gummy worms and half-eaten snack packs and the overfolded handouts, always with the same cringe face, cleaning up like she was a mom, then going through my notes, stretching out the crumpled papers and organizing them with plenty of clear tape and staples.

She had her own notebook in which she took my notes and transcribed them into girl language, with her flowery script, hearts practically over every "i" so I could hardly read them.

And then she went through the courses, one by one, every

day, what did I do in math, what about history, what about Connelly's class.

And I tried to work with her, but it was pointless. Whenever we tried, she would leave screaming or I would leave agitated for the rest of the day or Jamie would interrupt us, asking if we could just be a little quieter, so she could hear the TV.

I didn't know exactly what Lindsey was getting paid, but after me, she had to move on to Jamie's work, so you could not envy being Lindsey at that point.

It lasted until the day I came home without my *Of Mice and Men* book and she threw a tantrum, saying if I wasn't going to try, why should she? And I lied and told her I read the whole book at school, during a study period, which I was required to have as part of my 504 program. So she quizzed me, who was Lennie? What did Lennie have in his pocket? Why was Lennie always talking about rabbits? Who was Curley? What happened to Curley's wife?

And, of course, no way could I answer any of Lindsey's questions.

Which led to me being all frustrated and her getting in my face and calling me a hopeless moron, sounding a lot like Jacob.

Which, of course, led to me pushing her, which I didn't mean to do, but she *was* in my face and enough was enough and she landed on the bed anyways, but it was all she needed for her to tell my mom that I was physically abusing her, which was definitely not the case, as me and Jamie often had play-fights that were way more tough on both of us, being as Jamie was not afraid to fight back and drop-kick me like a pro wrestler. But no way had either me or Jamie ever play-fought with Lindsey. Or even so much as touched her before.

So while Lindsey was telling my mom what an animal I was, I flung myself onto the couch in the family room where Jamie was watching *As Told by Ginger*. When she looked up at me, she said, "You *do* know that *The Wild Thornberrys* is coming on in a few minutes?"

Which I understood to mean that she was not thrilled with the possibility of a family altercation that was going to interrupt her afternoon TV schedule.

Then a commercial hit, which meant Jamie could talk more freely. "What did Mom actually expect? You and Lindsey in the same room. Something was bound to happen."

But my mom was already downstairs, standing in front of us. "Did you push your sister, Steven?"

I have since learned what a rhetorical question is, and that was one of them, because the actual answer didn't matter. What followed was a telephone conversation with Jacob and a call to the doctor who prescribed the Adderall, who had already said to my mother that we should try to increase the dosage, because it wasn't working at the levels I was taking. Déjà vu all over again, having gone through the same drill years before with Ritalin.

The following Monday I was back with another old-lady tutor.

The extra dosage of Adderall did not make me any smarter. In fact, by the middle of October, I slipped into a miserable funk where life seemed completely hazed over, like everything else in the world was speeding up, leaving me behind. To make matters worse, I was becoming totally forgetful and oddly more psychic. Plus whenever I played sports, my heart would race like I was in the Olympics and I couldn't catch my breath. This sometimes also happened for no apparent reason even when I was sitting, just sitting in class.

Mostly in Connelly's class.

We were finished with *Of Mice and Men* (I got a 67 on the test) and then we started reading *To Kill a Mockingbird*. I had no clue what was going on with that book, even though I really did try to read it over and over again.

"Mr. Crashinsky, can you explain why Scout doesn't want to go back to school after the first day?"

So I start, "Well, because he . . ."

"He who?" Connelly's eyes brightened.

"Scout."

There was some laughter in the class.

"Mr. Crashinsky. Did you read the first two chapters?"

"Sure." I *had* actually read the assignment during study hall, big surprise, and I thought that I was ready. So I couldn't believe that I was being criticized, as I hadn't even said anything.

"Does anyone want to help Mr. Crashinsky?"

Sarah Cohen's hand shot into the air. "Steven, Scout is a girl."

I was jolted by this, like I was in a car accident or something. My heart started overpumping again. Reason being, I had no clue, I absolutely read the first two chapters and I had no fucking clue.

What kind of name was Scout for a girl anyway?

"I knew that."

"You said 'he,' Mr. Crashinsky," Connelly boomed. "That's why your fellow classmates were laughing."

A voice from the back of the class interrupted his flow of venom.

"I thought Scout was a boy too." This from the new kid, Newman.

I looked at him. Was he telling the truth or covering for me? I couldn't tell.

"I meant the other kid. The one who doesn't go back, ever." I could swear there was a kid in the book who didn't go to school after the first day. I was wishing I was him.

"Which other kid, Mr. Crashinsky?" he repeated. "Or should I call you Boo?"

"Boo who?" I asked. OK, I was pretty dazed, which had to be from the drug (being as Boo turns out to be a major part of the first chapter and I remembered seeing the word more than a few times during my attempts to read it).

Connelly repeated this. Loudly. *"Boo who?"*

"Don't cry," Burn yelled out, and everybody laughed and I didn't know why. So I looked at him and he mouthed "boo-hoo" again and I got it.

"Mr. Burnett, do you care to enlighten your friend with a little wisdom?"

And so Burn deflected for me and went on about Boo Radley, who he called Arthur and not Boo for some reason, and the rest of the characters, but tell you the truth, I just couldn't listen, because I wasn't caring about anything at that particular point: not Connelly, not English, not math or science or history or even girls, which was the most strange, because after all that time of superpopularity, I was suddenly in high school and no one seemed to be into me. Not girls, not even my good friends. It didn't help that the few times I saw Roxanne in the halls, she basically ignored me and acted like she either didn't see me or didn't care to notice that I was there.

And whatever it was that happened was getting worse, and what was worse than that was I didn't care.

Now Burn and Connelly were arguing over a point in the book, which I didn't get, and I don't think the rest of the class got either, and all the time Burn continued to sit in his new posture position, superstraight upright, using his hands to express how off base Connelly's opinion was. Connelly starts to raise his voice to get his point across, but Burn continues with his point, which I think the class thinks makes more sense than Connelly's point. In response Connelly actually says, "Why don't you start another fire or something?"

So the honeymoon was definitely over and it was back to

being us against him. Only I didn't know why, not for the life of me.

My mom got a call from my guidance counselor before I got home that afternoon, and apparently she put a call in to my doctor, who suggested that maybe I was having a bad reaction to Adderall. My mom asked if I was feeling any different, but I could swear that I had already told her over and over again about the dizziness and the racy heart and the fogginess.

So I was weaned off another medication. Only this one was supposed to be my last hope, since I'd already tried everything else. So now what?

In a few weeks, I was starting to feel like my old self again. But my old self wasn't all that much smarter.

And Connelly's class was no more tolerable, with Connelly mostly avoiding me but going after Burn almost every day with challenging questions. Burn responded with his own spin on things, and Connelly was not backing off, like he was testing to see if Burn had a breaking point.

Then, like two weeks later, the test on the book. I actually did OK for me, as in getting a 74, which I thought was pretty good until I compared it to other marks, as in Newman's 98 and even Bosco getting an 82, and I had to wonder, was Bosco actually smarter than me? How stupid was I really?

Except Burn failed. I saw the back of his paper, all red-marked up with a huge circle at the top. Which again made no sense as Burn knew everything about the book and probably could've taught a class on *To Kill a Mockingbird* if he wanted to, no question about it. And when Burn politely raised his hand to ask whether Connelly would reconsider the grade, Connelly ignored the question completely, like Burn wasn't even there.

* * *

"I'm slashing his tires," Burn told me and Newman in the lunch-room, after letting us peek into his backpack where he had this huge hunting knife. All I could think of was, the combination of Burn and a hunting knife was not a comfortable image, even if he was, on the surface, the completely reconstituted version of himself with virtually no outward signs of the kinds of crazy that I remembered from earlier years.

"You can't," I said. "They're watching us."

"They're always watching me," Burn told me, zipping up his pack. "But I'm watching them too."

He bailed on us, and even before he was gone, Newman and I exchanged our knowing glances for the very first time, some-thing that we would be doing the same way throughout high school, because we both knew, we totally *knew*, even then, that Burn was going to end up doing something supremely fucked up.

Just a matter of time. At least that was our opinion. The rest of the school seemed to embrace the new Burn, who had developed this huge social life, high-fiving everyone in the hall-ways, joking around with other teachers and getting involved in after-school activities. Instead of holding a grudge about the *Mockingbird* test or trying to get some kind of teenage revenge, he went direct to Principal Singh and argued his case, and somehow they got Connelly to reconsider the mark.

And then Burn showed up one morning during intramurals to tell me that he heard that me and Pete were going to his aunt's for Thanksgiving and he couldn't wait because he had something to show us, something absolutely amazing. And all I could think of was the trouble I had gotten into the last time he used those words. Actually, that wasn't the only thing I thought about. I couldn't help but wonder how my mom could ever have agreed to expose us to another Thanksgiving dinner with the family that basically blew apart the holiday two years before, not that I was blaming them for anything, since Burn did save my life and all. I was also thinking that maybe it wouldn't be so bad this time. I couldn't help but think about Roxanne, and while I didn't think that making out was a possibility at this point, I was hoping that she maybe would be nice to me again, or even notice me in her sarcastic Roxanne way.

And after the second marking period, I got my grades, and they weren't good at all, worse than I thought. But there were other kids who were doing worse, like Callahan and Shaun Leary, who we called Peanut because of his severe allergies to nuts. Oh yeah, and I got like a B+ in science, so clearly I could learn if I wanted to, at least according to Jacob. The good news was that I didn't have to deal with him immediately as he was off to eastern Europe with Felicia for the holidays.

So Thanksgiving Day came, and my mother spent the morning in the kitchen, working on the turkey and preparing side dishes while Lindsey followed behind her, tracing her every step, in full-tantrum mode, whining about how horrible Roxanne was and asking over and over again why my mom had ever agreed to go to the Burnetts', but my mom just wasn't having it as her mind was already made up.

Then it was us and Pete's family and some older adults from our town, all assembled that afternoon at Burn's aunt's house, the one that smelled like urine, where Burn and his family were still living. Well, all of us except Roxanne, who had apparently spent the night with friends in Manhattan, which she was doing a lot, according to Burn, because she didn't have many friends at Meadows. Mrs. Burnett kept promising that Roxanne was on her way and that it would only be a few more minutes, doing what she could to keep us out of the dining room until her daughter showed up.

It was after six when she finally did, dressed in goth clothing, all pasty-white skin and jet-black spiky hair, looking like a holdover from Halloween. The thing I noticed most was the black circles around her eyes. It was kind of unsettling.

I overheard Lindsey from behind me whisper to no one in particular, "She's absolutely stoned."

Before Roxanne could even say anything, Mrs. Burnett was ushering her into a far corner of the house where you could hear the two of them arguing, but you couldn't make out the exact words. A few minutes later, it was me, Lindsey, Jamie, Pete and his brothers Bernie and Joe, and Burn, and Roxanne all sitting around the table in the kitchen while the adults were in the dining room, apparently having mastered the seating arrangement issues this time around. Not that I was worried, being as there were no milfs at this Thanksgiving.

I noticed Burn staring at his sister more or less constantly, more like he was worried about her than angry with her.

Watching him watching her made me nervous, like I was on the Adderall again. Something was definitely up.

It was Jamie who broke the tension, saying that she wanted to eat quickly so she could get home for a Nick special, which got us all talking, and then Roxanne asked how I was enjoying Connelly's class. This being the first time she talked to me in a very long time, I took it as a good sign, although she didn't seem to have the usual fire in her eyes when she said it.

It was Lindsey who asked her about the Connelly letter. "I didn't know that anyone actually liked him as a teacher," Lindsey said.

To which Roxanne confessed, "I fucking hated him."

To which I had to ask, "Then why send a letter to Principal Singh to support him?"

Roxanne looked at Burn, and when she answered, her answer was directed at him.

"Revenge is sweet," she said, with a forced smile that told us there was still something between the two of them that apparently had been resolved with the letter.

That wasn't the end of it either. After we were clearing the plates off the table, for just a minute, it was just me and Roxanne in the kitchen, and I had to say, "But now I'm stuck with Connelly, too, because of your letter. That's not fair."

To which Roxanne said, "It's your own fault. You were supposed to make out with me before anyone else. You broke your promise. Now no one is interested in you anyway. As I said, revenge is sweet."

While this seemed to be a phrase that I was destined to hear from the Burnetts every Thanksgiving, this time I noticed that there was no conviction in her voice when she said it. She was going through the motions, but there was something so un-Roxanne about the way she talked that I had to wonder was it her or was it something I did? But then my mind filled with concern about what she meant about no one being interested in me, even though I knew that she liked to put me off my game. Was she fucking with me, or was something else going on?

Then Burn came back into the kitchen with Pete, talking about the incredible thing that he promised to show us. Then Roxanne was gone, and me and Pete followed Burn out the back door, down the rolling lawn behind the huge Victorian house, to the freestanding garage all the way at the back edge of the property, which was a pretty long walk from the house. Burn gave us flashlights and swore us to secrecy before he would let us in, because, he explained, he had something in there that no other kid had ever had before, and if we told anyone, he'd get into major-league trouble.

Me and Pete exchanged glances. How dangerous was this going to be?

So Burn opens the garage doors and we step inside, hit by the overwhelming smell of supermoist cut grass, skunk, and dog shit. We don't see anything, but we hear this scratching sound behind all this old landscaping equipment, and I proceed with caution, checking around to make sure that I can bolt if I need to run out.

Burn leads us to the back, where the smell gets stronger, switches on the light, and there, on the bottom shelf of this huge floor-to-ceiling shelving unit, is a cage, which is covered up.

He pulls the sheet off it. "I caught a baby fox back in October," he tells us, revealing a very spectacular animal with the shiniest red fur.

"I've been training it."

"Dude, you can't train a fox," Pete says, carefully choosing his words. (Keep in mind he already had an altercation with Burn over animals in the past.)

"Well, I am," he said. "Training it." And with that Burn sticks his hand into the cage and starts petting it, and the fox doesn't seem to mind. Then he reaches around and undoes the latch, carefully, gingerly moving the fox forward out of the cage.

"Go ahead," he says. "She likes being touched."

We don't move.

"Go ahead," he demands, like orders us, and so Pete does it, sticks out his hand and carefully touches, then pets the animal.

But I do not. I know something is wrong with this. I don't know what it is, but I know it's beyond trouble. Meanwhile, Pete is having the best time with the fox, as they start to feed it from a bucket that Burn kept by the side of the shelf.

So I ask Burn where he got it, the fox, and he tells me that he built a trap for raccoons but caught the fox instead, and if either of us, me or Pete, tells anyone, he will seriously kick our asses, because it's illegal and all, he's checked the laws as to wildlife. Pete and I look at each other: no way we're telling anyone.

I get close to the animal's face, stare at it. It stares back at me with empty black eyes, reminding me more than a little of Burn's sister in a weird way. It is cute and all, but there is something in its eyes that tells me it knows that it doesn't belong there and will never belong to Burn. It's a matter of time, I tell myself, before something goes wrong. I even mention this to Burn, telling him, "Dude, a fox is not a dog. A fox is always a fox and always will be a fox."

Burn just shrugs me off, like I don't get it. And, all in all, he actually seems pretty happy for Burn. I watch him with his face up against the cage, making cooing sounds to this animal as he places it back into the cage, and I actually believe for a minute that he's a normal kid, just like the rest of us.

So if you asked me, at that moment, how Burn was adjusting to life in Westchester and Meadows High School, I would have said, "Fine, just fine." I mean, yeah, he had his problems, like Connelly, who was always riding him, and he still acted weird (like carrying a knife and saying weird shit), but mostly he sounded and acted normal. In fact, better than normal, as he was still spending all this time with April and bragging about the number of times he got head to kids who had never gotten any. And he was getting like all A's except for Connelly's class and he had all these friends, so I would have said, "Fine, just fine." I mean, there were a whole lot of kids doing a whole lot worse.

It turns out that I was right and wrong at the same time.

Right, because I fucking knew the fox was going to be trouble.

The Monday after Thanksgiving, Burn didn't show for Connelly's class, and during math I get pulled into the principal's office, where Pete was already waiting, looking nervous, like he failed something. The school nurse comes out, looks at me with an unhappy snarl, like she was going to bite me. As she comes over, Pete whispers, "They found the fox."

"We are trying to reach your parents, Mr. Crashinsky." Her voice over his.

"Where's Burn?" I ask her and him at the same time.

"Apparently, Burn is having a meltdown," Pete tells me. "I'm in deep shit. He's gonna come after me, I know it."

"Do you have any idea how to get in touch with your mother?" The nurse at me, again chiming in over Pete.

"Did you try her cell?" I already have my cell phone out, and I'm calling my mom as the nurse is standing over me.

"No luck." My phone continues to ring.

"I might have to get the shots," Pete is saying. "My parents are taking me. They're on their way."

"What shots?"

"Rabies."

"What the fuck?" I say, and I realize that the nurse is still standing over me as I try to reach my mom again.

"Mr. Crashinsky, did you or did you not touch the animal."

"No, ma'am, I did not." Which was true. "Is it . . . Does it have . . . ?" I'm starting to think about those horror movies where people start foaming at the mouth and then turn into zombies. And then you die.

But I did not touch that animal, not for a second.

"So does the fox . . ." I ask again, "you know . . . have rabies?"

"They are testing it now."

Pete looks at me on this, crosses his finger over his throat, and tells me, "Burn is going to kill me." He is apparently more afraid of Burn than of rabies. This was all-out funny to me. Or it would have been, except for the fact that I truly was worried about whether or not I could have a dose of rabies.

Now Principal Singh was in the waiting room with us, asking the nurse if we are OK, but clearly neither of us is showing signs of rabies at that very moment, so why wouldn't we be OK?

Then I think . . . Burn. Does he have it? Will I have to get the shots? Will my whole family? Then my phone rings. My mom. I hand it over to Singh, and he explains in front of me that he heard from a teacher that Pete happened to mention to someone in school that Burn had a fox in his garage, and during Thanksgiving break, the boys, Pete and me and Burn, played with it. And it also turns out that there were a number of reports in upper Westchester county involving rabies. He told my mom that he already spoke with the county animal protection unit, so to be on the safe side, they were recommending that the kids (as in Burn and Pete and me) be inoculated, which, according to him, we could do immediately. Or we could wait for the tests, but Pete's parents were not going to wait, because better safe than sorry, and they were on their way to bring him to the doctor.

Singh wasn't sure how long the tests on the animal would take, but the animal was now in the possession of the county health department and they would be euthanizing it to make a determination.

Pete again with his finger across his throat, in case I didn't get the drift, which I did, as in they were killing Burn's fox, even as we sat there.

When Burn found out it was Pete who gave him up, I wouldn't want to be Pete.

But then again, with the prospect of rabies shots and testing looming in front of my eyes, I didn't want to be me either. I kept thinking about how those shots were supposed to be the most painful shots ever, and I remembered hearing that they give them to you in your stomach, so I couldn't help blurting out again and again, "I didn't touch it. I didn't even get close to it."

Pete backed me up. "Swear to Christ, he didn't. Just me and Burn."

The tests were negative, which in medicine is a good thing, as in the fox, now dead, did not have rabies.

Not so much for Burn. He stopped going to classes, and no one heard from him. I wondered if this was another case of him not being able to cope and having to go off to one of his special schools again. Maddy told me that Sarah told her that he broke it off with April over the phone and he wasn't doing good at all.

Meantime, Connelly had a field day when he heard the news about the fox and actually gave us a writing assignment that he thought was relevant. We had to write a short story about an animal that lived in our area. He even had Sarah stand at the blackboard and write down the names of each, with her new breasts bouncing up and down with every chalk stroke, as we called the names. Skunk, squirrel, raccoon, turkey, hawk, eagle, coyote, fox, rabbit. Someone yelled out bear, and someone else yelled out Mrs. Fincher, who was an old-lady teacher who taught the other freshman English class and was known to occasionally rip a fart when she was giving her lectures.

Someone, I think it was Newman, made a farting sound at the mention of her name. Connelly actually cracked a smile, and, for a second, I thought of him as human, instead of the monster that he was.

And then, on my way to gym, I saw Roxanne talking with some friends. Her hair was still jet-black, but she was back to wearing regular clothes, looking way less like a vampire. I waved to her, unsure whether I should ask about her brother or whether she would even talk to me at all. Instead of waving back, she nodded for me to approach her, which I did, cautiously.

"You've been a really good friend to my brother," she said in a voice that had absolutely no trace of sarcasm in it. She was speaking to me quietly for the first time, and I was listening differently, reluctantly letting my guard down with her, which I knew was an incredibly stupid thing to do.

"Not so much" is all I ended up saying.

"Listen," she said, hesitating before speaking, "I shouldn't have said that thing that I said to you last week. You know, during Thanksgiving, about no one being interested in you anymore. Well, that's just not true. I only said it because I frickin' hate your sister, and I heard that you were struggling this year, so that was wrong of me. You shouldn't let this place beat you, because you are so much better than that, and I don't know if anyone else ever told you. So don't stop being you just because it gets harder."

She leaned forward and kissed me on the forehead, which was totally and completely unnerving, because of all things, Roxanne talking to me like a friend, like an older sister, was the very last thing in the world I would ever have expected.

"He's coming back today," she added. "Please watch over him. I don't think he's taking the whole fox thing well at all. He's . . . fragile."

The bell rang. I would never make it to class. I wouldn't have moved, except Roxanne had already left, leaving me standing there alone.

So when I finally ran into Burn later that day, I was well prepared for him not to be the almost normal version of himself that I remembered from Thanksgiving.

"Murderer," he mumbled at me as he passed me in the hall.

I should have said something back, but because of Roxanne, I just kept going.

When Burn ran into Pete, Pete was fully armed and ready, as he was apparently preparing for some kind of confrontation. So when Burn called him a murderer, Pete gave it right back to Burn, telling him that Burn had no one to blame but himself, that the fox was dead because of him, not because of me or Pete or anyone else. Because if Burn hadn't caught it and tried to keep it, the fox might still be alive somewhere. This was in the cafeteria, so you couldn't help but think back to middle school and the Panthers incident.

Only this time it ended differently. This time, Burn actually apologized to Pete and sat down quietly, by himself at one of the girls' tables, and silently ate his lunch. Rumor had it that he was mumbling to himself, repeating the word "murderer" a few times.

When the new Burn settled back into his classes, he was like a pod person from a science fiction movie. This Burn had no emotions whatsoever, didn't talk to anyone or even sound like himself.

Too Down.

I wanted to tell him, dude, it was only a fox. But, tell you the truth, I was afraid to say anything. I kept asking myself, what did Roxanne expect me to do, and couldn't come up with an answer. So I backed off.

Even Connelly seemed to back off when it came to dealing with Burn.

Not so much when it came to me, but that was OK, because thanks to Roxanne talking to me in the hallway, I started to feel my spark coming back, and no bony middle-aged pointy-nosed English teacher was going to fuck with it again.

CHAPTER TWELVE

THE REALLY BAD INTERVIEW

About a week after the picture of me with the Westchester Mall girls and the blunt appeared in the *New York Post*, I got the all-clear signal that it was OK to go back home. Thankfully, Newman's parents let me stay in their guest room, eat their food, and hang by their pool while a group of reporters were camping out at the edge of my mom's property, waiting for me to show up.

I had very strict instructions from Jacob to avoid the press at all costs. More specifically, the morning after that shit went down, I had to sit through a meeting with his "experts" to talk about the impact of the weed-smoking photo on his business. My agent, Sally Levine, was there, joined by this superheavy woman with sunken eyes named Olivia, a publicist who worked with my dad's firm. No one said anything until the lawyer showed up, the very same bald guy who handled my book deal.

He told the group that based on the photograph alone, it was unlikely for the authorities to pursue any criminal charges, although he couldn't rule it out entirely. After all, while the image seemed relatively clear, it wasn't conclusively marijuana, and possession of small amounts had been decriminalized in New York State, so there was not much they were going to do about it. Plus the images of the girl's faces in the photograph had been blurred out, making it difficult for the police to identify the witnesses.

Then it was Olivia's turn. She was convinced that in a few days it would blow over and the press would be on to the next story. "Let it die," she kept saying, "just let it die," which, in case there was any doubt on my part (not that that was possible), Sally interrupted and made extremely clear that "let it die" meant lay low, disappear, and no matter what, do not engage in any discussion or interact in any way with anyone who has a microphone or a camera. She added that while she was disappointed in me, the publishers did not expect me to be a saint. So she did not anticipate that they would invoke the morals clause in the agreement that would permit them to cancel the book.

No guarantees, but if I kept working hard and continued to deliver, I should be fine.

And to prevent any missteps, she spent a portion of the morning going through my plans for the next chapters, while my father worked it out with my mom to have my laptop and some of my stuff delivered to Newman's house, which was absolutely fine with Alex's mom, being as me and my boys stayed there often enough over the summer and she was used to cleaning up after us.

The four of them prepped me on ways to avoid any further controversy, to keep out of public places that I was known to frequent, not to answer my cell unless I recognized the number, and if cornered by a member of the press, to say nothing and hand them Olivia's card, explaining that they should talk to my publicist.

So by the time I left, I had a pretty clear path as to what I should and should not do. Of course, leaving with my father's bag of weed secured safely in my back pocket had to be among the "should not do's." But it seemed like a safe bet that he would never ask me about it. I felt like I needed a reward for getting through the night and the morning with him.

The next thing I know, I'm at the corner of Seventy-Second Street in my BMW, staring up at the red light and down at the palm of my hand, which contained a perfectly circular green and purple nugg, having gingerly removed it from the bag, just to examine the sparkling crystals in the daylight.

Ironically, just as a cop car pulls alongside me.

Green light. I let him go first and slip the nugg carefully back into the plastic bag. All except for a small piece, which I drop into a bowl and light up. Just a taste for the ride. And it is sweet, no burn going down even as deep as I inhale. Three hits later, I am actually thinking about pulling over because Jacob's trees are so overwhelming, and instead take one more hit and keep going, most definitely another "should not do." Also among the "should not do's" was stopping off anywhere along the way to Newman's. But after trying to reach Christina a bunch of times and getting no answer, I had to wonder whether I finally went over the line with her this time. Not so much me, but maybe Jacob scared her off for good. Or maybe her parents told her not to have anything to do with me after seeing the picture.

And being as Claudia had texted me more than a few times, promising that she had nothing to do with the picture being printed and that she would make it up to me, I pretty much had no choice but to make a pit stop at the Westchester Mall again, where I was the recipient of round two from her in the parking lot, in the middle of a Saturday afternoon, surrounded by cars and oblivious shoppers. And while the first round a few nights before was excellent, after a few more hits from Jacob's weed, I was literally in outer space. It was more than just Claudia (who unquestionably had the technique of a professional); it was more than the spontaneous gratification of getting exactly what you want almost immediately after you think of it. It was unquestionably Jacob's weed, which fogged my mind and cleared my mental vision at the same time and got me to thinking, maybe for the first time, about my father and his wife, and did Felicia smoke too, I hadn't thought about that earlier, which got me to thinking about her even more and during the moment of impact, it was like Claudia wasn't even there.

And so, supremely relaxed in the backseat of my BMW, I held Claudia like she was special, and she asked me if she did good and I said that she did and she asked me if I forgave her because even though her friends released the picture of me to the press, she didn't even know and she wouldn't have let them because she really, really liked me.

And my phone buzzed so I picked it up. Christina texting me. "Where are you?"

It was almost like she knew that I was with another girl. This was the second time in a row that she broke into my buzz with Claudia.

Almost.

At least no pictures were taken this time, and I found it hard not to like Claudia at least a little, with her laughing and me laughing just like the first time, like everything in the world was a joke, and I knew that there was no way I was not going to forgive this girl. Plus, with the increasing odds that nothing was ever going to happen between me and Christina, I figured what was the harm? After all, there were five weeks left of summer. Christina was headed to Princeton, I was headed to Boston, and it wasn't like we would actually be seeing each other when summer ended.

So I made it to Newman's without committing any more "should not do's" and stayed there for the week, writing, partying, and still not connecting with Christina. I mostly avoided "should not do's" entirely, unless you count driving by my house a few times in the passenger seat of Alex's car to taunt the few remaining reporters who were hoping to catch a glimpse of me. And OK, I will admit to another quick visit to see Claudia again.

* * *

And then, just like Olivia predicted, the reporters were all gone one morning, on to the next story, and I was free to return to my house without anyone being the wiser.

Medusa greets me at the door with a new pig ear, as if she anticipated my return, and I immediately head into the family room, where Jamie is engrossed in a Disney Channel movie.

"Christina Haines called for you" is all she says. I try to interrupt her to find out more, but she is quickly dismissive, telling me that our mom is coming home to take her shopping and she wants to finish the movie. I ask more questions, not understanding why Christina would call on the house phone when she wasn't returning my texts. Something seems strange to me. But Jamie could not be distracted. No way could I compete with *High School Musical*, even if it was the sequel and even if she had already seen it like thirty times.

Well, at least Medusa was happy I was home.

Hours later, I finally get a text from Christina that she needed to see me. She shows up at my door minutes later in a bright yellow dress, all made up like she's going to a party, and walks in like she knows the layout of my house, up the steps with me and Medusa watching her, leaving us to follow her into the living room. She asks whether anyone else is home, and I begin to wonder what exactly she has in mind. She sits down on the couch, pats the cushion like I'm supposed to sit next to her, which I do, with Medusa trailing us looking for attention, pig ear dangling from the corner of her mouth.

Then she tells me, yes, she got my text messages and was sorry she didn't call, that she was in the Hamptons for some family reunion thing and needed time to think.

I'm wondering what there is to think about, given that we have a while before anyone comes home and the house is completely empty, and she asks:

"I need to know. Did you have sex with any of the girls in the picture? I know you said that you didn't, but I need to know the truth, Steven. Did you?"

I wondered where this was coming from, given that I already answered this question from her. But I also know that I'm great at lying, so even if I thought that what I did with Claudia counted as sex, which I didn't, then the answer would have been no anyways.

"We went through this before, Christina. Me and Newman and Pete met them at the mall. I was winging for my friends is all." Me, wondering why when I tell certain nontruths, they come out sounding all rhymy. Maybe I'm not as good at lying as I think I am, who could tell?

"Winging for your friends? Well, that certainly backfired, didn't it?" She snickered in her dramatic actressy way, with her hands flying up, and I agreed, laughing out loud and figuring that we were beyond this discussion. To be honest, I was actually a little uncomfortable with her on account of her witnessing the father-son breakdown firsthand (not the kind of thing you want a girl to see), so truth be told, I was feeling more than a little nervous this particular afternoon with her.

And then she tells me that it's time for a serious talk, because we both have been avoiding the obvious (of course, leave it to me not to have any clue as to what the "obvious" was), and she wants to know am I "in" or not, and I ask what does she mean by "in" and she says in a relationship with her.

I'm thinking that the time is running down on the house being empty, and if "in" means IN, then maybe I'm IN, as in right now. Also, I am sure that if I don't say "in," then I lose this chance now and possibly forever. Let's face it, at the end of the day, it's all about how much you can get, so I say "in." I say this pretty convincingly. But she just shakes her head, like she totally knows why I said "in" in the first place, so maybe I didn't sound all that convincing after all.

"You don't get it, do you?" she says.

"Am I supposed to?" I asked. "You know, get it?"

"I thought you would be honest enough to admit it," she answered.

"OK, what, exactly, are we talking about?"

"Love. Steven. As in, I'm in love with you. And you're in love with me."

"You are? I am?"

She had me so confused at that moment, I actually wondered if she was right. I mean, I *did* think about this girl all the time, and it felt good, for some odd reason, being with her. But you couldn't exactly call that love, not the kind of love that I already knew about.

That was one fucked-up word, and it didn't apply here. Besides me, none of my close friends had actually been in love, had they? Not Newman or Pete or Kenny. Sure, we had girl-friends, but in the end it was always about hookups, not about the actual girls. And none of those hookups ever lasted that long, a few months maybe. And, sure, there were other guys, like Bosco for example, who was obsessed with Amanda Jenkins since like eighth grade, or Bobby and Ashley, who went virtu-ally everywhere together. Or Mark Duncan, who never quite got over his brief period as Kelly's boyfriend and then spent senior year brooding after she dumped him. And of course, Burn and Christina.

These guys all were in love.

And they were all losers.

"Didn't you understand that when we were talking the other night? When I was talking about connecting? Didn't you see that in your father's apartment? Can you really deny that we have something special?"

Her eyes were watering up, and I noticed actual tears. I was *not* good at girl tears, and I most definitely needed to find a way out of this conversation.

"Can't we talk about something else?"

"No," she said emphatically. "Your turn."

"Look, I'm not in love with you, Christina" is what I finally told her.

"Of course you are" is what she said, smiling through her tears now, wiping them away.

"How are you so sure?"

"Because of the way you treat me. You never treat girls with respect, Steven, in case you haven't noticed. Except for me. How do you explain that? And if I'm wrong, why do you always seem a little nervous around me? And why is it that you almost never look me in the eyes?"

I looked into her eyes. What I saw there made me really uncomfortable for some reason. She had the same look that she had whenever she was up on stage singing to an audience, like she could, if she wanted to, suck them all in and make them her bitches. Well, I wasn't going to be her bitch. Even if she had a few good points, which I will concede. And I definitely did treat her differently, but that was because she was fun in a different way, and I was always afraid that if I said the wrong thing, I would spoil that fun.

"The point is," she said, "you have feelings for me even if you're not capable of acknowledging them out loud."

"OK, feelings," I admitted. (I may have done an eye roll saying this, but it was mostly to avoid looking into her eyes, which tell you the truth were scaring me with the intensity of her gaze.)

"Feelings," she echoed. "What *kind* of feelings?"

"Why do we have to call it anything?" I asked. "Why can't they just be feelings?"

"If I told you that you had to say it or I was going to leave and you would never see me again, would you let me leave?" This girl never failed to confuse me, as this seemed to be another SAT question in its complexity. And I didn't exactly know the answer. Did I think I could say those words in all honesty and actually mean it at the risk of losing her forever?

"If you could just walk away and never see me again because I didn't give you the right response, then you must not actually be in love with me." That is what I actually said, which was unbelievably quick thinking and totally a college-level answer for a Princeton girl because she actually laughed and said:

"Good answer."

And then my mom came in with Jamie, and we were suddenly done with the entire conversation and having snacks. And Jamie being Jamie glanced at Christina, then, going over to the refrigerator, studied Christina more carefully from a greater distance, before going wordlessly to the family room, undoubtedly to watch more television.

And before my mom could hook Christina into a conversation, which she was very clearly trying to do, I walked her to her car, where she gives me this really slow kiss, looking into my eyes with this new intensity, just to make sure that I got the point. I open the car door for her, all gentlemanly, and close it behind her. As she turns the ignition on, she rolls down the window and tells me:

"You should know. I'm considering being with you."

Leave it to a dramagirl to make everything such a big production.

"Then what about tonight?" I ask, not missing a single beat, without even considering that there is probably no place to go.

"Not yet. It bothers me that you are always drunk or stoned when we see each other at night." She suddenly snapped, "You've probably never been with a girl unless you were drunk or stoned or both. That's not how it should be with us."

Fact was, as I quickly ran through my mental list of

experiences, I was thinking that she may have a point—more or less, except for one girl. Even with Claudia, as casual as that was, I was high all three times. OK, so, except for the one, I was always fucked up. Thing is, I'm pretty much always fucked up anyways. This is who I am.

"What's the difference?" I asked her.

"It's not real that way, Steven, don't you see that? You can have sex and still not have an intimate connection. That's what you do. All the time."

"That's just not true," I answered hesitantly, not wanting to get into the truth, which she wouldn't understand anyways. "You know, being on weed doesn't change anything. It just makes things better. Maybe you should try getting high instead of criticizing it all the time."

"OK. I will if you will."

"Will what?" Trying to follow this girl was sometimes an effort that my scattered mind just would not permit.

"I will get high with you if you can stay straight until we are together. Do we have a deal?"

"What are we waiting for exactly? Why can't we be together tonight?" Still not giving up.

"Not tonight . . ." She was deep in thought for a minute. "No weed for you until we're together. And I choose where and when we're together."

"OK, but it has to be like within the week," I confirmed, knowing all the time that Jacob's perfect weed was in my pocket and no way would I be able to last that long, but also there would be no way for her to check up on me either.

"OK, then," she said, turning all business, and about to shift her car into drive, like everything was completely solved. Only I was still confused, and so I had to ask just to be sure.

"Just so we're clear. You're agreeing that in a week, we will be together, as in *together*?"

"If you can stay straight, yes. I will be with you."

I nodded, still not sure. "We *are* talking sex, right?" I had to ask, better safe than sorry.

"Yes," she answered. "But I get to choose the place and the time."

Her car lurched forward. We were done talking, which was a good thing, because talking was definitely tiring me out.

And she was gone, leaving me feeling both relief and an odd craving for her. Maybe she was right; I couldn't tell. Whatever I was feeling, it didn't necessarily feel good.

I went back into the house and dropped down onto the couch next to Jamie, who was back to watching *High School Musical* again while Medusa crunched on the last bits of the pig ear. Good old Jamie. Good old Medusa.

I make her switch to *SpongeBob*, which she does, reluctantly. So we watch in silence as we always do. But this time, I'm not watching at all, even though it's one of my favorites, "Free Balloon Day," with SpongeBob and Patrick stealing a balloon which was otherwise free anyways, but I'm not into it because all I can think of is, what if Christina is right about us? Given my experiences, wouldn't I know?

After the episode, I grab the clicker and channel surf. Jamie just starts talking out loud, not necessarily to me or anyone in particular (she does this sometimes as if she's talking to the television).

"It'll never work."

She is somehow on my wavelength, because I was still thinking about whether a relationship was possible with Christina and if I even wanted one at all.

I clicker-switched to Cartoon Network, then back to Nick.

"Why not?" I ask her.

"She's too smart for you."

Usually Jamie will say these kinds of comments sarcastically to engage me in some kind of fight, which we always are doing with each other. But this time, I got the feeling that she was saying this to protect me, with the same amount of conviction in her voice that I usually have when I'm protecting her from something.

"Maybe I should talk to Felicia" is what I tell her. "No one is smarter than Felicia."

Jamie nods. "I know you think so, but in the end, she married Dad, didn't she?"

SpongeBob is on again, so we are done talking.

Two nights later, I break my promise to Christina, because me and the entire Club Crew, with the exception of Newman, end up meeting at the nature preserve. At first I decline when the bong is passed around, but then with the fragrant aroma wafting around me, I can no longer hold out, and as a compromise I decide on a few hits and out. Except since I have a small chunk of my father's excellent weed with me, I drop a small nugg into the bowl, knowing that one bong hit of that stuff is the equivalent of like an entire blunt, perfect in aroma, taste, and effectiveness.

Fully relaxed, we end up at Pinky's, where we totally pig out on burgers and onion rings. A superpolished-looking guy, who I recognize as a reporter from one of the morning television shows I did, heads over to us supercasually. Immediately suspicious, I back away from the table, but he's got no camera and just wants to introduce himself, or so he claims. I tell him I don't do interviews, reach into my back pocket to hand him Olivia's card, and instead feel the aluminum-foiled ball that encases a portion of Jacob's most excellent weed. No cards in there anymore; I don't even remember what I did with them.

To make matters worse, my friends are all about meeting him as he's a celebrity and all, so handshakes all around. And he ends up sitting with us, talking up the reporting business with Kenny and Evan and Bosco, all about who he's met and who's a bitch and who's hotter in person. I'm wishing Newman was there, because Newman would spot the setup a mile away, but the rest of the Crew is eating up these stories and having fun, like it's not obvious why the guy is there, at least not *so* obvious, until he casually mentions that one of the girls in the *Post* picture has just given an interview, and while I didn't have to comment on it, if I wanted to, to set the record straight, he could arrange it.

And while I'm sure that it's not Claudia, because Claudia wouldn't do that to me, my paranoia gets refocused in my mind, and the guy seems so friendly that I start to think what would it matter, me answering a few questions. Like he said, set the record straight.

Next thing I know, we are all outside, in the back lot at Pinky's, where he has this setup, two chairs and a series of floodlights set up over the chairs. He offers me a chocolate milk shake, and then suddenly I am sitting in this seat across from him in semidarkness as he leans over to me and asks, "Are you ready?"

And before I can tell him, "Actually, no," the lights are on me and the cameras are rolling.

And this is how it goes:

Newsguy: "You all remember Steven Crashinsky, who was a guest on our show earlier this year after dramatically negotiating a hostage crisis at his school in Westchester, New York, a sleepy suburb of New York City. For those of you who haven't heard, Steven's recently been in the news for a very different reason."

He turns to me.

"Several photos have been published with you holding what appears to be a marijuana cigarette in hand with your arms around several unidentified women." He is suddenly holding a giant poster version of the image.

Me: "Girls. They're in their teens. I don't know if you can call them women."

Newsguy: "Are they friends of yours?"

Me: "Acquaintances. I wouldn't call them friends, no. Actually, I met them on Facebook, and that was the first time that we spent time together. And the last." (No point in getting into the Claudia thing.)

Newsguy: "How do you answer the charge that what you're holding is marijuana?"

Me, suddenly realizing that I couldn't actually lie outright, even though I'm all about lying when it is necessary: "I deeply regret my actions that evening and recognize that they were irresponsible." (Thinking in my ridiculously stoned mind that somehow Sally would be proud of me.) "I am now involved with a very important person in my life in a relationship that I believe will prevent this kind of mistake in the future."

Newsguy: "So you're not denying it was marijuana, then?"

Me: "No, I never said one way or the other. But I thought you said that we would talk about the future, not the past."

Newsguy: "But with all due respect, this incident happened just a week ago. We're not talking several years or even months. And the point is, what people are asking is whether you were smoking marijuana."

Me (getting a little irritated, looking for my friends, who were out of my line of sight): "Yeah, it was marijuana."

Newsguy: "Was this a one-time event?"

Me: "With these girls, sure."

Newsguy: "No, Steven, with all due respect, I'm asking if you frequently smoke marijuana. If you smoked it before the night that these pictures were taken, if you have smoked since then."

I'm looking around, getting a little annoyed, thinking you

know what, this guy probably gets high every night and now he's acting like it's such a major bad thing. I'm thinking about Felicia dropping the bag of Jacob's perfect weed onto my father's coffee table.

Newsguy: "Steven?"

Me: "You know what? Sure. Sure I've smoked before. Sure I've smoked since. We're just talking about weed here, aren't we? Am I missing the point or are you? Because frankly there is nothing wrong with smoking a little weed now and then. In fact, as you may remember from our last interview, the press made a big thing out of me having attention deficit disorder. So you know what? It is a known fact that marijuana helps people with ADD to focus. In fact, in case you're forgetting, you can get medical marijuana legally in California. So yeah, I smoke weed. For medicinal purposes."

Newsguy (actually breaking into a smile for just a second, but then going back in the next instant to being a newsguy): "I'm not sure I understand. Are you saying that you have a prescription?"

Me: "No, all's I'm saying is that it helps me to focus sometimes. Is that such a bad thing?"

Newsguy: "So then are you advocating that people with ADD smoke marijuana?"

Me: "No, I'm not whatever-you-call-it for anything. Look, I'm just an eighteen-year-old kid looking to have a little fun in my last summer before college. Clearly, those pictures show a few people having a good time. When was the last time you had a good time?"

Newsguy: "This isn't about me."

Me: "Yeah, but when was the last time you smoked weed? The truth. If you're gonna ask me that, then don't I have a right to know about you?"

Newsguy (definitely uncomfortable, so I'm thinking maybe

I got him and he can be the news story instead of me): "Steven, what I'm hearing from you is that you're making light of your use of what is currently an illegal substance. And that while you began this interview with apologies, it seems that you are unrepentant."

Me: "Actually, it seems to me that you are making a big deal out of nothing. Like every kid, virtually every kid in my high school, has gotten high from time to time. And it's just not in my school, it's every school throughout the country. And it's every college. And it's probably every office and business too. If you polled the people around us right now, like probably half of them are still getting high. Probably even you, like I said before. Even my father still smokes weed now and then. Even at his age. So why are we making such a big deal out of these pictures?"

OK, here there is a superlong pause. Long enough to fit an entire commercial between what I just said and the next sentence.

Newsguy: "Are you saying that your father smokes marijuana? How do you know this?"

As soon as the newsguy repeated what I said, I know that I have just gone too far, and I know there's no turning back. I know immediately that this is worse than totaling my car or burning down the house, this is worse than getting arrested for some major crime. This is Bad, with a capital "B," as in bringing Jacob into this is a mistake that I know I will be living with for a very, very long time. I have nothing left to say this guy, this motherfucker who ambushed me with kindness and a chocolate shake.

Newsguy: "Steven, how do you know this?"

Me: "Same way I know you smoke weed. It's in your eyes."

This is exactly what they played on the morning show at exactly 7:42 the next morning, cutting to a commercial after my last line. By the time the segment aired on national television,

I knew I was fucked. No one had to tell me that I was fucked. I had been up all night preparing for the consequences.

At 7:48, the house phone started ringing, but no one picked it up, being as my mom was already at the gym and Jamie was still sleeping. I stared at the phone and then stared back at the TV screen, where some middle-aged lady was trying to cope with her joint pains and was advised to take a medication with a gazillion side effects.

The machine ended up picking up the call; no way was I touching the phone. I expected to hear Jacob's voice on the other end. What I heard was an unexpected female voice, identifying herself as "Olivia Swanson, your father's publicist."

The message she left was: "Your father has been informed about your failure to comply with his instructions. He has advised me to inform you that you are on your own. In case you are not clear what that means, you shouldn't expect any financial support of any kind. You shouldn't attempt to contact him or his wife again because he is done with you."

All I heard were the words "or his wife."

These words echoed in my mind.

Fuckme. Fuckme big-time.

CHAPTER THIRTEEN

HOW POKER SAVED BURN

"You're getting fat, Steven" was the way Jamie put it between TV shows, staring down into my bowl of cold spaghetti. "Maybe you should stop eating crap all the time."

OK, so I started to grow a bit of a gut.

It was a few months after the fox incident, after the holidays, well into winter, and I was constantly hungry. After months of not being able to eat from the Adderall and getting practically anorexic, my appetite had returned with a vengeance, and I couldn't stop myself from grabbing stuff out of the refrigerator and the pantry every afternoon after school, after dinner, and late into the night. Hard pretzels, soft cooked ones, chips, nachos, cookies, brownies, string cheese, peanut butter and jelly on rice cakes, cream cheese on a bagel, pita chips, ice cream, Lunchables, Hot Pockets, Tastykakes, Funny Bones, Pop-Tarts, Cap'n Crunch, Frosted Flakes, Golden Grahams, Froot Loops, Waffle Crisps, Fruity Pebbles, and practically every other snack or cereal you could name. Nothing was safe if it was in my house.

As expected, my doctor decided against trying me on any other ADD medications, so I was pretty much on my own, which wasn't making school any easier. Instead of medication, I had to see her once a month. Mostly we talked about school and she tried to get me to tell her how I was feeling, but except for school, I was starting to feel pretty good again, so we didn't have much to talk about.

Jamie started seeing the same doctor as me. Not because she

had ADD, but because she lacked friends, which shouldn't have surprised anyone being as she spent most of her time in front of the television (which was what she did even when her friends came over, whenever one came over).

Point was, the bar mitzvah and party cycle had started for her grade, and she wasn't getting any invites, which made my mom nervous about Jamie's ability to socialize, so my mom took her to my doctor, who recommended talk therapy and some kind of mood medication, saying that she thought that Jamie was suffering from depression. To me, she was just Jamie, and that was the way she was for as long as I knew her.

Also, she couldn't have been depressed, as she was always laughing at *SpongeBob*.

Plus she did good enough in school, so what did anyone want from her?

Plus she was totally captivated by Medusa, and took total responsibility for feeding and walking her, even though we all secretly knew that since we got the dog, Medusa had basically bonded to me as her master and followed me everywhere and never got all that excited playing with Jamie on her own.

Lindsey was also being nice to her, which meant that my mom must have put her up to it, because Lindsey was never nice without a motive. Speaking of Lindsey, her friends were always over. But, unlike the year before, now they had no interest in me, which didn't matter to me one bit because none of her friends were anywhere near hot anyways. Instead, they had basically accepted Jamie as if she was one of their group, which also meant that my mom must have put them up to it, because no way had they ever paid any attention to her on their own.

"I *am* not," I told her, scooping the last of the spaghetti into my mouth. "I'm just putting on the weight I lost." I didn't want to say it, but Jamie had also put on weight. Maybe it was the new medication, or maybe it just an age thing, but she had always been a superskinny kid and was now getting fuller looking.

She leaned over and grabbed my belly flab, which pissed me off, and we were in a full-on fight when my mom came home, with Medusa barking away at both of us, stepping in to join us, then stepping back cautiously.

"Enough!"

My mom yelled this, peering into the family room, packages in hand. One look at her face and we both knew, *we totally knew* that something was very wrong. So we immediately cut out the physical stuff and sat there, not moving. Even Medusa quickly laid her head down on the carpet, playtime most definitely over.

"Shouldn't we find out what happened?" I finally asked, thinking that whatever the news was, it was definitely a major thing, like a life-changing thing.

Jamie either wasn't as paranoid as me or just didn't want to know. She was back to switching channels and came across a *Simpsons* episode. "Did you ever notice how much Maggie looks like Lisa?"

I looked hard at her. She couldn't be depressed. The doctor definitely must've gotten that wrong.

Lindsey was first with the question. All of us in the kitchen, with our mom being uncharacteristically quiet, doing her supercleaning thing, which is what she always did when something bothered her.

"OK, so, what's going on?" Lindsey finally asked.

"Oh, don't tell me you haven't you heard," she answered, as if accusing Lindsey of something, in a tone that she never, ever used on Lindsey. "I would have thought the news would be all over school by now," she added, working with her special polishing spray and rag, shining the kitchen counter, instinctively following whatever path I took during an eating binge. As usual, I had left several food containers out, along with multiple forks and spoons, each with half-eaten samples of whatever was in the refrigerator. Usually, she would make me clean up after myself. Not today. Today, everything was already cleared off, gone.

"What news?" Now even Jamie was full-on curious.

"Roxanne Burnett is in the hospital," my mom said, looking at Jamie like she wasn't sure if Jamie should be included in the conversation. But no way was Jamie leaving now. This was getting as interesting to her as a Nickelodeon show.

"She tried to . . . hurt . . . herself." My mom, choosing her words very carefully. Too carefully for me, as I wasn't understanding what she meant.

"Ugh," Lindsey said with a typical sigh. "She *so* craves attention."

My mother dropped the polishing rag and practically yelled, "Lindsey, this is not a joke!"

I was in momentary shock. Like maybe I was missing something. So Roxanne was in the hospital, I was sure she was fine. Still, Lindsey's comments irritated me to the point of almost hitting her for being such an uncaring bitch. My mom actually looked like I felt, and I thought for an instant that she was going to reflexively let her hand fly, but Caroline Prescott always maintained control and never actually hit any of her kids.

"Do you understand the seriousness of this?"

Lindsey was smart enough to get the point. I was not, however, and was still not clear on the whole thing until my mother explained it more simplistically:

"She tried to kill herself."

So now it all made sense in a rush of logic to my brain, which left me dizzy, queasy, unable to move, as if someone had sucker punched me in the solar plexus. I started to gag, which I suppressed, then thought about the last time I talked with Roxanne in the halls of Meadows, with me leaving, thinking that there was something different about her, not just in the way she talked to me, but in the total lack of energy behind her voice. Should I have known?

We all asked different questions at the same time.

Jamie: "How?"

Lindsey: "Was it one of those goth things?"

Me: "Is she OK?"

The answers, all at once, were "pills, I don't know what a goth thing is, yes." My mom took a deep breath. "She's alive. They said that she'll be all right. Someone found her in her mom's car this morning with a bottle of vodka and an empty vial of pills."

"I heard that she was into weird stuff," Lindsey said casually, not backing off her uncaring tone, as if to defy my mom. She didn't realize how close she came to being beaten to a pulp. I would have hit her, except that I didn't understand why the news was so upsetting to me. After all, this was Burn's sister. They had a history of crazy, so why should I be so surprised? I had a momentary flash of an image of Roxanne, lying across the front seats of her mother's Prius, unconscious, with her head on the passenger door armrest, her hand outstretched and open, inches from an empty Grey Goose bottle, drool seeping into the seats as someone (a cop?) peered into the driver's side window. The vision startled me back to reality and made me gag again.

"Elaine is beside herself," my mom said, referring to Mrs. Burnett. I had forgotten that Mrs. Burnett had a first name, not remembering when or whether I ever heard it before. "She's at the hospital with Roxanne. Really, she's been through enough, losing her husband, then having to deal with David, and her health issues. Now, Roxanne. Although, in my opinion, she should have seen this coming."

More cleaning, leaving us to think about what happened.

Then directed at me:

"I hope you don't mind. I told her that David could stay here for a few days."

Immediately, my intense panic gravitated from Roxanne to her brother. The type of panic I was having now was a different type of panic, but the level of panic was about the same, as in off-the-charts panic. Off-the-charts because Burn was, well, Burn, and you couldn't predict what he was going to be like at any given time. So even though he had become subdued, almost sleepy, in school recently, I more or less knew how his mind worked, the way it twisted things sometimes. I didn't know what kind of relationship he had with his sister, but his mind had to be spinning beyond any measure of control.

I had another momentary flash of an image, this one of him lying in our guest room in the dark while the rest of us were asleep, with his eyes open and unblinking, staring at the ceiling, maybe cracking under the pressure of having a suicidal sister. And it crossed my mind, what if he went completely over the edge when he was here, and decided to kill himself or, worse, kill my entire family in the middle of the night? I couldn't say that this was impossible. In fact, in the psychic part of my brain, the part that was able to concoct these clear images, I believed we were all in danger if he stayed over.

And so my heart was beating with a totally uncomfortable drumroll, and I wasn't about to let this happen.

"I don't think that's a good idea," I told my mom. Lindsey echoed my sentiment, looking like she was thinking what I was thinking, and adding some pretty harsh words on her own.

But Mom didn't listen to us, not to Lindsey, not to me, because I couldn't exactly describe to her the real problem of having Burn sleep under our roof.

Because he wouldn't.

Sleep. I mean, he didn't. Sleep.

So neither would I. Not for as long as he stayed here.

A few hours later, there was Burn, in a red University of Maryland sweatshirt, hood over his head, practically covering his face in shadows, with his laptop and his backpack, following my mom into the house, nodding to me from under the hood.

He sat at the kitchen counter, opened his laptop, and waited for it to boot up.

"Thanks for having me," he said to my mom, not at all convincing. "Although, as my mom probably told you, I prefer to stay at my aunt's house."

"Well, we are here for you, David," said my mom in her most articulate mother voice, overpronouncing every word, which she sometimes does and which I always found supremely embarrassing.

She fed him. Warm plate of leftovers. I felt obligated to sit across from him while he ate, even through he never looked at me. He didn't look at my mother either. Only at his laptop. So I continued to watch, thinking about what would I do if it was me and I had to go to his house for some reason.

"Sorry about your sister," I told him when we finally talked.

He was cross-legged on the family room floor, his laptop in the circular space between his legs, typing away, staring both at the computer screen in front of him and the TV above his head on the wall of the family room. Jamie was in her usual position, at the corner of the couch. On TV, DJ was yelling about something that Michelle did, so everything was normal on *Full House*.

But not in mine.

"She doesn't want to see me," Burn said, banging on his keyboard.

"How come?"

"She knows I will have questions for her, and she's not going to want to answer them."

"You mean like why she did it?"

"No. I know why she did it," he said. "She was always talking about it, so I figured one day she would try." He sat up. "No. I need to know how far she got. And whether there was anything on the other side. Have you ever thought about it, Crash?"

"Thought about what?" As always, I had no clue.

"Suicide," he said, and I told him "no way," because trust me, it never once entered my mind.

"I have," he said. "But mostly, I would like other people to die." Which confirmed all the more that I should be uncomfortable with him under the same roof as my family. "You know, the ones that fuck with us." He tried to rationalize his thoughts, but to me they sounded crazy as always. "You know, like Connelly. Don't tell me for a minute that you haven't thought life would be better if Connelly just went down."

OK, actually, I had thought about that, but not in a realistic way, just like, in the middle of class when he picked on me for no apparent reason, I did wish him dead, and sometimes I even visualized him going down suddenly midsentence with an extreme heart attack that would leave his twitching body clinging to life. So I kind of got what Burn was saying.

"Well, maybe Connelly," I confessed.

"What about you, Jamie," he asked. "Did you ever think, what would it be like if you killed yourself?"

I was sure that Jamie would only be annoyed. After all, Burn was interrupting *Full House,* and you had to know that no one ever talked to Jamie during *Full House.*

Except that she actually seemed interested in our conversation.

"I used to," she said, which blew me away. "When I was younger."

I wondered if maybe the doctor was right after all, in giving her drugs. I also wondered if I should tell my mom, except that would only panic her more, because lately all of her panic seemed to be focused on Jamie.

"Sometimes I think about really creative ways to do it," Burn said, and I didn't know if he meant killing himself or others. "Like driving off a cliff or jumping in front of a speeding train, you know, where you are instantly killed. I wouldn't want to pull a Roxanne and fuck up the attempt."

"Me neither," said Jamie, and I was beginning to get beyond freaked at this conversation.

The next day, Burn decided that he would go to school, and rode in with us in my mom's car. He was still in his University of Maryland sweatshirt, and you could hardly see his face. I'm sure he hadn't slept at all.

As expected, I hadn't slept much either. I lay awake most of the night, listening to every creak and crack, waiting for sounds to come out from the guest bedroom, waiting for footsteps in the hallway, thinking all the time that Burn would be getting up and checking us out, standing over us as we slept.

I had to be ready for him.

The news about Roxanne, was, of course, all over school. People were coming up to Burn, saying that they were sorry to hear about his sister. He mostly ignored them, never removing the sweatshirt hood, and while normally some teacher or the assistant principal would have said something about the hood thing, no one was going to fuck with Burn under these circumstances.

Burn ended up staying with us for the rest of the week. Which meant me staying up all night every night to make sure he wasn't going to go off the deep end in my house and kill us all.

Tuesday night he finally talked more about Roxanne, who, I found out, had been sent to a special psychiatric clinic for drug abusers and suiciders. Apparently he had gone to see her that afternoon with his aunt, and she was doing OK, not talking about what had happened even though he tried to get her to tell him stuff.

Wednesday night he helped me with my English paper.

Thursday I got home after practice to find him hanging with Jamie on the couch, but get this, the TV wasn't on and they were talking.

That was it, as far as I was concerned, because Jamie had no idea how corrupt his mind could be, and Jamie was innocent about mostly everything except the stuff she learned on TV. I knew instantly that for as long he continued to stay at my house, I would have to be home whenever he was there. No way could I chance him talking to her again about suicide or anything else for that matter.

Short version, he had to go.

Except Friday, he was still there. I had to wonder what had happened to Mrs. Burnett after all this time. Had she abandoned him?

For what it was worth, Lindsey, being Lindsey, never actually said one word to Burn in all that time. Not a single word, got to give her credit, not even to ask how Roxanne was. But of course, Lindsey, being Lindsey, didn't care, so no need to pretend.

Which left me home on a Friday night while my boys were playing poker at Pete's house because Burn said he hated card games, didn't think they were challenging enough, complained that it was all about luck, not skill, so it didn't matter who won and lost really, did I want to play chess; because that he could do, but, of course, I refused to play chess or any other game with him. So we sat in front of the TV watching movies, with him laughing sometimes when nothing was funny and seeming to get all teary-eyed during, like, *Everybody Loves Raymond*, I swear I'm not making this up.

Kenny called, "Where are you? Aren't you playing?"

Then Newman called, "You gotta ditch him, Crash. The game's not the same without you. And definitely don't bring him, no one wants him to play."

Here's the thing: We had learned during the course of freshman year that most of the girls in our grade had no desire to do anything with us and started partying with the sophomores. Not like it mattered to most of us, as we totally bonded over poker, which we played every Friday and Saturday night, switching houses, except for Pete's house, because his parents were like superreligious and thought that poker was gambling, which made it totally inappropriate and against the church. His mom even called my mom to ask whether my mom was concerned that we were developing into gambling addicts or some such thing. My mom dismissed the comments, but apparently Pete's mom was riling up some other parents like Newman's mom and Evan's, who actually had a talk with us as a group when we were at his house, and we had to assure her that we had everything under control.

Which it pretty much was, except that as the winter wore on, a few of us would sneak six-packs and vodka, and this is how we started drinking as a group. Also, we had other secrets.

Which brings me back to Burn, because by Friday, he was not looking so good, mostly nodding to himself and, as I said, laughing one moment, then supersad the next. Getting totally into the lyrics of *American Idiot* like it was the Bible and reading them to Jamie, trying to convince her how important they were.

Good news was he went home Saturday. And me and Jamie were picked up by limo that afternoon and taken into Manhattan to spend time with Jacob and Felicia, which for me was perfect, because while I continued to hate seeing Jacob, Felicia was the only adult I could talk to. And I desperately needed to talk to someone.

I finally had my chance later that afternoon, with Jamie disappearing into what was designated as the "girls'" bedroom in their apartment, doing her TV thing, and my father on his business calls, so it was just Felicia and me, sitting on the couch together, as if she knew that I need to spend time with her alone.

First things first. I told her about Jamie's conversations with Burn, and she said that she wasn't surprised, given all that Jamie and the rest of us had been through, with our parents divorcing and other changes, not to mention having a sister like Lindsey who excelled in everything, and, no offense, but I wasn't the easiest kid. Besides, kids react to things the way they do, they just do, each one different from the next. She agreed with me that she didn't see Jamie as suicidal or anything, but she did think it was a good idea to mention it to my mom, who should have a talk with Jamie's therapist. Also, she promised that she would have her own conversation with Jamie, just so she could confirm for herself that Jamie had no intention of hurting herself.

Which brought us to talking about Roxanne, which was natural since we were talking about suicide and all and she had heard about what happened. She asked how I was handling the news. I said it wasn't about me. She just shook her head, like my answer was not the one that she was looking for, and said, "Of course, it's about you. You have feelings for this girl." Which was a statement from her, not a question, like there was no doubt in her mind.

And that made me real quiet because, OK, in my mind, there was something special about Roxanne, and sometimes I thought about her even when I hadn't seen her for a while. But she was also two years older than me, and, not gonna lie, pretty much out of control, even before she tried to kill herself.

Plus she was Burn's sister.

So no, it wasn't about me, even though on some level, it was. So I said "yeah," knowing that what I said would stay between us, because that's the way Felicia always was.

After she finally got the answer she was looking for, she was the one who got real quiet. It looked like she was trying to decide whether to tell me something that she never told anyone before, and she even said as much, that there was something she never talked about, not even to my father.

And then she told me.

There was a time when things were not so good for her when she was around Roxanne's age, back in her country, when some things happened to her that were unspeakably bad.

And I asked how bad, wanting to know exactly. And she paused again and told me that when she was Roxanne's age, someone she trusted betrayed her, and when she had nowhere to turn, she tried to do it too, tried to kill herself, just like Roxanne. And someone saved her life.

She told me this with an honesty that I had not seen before in anyone else and in a voice that seemed to take her back to that time in her life so completely that, for a fleeting second, I could actually see the pain in her eyes that she had experienced at that time.

I pretended not to be shocked, which I was, not going to lie. Because it never occurred to me that anyone would want to kill themselves, least of all someone as beautiful and totally together as Felicia. If she could imagine herself dead, then what about regular people?

Also, I could tell that there was something else that she wasn't telling me, something that she was still dealing with, something that she couldn't tell anyone.

Now I knew something about her that even Jacob didn't know, something that she trusted me with in complete confidence. So now we were even.

Thinking back now, that may have been my first adult moment. Even then, I felt weighted by the responsibility of knowing something that I shouldn't, at my age, have known.

"And because you understand now, you must be there for Roxanne," she told me. "You neet to visit her in de hospital. To tell her that you care about her." Felicia took my hand. "Dis is empordint, Cresh. She neets to know someone is dere for hir."

"Why does it have to be me?" I bounced back when I realized what she was trying to tell me. Like no way could I get to whatever mental institution they were keeping Roxanne at in the first place, even if I wanted to go, which, of course, I did not. Not in the least.

"If not you, den who? I remember her. She is a very sensatif soul. She must be nurtured, Cresh. And she likes you. She trusts you. No, I think it must be you. Hir own brother is useless, no?"

"I'm gonna take a pass on this," I said emphatically, imagining myself wandering around the hospital with zombie psychos reaching out to me, like in one of those horror movies or at the very least an episode of *The Simpsons Treehouse of Horror.*

"You cannot take a pess on dis," she responded. "If it was Jammie, vood you be dere?"

"Roxanne is not Jamie," I told her. "Besides, I'm pretty sure Roxanne didn't mean to kill herself. More likely, she was just experimenting. . . ." This was me repeating a line that I heard from my mother, who said it to a neighbor on the phone.

Felicia looked at me sternly, pointing those eyes of hers at me like spotlights, eyebrows up, head pointed down, watching me. "CRESHHHH . . . Veren't you listening to me at all?" Which was all she needed to say, because the way she looked at me, I knew I was out of excuses, because now I understood why Felicia had confided in me in the first place. It wasn't for me at all, but for Roxanne, a girl she hardly knew.

"It's settled den. I vill haf a car take you dere tomorrow. Ve vill neet to get dee adderess," she told me, leaning her hands on my legs and pushing herself up off the couch. "Dere is sometink else," she said, leaving me to watch her move as she left the room. "Sometink that somevon vonce gave me."

She returned, holding something I couldn't see, her hands cupped together. Then, kneeling down over the couch, she opened her hands and scattered what appeared to be dried beans across the coffee table. Maybe a dozen, at most, white beans, the kind my mom uses to make soup.

I stared down at the beans, wondering if this was some kind of Slovakian ritual or something.

"You must give deese to her."

"Beans?"

"Not just beanz," she told me. "Magik beanz."

OK. I stared at those beans for a really long time in silence. They didn't jump, they didn't move, and they weren't pretty or spotted or at all unusual. Absolutely nothing was magical about them. They were beans. *Just beans.* I couldn't help but to point this out.

"There is nothing magical about them."

"How can you be so certin dat dey are not magik? Haf you askt dem to grant your vish? Haf you pictured sometink in your mind and held dem? Haf you tossed dem into a corner and vatched dem fall or used dem to predikt de future? If you haf not tried deeze tings, how are you so sure dey are not magik?"

"OK, I can't say for sure." But in my mind, I was saying for sure. These were ordinary, run-of-the-mill beans. Beans for cooking, beans for eating (well, not for me as I hate beans), but magic? Not so much.

"Besides," she told me, "dey are not intendit for you. Dey are for Roxanne. It is only your job to convince her that dey are magik."

"So let me get this straight. Not only do I have to go to a hospital for psychos, but I have to give one of the psychos these beans, plus convince her that they are magic beans."

"Dat is how it verks."

"What if they decide to keep me there? I mean, if Roxanne tells anyone that I am trying to give her magic beans, they'll think I'm as crazy as everyone else." Which got Felicia to laugh, and she totally lit up a room when she laughed.

"I see your point," she said. "Still, dis is vat you musdew."

I gathered up the beans and held them in my hand. They felt like they looked: ordinary, run-of-the-mill beans. She handed me a small plastic bag.

I dropped them in, staring at her in disbelief.

"It's settled, den," she said, dismissing me with a wave of her hand. "One other tink, maybe you shoot cut down on de carbs, Steefin. You are gaining weight."

I instinctively sucked in my gut, not that I had one, at least I didn't think so, but I was starting to get a complex.

"It's settled then" is all I had to say.

Which is how I found myself standing at the front desk of this sprawling hospital building in the middle of the Westchester woods, in the middle of a midwinter Sunday afternoon, while my friends were at Evan's house, watching the football playoffs, playing poker, and eating box after box of Mario's pizza.

As promised, Felicia arranged for a limo to take me on this superlong drive to get me there. Then I panicked when my name was announced to the nurse lady, who put in a call and informed me that Roxanne would be there shortly.

Nervously, I checked out the lobby, which to be honest looked more like a hotel than a mental hospital. There were a few people, all different ages, wandering around, none of them dressed for winter, so I had to believe they were patients, which made them crazy, didn't it? Crazy or drug addicts.

And then there was Roxanne, coming down the stairs in a pair of old sweatpants and her brother's University of Maryland sweatshirt, her hair not combed at all, with all these clips sticking out, looking pale and pasty and pimply, and I couldn't help but notice again the strong resemblance between her and her brother, which only made things stranger for me.

She drifted over to me. Slowly, like she was on drugs or something. She looked as if she didn't have enough strength to talk.

"Crashinsky?" she exclaimed in total disbelief. "What the frig are you doing here?" Sounding very much like the Roxanne I knew.

"Visiting you?" I asked more than said.

"Why, in fuck's name?"

This was a tougher question than I was prepared for. I couldn't tell her the truth, which was that Felicia convinced me to go, as she would have no idea what I was talking about.

"I thought it would be a good idea?"

"Who the frig brought you here?"

"My dad got this limo for me."

"Your dad's fucked up," she said, still superhostile for some reason I did not know.

"Yeah, my dad's pretty fucked up," I answered. "But his girlfriend is cool."

Apparently that line got through to Roxanne, who was suddenly twirling a piece of her hair with her forefinger. When she lifted the twirled hair up, I saw that underneath she had shaved a part of her head. A jagged pattern, like she had attempted it on her own, then stopped midway. I tried not to look, which of course made me stare.

"Yeah, I know, I fucked myself pretty good," she said, noticing me noticing her. "You wanna sit down?" She gestured over to the huge modular couches in the center of the room, where other random, spacey-looking people were sitting. I did not want to sit with them but couldn't tell her that. Those people could be friends of hers for all I knew.

She wrapped her arm around mine and escorted me, whispering, "Don't worry, those fuckheads will move when they hear us talking," as if reading my mind.

"Yeah, OK," I said, realizing that she realized just how uncomfortable I was.

We sat down on one end of the main couch. Just as Roxanne predicted, the others on the same couch moved simultaneously to other couches, giving us some privacy.

"They watch us here, like, every fucking move we make."

I looked around the room and noticed two black men in white uniforms doing nothing but looking around. They were conspicuous as they were the only black people there, besides the receptionist.

"I don't fucking get why you're here," she said again.

"Just thought it would be a good thing to do. Like I said, I was at my dad's apartment, talking to Felicia. And she agreed. So here I am."

This seemed to satisfy her. "I can't believe she's still with him." Then, switching gears, "What the fuck are people at school saying about me?"

"To tell you the truth, I didn't hear anything at all." Which of course could not be further from the truth.

"Don't you fucking lie to me, Crashinsky. I'll cut your fucking heart out." Still twirling her hair, or what was left of it.

"Most kids in my grade know you only as Burn's sister. I don't have to tell you that I don't spend much time talking to Lindsey, so what the fuck do I know?"

"Still, they must be talking. And you're not. Not being honest with me."

I was caught in a tough place, not willing to tell her what I knew, but knowing that Roxanne was relentless. And also, being a Burnett, smart enough to catch me if I lied.

"They say you were drugged out. That you were doing all kinds of stuff. You know, weed, coke, heroin."

"What else?"

"You were like hanging out with a bunch of older people in the city."

"What else?"

"That you, you know, would have sex with anyone . . ."

"What else?

"That you were always crazy."

She nodded, seemingly to herself, like she had finally gotten the right answer.

"What do you think?"

"I dunno." Which was honest, because honestly I hadn't thought about it like that, actually, but I guessed that I believed everything I heard, believed that she was on drugs, that she was into stuff that she shouldn't have been, and yeah, a little crazy, although not as crazy as her brother. "You did seem different to me that day in the hallway, when we were talking about your brother, and so I'm thinking, maybe I should have noticed."

"How could you? You don't know me," she said. "Not really."

I wanted to tell her that everything she told me about being better than that, about being special, applied to her, because she was special too. What came out was:

"Did you really try to kill yourself?"

"Yeah, Crashinsky." She kept nodding. "I really did."

"I just don't get it" is what I said, only because if I didn't say anything, neither of us was going to say anything. At that instant I wondered what the hell I was really doing there and thinking when was it the right time to give her the beans. It seemed like such a stupid idea now that I was there in person. So after I said "I just don't get it," we sat in silence, which was what I was afraid of. I started looking around at the others in the room, and I turned away from her, which must have made her more comfortable talking, because she started, real softly, almost whispering . . .

"I was tired. Tired of living in my aunt's house, tired of having to go to school with assholes who are only worried about who's hotter than who and who's taking them to the prom, tired of girls like your sister making snide remarks every time they passed me in the halls, tired of being called a slut and a whore because I have older friends and different interests, tired of listening to my mom complain about David, tired of David banging on his laptop all night and making weird sounds since he doesn't sleep, tired of him having these incredibly angry tirades and tired of him bursting into my room in my house—no, my fucking aunt's house—to tell me that he thinks nine-eleven was a conspiracy and that maybe our dad wasn't dead at all, maybe it was aliens or something that transported everyone in the towers to another planet or another dimension or some other bullshit theory of the moment that he comes up with, tired of wondering what life would have been like if my father was on one of his business trips that week instead of in his office, tired of watching my mom go from one therapy treatment to another, tired of having her tell me that I had to be more like the other kids in school and that I wasn't allowed to visit my friends in the city and that if I stayed out one more time past midnight I wasn't permitted to come back home, tired of watching other people get fucked-up drunk and sloppy, tired of not being able to drive because my mom doesn't trust me . . ."

By the time she finished, she was no longer whispering. Actually, she was getting louder and louder, with no shortage of anger coming from her voice, and everyone in the room was turned to listen, even as I turned to look at her too, thinking maybe I could stop her at that point, although she was finally sounding like the Roxanne I knew, which almost made me smile, except of course under the circumstances and all, maybe not. And then she said:

"So do you *get it* now, Crashinsky?"

"Yeah," I said, trying to calm her down. "You were tired."

This got her to laugh. At least she knew I was paying attention.

"I still don't know what the frig you're doing here."

This was my opening, I figured.

I reached into my pocket.

And pulled out the plastic bag. "This is for you," I told her.

"I'm not allowed to accept anything from anyone," she started to say, even as I opened the bag to hand the beans to her. And at the same time, the two black men in the white uniforms were practically on top of us, grabbing the bag, but as they reached for it, I pulled it away so fast that the bag split in half, sending the beans popping up into the air and shooting into different directions, some spilling onto the couch, others flying across the room.

"He's giving her pills!" one of the men said, trying to hold me down. Roxanne backed away.

"They're not pills!" I said.

Roxanne picked one up and examined it. "What the fuck, Crash?"

"They're beans," I said, knowing that was maybe the

stupidest thing I'd ever said in my life, and that this bean thing was the stupidest thing I ever did. Thank you, Felicia.

"Fucking beans?" said Roxanne and one of the men at the same time.

"Just beans," I said.

"What the fuck, Crash?" By now everyone but me was holding a few of the beans, and I could see how they had confused them for pills. They did kind of look exactly like pills.

Then, Roxanne yelling at me: "This is a rehab clinic, for Christ's sake! I'm not supposed to accept anything from anyone, not unless it goes through them"—pointing at the guards.

Again, thank you, Felicia, for sending me to a rehab clinic with a bag full of things that could be mistaken for pills and getting a suicide girl all worked up.

The other guy in the white uniform, the one not holding me down, had scooped up most of the beans. He held them out to me in his giant hand.

"How many?" he asked in a deep Caribbean accent.

"I dunno. Like twelve maybe."

They recovered nine. I had to explain. To her and them.

"They're supposed to be magic beans. I mean, they are. Magic beans . . . ," I started to explain to the group. "Actually no, they're just normal cooking beans, but my father's girlfriend gave them to me and she told me that when she was younger, she tried to, you know, kill herself, and like these magic beans, well, not these beans, other beans, kind of saved her life, and so I thought it would be a good idea to give Roxanne some magic beans, which according to Felicia . . . my father's girlfriend . . . if you make a wish and I dunno maybe plant them or something, your wish comes true and like how could we be sure that they aren't magic, after all, they totally worked for her, for Felicia, and so I figured that maybe they would work for her, Roxanne." Now I was looking at her instead of the guards, and I repeated,

"Maybe they would work for you."

And she was shaking her head in disbelief.

"Fucking beans?" she said again, and by now there were two other people standing over us, some doctor guy and a nurse lady. So we had a crowd, with two new people checking out the beans to determine whether they were, in fact, beans, and I actually began to wonder, just for a second, what if they weren't beans at all, even though I knew of course they were. But what if either by mistake or magic, Felicia had given me something else?

I panicked a little. At least until I heard the voices around me.

"Beans," said one of the black guys in the white uniforms.

"Beans," said the doctor guy.

"Beans," said the nurse.

"Motherfucking beans." Roxanne was holding one of them and totally laughing now. "Motherfucking magic beans," she repeated, in actual hysterics.

The two men in the white uniforms were also laughing now.

"False alarm," said the doctor guy.

"Unusual," said the nurse.

"Still, rules are rules," said the man with the Caribbean accent. "Nothing from the outside world." He took the single bean that Roxanne was still holding and folded it into his giant hand, where it took its place among the other beans. "You can have these when you leave," he told her. "We wouldn't want you growing a beanstalk and escaping from us." He said this with a deep laugh. Which made all of the others laugh.

And we were soon by ourselves again and Roxanne was all smiles, like I made a difference, like something changed for her. For the first time since I got there she was looking at me like she was really glad to see me.

"Fucking beans," she repeated. "They must be fucking

magic, Crash, because right now I'm thinking that they are the best present I ever got in my life." Then she switched to serious. "Tell me again about Felicia."

And so I did, explaining how when Felicia was Roxanne's age, she still lived in whatever country she was from and things got tough, and whatever else Felicia told me, I told Roxanne. And I explained that Felicia wanted me to tell her, Roxanne, that she got through it, that Roxanne would get through it. And then one day she would look back on the experience from an entirely different place, with different eyes and a different perspective.

And Roxanne said, "Yeah, she ended up with your dad. A fate worse than death, if you ask me, even though he's an attractive enough man, I'll give him that."

Which caused her to laugh again, which caused me to laugh too, and it caused me to consider my own father in a different light, if just for a second. Did he have some kind of magic that I could actually learn from?

Then she said, "Speaking of a fate worse than death, I heard David was staying at your house." And I told her that he had been, but not anymore, and she admitted that she didn't totally trust her brother, not that he would do anything bad to her, that she tried to be close to him; and once in a while tried to talk to him about stuff, like during those nights when he kept the fox in the garage they would spend time talking together, but otherwise, he was either preoccupied with one of his obsessions or angry for no reason, or too inquisitive, asking her so many questions that she would just give up trying, even though her mother often begged her to keep an eye on him.

And then I said something that made her laugh again. What I said was "I'm sure Lindsey says the same thing about me."

"Yeah . . . Lindsey" was all she said.

Then it was time to go, as the limo driver was in the lobby now, looking for me and tapping his watch.

Roxanne walked me over to the front door and stood on her tiptoes and held my face in her hands as she gently kissed me and said this:

"I'm going to admit it, I'm glad you came. I didn't think that I wanted to see anyone ever again, but I'm glad you came."

I was going to tell her before I left that she was special too, but I couldn't get the words out, and besides, just as I turned to get into the limo, Roxanne yelled out, "I'll be out of here in a month. Maybe you should lose a little frickin' weight by then, Crashinsky," sounding exactly like the Roxanne I knew.

OK. Thank you, Felicia. For real.

My mom got me on one of those programs where they prepare special microwavable portions for all of my meals, which I pretty much stuck to during the day, and I stopped eating all of the hard pretzels, soft cooked ones, chips, nachos, cookies, brownies, string cheese, peanut butter and jelly on rice cakes, cream cheese on a bagel, pita chips, ice cream, Lunchables, Hot Pockets, Tastykakes, Funny Bones, Pop-Tarts, Cap'n Crunch, Frosted Flakes, Golden Grahams, Froot Loops, Waffle Crisps, Fruity Pebbles, and practically every other snack or cereal you could name.

And I started working out with Newman, who was all about going to the gym and running, like, miles after school, and he suggested that I join the track team to get back into shape. We all needed to work out and get into shape, because it wasn't only me. Most of my friends had gained weight during the course of freshman year, being as we were always eating.

It wasn't just eating after school that was the problem.

We had discovered something that made the poker more interesting, that made everything on TV more intense, that made every video game that we ever owned worth playing again, like it was for the first time, that made going to the movies like a day in the amusement park. Get the picture?

If so, you should have guessed by now:

We had discovered the magic of weed.

We were, in fact, lighting up every weekend night and some-times during the week after school, which is what made all of the stuff I ate taste like it tasted the very first time. Plus it actu-ally helped me study, so for the first time in my school career, I was actually getting B's on my own. So in my mind, marijuana was the real magic bean.

Only I couldn't tell that to Felicia and certainly couldn't tell it to Roxanne, who, after all, was apparently a drug addict. That was what they were actually saying in school about her—that she was a drug addict slut who went with guys in the city for money, which I didn't believe but didn't ask her about. I couldn't ask her about it.

A month went by and I was doing OK on my diet; OK except for not being able to stop myself from eating when I was blazed, so I didn't even realize that a month had gone by until one Friday my mom picked me up from school and on the way home mentioned that Roxanne was coming back to school. I could tell by the way that she was talking that the conversation wasn't about Roxanne at all, because she was going on about how Mrs. Burnett was going through a difficult time, and while Roxanne was better and the doctors assured her that Roxanne wasn't going to do it again and was going to see a therapist, David was not doing well at all, as it seems he had completely disassoci-ated himself from everyone and was withdrawing further into his own world and was not willing to see anyone and was blow-ing up at his mom practically all the time.

I stopped listening to her and played around with the satel-lite radio in the new Mercedes she got because she was doing superwell at work selling houses in the neighborhood, so I was scanning the stations when she asked:

"So can you take David with you tonight?"

Which meant the poker game.

No way were any of my friends going to let him play, but that wasn't going to be a problem, because no way would Burn play. He had already told me that he hated cards. Except that he apparently had no choice, because his mother wanted him out of the house that night so there would not be any conflicts between him and Roxanne on her first night back.

Which is how he ended up going with me to Evan's house that night. As in, my mother drove us both.

Of course, I called my boys in advance to warn them.

Pete looked ready for a fight when we showed up, like no way was he gonna take any shit whatsoever from Burn. Only, after one look at Burn Pete backed off.

Fist bumps around, even from Pete, welcome to the game, all smiles, and I wondered whether Burn even had any idea that Pete still hated him so much after the fox incident. Of course, Burn being Burn, he probably did know and it didn't matter to him. Besides, from how it looked on that particular night, he was completely in his own Burn world anyways, even suggesting that he would watch, not play, the first game.

And so we started, cards being dealt around the table. Me, Newman, Bosco, Evan, Pete, with Burn on a barstool watching us, mostly me, sitting over my shoulder. Which, of course, made me extremely uncomfortable, to the point of complete annoyance.

We started with dimes, worked toward quarters. Kenny showed up, and I knew he was bringing stuff, which presented a problem, because while we would be able to sneak out of Evan's house and go for our usual walk while we passed around a joint, what the fuck were we going to do with Burn?

I, for one, was itching for the weed by then. My hunger for it had been building all week, having had no opportunities since our last game. So between the weedlust and the fact that I could not concentrate on the game being as I could constantly feel Burn hovering over every move I made, and so even though I was on a superhot streak, with me winning every hand that mattered, I asked them to deal me out.

"You wanna take my place?" I asked Burn.

He shook his head no. Still no.

Kenny stepped in and sat in my seat. Pete made a nasty comment about me always winning, which had a tendency to be true, but when I looked over at him, I saw from the look on his face that his comment wasn't about poker at all, it was like, what are you going to do about Burn?

And also, while they didn't have to say so, Newman and Evan were looking at me like, he's your problem, Crash. He's always your fucking problem. Do something so we can get on with it.

"I'm going for a walk" is what I said, heading out the sliding glass doors into the backyard, not noticing that Burn had followed me, like a watchdog.

"Hold up."

"What?" Me, all irritated, wanting him to know.

"What?" Like he didn't know.

"Are you going to fucking play or not?" I asked. "If not, why'd you come?"

"You know why I'm here," he said softly, like he was hurt or something.

"Still, as long as you're here . . ."

"I'm not ready yet. Bosco is easy. Every time he has a pair or better, he taps his fingers on the table, like he's playing the piano; the faster he goes, the better his hand. Evan makes this chewing face, like he's ready to eat. Newman is harder, so you have to watch his eyes, but if he's sure he can win, he nods slightly, just once, like he knows he's being watched but is nevertheless compelled to do it, almost like a dare. I can beat them all."

I was pretty impressed at this, but I was still mostly annoyed. "So?"

"So there's still you. I've seen your cards, seen your picks, seen the way you bet, and none of it is, in any way, logical. Everything you do is, and I fucking hate this expression, totally random. Completely luck of the draw, as the saying goes. But that can't be, since even the luckiest guy can't win as consistently as you do. I've tried to calculate the odds on this; it's impossible. You should not be winning at all. Yet you mostly do. And when you fold—and sometimes you fold even when you have good cards—you are almost always right. I have watched you do this twice. What the fuck, Crash?"

When he said this, he reminded me exactly of his sister, and I could see the resemblance again.

Still, I already knew about Bosco with his drumming hands but had no idea about the others. And the truth was, everything I did in the game was instinct. The only reason I never questioned it was that I kept winning.

"There is, however one little thing that you do. . . ." He smiled at me. And I knew he wasn't going to tell me. He wasn't, because he was probably just making it up to get under my skin, in a way that only he could actually do. But also, knowing how Burn was Burn, there probably *was* something he picked up. After all, if he picked up Newman's tell . . .

I felt exposed. And more irritated, since he confirmed that he was watching me, which is what I thought in the first place.

"Fine. I'll sit out," I told him. "See what you can do without me."

"No. I need you to play. No one wants me here. Most of the others hate me. Maybe with the exception of Newman."

He was dead on. Except maybe for Kenny, who respected

that Burn was a genius, and who, on a good day, could maybe even out-genius Newman. Point was, all three of them, Newman, Kenny, and Burn, had a smart thing: a never-spoken-about competition, but also a bond, which I was not unhappy about not sharing with them.

"Know what I think?" I asked him. "I think you're afraid to play. I think you're afraid you might have a good time."

"Oooh, Mr. Psychologeeeeeeeeeee." Burn laughed. "Do me a favor, save it for my sister."

I looked at him but didn't say anything. I wondered what he knew about my visit. We were out in the front of Evan's house now, which gave the others an opportunity to sneak out the back and file into Evan's garage.

Burn looked surprised that I was surprised. "Did you think I didn't know that you visited my sister in the hospital?"

I didn't know that it was a secret; still, I never actually told anyone except Felicia, and of course Roxanne and Jamie knew. But not even my mom.

"Don't you get it, Crash? I know everything. I know that your father is getting married," he said.

Actually, *I* didn't know that, and he must have seen it in my expression. "Didn't anyone tell you? I know that your mom is having a problem with the guy she's dating, and that she's afraid he's not willing to commit to her and she really likes him. I know that Lindsey is still a bitch, but she'll be getting hers soon enough because someone in school is out to out-bitch her. What else do you want to know, Crash?"

I stood there, absorbing, listening, not wanting to hear more, but needing to know. Thinking first, why didn't she, as in Felicia, tell me?

My first thought: Good for my dad. Better for me, since my relationship with him was all about Felicia anyways and without her he would be intolerable again. Not good for my mom. I felt sad for her. Not interested in Lindsey. Really not. He probably got all the facts from his mother, who talked to my mom.

Or not.

"Are you IMing with Jamie?" I asked suspiciously.

"Sometimes. You have a problem with that?"

"Yeah. Stay away from my sister, you freak."

Most guys would have considered those words to be fighting words, but Burn being Burn took it for what it was worth and laughed. Which also got me thinking that I had to tell my mom to make sure that Jamie did not have anything to do with this psycho.

"Which reminds me," he said, "my sister did tell me to say hello to you. That's what she said, tell Crashinsky I said hello. Plus she gave me a present and said I could share it with you." He reached into the back pocket of his jeans and pulled out a plastic bag filled with weed. "Obviously she can't have access to this type of stuff anymore. Did you ever get high, Crash?"

So apparently, he didn't know as much as he claimed. I wasn't sure what to tell him. So I didn't say anything, while he reached into the bag and extracted a joint.

"I've been smoking her stuff since she told me about her stash when she was in the hospital. I was supposed to get rid of it, which in a way, I'm doing now."

He lit up.

And coughed. And handed it to me.

I took a hit, then another, and coughed hard, feeling it burn all the way in the back of my throat, as if I had swallowed fire, and it continued to burn all the way back to Evan's house, where even spiked Gatorade did not do much to ease the feeling that my lungs were searing.

I sat down at the poker table, thinking that it still hurt, but feeling nothing at all.

. . . Until it hit me, almost knocking me over.

This was, of course, before I became a weed connoisseur, with the tolerance of a Jamaican farmer.

It hit me so strong, in fact, that I apparently just sat there until Newman (not knowing I was blazed, since we had not smoked together) informed me that I had lost another hand, and I looked down to see my remaining poker chips spread out, most of my winnings gone, and my cards, none of which matched together in any way, displayed for all to see.

And there was Burn on the other side of the poker table, holding three tens and smiling at me. He could handle. I could not. He was finally playing. And apparently winning. His chips, which apparently included a good portion of mine, were stacked higher than anyone else's at the table.

Where the fuck was I all that time?

"Your luck seems to have run its course," Burn said to me, hauling in the kitty.

Pete was looking at him suspiciously, as if somehow, during my walk with Burn, he had put me under some kind of spell or something. Remember, no one except Burn knew I was baked.

I wasn't feeling all that good. Not good at all. I was ready to quit.

Except I had a feeling that I could win, which, when I get it, I always do. So rather than give my seat up, I anted up for the next round, thinking that I could win everything back, as long as I didn't look at Burn, as long as I treated him like any other player.

Which is exactly what I did, as in not thinking at all, even though Roxanne's weed was making me overthink, which is something that I almost never did, as it makes my brain hurt.

And soon enough, I was back to where I was at just before I went for a walk with Burn.

And then it was just the two of us left, everyone else out.

And I was still high, feeling no letdown from the strength of this weed, and knowing this is the last hand of the night.

And Burn suggests we switch from Texas hold'em to five-card, which is fine with me.

And Burn deals, passing me cards, and us betting and me having nothing, well not nothing, actually, three random hearts is all, and we bet and we raise and we raise again. And I ask for two cards and he asks for one.

And then I look at him for the first time since we started playing, and he looks at me, and I know, *I totally know* that he is holding three aces and two other cards, and I am sure, totally and completely confident, bet on it positive, that those other two cards, whatever they are, are also a pair.

Which would give him a full house.

There are only three hands that beat a full house with three aces: four of a kind, straight flush, royal flush. But only one of those hands was even remotely possible for me, because I knew I didn't have four of a kind or a royal flush.

I had a seven of hearts, a nine of hearts, and a jack of hearts. So all this time, I had been going for a regular flush, which meant any five hearts, except that if I was right about what Burn was holding, then just another two hearts, which I had a decent possibility of getting, would not be good enough.

So I pick up the two cards that he slid across the poker table.

I stare at Burn and he stares at me, and I can see from his eyes that he knows he won, but because I'm so baked, and because he is looking deeply into me, trying to figure out what's in my head, I can, for some odd reason, see directly into his . . .

Mind.

And what I see in his mind is the fox and what they did to the fox. He's still totally freshly pissed off about it even though it was months ago, and he's planning some kind of revenge but doesn't know who to go after. He just wants revenge. And then Connelly is in there. And so is the World Trade Center, smoke billowing from the towers. And then I see Roxanne, and how what happened to Roxanne was, in a way, at least to him, at least partially his fault. Like he knew that she was broken and couldn't fix her, because he was broken too, maybe even worse than she was, and he was jealous because she was able to lead a normal life if she wanted to and he couldn't, and then there was something that I couldn't see in there, something that I didn't want to see.

Because the deeper I looked, the more stoned I felt, and the more totally and completely anxious I became, until I could feel my own heart beating rapidly in my chest and I wondered whether somehow it was syncing with his . . .

Heart.

I had hearts.

Which was totally freaking me out.

Except that suddenly, in with all of the mashed-up images in Burn's mind, at that very next moment, was the feeling of winning. Not just winning, but beating me. Which should have been easy, beyond easy with the cards that I *knew* he was holding. And he knew it too, but he also was anxious, *very* anxious, because even with his near-perfect hand, and even with his perfect sense of logic, he could not know for sure, and not being able to rely on the odds was driving him crazy with anticipation.

And in his mind, from what I could tell, it really, really mattered.

Winning.

Because the universe doesn't give you an ace-high full house if it doesn't want you to win.

Except that the two cards that I turned over happened to be, just like Burn said about me earlier, the exact cards I needed.

Eight of hearts.

Ten of hearts.

Straight flush.

I stared down at the pool of money, almost every cent that everyone brought that night. Over three hundred dollars, well over three hundred dollars. And it was Burn's turn to bet.

"All in, plus twenty," he said, still staring at me with those intense eyes.

I looked away, breaking the connection, and it immediately hit me that something inside him would snap if he lost, something that would ripple through his psyche and infect others around him. And his sister, being so fragile, didn't stand a chance. I know it sounds crazy, but I knew this every bit as much as I knew what cards he had in his hand. And in that second, I understood that I had a choice. Saving Roxanne wasn't about going to the hospital to reach her. The universe was testing me, and somehow she was the bait. Saving Roxanne was all about doing the right thing now.

"I fold," I said.

"C'mon, Crash, don't be a baby now. Last hand of the night. What the fuck."

"Sorry. I'm out. No more cash."

"I'll lend you the twenty," Burn said to me.

"Fuck it," Pete said from the sidelines. "I'll give you the twenty. Destroy that motherfucker."

"No," I told him. "I'm out."

"Fine," he said, reaching for the entire kitty, confidently smiling. And when I looked into his eyes again, everything was completely gone. No fox, no Connelly, no World Trade Center, no Roxanne being infected or anything. Disappeared, as if I had imagined it, which maybe I had, but I didn't think so. Just the win, just the money was there, as he flipped one card over, then the next and the next, revealing, oddly, three aces and two fives.

Fuckme. I did see it.

"Would've beat you anyway," he said, ear-to-ear grin.

I nodded.

"What did you have?" he asked.

"Nothing," I said. "I was bluffing."

"C'mon, Crash, you never bluff. You always have luck on your side."

"Not this hand."

He reached across the table and I knew, *I totally knew* that if he saw my cards, the damage would be irreparable. I couldn't let him do that.

So, stoned as I was, I stood up and pushed the table toward him, scattering the money and pushing my cards quickly into the remaining deck.

Shocking everyone with my actions.

"What the fuck, Crash?"

"Nice play" is all I said, walking away.

"What a sore loser," someone said.

CHAPTER FOURTEEN

GETTING HIGH IN WOODSTOCK

Call me lucky.

After the brutal interview outside Pinky's, I pretty much figured that life as I knew it was over, especially since my father had his publicist essentially break up with me by voice mail. All before eight A.M. the next morning.

By noon, there was a huge buzz on the internet about the Westchester Teen Hero who outed his father as a marijuana smoker on national television, all with links to a YouTube page showing the entire interview, along with additional links to earlier interviews that I had done after 4/21.

By one P.M., there was a traffic jam of reporters in trucks lined up along my street. The heat was most definitely on, and it was immediately back to Newman's house, where Mrs. Newman was not so friendly to me this go-round. This time, there was talk between Mrs. Newman and my mom about my entire family relocating for the short period. But no way was Caroline Prescott going to bow to pressure; she made it clear that I wasn't to go home until she said it was OK, but she also insisted that my mistakes were not going to disrupt her schedule.

When my mom stopped by Newman's to drop off my things, she seemed disappointed in me, not necessarily angry, and I had somehow convinced myself that she was secretly happy about the turn of events, because, let's face it, given their less-than-amicable divorce and the continuing negative feelings over the years, she wasn't about to suddenly develop any deep sympathy for Jacob Crashinsky. And she most definitely did not develop a relationship with or even, to my knowledge, ever talk to Felicia. I guess you don't come to a person's house and eat their turkey if you're fucking their husband. (Sorry, Felicia, my mom has a point, even though it did end up saving my life.)

Christina and some of her friends came over to spend some time with me and Newman and to share a bottle of wine by his pool, and while she called me a total douchebag (which she kept pronouncing "dewich" for some reason), she also said that I looked good on TV, and even though I should have known better—after all, she was there with me when my father gave me very explicit instructions on not talking to the press—she also understood how hard it must be to ignore reporters when they ambush you, which was the way I described the interview to all of my friends who weren't there. Like my mom, Christina was disappointed, but not necessarily angry, and by the end of the night was even affectionate, thanks to a few too many glasses of chardonnay.

Long story short, it looked like we were still on, although I was pretty sure that she was also checking to see whether I was making good on my promise to stay away from weed. Joint after joint came and went in my direction without so much as a single public hit, and I was, to be honest with you, getting tired of the straightness and all.

Back to luck. Having just finished writing the poker chapter, I had to think that maybe Burn was totally right about me being beyond lucky.

To prove my point, consider this: not two days after my interview, the most amazing thing happened, which totally diverted attention from me and Jacob, as in people were all still talking about weed, but instead of talking about me and weed and Jacob and weed, they were talking about the movie that had just opened and was number two at the box office that weekend, and the only reason it was not number one at the box office was that *The Dark Knight* was still kicking ass over virtually every other movie.

The film that was number two, the film that I am referring to was, of course, *Pineapple Express*, which opened big and was about nothing *except* weed. My new hero, Seth Rogen, was all over the late-night shows and stuff, talking about how great weed is, and there was also this TV commentary guy saying that it wasn't right, the public "vilifying Mr. Crashinsky" while at the same time letting Mr. Rogen "extol" the virtues of marijuana.

So thank you, Seth Rogen, wherever you are, even though, tell you the truth, I didn't think *Pineapple Express* was all that. Of course, I was blazed when I saw it, which should have made me the perfect audience.

I had even heard that Seth mentioned my name in one of his interviews and suggested that maybe I should be in the sequel, so thank you again, Seth Rogen. Give my agent a call; I might be available around Christmastime, unless the Sandler people call first.

And even if you don't consider that lucky, consider this: The talk shows decided to take my weed claims seriously, and a couple of them followed up with stories about doctors who were actually recommending weed as a possible alternative to stimulants like Adderall for treatment of ADHD, and suddenly there's this whole big debate where my name is being mentioned, but this time as a spokesperson for kids with ADHD, advocating for alternatives to the traditional medicines, like I was some kind of medical pioneer or something.

And, get this, apparently all that coverage only made the book all the more valuable to my publisher, because Sally kept emailing me, requesting additional chapters.

If not for luck, what were the odds of that happening? For all I know (and again, I suck at math), greater than the odds of pulling a straight flush against a full house, don't you think?

By the time that I picked Christina up for our "excursion," as she called it, I was on day five of no weed (except for the *Pineapple Express* night out, which shouldn't count; well, that and the nature center) and also of avoiding Claudia's "sexts," which meant my impatience was gnawing at me like a splinter that I couldn't remove but could constantly feel, all based on the fact that Christina was going to make good on her promise. As I may have mentioned, I have never been very good at waiting for anything. Part of the ADHD thing, but knowing that didn't make it any easier.

Anyways, seeing as how it was looking like a better and better idea to get out of town for a while, and being as I had the book to work on, she suggested we go to her uncle's cabin in upstate New York, somewhere in the deep woods, about twenty minutes away from Woodstock and about the same distance from Hunter and Belleayre mountains. Christina's uncle and his family rarely used it during the summer months, as they were skiers, which she explained as I turned onto the New York Thruway. We both had cover stories: She was going with friends; I was going away for the weekend with my boys, which my mom actually thought was a good idea under the circumstances.

For insurance, I brought a cooler filled with water bottles containing Kenny's distilled vodka. In my laptop case there was a sizable nugg of "Jacob's Gold." (Yes, I had named it. After all, it seemed like more than a coincidence that a movie in honor of very special pot came out only days after I discovered that very thing in my father's apartment.) Another, smaller nugg was in my glove compartment, and several prerolled joints in a canister in my jeans pocket. I was totally covered.

I should have been in vacation mode. Sitting beside me, with her hair blowing back as she opened the car window, was a very hot girl who looked like an actress and moved like a dancer, who was wearing a slinky shirt that exposed her left shoulder and skinny bra strap and who smelled like flowers. I was driving into the middle of nowhere with this girl to have a total night of passion. So I should have been in vacation mode.

Except I was extremely anxious, not just irritable, but . . . jumpy.

She noticed and asked if I was all right.

So I told her about this unnerving feeling I was getting now that I was all over the news. It had to do with the fact that I was pretty sure that Burn had somehow seen the report; after all, they must have television in the institution where they placed him. I admitted that I had Newman do a check on the internet to find out Burn's exact location, and we found out that he was currently in a psychiatric facility for criminal patients in upstate New York, a few hours from the location that Christina and I were traveling to.

"And you're actually worried about David? Really?"

In my mind, I could practically see him as he was that very minute, in the middle of a summer morning, with all of the rest of us going on with our lives: him in a hospital gown, maybe sedated, looking like he did on 4/21, with his eyes staring inward, pacing the hospital floor. He once told me that he stayed in the city with his sister a few nights the summer before junior year, and that everyone there was rolling on ecstasy, having this relaxed, intimate time, when one of his sister's friends curls up next to him and tells him that she's all into tigers, that she wanted to be an animal trainer, and that he reminded her of one of them. When he asked what she meant, she said that she didn't think that he could ever be tamed, not really. So now I pictured Burn reaching out from whatever cage he was in and telling me *I am as dangerous as you think. And, one day, there will be no bars between us and your luck will run out and I will devour you.* I hear all this in my mind, and it's coming to me in Burn's voice, loud and clear. I also know that I am not smart enough to deal with Burn a second time.

"Aren't you?" I asked.

"Not really. After all he *is* locked away, and I'm sure there's adequate security," she said, confidently.

"Yeah, but what if they don't understand how brilliant he really is? Can they possibly know for sure?"

"Did you ever think of contacting him?" she asked casually, as I followed the GPS, turning off the highway onto Route 28.

"Are you fucking nuts?" I almost yelled. "Or did you simply forget that this guy came within a hair of killing us all?"

"Pishposh," she said, one of those expressions she used from time to time, in her actressy voice. "And could you please refrain from cursing when we're alone? I find it offensive."

"OK, he had practically the whole school wired with explosives. He left a list of people, and both of our names were on it. And now we're on our way to your uncle's place in the middle of the woods. And somehow I have this feeling that David Burnett knows we're together. Maybe from Franklin; I heard he keeps in touch with Franklin. Maybe he watches the news and sees me on it, and he calls or emails or whatever you can do from wherever he is. So pishposh you."

"Steven, you can't use pishposh that way," she scolded. "I was using it to denote sarcasm, or rather to denote that you were overstating the obvious. Clearly, I was teasing you when I asked if you thought of contacting him, and yet you failed to appreciate how flippant I was, because you seem to be too wrapped up in this sudden paranoia over David's very unanticipated and unlikely release."

"Meaning?" Me, not getting her point.

"I was being playful," she said, as she placed her hand

on my thigh and stretched her fingers upward, but not quite touching me.

"Pishposh," I answered. "Pish FUCKING posh." This, as my hand crept up her skirt thing until it touched too high and she slapped it away.

"Yeah, pish fucking posh, Crash." She laughed, and I felt that I finally got her down to my level. After all, she almost never cursed, and she certainly had never called me Crash before. Plus she was displaying genuine laughter, and her real laughter was amazingly musical and infectious. So now I had a pocketful of Jacob's Gold and Christina cursing and calling me Crash and making jokes and laughing. Good times. I reached into my pocket and pulled out the canister of prerolled joints, flicking one directly into my mouth and lighting up.

"What are you doing?" All the casualness drained from her voice in an instant.

"What? You promised." I took my first hit.

"Not now, Steven, and not while you are driving," she barked. "Put that away."

"We had a deal." I did not fail to notice that she returned to my actual name. I took another hit.

"A deal that I would smoke when we got to my uncle's. Not while we're driving." Sounding again like a mom and not a kid.

One last deep hit and I snubbed it and leaned back, and soon we were driving down Tinker Street, the main road in Woodstock. As I stared out the window, there was nothing particularly special about this town; normal people dressed in jeans and khakis walking around like it was some Westchester village with clothing shops and restaurants.

Only as I slowed to turn into the municipal parking lot, Jacob's Gold hit me full on, and suddenly the town appeared more colorful than I previously recognized, mountains surrounding us and vibrant flowers dotting the side street, decaying art sculptures along the back of a building where a heavy woman in a crinkled blue dress was lifting paintings out of an old VW van that was not only old, it was rusted-out old and painted in psychedelic colors and for me it was like peering into the past. And in perfect synchronicity, like *Dark Side of the Moon/The Wizard of Oz* synchronicity, the Grateful Dead channel saw fit to broadcast "Saint Stephen," maybe the Dead's trippiest song (this according to Newman, who was into the Dead more than any other kid my age).

"Steven." Her voice from a distance. I had almost forgotten she was there. "Do you want me to try it or not?"

Me thinking, they always come around, almost laughing a genuine laugh, I relight the joint and pass it to her. I am stardust. I am golden.

"You are what?" said Christina with a practiced inhale (more experienced than she let on), apparently pointing out that I had been talking out loud and not knowing it. I made a mental note to be more careful.

So we got lit together, listening to a few Dead songs, before getting out of the car. And because even walking was no longer automatic, we headed into the first restaurant we passed.

So lunch was a pretty incredible lunch experience, with her giggling at practically everything I said and mimicking the waitress, like almost exactly duplicating her every mannerism, Christina was *that* good as an actress, and I started thinking about how the rest of the trip was going to go, with me and Christina getting along so well and how was I going to get a refill of Jacob's stuff, being as he had stopped talking to me, which of course made me think about Felicia, and I was instantly saddened by the thought that she wasn't talking to me either.

Except that couldn't last, could it? I was still the guy's son.

"Steven."

"Yeah?"

"The check," Christina said, going through her purse for some cash. I told her, no way, your cash is no good here, I had it, and produced my debit card, dropping it onto the bill.

And the waitress picked it up and came back.

"Your card has been declined."

I was suddenly not so stoned anymore. "Can't be," I said.

"I tried it twice. No go."

There should have been like three hundred on the card.

I anted up the cash, which pretty much tapped me out. I anticipated getting more from the ATM. We found one a few blocks away. And I tried twice to withdraw a hundred and both times it said "insufficient funds." I checked the balance and it was down to like five dollars, which meant that my account, which would replenish every Sunday, apparently had not been replenished.

Or rather Jacob forgot to put the funds in, as was our deal from the beginning of the summer. Me writing, and him dropping two hundred a week into the account as my spending money. Jacob, so purposeful in everything he did, would not have forgotten.

Now I was faced with a dilemma. Call him and pretend like everything is fine and find out what's going on, or tell him about my card being tapped out.

In the meantime, we needed to go shopping for food and other things to bring with us to the cabin, and Christina said that she could cover whatever we would buy. So while she bought supplies, I stayed in the car, sitting in the parking lot, because Christina assured me that once we left town there would be no way to get a phone signal, as we were going deeper into the Catskill Forest.

And I reluctantly called him.

"Hi Maria," I said casually to his assistant. "Can I speak to my dad?"

"Hold on," she answered curtly. Something was up, because she was usually so bubbly and inquisitive, like "Steven, how's your summer?" or "How are your sisters?" or whatever. I tried not to read too much into it, remembering that I was still high, even though I no longer felt so high at the moment.

"Hello, Steefin."

It was Her. My mind raced; my heart pounded. Act normal. She was away last week, maybe she knew nothing. Or if she did, it had to have blown over by now. Except she called me Steefin, not Cresh, which meant that something was up. Except she did that sometimes too. But always when she was being serious.

"Hi, Felicia. How was your trip?" I asked, trying to be as casual as possible.

"Complitly rueened, if you vont to know."

"Sorry," I said, thinking maybe she had other things on her mind besides my interview, and maybe the way she sounded had nothing to do with me at all. Maybe she knew what I knew, that the whole thing was blown totally out of proportion.

"You shoot be," she responded angrily. "Do you know vot ve are dealing veet because of vot you said on television?"

"I was set up. Totally ambushed." Me, quickly taking the defensive. Of course, I had no idea what they could be dealing with.

"How *coot you*, Steefin? How coot you betray my confeedince like that? I trusted you."

OK, I thought, so it was out in the open. So let's get past it, I remember thinking, let's move on. Except, I couldn't think of anything to say, so there was silence instead and then she said:

"I thought you were better than that."

Then she was gone and Jacob was on the phone, and I couldn't even tell you what he was saying, because he was rambling on about not calling him again, and all the time he was talking, all I could think of was what his wife had just said to me.

No question. We were done. Seriously, every word echoed into my still-stoned brain and I heard it over and over again and there wasn't even a trace of her usual accent in the words.

"I thought you were better than that." With almost no accent at all.

Like she was the one who made the mistake, not me. Only her mistake was in believing in me, and now she found out that I was not the person she thought I was.

Bear in mind that in my past I had heard some pretty vile things directed toward me from teachers, and prior to 4/21, my guidance counselor wasn't exactly a huge fan, and sometimes other kids' parents used me as an example of someone their kids shouldn't be like. And all that time, throughout high school, none of that mattered, because there was one single adult who knew better. Only now that one single adult who knew better was finally admitting that she was wrong, which made everyone else right.

If it had been anyone else on the other end of the phone, I would have come up with any number of excuses. But now I racked my brain for a way to rationalize what I said during the interview, how I divulged a secret that she shared with me, which she did only because she loved me and didn't want to see me hurt by the man who she made her life with. She trusted me, and I stabbed her in the back.

I was suddenly overwhelmed with remorse.

Remorse, when you are stoned, is not something that you want to feel, trust me on this.

But that didn't stop me from screaming at her husband, who was a douchebag anyways and who never shut the fuck up for a guy who didn't want to say anything to me.

My turn.

"We had a deal. It's my money, and I need you to put it into my account now."

"Grow up, Steven." I detected a distinct pleasure in his voice.

"If you don't put it into my account, I will stop writing."

"Do what you have to do."

"What I have to do is get my money since I earned it and you are just holding it for me as my manager. You know what? You're fired." This is actually, word for word, what I told my own father, like who the fuck was I?

"Fine. I resign." He laughed that laugh-thing he did, and I could tell he was gloating. "Do me one more favor," he said before hanging up on me. "Lose my number."

This is what my father actually told me.

And still the words of my stepmother echoed more sharply: *I thought you were better than that.*

When Christina returned from the store, she could not help but notice that I was visibly shaken.

"What did he say?" she asked.

"It's not what he said," I told her. I was about to explain, but really, there was nothing to explain. I would get over it, I thought. Eventually. Maybe.

But for now, the war was not over. I was not going to let Jacob win. After all, I had a weapon of last resort in my never-ending battle with him, one that I hadn't used in a long time.

My next call would not be wasted.

"Mom? Dad cut me off. I'm stuck upstate without any money."

CHAPTER FIFTEEN

CABIN FEVER, OR, CHRISTINA AND THE REALLY, REALLY DARK NIGHT

A word or two about my mom.

Caroline Prescott Crashinsky, now back to just Caroline Prescott after the divorce, as I mentioned before, puts up with a lot of shit, but if you back her up against the corner, she too has tiger in her and is absolutely capable of pouncing, and, if necessary, going in for the kill.

She is funny. Like when some relative told her that she might be a distant blood relative to George Bush, she threatened to have her blood removed.

She has always been considered by my friends to be a milf, skinny and athletic (she never misses a spin class and now has her own full gym setup in the basement, which she uses every day before the rest of us are up, greeting us at breakfast covered in sweat), and even at like forty-five, she looks like a high school kid.

She never gets sick. Maybe once she was too tired to make dinner, but the next day she was back to full speed.

She will be your most loyal supporter, and if she likes you, she will never say anything bad about you, even though she knows you're not perfect. Not only that, she will defend you relentlessly when others are on your case. I have seen her react to her own friends when these women started talking behind each other's backs. Well, don't do that in front of my mom, because she will come after you and then cut you to the bone. Then cut you off.

She has lost a number of friends that way. All seemingly without regret.

Also, fuck with her kids, whether you're a teacher, a coach, or someone at work (for Lindsey, not me, as I never had an actual job), and Caroline Prescott will come to their defense like a true warrior. For example, whenever a teacher was not giving me the benefit of the doubt, I would mention to Caroline that I wasn't getting the benefits of my special ed program, and she would immediately be on the phone with the guidance counselor or even the principal if necessary, and right away I would have the opportunity to make up a test, rewrite a paper, or get out of some kind of trouble.

She was either supertough to begin with, or supertough as a result of dealing for like fifteen years with a man who was like a military general, even to her. She took it most of the time, but when she had enough, even Jacob would run for the hills. And then, after she kicked Jacob out, there was no turning back for him, no second chances, no room for further discussion, and she never let on for even a second that she was hurt or anything. I once heard her on the phone saying to someone "you just live through it and move on . . ."

This seemed to be her philosophy about everything, which apparently got her through the days when we were sick and she was alone, or we were in trouble at school and she was alone, or one of us had soccer and the other had basketball at the same time and she had to be in two places at once and she was alone, or she had to deal with urgent calls from a teacher which resulted in morning meetings with the principal and she was alone.

And in spite of that, she would always ask how we were doing and always be concerned that we were not doing great, even Lindsey, who pretty much never had an issue with anything.

So on the rare occasion that she went into a rage, sometimes for no apparent reason, all three of us kids knew to totally back off and give her space.

Point is, even though I have (had?) a special relationship

with my father's second wife, his first wife is my true hero.

That said, I'm not going to lie to you, I've totally learned how to play her. That is what I do and she knows it, but it doesn't matter, because in the end, she can't deny me anything. There are certain rules that I follow: Say, if I'm too drunk or stoned, I will stay out so as to avoid the possibility of being caught by her, or wait until I know she's asleep (sorry, Mom, but you are pretty clueless). And I call her a lot, just to tell her where I am, even though like 90 percent of the time I totally lie about it. As in Mom, I'm out playing basketball, when I'm actually rolling at a concert, you know the drill. Again, sorry, Mom.

Oh yeah, and I have never, not ever, let on that I have (had) a close relationship with my father's new wife. Mostly, I tell my mom that Felicia is OK or some kind of easy compliment. This is because I truly believe that if she found out how much I confided in Felicia, she would be heartbroken, so I have been supercareful about this. Jamie does the same thing, I have noticed, even though we have never talked about it.

Which brings me to the point of getting my mom to go after my father now:

They have an arrangement. Jacob takes care of all of our financial needs; she does everything else. When he fails in this regard, she is immediately on the phone with him.

So I get off the phone with her, comforted by the fact that Caroline Prescott would restore order in the galaxy and by the next morning, my bank account would be properly replenished. She just about said as much during our brief conversation, which ended with her usual "Stay safe, Steven, stay smart." And then always adding an emphatic *"please"* at the end, which was her way of telling me that she loved me but didn't completely trust me.

So I should have been completely relaxed, totally psyched

for the ultimate summer vacay, me and my "girlfriend," alone in a cabin in the woods, no one to possibly get to us, and full confidence in Christina since she already delivered on the first promise she made to me, as in having gotten high with me and totally loosened up. Now, all I had to do was to concentrate on how to get promise number two accomplished.

Problem was, I could not get Felicia's voice out of my head, playing like a skipping CD. Click, click click, I thought you were better than that. I thought you were better than that. I thought you were better than that . . . which was turning into a total cockblocker for me.

Christina's uncle's "cabin" was not a cabin at all, but a multi-level redwood house in the woods with a deck on the upper level that wrapped around all sides and had multiple stairs leading up the front and the back. To get to the house we had to turn off the winding mountain road, down a gravel road, past two other houses on the left, nothing but woods on the right, until we stopped at the end, number 1221, with a crooked sign that said "Haines." I looked past the house to the sloping lawn in the back that separated the property from the forest with a row of pine trees, and I breathed in the mountain air while Christina fumbled with the lawn ornaments that led up the path until she found the one that was, in reality, a key holder.

We entered the lower level, which smelled of firewood and mildew (oddly like my Aunt Randi's one-time boyfriend), past the semicircular couch that faced a giant flat-screen TV and a fireplace at the same time, up the stairs to the open living room area, which had a superhigh ceiling and a series of floor-to-ceiling windows that opened out to the deck in the back. To the right, the bedroom.

Christina led the way into the rustic room that looked fit for a cowboy, more floor-to-ceiling sliding glass doors. I dropped my bag onto the bed, unlocked one of the sliders, and stepped out to the deck, where there was this ginormous hot tub, and I heard Evan's voice in the back of my head saying "Sweeeeeet . . ."

I realized that I was still mostly high but coming down and needing another hit of Jacob's Gold. Then I heard the voice again: *I thought you were better than that.*

Fuckme.

My cell had a "Searching for Service" warning, then an X. At least no one could get to me now.

Down and up a few times with the other packages, and back in the master bedroom, I noticed the pictures on the wall, I assumed they were her uncle and his family. Gray-bearded guy with a tough-looking wife and two young girls who looked like their mom. One set of pictures with them skiing. Another set of the entire family on horseback. Another that must've been taken in the Caribbean, aqua-blue water, all four in bathing suits. If I stared long enough, I could practically hear their voices echoing in the house, the little girls in snow-crusted wool caps, squealing for hot chocolate as their father yanked off their ski boots one by one. There was never any happiness like that in my family. Vacations made life even more miserable, with Jacob constantly watching me, waiting to criticize everything I did, and my mom yelling at him, and my sisters watching Jacob and me in horror and total annoyance. No wonder I sucked at skiing.

"Are you OK?" Christina asked, keeping her distance.

"I'm thinking maybe we should light up again," I said, trying to cover, realizing why I was there in the first place. Newman's voice was the next sound to echo through my mind with a very clear *snap out of it, Crash*, which I had every intention of doing.

"Really?" She sounded disappointed. "I thought we'd wait on that. Until later tonight. In the meantime, I have a surprise . . ."

She left the room with me wondering what kind of surprise she had in mind.

I wandered out onto the deck. Supernice day, not a cloud in the sky. The air was crisp and a little cool. First breeze of fall. It hit me that in a few short weeks I would be in college, we would all be in college. And I'd be far from my closest friends and far from the girl who was with me now. It also hit me that no way was I going to be able to finish the book in time, even though I brought my laptop with me. This thought only served to increase my anxiety level. I twiddled with the canister in my pocket, unscrewed the lid, and inhaled the sweet weed smell of Jacob's Gold.

It did not, as I expected it to, relax me at all.

Then Christina returned, all happy, with a bottle of champagne and two glasses. She popped open the bottle and we sat on the deck chairs next to each other, me with my glass, Christina with hers. Cheers.

"If it helps at all, you should know that it isn't you," she said. OK, I have already admitted that there were times when I wasn't exactly sure what she was ever talking about. So this was nothing new. Except, this time, I *really* had no clue at all.

"*What* isn't me?" I had to ask, remembering Mrs. Barbash telling us all in biology class that there are no stupid questions. And then yelling at me when I asked a question that she thought was stupid. I have been careful ever since.

"Your father is an asshole, Steven," she laughed. "I just had to say it."

This caused me to laugh out loud. Because here she was, one of the smartest girls in my school, and she was just figuring out what seemed to me to be the most obvious thing in the universe.

"Yeah, he is" is all I said, downing the champagne and watching her do the same. And watching her, it hit me.

How could I not have noticed it before?

She was nervous.

Visibly uncomfortable.

Her hand had a slight tremor when she placed the empty glass on the small table between us. And maybe when she said that it wasn't me, she was really referring to the fact that I wasn't really the agitated one. Maybe I was picking up the jitteriness from her, as I sometimes did from other kids. I almost always picked it up from Burn whenever we were in the same room together, especially whenever he showed up at our lunch table or I sat next to him in a class. There were other kids who left me feeling that way, mostly after I smoked megadoses of weed. I picked up on other people's energies all the time. It was Felicia who first pointed that out to me; one of my unusual talents, she said.

I had gotten used to that feeling by now and sometimes forgot I did it. Seeing as Christina was so nervous, and knowing what I know, I regained control of the situation, grabbed the bottle, and poured us both another glass. Problem easily solved thanks to Don Perignon.

"Steven, he treats you like dirt, like you're a failure, which you're not. It's truly embarrassing, and I'm sorry for you." She continued, "If you want to know the truth, it makes me really angry. I know I have no right to be, but I don't like the way he talks to you at all."

"Well, I apparently got him back, didn't I?" I said, downing my second glass. My confidence was returning with every gulp.

"You definitely did." She laughed back and downed her glass. Who knew Christina was going to be so much fun? I repoured for both of us.

"I have another bottle of Dom," she said. And now I burst out laughing, because I had no fucking clue that it was Dom with an "m" all this time. But there it was on the bottle, like who changed it and didn't send me the text?

"What are you laughing at?" she asked.

"Just . . . this is nice."

Now I started thinking about exactly how I was going to close this deal. I mean, we both knew what we were there for, and we were apparently only a few drinks away from homerunsville. I settled into the chair, more comfortably. The mountain air was refreshing and revitalizing; no, beyond that, it was totally motherfucking relaxing.

More importantly, Felicia's voice and her accusation were settling somewhere in the recesses of my brain, and the echo wasn't as overwhelming as it was earlier. Thank you, *Dom* Pérignon, wherever you are.

"Steven, I know it's not my business, but I just can't stand by and say nothing when someone I care about is getting hurt like he hurts you."

OK, now I'm starting to feel like we should be moving on from this conversation, because honestly, it *is* a bit of a sore spot, my lack of a relationship with Jacob, and now I'm wondering is she trying to get me to open up or something. Because that's not going to happen. And if she keeps going, it's only going to piss me off and ruin everything. She, of course, doesn't know this, as she has no idea how short my fuse can be about certain things.

"What makes him think he's better than everyone else?"

"I don't know." I took another sip.

"And what's up with that wife of his? I know you are like BFFs with her, but if you ask me, she's more than a little strange."

This stopped me cold. "What do you mean?"

"She's so . . . I don't know . . . calculating," Christina shot back. "If you ask me, she's sneaky."

This came as a shock. No one to my knowledge had ever said a bad word about Felicia. I was caught between total loyalty, as in ready for battle over my stepmother's honor, and . . . curiosity. "In what way?" I asked.

"I just get the sense that she doesn't really belong with your father. Maybe it's, like, a career move for her, or something like that. I've heard about these women who come over from eastern Europe. . . ."

"That's it? That's all you got?" I snorted, defensively. "That she's from eastern Europe and she seems sneaky to you? She speaks like five languages, grew up in a culture that values a certain standard of excellence that we as Americans don't have, like etiquette and posture and stuff, and she studied music and art, plays Beethoven and jazz on the piano, and knows more about U.S. history than most of our high school teachers and holds her own in a business of cutthroat men twice her age and you think she's sneaky because she's different from the people you know." OK, I was back to getting defensive out of loyalty, so much so that I had just delivered the exact same speech that I heard Felicia once give to Lindsey when Lindsey asked her why she always had to look perfect.

"Steven, I knew you were going to react badly. I'm sorry I brought it up. It's just . . . I think you trust her too much." Neither of us were drinking during this part of our conversation, and it got me thinking that trusting Felicia wasn't the problem, because whenever I trusted her, it always worked out well for me. *She* was the one who trusted me and got betrayed, and didn't she tell me, back before I visited Roxanne in the hospital, that the reason she tried to commit suicide was because someone betrayed her, someone she trusted?

Another mountain breeze brought me back. Eyes on the prize, Crash, eyes on the prize. And with my attention back on Christina, it hit me:

How could I not have noticed it before?

She was jealous of my relationship with Felicia. She was so into me that it bothered her that I had feelings for my stepmom. Maybe I was too obvious about it when Christina was at my father's apartment. Still, I wasn't going to sell out my stepmother for any reason, not after everything she had done for me.

I was better than that.

Except I did not feel compelled to have my entire night ruined just to prove the point at that particular moment. As in, I almost called Christina on it, and I almost told her my impression of her being jealous and all, but I decided against it and instead totally caught her off guard by saying this:

"Christina, here we are, totally and completely cut off from the world, enjoying time together in a perfect setting on a perfect day. Why are we talking about them? Why aren't we talking about us?"

She laughed. "Give you this, Crashinsky, you can be so smoooooth sometimes."

She left her chair and joined me in mine. As she stood, I could see that she was tipsy. She almost dropped her champagne glass, and I quickly caught it in one hand and placed it on the table next to my glass, both empty.

"See?" she said, climbing closer. "Smoooooth."

I glanced at the bottle. It was almost empty, maybe enough for one more glass. Guess who would be drinking the rest of that? Call me evil if you want, but you always have to have a plan.

She was getting very comfortable on my lap now, feeling very warm, and staring down at me with drunken eyes and moist lips. I most definitely did not want to remind her that only a week before she was giving me such a hard time about only hooking up when I was either drunk or stoned. Not a good time to win that argument.

I almost laughed again. Instead, I kissed her gently, pulled back, took a fake swig of the bottle, and handed it to her to let her down the rest. Insurance.

Now she was the aggressor, kissing me. Very, very deeply,

and I could taste the cold champagne and the warmth of her mouth at the same time. I wished that she had let me light up for this occasion and itched for a hit, but was determined not to let my mind wander any more than it already was.

Now her body was pressed really, really close to mine, and I was, tell you the truth, too ready.

And then she whispered to me:

"You should know. This is my first time."

This I found incredible to believe. I mean, she had been in plays in the city, had flown out to Hollywood a bunch of times on auditions, hung with actors, spent a summer in Barcelona, had other boyfriends, even college boyfriends. She was, as girls go, pretty popular and definitely no prude, plus amazingly hot. And in all this time no one had actually tapped her before? I confess that I actually thought that Burn did back in sophomore year, although I found out after the Massachusetts incident that he didn't. Still, there were so many opportunities for a girl like Christina that I found this information unfathomable.

Even more incredible than the fact that she hadn't done it before was the fact that she actually chose me as her first. She had to know that I was not really boyfriend material, not someone who, as a girl, you would want to tell your *Sex and the City* friends about later in life. I was the guy who nailed you *after* you had your first experience with Mr. Real Boyfriend, maybe after that relationship went south, maybe because he dumped you and you needed a rebound thing. I was the horse you got back on after falling off with someone else.

So the pressure was on. I tried to be all casual about it, but I let slip out the following:

"No way."

It definitely ruined the mood, because now instead of a mutual drunken exploration, we were suddenly talking about it, me asking questions, her answering, no, no, no, not that one, me asking exactly how far she went before, and her answering well, yeah, this, but not that, and me asking was she sure about us doing it, and she said that it was something she had thought about for a long time and it had to be me, not just because I saved her life in Massachusetts and again on 4/21, and no she didn't expect that we would necessarily be together for the rest of our lives, but despite my flaws, there was something special about me, about us, and she was ready for it to be us. And all I could think of at the moment was David Burnett sitting in a cell somewhere, not approving one bit.

And I tried making out with her again, but it felt drastically different. I didn't know if she recognized it too, but we continued kissing, and this time my hands were exploring, because I wasn't going to let on that something had changed.

And when my hands started moving down her body, she stopped and said that she didn't want to do anything outside, not where someone could be watching, even though there were no other houses or people anywhere near where we were, and no possibility of being seen by anyone.

So she got up and I followed her into the bedroom, her leading me by the hand.

And when she got there, she made me sit on the bed and she took her iPhone out and set it into her uncle's music player, so we had music, not the usual techno stuff that I like, but, like, guitar music and some folk singer, and it seemed like she made a special playlist of songs that must have been important to her (I wondered what the title of the playlist was—songs to get your cherry popped by or something).

With the music going, she stepped between my open legs and slipped out of her dress and was, surprise, wearing absolutely nothing underneath. She was incredible to look at, which I already partially knew, having seen her in a bikini a bunch of times. Still, naked is naked, and you never know exactly what you're going to get until you see everything, and while her body was flawless, she looked *sooo* naked and pale standing in front of me that there was an awkward moment where I didn't know exactly what to do.

Until she took my hand again and moved it onto her body. And since she had this thing pretty much all planned out the way she wanted, I didn't think I should do anything that would interfere with her plans.

And then we were both naked and then she turned all business. Did I have condoms, which I did, but I explained that I don't like them, and she said "pishposh," which seemed to mean put one on if you're going near me. So I got a pack out of my suitcase.

And sure I was all excited, as in full and complete attention, but then we were doing everything so mechanically, as if she had to make sure to get everything in this first time, and I felt kind of like I was the girl, as in, was she just using me to get it over with?

This thought, or maybe the champagne, made it difficult for me to finish, so we were going at it for a long time, and when she was done, she actually asked about me, seemingly concerned, and I told her that the bag was hurting. So she let me take it off and then used other methods on me, but nothing was happening so I started thinking about different things to keep me in the moment, and then during the actual moment of impact, I wasn't thinking about her at all.

Instead I couldn't help myself, someone else seemed to invade my mind and wouldn't leave, and soon that other person was the only one I could think about and . . . get this:

It was Claudia.

"Was it OK for you?" Christina asked me.

And, of course, I said it was great, even though it was kind of weird, and she cuddled with me and started to play again, trying to restart, but I was done for the moment, as in I was hurting, but wouldn't, couldn't admit it to her. She finally gave up and draped herself in a sheet and went off to the bathroom, leaving me alone to think about why I couldn't stop thinking about Claudia.

Maybe it was because what I really wanted was a slut, because a slut is up for anything, and even though Christina seemed like she *could* get into it . . . *eventually*, she was not there yet, not on my level, as I too was, and remain, a manwhore (just calling it as it is).

Christina emerged from the bathroom in her bathing suit and announced that it was hot tub time, and I found my suit and got another bottle of champagne. So far, no blinding headache, which I almost always got from champagne, so, as always, I had to continue to tempt fate, opening the second bottle and taking a selfish gulp.

We settled into the tub and passed the bottle between us. The water was at first boilingly hot and I felt like I was being cooked alive, but then as I got used to it, it felt good. She seemed happy, so I asked her if she was and she said, "Relieved." And I asked her what she meant, and she explained that she had put too much pressure on herself about it, so she was glad it was over and she didn't think it was great for me, but promised, "I'll do better next time."

And we continued to drink until the second bottle was done, and while I'm used to drinking big-time and handling my alcohol, the combination of champagne and steam got me to a point of total zombiness. Yet it didn't seem to affect her at all.

I wanted to get out, but couldn't admit it, so I fell deeper into a comalike state and she started getting frisky again and I started feeling sick.

I crawled out and made my way to a deck chair, where I passed out.

* * *

When I woke up, it was pitch-black out, beyond the darkness of summer camp, no lights from anywhere all, except for this magnificently starry sky. For a moment I forgot where I was, and when it hit me, I was more than a little spooked by the extreme darkness. Plus I was cold, not just cold, but freezing, as the temperature had dropped and I was still in my wet bathing suit. I was, in fact, shivering uncontrollably.

I stumbled back into the bedroom and called out for Christina. No answer.

Freaky.

"Christina?"

I glanced at the clock radio. 11:25. How long had I been out? I climbed into a pair of jeans and a T-shirt and went from room to room, getting increasingly nervous. Could she somehow still be in the hot tub? What if she had drowned?

I was saved from my panic by the sound of her voice. She had apparently snuck down to the lower level, settled comfortably into the modular couch, and was playing with my MacBook, all curled up, eating frozen pizza, occasionally looking up at the huge TV, where some movie was playing.

"Want some?" offering me a slice.

And, that's when I noticed what she was doing.

From across the room I assumed that she was on Facebook or IMing her friends, or going on whatever websites girls go onto (as opposed to me and my friends who are all into all of those free porn sites).

She was doing none of those things.

Instead, she was reading one of the chapters from my book. I noticed my writing on the screen and quickly grabbed the computer away from her.

"What the fuck?" I practically screamed at her. Not only had she gotten into the files that contained the chapters about

McAllister and Meadows, stuff she mostly already knew about, but what was worse, she was reading one of the present-day chapters, the one titled "Another Night of Partying with Jungle Juice and Weed" which was about the party at Kelly's earlier this summer. Her reading any of this was a major violation as far as I was concerned.

"I thought you said I could read it," she said defensively.

"That's a lie!" is what I shouted, although I may have kind of told her I would let her read some of it when she asked when we were driving up. But even if I did, I meant the few chapters that I already sent to Sally.

"OK, maybe I should have asked," she responded. "But you were passed out and I couldn't wake you, and seeing as you said it was OK . . . I didn't know that you were writing about us now, this summer." Which made me feel even more exposed.

"My agent," I started. "Sally . . . wanted my current impressions, after everything went down, not just the events leading up to 4/21. So there are some chapters that deal with the time after, some of those chapters aren't chapters yet, just segments."

"You mean like the interview," she responded, and I thought fuckme, how much did she actually read. Problem being that some of these segments not only contained my notes for the main part of book but also detailed my trips to the Westchester Mall with Claudia, stealing my father's weed, and worse, way worse than that, was the fact that almost every entry talked about Christina, at length.

"Like the interview," I repeated. "These segments aren't ready for anyone. I don't even know if I would send any of them to Sally."

"Well, you should. It's all really good, Steven."

"How much did you read?" I demanded, still on fire with anger, but, not gonna lie, besides being really pissed off and feeling violated that she had seen what I considered to be my secret stuff which also contained plenty of stuff about her, I kind of liked the idea that she liked what she read. So I was in conflict mode, as in, do I stay mad or let it go so I could find out more?

"How much?" I repeated.

"Whatever I could open," she said. "The chapters are all different files, so I didn't know where to start, really." Which seemed like an honest answer, but which got me nowhere in terms of whether or not she had seen stuff about her. I didn't exactly know how to ask.

"Like?"

"Like how Burn saved you from going to military school."

"And?"

"Your visit with Roxanne. That was really sad and actually hilarious, at the same time."

"And?"

"And OK, I get now why you are so devoted to Felicia and how she's been there for you. So I apologize for what I said about her before." She seemed sincere, but I sensed that she was being purposely evasive.

"And?"

"And, OK, I did look at some of the stuff with my name in it, I mean, you can't blame me. I couldn't help but notice that you have this section called 'Christina and the Dark Night,' so I had to . . ."

I panicked, and tried to concentrate on the section that was displayed on my laptop screen, and it instantly took me back to the moment we were driving to the movie theater. As she talked, I scrolled down and reread what I had written, and from what I could tell, this part wasn't so bad if she read it. It seemed mostly complimentary to her, so it looked OK.

Also, as I read about my reaction to Claudia calling me constantly, I wondered whether she knew about the sex part, as in head from Claudia. Christina, like everyone in the entire universe, had seen the picture with me and her and the blunt, so it shouldn't have been a surprise. Except she made me swear that I hadn't had sex with Claudia, sex of any sort, and I may have stretched that particular interpretation a bit.

Anyways, I probably didn't have anything to worry about, seeing as how she didn't bring it up and instead kept apologizing to me, and, in a total Crash move, she even tried to convince me that she was actually doing *me* a favor, that she had always known, even back in middle school, that I had this great potential that I wasn't using, which the book clearly showed, and that the summer stuff was so good in her mind, at least from what she read, that it had to somehow be included in the actual book and she even went so far as to insist that I send an email to Sally and attach the segments, so that Sally would get them all at once and could see for herself.

She got me so psyched about it that I followed her instructions. And as soon as I hit send, I got back a confirming email from Sally, saying that she would read them and get back to me. It was after midnight. Did that woman ever stop working? Probably not, as she was one of my father's people, and they all seemed like they worked 24/7 with their BlackBerrys and iPhones attached to them, buzzing at whatever hours of the day and night.

In the meantime, I was still shivering from being cold, so I draped a blanket over my shoulders and followed Christina up the stairs and into the kitchen, carrying the remainder of the pizza, which I practically inhaled, though it seemed to do nothing for my appetite. In addition, I still felt half frozen, and for some reason not thawing out.

She made some more food, and I borrowed one of her uncle's sweatshirts from the closet. She looked at me like it might not be such a great idea, but didn't say anything.

We ate the rest of the stuff we bought and I was feeling better. And then we went back to the family room and had a follow-up, this time on the couch, and still she was more bossy than into it, or so it seemed to me. It was better but not brag-worthy. And we were both pretty gone afterward, lying across each other on the couch, which I thought would be a good time for—you guessed it—weed.

So I reached over to the pouch containing the second stash of Jacob's Gold along with one of my favorite glass pipes and lit up without asking, no point in having to argue if she said no. But she didn't complain, she even took a hit, although it didn't look like she was doing much inhaling, and I ended up finishing the bowl and packing another. Then I lay back down and asked her to tell me about her thing with Burn during sophomore year. I hardly saw Burn during sophomore year, so I was thinking, if Christina could cover sophomore year, that would help me to fill in the gap.

Thanks to Jacob's Gold, I was able to close my eyes as she talked and could totally visualize her version of the story, picturing her and him in chemistry with Ms. Reynolds, the superdyke teacher with arms like a wrestler and a face that was almost but not quite manly and a smell like salt-and-vinegar potato chips.

So there she is, the second day of sophomore year (I am picturing her in one of those sundresses, which she wears a lot), when Burn announces to the class that he's going to marry her. Thing is, up to that point, she had never interacted with him before. She only knew him as the boy who cried during her performance in *West Side Story*, and then as April's boyfriend, and then as a boy who was asking about her a lot during freshman year. So she didn't even know that he was in her class, but then here was Reynolds taking attendance, and when Ms. Reynolds gets to Burn's name, he yells "PRESENT" at the top of his lungs (I guess he was back to being Up on the scale of Up and Down), and then Burn proceeds to volunteer that in ten years' time, on this date, as in September 6, he would be getting married, and he officially wanted to invite the rest of the class to his wedding, which of course would be with Christina Haines, and please RSVP by the end of class to reserve a seat at the reception.

So of course Christina puts her head down, hand over her eyes all embarrassed, not thinking it was cute at all, but not thinking it was all that strange coming from Burn, because, among other things, Burn was also known by then for these insane outbursts, which made him kind of famous for being "so random," which at the time was an expression girls used for virtually everything, except in Burn's case it was actually totally and completely true.

So she is about to leave Ms. Reynolds's class, sneak out, knowing in her bones that Burn is going to try to talk to her and she skulks toward the back exit, but he beats her to the door and, with an open notebook, starts to ask every kid in the class, well, are you coming to the wedding or not, and will you be having the fish or the prime rib, and most kids laugh but then he gets to Christina and she looks at him dead on and says, "David Burnett, I don't think this is funny."

And he says, "It's our destiny, Christina," and she says, "it's not *my* destiny," and he says, "well it *is* mine."

And now she is arguing with him, and this goes on until everyone else is gone and they are both late for their next class, and she tells him again that it can't be destiny for only one person, not both, it's not physically possible, and he says this, he says, "I know physics, Christina, and it *is* possible that something can be in two places at the same time. Consider quantum mechanics. And by the way, nothing is actually random."

So next class is Spanish, and guess who's in her class again.

Sure enough there might actually be something to this destiny thing, because he, Burn, sits right behind her; both of them are late. Señorita Sanchez calls attendance, and guess what, there's Burn again, announcing to another class that there will be a wedding in ten years' time, September 6, who wants to come, and do they want the chicken or the steak, and he whispers to Christina, who is already totally fed up with him:

"Destiny."

So she flees, and then next class is American history, and guess who's in her class again? Yep, and the wedding thing for the third time. Only this time it's the grilled salmon or the rack of lamb.

Me, I didn't see any of this, and didn't really see much of either of them in tenth grade at all. I was busy with my boys, mostly.

Back to Christina, still with me on the couch, I am totally picturing her dilemma first day of school. She's explaining how there she was, three classes in a row with a total lunatic who even if you pretend not to notice him is constantly staring at you, at your back, at your profile from across the room, at your hands when you're writing, at your feet when you slip them out of your flip-flops, which is how she described it. And when I asked how she knew he was watching, she said, "Crash, when you're a girl, you just know," which made me wonder what they knew about me.

But back to Christina, because by the end of that first week, she was thinking, what was she going to do about this guy in her classes who totally freaked her out? And then sometime in the middle of the second week, Burn did the most unexpected thing:

He totally backed off.

After all that over-the-top talk about destiny and how they were meant to be together and how she was his soul mate, he just stopped. Cold. And instead, he started pretending that she didn't exist, so no more staring or making her feel uncomfortable or defensive, no more outbursts about her in class or to her friends. And she even had to ask some of them, was he still watching her, because it didn't make sense that he suddenly stopped.

But he did. He started hanging with Paige Thompson, who was one of the black girls, before she moved to Boston. But Paige was superfriendly with Zoë who was also superfriendly with April Walker, who now hated him because of his overwhelming obsession with Christina, even when they were going out, which meant that Zoë wasn't about to let Paige hang with Burn for too long. Plus Zoë was in chorus with Christina and was also into acting, so she knew about Burn's proposals and relentless pursuit of Christina even though he was no longer relentlessly pursuing, but that all got back to Paige and kind of scared Paige off.

So it seemed that Christina was finally free of him, except, she admitted, which she never admitted before, she kind of missed the attention, because despite everything else, she always thought that he, Burn, was essentially harmless, despite his reputation, or so she was beginning to believe after weeks of being in the same classes. Oddly as it turned out, *she* actually began watching *him*, not in the same way he had been watching her when he was watching her, but she was becoming curious, especially as to how he could go from like superobsessive to nothing at all, as in not even acknowledging her. Did he forget or did he just get over it, the whole destiny thing?

So she finally asked him, not directly, you don't go direct on something like this in high school, but through channels, as in Zoë, who asked her sister Farrah, who knew Roxanne. But Roxanne either didn't know or wouldn't say anything about her brother and his motives, so dead end there, but not completely, as Roxanne suggested she ask Kenny, because Kenny was always over at their house doing something with David on the internet. But Kenny never really talked to girls, so that left Zoë to talk to Evan who talked to Kenny who talked to Burn who said, when he was asked why he stopped talking to Christina, that it didn't matter whether they talked because, talk or not, "destiny is destiny."

So destiny was basically still involved, or so it seemed to Christina, which meant that he, Burn, pretty much still believed that in ten years they were destined to be married. And it began to bother her again that he still believed it, and it bothered her enough that a few days later, she had to let him know that he was wrong, but she couldn't just come out and tell him, since he hadn't brought it up again. So instead, being as he sat behind her in Spanish, she simply asked if he thought the Mexican cultural section was going to be on the quiz although she definitely knew the answer to that, as in, of course it was, why would they put it into the book if it wasn't going to be on the quiz. Which is exactly what Burn told her in an overly sarcastic voice.

And that was their entire conversation, leaving her feeling so Cady from *Mean Girls*. Did he, Burn, know the scene in that movie? Because she had just played it out so completely and he must have seen it, she thought, as Burn was one of those guys who saw every movie, especially since, everyone knew, he never slept.

So now she had to know if he knew about the *Mean Girls* scene with Cady asking Aaron Samuels a question that she already knew the answer to, because if he did know the scene, then he was probably thinking that she was thinking about him, not thinking about whether or not Mexican culture was on the quiz, because who was she kidding, he knew that she knew what was on the quiz. So she couldn't help but feel stupid, and knowing she couldn't take it back, she promised herself she wouldn't ever talk to him again or even look his way so he would have to take it as just a random question and not a *Mean Girls* thing at all.

OK, I absolutely would not have been able to follow the

whole Christina drama-story thing at all if I hadn't been blazed on Jacob's Gold, because my mind would have gone to so many places while she talked that I would have absorbed absolutely nothing. But now, every time my mind started to wander, this particular strain of weed allowed me to focus again, to get into Christina's mind so I could tell her story.

Except that I started to feel like my mind was spinning the way her mind seemed to spin, which was, in a way, the same felling that I got when I connected with Burn.

So Christina stopped driving herself wacko and started actually not thinking about Burn at all, even though he was in so many of her classes. After all, she had tons of friends in every class, so she never actually had a free minute to talk to him or even be in a position where he could talk to her, which was fine as far as she was concerned. Except that the Mexican cultural chapter was, in fact, on the quiz, and when they got them back a week later, she saw that she got a 94 and felt just fine, but then he tapped her on the shoulder, and when she turned, she noticed his grade, which was 100, even though every word had to be in Spanish and Señorita Sanchez was unforgiving when it came to using the correct tense and spelling and even accents. Burn said he noticed that she didn't get the Mexican cultural questions right, and did she somehow forget that he told her it was going to be on the quiz?

And that was the way it pretty much was, with them not saying anything to each other for weeks on end, and then one question, one answer, then back to not saying anything at all. Which took them through October and no more issues with destiny, at least until Halloween, when Kelly had one of what would become her famous parties, the ones where her parents went to sleep early, leaving kids to come and go totally unsupervised, which also allowed kids from other grades to show up with bottles of bottled water that wasn't bottled water at all.

I remembered this particular party, at least the first half of it. The second half was mostly a haze of beer pong and vodka shots. I didn't even remember that Christina was there. Or Burn, who hardly ever went to parties.

But there she was, according to her, in her Dorothy from *The Wizard of Oz* costume, or so she remembered, and Burn, who was working on getting drunk, was there with Paige, who was already drunker than drunk. And Burn bumped into her, Christina, seemingly by accident, but nothing with Burn was ever an accident, and he said, "Sorry," and she said, "It's OK," and he said, "Not about bumping into you, I couldn't help bumping into you. Sorry that I was such an asshole the first week of school," and she said, "It's OK," and then they were done, so she figured that they wouldn't talk again until maybe Christmas based on their pattern.

Except that when she got into class on Monday, there was a note waiting for her, which she opened and read even though Ms. Reynolds was watching. What the note said was "Can we start over?" and she wrote back "Why?" and he sent her back a note that said:

"Because you matter. And I can make you a better singer."

She read his note in the bathroom, in the privacy of a stall, at lunch between classes, and she prepared a note to give him back during American history, which simply said, "How?" His note back to her, which intrigued her, said:

"Because your voice is so absolutely incredible that songs should be made just for it, songs that are sung so loudly and clearly that it would break mirrors with its absolute brilliance. And because I hear things differently than everyone else you have ever sung for."

So even though she had been to the best vocal coaches in Manhattan, and even though she only took advice from professionals, practicing her breathing exercises every day and working tirelessly on songs from Broadway to Madonna to Kelly Clarkson and Alicia Keys and other singers like Karen Carpenter and Dusty Springfield and Aretha Franklin and Joni Mitchell and Patti LuPone and Patti LaBelle because she wanted her voice to be *that* good, and even though so many people had told her that it was, or could be, as in *that* good, she still didn't believe it, not deep down where it mattered, and until she believed it she knew that she could never be *that* good. And what she also knew was that even though she didn't believe she could be *that* good, Burn believed that she could be *that* good.

So she said, "OK, teach me what you know."

So they started to spend time together, after school, on weekends, going to movies, going into the city to see musicals, going to concerts, and she always felt a little uncomfortable with him, partially because she knew that he still believed in the whole destiny thing, but mostly because, when it came down to it, he looked at her differently than any kid, or for that matter, any adult, had ever looked at her before. With eyes that seemed to love and question at the same time, at least that was how she interpreted the look he was always giving her. Like, when she was sitting in a show and watching the performers, and knowing at the same time that he was watching her, never the stage, that he didn't care at all about the performers. All that mattered to him was her and how she experienced things.

There was also something very old about him, which she sensed. Almost nothing teenage at all. He was, for one thing, so serious about everything that she frequently needed a break from him. But, despite his shortcomings, he was, in fact, teaching her something about singing that no one had ever taught her before. He was not teaching her how to sing. He didn't know anything at all about technique, about breathing, about anticipating a note or a phrase.

What he knew was how to get "inside" a song and how to

turn it into something that mattered in your own life. Like take just one song and really put yourself into it. Not just the words but, more importantly, the melody. Every note, he told her, actually matters. Every note was a second that would be lost unless you totally experienced it with every part of your being.

And she sang for him, giving him everything she learned from the best songs that she did, and he just listened, sitting back, as if taking notes in his head. And then he made her sing again, this time twice as slow, next time the same thing except with raging anger, next time with frustration, and then finally he made her sing the same song with no words at all, just concentrate on the notes, he told her. What he said was that you had to be naked, stripped of everything but your essence if you were going to get it right. It was just you and the sound.

And even if she didn't completely understand him, she sensed that everything he told her, he told her because he believed that he could make her better. And he seemed not to doubt himself at all, so self-assured about what he heard, that when they managed to sneak into the empty auditorium of the high school one afternoon, she stood at the edge of the stage and he went to the back row, and she finally and completely stripped herself of everything but the sound, listening to herself for the first time as if she was in the back row with him and her voice came from another place, from another person she didn't know or even recognize for a second.

And it was absolutely incredible, which brought tears to her eyes because she realized that for the very first time, she heard herself the way he heard her, and because when she was in the zone she could move him to tears. His eyes were always welling up with tears, and he would let them flow freely, without embarrassment, which of course was at first completely uncomfortable for her, but then finally, finally, after working with him for so many months, she completely understood.

What's more, her vocal coach noticed, not only noticed, but complimented her practically to the point of exaltation, and asked what had changed, because there was suddenly something more mature about her, as he put it, something that he considered to be unteachable. A sense of timelessness that few singers, even the greatest ones, ever get to.

And so he asked, what made her change? And she wouldn't tell, not because she was afraid to give David credit, but because a selfish part of her wanted to keep the credit for herself.

And not only her vocal coach, but Mr. Morris, who conducted the chorus and was in charge of the musical productions at school, and then even other kids who heard her sing, and even her parents.

They all knew. Something was different.

She was actually, finally, really *that* good.

And months went by, into the spring of sophomore year, and they, she and Burn, continued to spend time together. At first he hardly talked about himself, but then he talked incessantly, about his aunt and living at her house; about school and being a genius, or at least being radically different from everyone else; about being bipolar, which he didn't believe he was for a minute, but was labeled anyways; about medications and how none of them worked; about marijuana and cocaine and ecstasy and all of the other things he tried; about his research on the internet about virtually everything; about the kids in our grade and the juniors and seniors; about Roxanne, who was always getting into trouble with her mom for her adventurousness, and sometimes stayed out for weeks without coming home, which worried him especially after the suicide attempt; about the people he met through Roxanne; about his mom and her problems and her New Age philosophies and all the self-help books she was always reading; and then, finally, about living in the shadow of the memory of the World Trade Center, remembering how his father took him there as a kid, remembering how incredibly big the towers were and how the wind between the buildings practically lifted him skyward the first time he visited his dad at work, remembering how proud he was of his father as he sat in his father's chair and looked across the huge office out at the world outside and the convergence of rivers.

He remembered pressing his nose against the window in his father's office on the eighty-somethingth floor, feeling the extreme cold when he made contact with the glass, staring down at the miniature people and the insignificant reality that everyone below was living, and he remembered thinking how his father must have been some kind of god with the power over life and death if he spent so much of his time at work so close to the heavens. And then, 9/11 and *nothing*, not a chance to say good-bye. And his last memory of his father, the one that lingered in his mind, that kept him going, was an end-of-summer barbecue on that Sunday before the Tuesday that was 9/11. Remembering how he spilled the pitcher of ice tea and his mother was all over him for that, but not his father, working the grill and turning the hot dogs with a practiced perfection like he did for so many summer Sundays before then and everyone expected he would do for all those summer Sundays to come. Don't worry about the tea, we can always make another pitcher; we can't always make another boy, honey. Or something like that.

And then into the blackness and the smoke. Where was my dad in all that rubble? Somehow he must have made it out.

He must have.

He must have.

He must have.

But there was no word, no sign, no signal from other worlds that might be but probably were not, that life on this planet was anything more than simple, inconsequential short-term existence, no spirit in the sky that you became a part of or could communicate back from, because if there was, his father would have found a way.

Again, maybe it was the magic of Jacob's Gold making me more observant, or maybe Christina was feeling the effects of it too, though she had only taken a few hits, but in describing for me what Burn had described to her a few years before our time together on her uncle's couch, in the middle of the woods, in the middle of the night, in the middle of another summer, Christina Haines totally and completely morphed into David Burnett, as in totally surrendering to his mannerisms, his speech patterns, the way he talked, and even the tone of his voice. It was spooky, in a way, and it made me realize what an incredible actress she actually was or was going to be.

She continued with her Burn impression, explaining that there were times of overwhelming grief, followed by times of overwhelming sadness, but mostly there was overwhelming anger at that fact that he and Roxanne and his mom were the real living victims of terrorism. And he learned soon enough, at least in his fragile but genius mind, that the real culprits were not the Osama bin Ladens of the world, but the U.S. military-industrial complex, whatever that was. Whatever it was, according to Burn, it was responsible for the destruction of the Twin Towers and for U.S. involvement in Afghanistan and Iraq. Guys like Cheney and Rumsfeld and other members of the Bush administration were responsible, and Burn said he was going to prove it one day.

The point, she explained to me, was that Burn was consumed with every theory on 9/11 and had an extensive database of everything ever written on the subject, which I already knew from Roxanne.

Which led me to get Christina back into focusing on her

relationship with Burn, and so I asked were they hooking up at that time. She said that for months Burn never even tried, not while he was working with her on her music, but by spring, when all he could talk about was his 9/11 theories, he started in with her, and she kind of felt obligated to comply, as in making out and not much more, which he didn't seem to mind at all. But then one day they were at a party, and I was there and apparently I was doing my thing, which of course was to get totally shitfaced, and Burn noticed the way she was noticing me, which got him all kinds of jealous, and apparently that was when he told her that we, he and I, were "connected" in some cosmic way, and it didn't surprise him that she had feelings for me, because the three of us were connected in a way that he didn't exactly understand yet.

Except that, after seeing how his girlfriend, the person *he considered to be his girlfriend*, was interested in someone else, he tried to close the deal with her, as in bringing it to the next level the next time they were alone, and she had to tell him, "David, I don't like you like that," and he said, "You mean the way you like Crash," and she said, "Steven has nothing to do with it," and he said, "Then how do you like me?" and she said, "As a friend." And he shook his head, kept shaking his head like he was listening to some kind of music that only he could hear, and he did this for a while, finally repeating "as a friend . . ."

And that was it.

He stopped calling, stopped returning her calls, stopped responding to instant messages, stopped coming over or making plans.

He just moved on to something else, whatever that was, and sure she was sad, but in a way it made sense, because he would never be more than a friend to her, and that would never be good enough for him, because, as he said, she was *his* destiny, but he wasn't hers.

And so ended sophomore year for her, and she didn't want to talk about the problems that she had with him junior year. She confessed that she hated it when other people used the word "abduction" after the Massachusetts incident, because even though she wasn't a willing participant, she never actually felt that her life was in danger. He never actually threatened her; he just refused to take her home.

Still, she said, it could have been different if I hadn't showed up to save her.

She leaned over and kissed me, in a completely nonsexual way, but in a way that reminded me of our connection and my willingness to risk my life for her, which, despite everything else I may have thought until that moment, was evidence that maybe I had feelings for this girl, no matter what I pretended or even told myself at any given moment.

So maybe I did deserve to be there with her.

And literally minutes after finishing the story, she was sound asleep. But not me, as I was still wired from the food, the weed, and the sex and having already had a major nap. So I started flipping the channels and retorching my bowl. Another chunk of Jacob's Gold, burning it nice and easy, taking slow, unhurried hits, flipping through infomercials and an old *Chappelle's Show* on Comedy Central. Next some real old black-and-white movie, and then Pete's favorite horror movie of all time, *Cabin Fever*, and the scene where the girl shaves her legs and chunks of flesh come off. And being as we were in a cabin in the middle of the woods and I was flying high, I thought it best to switch to something more upbeat, and sure enough, I found *Happy Feet*, which I watched but was still feeling too cold to handle, still kind of shivering from the hot tub, cold nap, and then . . .

Pop.

Then . . .

Total darkness.

The lights went out, the cable went out, the electricity stopped buzzing, and we were plunged into total and complete blackness.

And silence.

Now, I was suddenly seeing absolutely nothing, and hearing only the sound of Christina's rhythmic breathing, which normally would have sounded relaxing. Except that on top of that sound, I could hear, *and feel*, my own heart pumping, as on those rare occasions when you oversmoked, too many bong hits on kush, and you start wondering if somehow you finally went over the line, and your mind starts zipping past funny and relaxed and totally chill and somehow gets to Paranoia City. I have had this like two or three times in the past and have witnessed my friends go through it, so I know that when you start actually feeling your heart, it is not a good thing at all.

And, as bad as that typically is, I just learned that it is like a million, no a billion times worse when you are doing this in total and complete darkness.

"Stay calm, Crash."

I may have said this out loud. A part of me desperately needed to hear my own voice to make sure I was still OK.

I know that sounds fucked up, but you had to be there.

Then I waited, because I knew from experience that the heartbeat/breathing/panic thing would lift, as it always does. Only the more I waited, the more freaked out I was getting.

It occurred to me, just for a fleeting instant . . . what if I was actually dead? What if this is what it felt like to be dead?

So I got up and started pacing the room. Then I blindly crawled up the steps and found my way into the bedroom, to the sliding glass doors that led to the deck that led to the hot tub, and I stepped outside.

I looked out into the vast darkness and could see no other lights anywhere. Except for the incredible night sky. And I could feel that I was just a speck, on a speck of the planet, in a speck of the solar system, in a speck of a galaxy, which made me think that I was thinking just like Burn would have thought if he had stepped out of the darkness onto the deck that night instead of me, and maybe if things hadn't happened the way they did, it would have been him, not me, standing there on this particular night, having christened Christina as in being the first one for her.

It would have seemed the logical progression of things for him to be her first, and I had to wonder, did I somehow, several months ago, by saving the school and keeping him from killing himself and others, alter the course of the future?

Or did Burn alter the future by not going through with it?

Or what if I was meant to go to that military school after all, and by virtue of him stepping up that Thanksgiving Day, everything changed and was out of sync. And if somehow we *had* altered the future, could that affect the entire universe? And maybe my recognition of that fact caused the blackout, and now that I knew, everything would be somehow changed. Maybe it was just me and him left in a world of darkness.

Except that if I was thinking about Burn and he claimed to be connected to me, could he at that very moment be thinking about me? While it was way beyond midnight, he would still be up, because he never slept, and given that I once, probably more than once, got into his mind, as in the poker game, the question remained: Was he capable of doing the same with me?

And then it hit me.

Thinking about the poker game and how sure I was that he was holding a full house, I was now equally absolutely certain that Christina and I were not alone.

My mind started to spin at the thought of this. It was spinning not because I was stoned, but because I knew, without question, just like I knew his cards during our poker game years before, that I was right. David Burnett was here.

Except, how?

My mind answered this question as soon as it heard it, because I had to remind myself as I calculated during the car ride to the cabin, even though I hadn't told any friends where we were going, I was sure that Christina told a few of hers, including most probably Amanda Jenkins, who might have told Franklin Hawkings, who might have sent an email to Burn, maybe after Burn saw me on television. Maybe there was a phone call or two. Burn would have access to a phone, and there were actually people who, sick as it sounds, admired him and all.

So even if the world wasn't plunged into darkness with only two people left alive and the universe wasn't out of sync after all, it was absolutely possible that Burn knew exactly where we were.

And knowing where we were, Burn being Burn, he would figure out why we were here. And once he figured that out, there would be no way to contain him in any mental hospital, no matter how secure. He would find a way out. And if he managed to escape, the rest would be easy.

And that's when I heard the sounds. Rustling leaves in the distance, then around the other side of the house.

I was back to full-on heart palpitations again. This time from knowing beyond doubt that Burn was within shouting distance, possibly even inside the house at that very moment. And because I was absolutely positive he was there, I started yelling into the woods at the top of my lungs:

"David, I know you're out there. David, you can't fool me. I'm ready for you."

And then, through the sliding glass doors, a shadow of a figure.

Hard to make out, but my eyes were good enough to tell it

was a girl, not a guy.

"What are you doing?" Christina asked.

I instantly felt stupid. "The lights went out," I said.

"They always do around here," she said without a trace of fear. I wondered if she sensed mine. "They'll be back on in a few minutes."

And, as if on command, all the lights were suddenly back. Panic time was over. I was in control again. What an idiot, was all I could think. There is no Burn, no end of the world, no glitch in the universe. There is only Jacob's weed and a warm, very tired girl who wants to sleep with me.

I put my arm around her, feeling beyond exhausted, feeling chilled to the bone, and I let her lead me back into the room, where I fell asleep before my head hit the pillow and dreamed the dreams of a stoner.

And apparently kept sleeping until she woke me midday.

"Steven, you are extremely hot. Are you feeling OK?"

I was not, not at all. I was covered in sweat, burning up with fever. I could not move. I was having trouble even opening my eyes.

"We have to go home," she said.

"Not me," I whispered. "I'm not going anywhere." And drifted back off to sleep for a very, very long time.

When I awoke, it was dark again, and she was gone. I stumbled into the kitchen, feeling like shit. There was a note on the counter telling me that she had to go, but she would be back either tomorrow or the next day. In the meantime, she had worked it out that someone would deliver food and anything else I needed.

So not only was I sick, but I was sick and alone. Sick and alone and hungry and, tell you the truth, hating her more than a little at that point.

At least until I turned the note over. There on the flip side was her final paragraph:

> *I know you are probably cursing me by now, but I read more of your book, and you should know that you have real talent. You need to finish it before school starts. So I'm doing you a favor and you will thank me one day, maybe not today though. Get back to writing. There's nothing else to do here. And thank you for being you. You have not only saved my life, you have changed it forever. Love, C.*

It made me feel good about being me. And this from a girl I had just deflowered. Am I smoooooth or what?

And I felt smoooooth, until I checked the front window and realized that the bitch took my car.

And the one remaining nugg of Jacob's Gold, which was in the glove compartment.

Fuckme.

CHAPTER SIXTEEN
HOW BURN RUINED MY BIG NIGHT

These are some of the things that the Club Crew did during sophomore year:

- Went to school stoned, went to school drunk, went to school late, left school early.
- Started hanging out at Pinky's without our families.
- Drove without licenses (including getting Evan's father's car stuck in the swamp by the nature preserve).
- Partied, mostly with the girls in our grade, and even got two girls to kiss each other.
- Snuck out in the middle of the night, to hang with each other and some freshman girls.
- Played lots more poker than we did as freshmen, sometimes even with the guys in Prime Time, guys in our grade that we got along with mostly, but they were more into fighting than we were, plus they were all athletes and had football and lacrosse in common (not to say we weren't into sports, as almost all of us were on a team or two, but we were not the jocks that the Prime Time guys were).
- Got Xbox 360, which was big-time for teenage gamers, and so we all played *Call of Duty 2*, like, constantly, with the occasional *Madden* tournaments thrown in for good measure, mostly in Pete's rec room.
- Started having issues with some of the Prime Time guys over playing time in football and baseball, and even though I wasn't involved since I was a solid and reliable shortstop, I

had my boys' backs, knowing that Prime Time loved fighting more than they loved sports or girls.

- Also, one or two of us started having girlfriends. Me, I was still superclose friends with Annie Russo, but she was not about doing anything except occasionally kissing in tenth grade, which of course left Madelaine Brancato, who was totally into me, like everyone knew that Maddy was totally into me and would do anything to go out with me. So even though she was not part of the Herd Girls, which was the group of girls who we were hanging with more and more, and even though I didn't even really like her, I started hanging out with her because she liked me, and soon people in school were talking about us like we were a couple, which I did nothing to encourage, but I didn't exactly discourage it either, reason being, ever since my stretch of unpopularity as a freshman, I was not about to ignore any current opportunity, as I figured that was the best way to ensure future opportunities. In other words, I had a reputation to rebuild and to protect. And to be honest, even though I lost my gut and was in shape, my rep still wasn't actually all that great by the middle of sophomore year, because most of the Prime Time guys had gotten blow jobs, mostly from girls we used to hang with, girls who weren't even talking to us now. And what was worse, exactly *none* of the Club Crew guys had even had a touch, including me. And at the time, it was obvious to me, knowing Evan and Bosco and Kenny and Pete and Bobby and Newman the way I knew them, that it was up to me or maybe Bobby to get the ball rolling on any kind of meaningful experiences for us. So even though Maddy was not exactly what I had in mind, I figured that if she was into me that much, it was the best shot any of us had.
- Oh yeah, and during Thanksgiving week, we got into mad

trouble for hanging at Pete's house, problem being Pete and his family were on vacation in Cancún at the time. So we were having this great time until one of Pete's neighbors reported us and the cops showed up. We didn't get arrested or anything, thanks to some quick thinking by me and Annie Russo, with her claiming that we were there to water the plants and me adding, "and feed the fish," even though Pete had no fish to feed and didn't even own a fish tank. The cops took our names after we told them that we had the garage code, and by the time they talked to our parents, we had already prepared Pete, who talked to his parents, who separately talked to our parents, so while it ended up not being a police matter, we were in collective trouble with adults again, just like in eighth grade, with most of us grounded until Christmas.

- And oh yeah, we started partying even harder throughout the winter, with better weed and more access to alcohol, as in mostly supercheap vodka, but anything else we could get our hands on, counting on our older brothers or sisters to deliver the goods (not me, as Lindsey could not be relied upon for anything) or pillaging our parents' or uncles' or some other relatives' liquor cabinets, replacing the Ketel One and Grey Goose with Poland Spring and Deer Park.

- Wrestled, which I excelled in for my weight class, not because I was strong, but because I was quick.

- Toward the end of spring, discovering the nature preserve as a great place to pregame.

- Went to the movies a whole lot. These were the movies that we went to see during the school year, probably in order of when we saw them: *The 40-Year-Old Virgin* (overrated), *Wedding Crashers*, *Waiting . . .* (if you didn't see this, you have to, as everyone in it is famous now and you will never look at your ballsack the same afterward), the second *Saw* (fucked up), *Harry Potter and the Goblet of Fire* (best one, if you ask me), *Narnia*, *King Kong*, *The Polar Express* in IMAX 3D (blazing of course), *Underworld: Evolution* (not as good as the first one), *Big Momma's House 2* (totally stupid), *Final Destination 3* (just as good as the first one), *V for Vendetta* (fucked up), *Silent Hill* (not scary), *Mission: Impossible III* (OK), *X-3* (over the top), *Cars*, *Click* (finally a movie Duncan would go to), and by the time the second *Pirates of the Caribbean* opened it was summer and sophomore year was over.

Point of all this being, even though nothing special happened in tenth grade and we all pretty much lived our lives, just like kids in every other high school in America, everything that happened since happened because of who we were by the end of sophomore year.

More or less, anyways.

I still sucked at school, still was pretty good at baseball, though it was getting too boring for me, still hated my dad, but had nothing but mad respect for his girlfriend, soon to be my stepmom, had almost nothing to do with Lindsey, and Jamie was still watching TV with Medusa sprawled out on the couch beside her.

Which of course brings us to David Burnett.

After the now-famous poker game, he was invited again— not by me, by some of my friends—and while he never actually showed up to play again, he resumed his bond with Kenny and they started hanging out together, doing the same after-school activities, while I was shuttled for the rest of the school year to various after-school courses in hopes that one day I would simply catch on.

Burn's mom still talked to my mom regularly, but whatever

they talked about stayed between them, and I sensed that there was something going on that was not for teenage ears, as my mother often put it, something that didn't necessarily have to do with their children.

As for Roxanne, when she returned to school, it was as if the entire incident at the hospital had been wiped from her memory. I tried to approach her a few times, but she was dismissive and cold, not even her usual sarcastic self, and I chalked it up to her not wanting to remember anything that had happened to her. I had stopped approaching her, feeling very much like what I was at the time, a freshman boy trying to talk to a junior girl, as in totally and completely out of my league.

Not gonna lie, it stung, but it was also clear in my mind that she was, after all, a Burnett, and how could I ever have forgotten that being a Burnett comes with its own special hall pass for crazy?

Except her brother was so normal by tenth grade that pretty much everyone forgot he was actually crazy out of his mind. Everyone but me anyways, and I had very little exposure to him. He was big into lifting and was working out in the gym, like, every afternoon with the seniors on the football team. He even got onto the varsity wrestling team, which was just about the only place that he and I would see each other as I was on JV. So even though I didn't hang with him, he was hanging with other kids, wrestling, playing video games with them, and going to movies and concerts just like us, and, from what we heard from Kenny, still all about the internet and still a motherfucking genius and, of course, totally and completely and publicly in love with Christina Haines.

For me, I was just happy that I did not have to deal with him at all. And it was probably a good thing that I saw even less of his sister, who I understood was spending most of her time with people she knew in the city.

By late winter of sophomore year, for some odd reason, I started running into Burn more and more. Sometimes I would see him and Christina, and while I tried not to look at her, I remember noticing the way she noticed me and I thought it wasn't all that different from the way Madelaine Brancato looked at me. Except, of course, for the fact that according to everyone else at Meadows, Burn and Christina were totally in love, as in just like Burn had said, it was their destiny to be together. At least until they broke up unexpectedly in March of that year. Word spread quickly that the Christina/David universe had imploded and that they didn't even talk.

Me, I couldn't care less, being as I had more important concerns. After months of commitment to the pretend relationship that I was having with Maddy, I was, I convinced myself, finally locked in for my first blow job, as in Maddy was giving me signs that it could finally happen. The only issue was finding a place, as she wasn't letting me get her into any empty rooms at parties.

It was at one of Kelly's parties later that spring that I figured it all out.

Kelly hadn't had one of her famous parties since like Halloween, and this one was going to be off the hook, as in juniors and a few seniors, not just our grade.

Kids were party planning all day, bringing in coolers and ditching them at the edges of her property, away from parental view, behind trees, secured by rocks. This party was going to be a major event. We were closing in on the end of sophomore year, and probably this would be our last chance to celebrate before finals. Plus some kids were driving now, one or two of the sophomores and mostly all of the juniors, so we had access to everything. And I had a plan.

We pregamed at the nature preserve, like always, and I

invited Maddy and some of her friends this time. Lots of cheap alcohol, and me handing out constant refills to all of them, mostly her. No way was I going to screw the opportunity. By the time we got to Kelly's house, Maddy was full-on wasted.

Now the delicate part, as in making sure that she didn't drink anything else, which, I had carefully calculated, would bring her over the edge, given that she had only recently started drinking and didn't have any appreciation for what her limits could be. It was exceedingly clear that she was falling into the typical amateur's trap of thinking she wasn't drunk and that she could handle it.

So I managed to get us a quiet spot in Kelly's rec room and left her in the care of Evan as I headed for the tree where a beverage section was set up, intending to cut back on the alcohol content on anything she would get.

Along the way I checked the pool house, the most important component of my plan. No one was inside, as pretty much every guy in my grade knew that I had reserved it for the next step. I called Bosco over, told him to guard the door and not to let anyone in. One thing about Bosco, he never said no. So he did what he was told.

On the way back to the house, two redcups in hand, I ran into Christina, who was working on having her own good time. Clearly the drink she was holding was not her first.

"Hi, Steven."

"Where's Burn?" is what I asked.

"Didn't you hear? We're not spending time together anymore."

I actually had heard.

"Sorry," I said, noticing that she was stepping closer to me. For a fleeting instant, I thought that I could switch out. The pool house was reserved, and Christina, getting over Burn, might be a perfect candidate for a rebound hookup. I looked over at the pool house, and Bosco was still standing there like he was one of those English guards protecting the queen or something. No question, between Maddy and Christina, Christina would have been a far better choice.

Except that she had a way of intimidating me even back then, maybe because I felt like she thought we had a connection that could be more intense than I was ready for.

More importantly, if Burn found out, he would definitely not take it well. Thankfully, I was sober enough to hear an inner voice practically scream at me, *I will hunt you down, mother-fucker*, in a voice sounding exactly like Burn, and not the completely normal sophomore Burn who everyone thought was OK but the crazy Burn who I knew all too well, the one who went off the deep end when his fox got dissected.

"He talked about you a lot actually," she said. "Told me that you were like a brother to him when you guys were younger."

No question, he would have hunted me down and dissected me too. "Not so much" is what I answered, wondering how Burn could have ever said anything like that.

She moved in closer to me.

I glanced at the pool house. Bosco was leading people away from the entrance. Another thing you had to say about Bosco, he followed orders perfectly as long as you kept it simple for him.

"I think maybe we should talk," she said, touching my arm, me thinking that if Burn found out she even touched me, I was fucked. Still, there was a spark of something in her touch that almost made it worth it anyways. "We haven't talked since like eighth grade." Slurring her words slightly and touching my arm again.

"How's the acting thing going?" I fumbled for words.

"When we made out, do you remember?" she continued, her arm still on mine. "Why haven't we talked since then?"

I started not to think about Madelaine Brancato at all, or the fact that I had a girlfriend, even though in my mind she wasn't my girlfriend. Point being, Christina was making me forget about the original plan.

Until I saw Tyler out of the corner of my eye, leading Stacy Richman over to the pool house. And seeing that, I knew that I had better move quickly. Bosco would cave to one of the Prime Timers. He was, after all, the supreme pussy.

"Gotta go" is what I told her, leaving her and her extended arm and flying back into the rec room where Maddy was. Except she was now passed out.

I looked at Evan, hate in my eyes, and he quickly swore that he did everything he could to keep her up. "She just folded, Crash. Nothing I could do."

I wasn't giving up. The pool was open. No one was in it as the water was still winter cold, so what if I accidentally threw her in?

I tried to lift her up, but she was dead weight. No that wouldn't work, who was I kidding? Then another thought, leave her, go back and find Christina again. The night did not have to be a total loss.

Except Christina was now on the other side of the room, watching me attempt to lift Maddy, and I must have appeared to be a caveman or something because she had this look on, you know, that "you have *got* to be kidding" look, as I heard someone tell her, "Brancato was supposed to take care of him tonight."

I didn't know that everyone knew, but everyone knew now.

That was the last time Christina and I had any contact until junior year.

And my night of humiliation was far from over, because as soon as I left Maddy in a pile in the rec room, wandering back to the beverage tree again, I was stopped again by another girl, her voice practically coldcocking me from behind.

"Yo, Crashinsky," in that slightly raspy voice that oozed sarcasm.

I turned.

Despite her distinct emo look, she was easily one of the hottest-looking girls at the party, even though it took me a full second to recognize her latest appearance, bangs covering her right eye, piercings above her eyebrow, jet-black hair again, this time with added blue streaks, and underneath it all, as girl-pretty as she was when I first saw her in McAllister.

"Yo, Roxanne," I answered with a cautious nod, not knowing whether she was new Roxanne or old Roxanne and whether I was a friend or an annoying younger brother of an enemy.

"You *do* get high, don't you?" she asked. She gave me the blunt she was holding. I took a very tentative hit. She was with a mostly emo group that I heard she hung with. They all looked college; I knew one of them from town but mostly didn't recognize the others. I don't even know if she hung out with any other seniors from Meadows at that point.

"I didn't think we were talking anymore," I said, testing her and watching for a reaction.

"Heard you were hooking up with Brancato tonight. Came to watch."

"You heard wrong," I said, sounding as frustrated as I was and also trying to hide the fact that I was nervous around her.

"So you're still a virgin," she said more than asked. All her friends laughed. I *was,* not gonna lie, still a virgin, and she knew I was, and I also knew that she wasn't.

"So you're still crazy," I said more than asked, determined not to let her embarrass me in front of her loser friends. Still, I knew it was wrong to say and immediately felt terrible about it.

"Yeah," she said matter-of-factly. "No amount of frickin' beans is gonna change that," she said, laughing out loud, and

I understood that she was making a private joke to me and that she wasn't at all insulted by my comeback. In fact, she inhaled the blunt again, got close up, and told me to open my mouth, which for some reason, I did, as I could never say no to Roxanne.

"Inhale," she said as she passed the smoke into me in this liplock kiss thing. This completely turned me on, no surprise there. I hadn't done this before.

"It's called shotgunning, Crash," she said.

"I know that," I told her, even though, at the time, I didn't know it.

Then she whispered to me. "About the virginity thing. If you wanna go, just say the word. I owe you." This in a voice so low that her friends couldn't hear. It was just me and her and, from what I could tell, she was offering, really offering, not just messing around the way the girls in my grade would.

"You mean, now?"

"Whenever you want," she said.

I saw Bosco still guarding the pool house. I was rock hard and ready, and I still had everything in place.

And then I heard Burn's voice, as clear as a bell, in the back of my brain; this time it was saying *stay away from my sister.* So for the second time in less than an hour, my shot at changing my sexual status was ruined by a kid who wasn't even there. "I don't think David would approve," I told her.

"I won't tell him if you don't." She did that inhale, exhale shotgunning thing again, passing the smoke to me, but this time, also gently grinding herself against me, so she knew how ready I was.

"Someone will tell him. Your brother has his ways. He will definitely find out." Me, sounding defeated, not believing I was turning down a sure thing.

"Have it your way, Crash. Call me when you're ready." She laughed. "And you *will* call."

This time, it was all kiss and no smoke, and she knew she totally had me. And then I was standing there, fully stoned, still in kiss mode as she stepped back, and her friends were laughing at me and my stupid pose. As I straightened up, they were gone, and I was alone by the pool with massive wood hoping it wasn't showing and filled with mind spin, so much so that I was dizzy. It hit me that I now had exactly what I wanted: not only my first chance at a guaranteed path to manhood, but with a girl who has totally mesmerized me since elementary school, not gonna lie, and I had just balked at going through with it that very night with the one girl who totally would have rocked my world, because no question about it, Roxanne would have known exactly what she was doing. No question, now that Roxanne was even a remote possibility, Maddy was going to be a great disappointment, at best.

But I also had to deal with the cruel fact that she was probably teasing me in her Roxanne way, and who was I kidding, I was, in all probability, as much a toy to Roxanne as Maddy was to me.

Which brought me back to Maddy, because I did have the obligation to get her home, that was part of the deal, and maybe, just maybe, she was up by now, and if so, one last attempt wasn't going to hurt. At least it would be safe, even though all I could think about was Roxanne now, as she totally did a number on me. So one last attempt would allow me to refocus . . .

Except that across the property, Tyler and Stacy were pushing past Bosco, into the pool house, and Bosco just shrug-motioned to me that he had done all he could do and was officially resigning from his job. Fucking Bosco.

I headed back to the rec room, still spinning, thinking about Roxanne and the whole shotgunning feeling. And there, on the couch, sitting next to a now fully conscious Madelaine Brancato, was a fully sober David Burnett, totally making his move on her, and she seemed totally into it.

"Yo, Crash" is what he said, though he wasn't looking at me, he was looking at her, in fact with one arm around her and holding a redcup filled with, my guess, a fresh round of jungle juice. She was drinking again and looking at him, not me.

Which really pissed me off, not because I felt any jealousy whatsoever, which I totally did not, but because I could possibly have been, at that very moment, using the pool house with his sister, who as far as I knew he had no real care in the world for, at least no more feelings than I had for Lindsey.

Which reminded me to call Lindsey, because she was supposed to drive me home and we had a midnight curfew and it was now 11:45.

Fuckme.

I flipped open my cell phone, made the call. She complained, but I reminded her that our mom had already worked it out with her and that she had to drive Maddy home too. I heard her curse me and I hung up smiling, knowing that she was on her way and I would make her wait at the end of the driveway by Kelly's house for a good long time before I emerged from the party.

"Saw your sister," I told Burn, who was still all about Maddy.

"Heard she was here," he said, not looking at me. "She won't be for long; not her kind of scene. Definitely not enough action." From what I knew about him, this wasn't exactly the kind of party that he normally showed up to either.

"Christina is too," I said, wondering why I was baiting him. "I saw her by the pool."

"Yeah, well good for Christina," he answered, then whispered something in Maddy's ear which made her laugh, and I wanted to ask her, and everyone else, was I the only person left who realized this guy was still crazy? Because everyone was treating him like he was just a normal kid. No, better than a normal kid, like some kind of royalty, because he seemed to always get his way now that he was all jacked and everything.

I was thinking that I liked him better Down than Up. As for Up, he seemed way Up at the moment, like indestructible Up, one arm around Maddy, turning the other way to flirt with Amanda, who was on the couch with Bobby and who Burn knew was one of Christina's closest friends. So he was not only flirting with her but making her laugh, and I could tell Bobby was getting annoyed, because Bobby, being the most competitive member of Club Crew, knew what my goal for the night was, and Bobby was doing what he could to beat me at my own game (this was easily the third girl he was hitting on that night, although, come to think of it, I was also zero for three, as in Maddy, Christina, and Roxanne, but I had real shots at my three, at least two of the three, while his choices were near impossibilities).

Then Lindsey was calling my cell, which meant she was waiting. I signaled Maddy that our ride was there, and she dutifully pulled herself up from the couch, stumbled over to me with a quick "sorry," as I helped her maneuver around groups of other people. Her breath smelled like vodka and some kind of luncheon meat, not pleasant at all. I was, tell you the truth, buzzing with anger.

To make matters worse, as I was leaving, a crop of the hottest freshman girls showed up, all short skirts, tight shirts, and too much makeup.

"Hiiiiii, Crash," a few said in unison, all giggly.

I knew some of them liked me, which left me with a choice: I could bail on Maddy, avoid Lindsey and blow off my curfew and leave Maddy there, positive that she would get a ride with one of her friends' mothers or brothers, but that would cause a problem with respect to my future plans with her. Plus there was my mom to deal with the next day.

"I'm not feeling so good" is what Maddy said.

More luncheon meat smell.

Great. My anger level boosted, knowing that I was going to do the right thing anyways.

Down at the end of the driveway, Lindsey was already out of the car, looking for me.

"I called you like ten times."

"So I'm here."

"So you completely ruined my night."

"Yeah, well too bad," I said, wondering how Lindsey's night could be more ruined than mine. I shoved Maddy into the backseat of the car and got in after her, noticing for the first time that Lindsey's best friend, Erin, was in the front seat. We had made out once years before, when she was learning how to kiss and practicing on me. Unfortunately for Erin, she did not get any prettier, though she was mad smart, as in going to Harvard the following year smart. Lindsey, no slouch either, was accepted to U-Penn and Georgetown, causing a minor quake in the Caroline/Jacob coexistence treaty, because my mom was all about U-Penn and Jacob was insisting on Georgetown—to him there was no comparison.

I was fairly positive at that point in time that there would be no similar arguments when I graduated from high school, *if* that ever even happened.

Maddy burped loudly. Trust me, you do *not* want a description of what *that* smelled like.

Congratulations on Harvard, congratulations on Georgetown, she told the two older girls. They were clearly annoyed, offered totally nonenthusiastic thanks in return, clearly not wanting to talk, but Maddy would not stop, going on about how she wanted to go to Brown or Williams, like who in our grade even knew the names of colleges.

Why did I not stay at the party?

Lindsey interrupted Maddy to talk to me. "Dad called. He wants us to visit him next weekend."

"No way" is what I said, knowing there would be another party and another chance for success, if not with Maddy, then with someone else. I wasn't going to wait much longer.

"It's Felicia's birthday," she said, knowing that I wouldn't disappoint my father's girlfriend. "She's having some cousins come in from her country and she wants to introduce us."

"Good times," said Erin sarcastically. I later found out that she had just started having sex with some college guy who she met online. Didn't sound like a particularly Harvardy choice, if you ask me.

Lindsey stopped on Maple, slowed to a crawl, asked which house and Maddy pointed. Call me, is what she said when she got out of the car. Sure, is what I said, though I wouldn't, knowing that she would be all about IMing me by the time I got home anyways.

Door slam. Madelaine was not even across her lawn yet when Erin started in.

"She's just like her sister."

Lindsey: "I hate her sister. I hate all the Brancatos."

Erin: "Everyone hates her sister. Everone hates the Brancatos." Then, to me, "Steven, what do you see in her? She's not even pretty," which, OK, she wasn't, but she was, in her defense, a lot hotter than Erin.

Lindsey: "What do you think he sees in her?" As if I wasn't even there.

They went on like this all the way home, or at least most of the way, because no sooner did we pull up to my street when I got a text from Evan.

Looks like Bobby wins.

I call him. He tells me that Bobby is in the pool house

with April Walker. No contest. We all know that when April is shitfaced she will deliver. And April was shitfaced before I left. I saw her but didn't even consider it. I tell him that April shouldn't count, and Evan says he asked the rest of the Club Crew and it's unanimous, April counts. Bobby wins.

I stagger into the house, not realizing until I hit the kitchen that I am also shitfaced drunk, plus still stoned from Roxanne's superblunt. I will have to avoid Caroline Prescott and her obsessive questions. Only there she was at the top of steps, launching right in—as in where were you, who was there, how was Maddy, I saw Mrs. Brancato at the market, and did you see David, I heard from Elaine that David decided to go to the party, good for him, he had a hard time dealing with the breakup with that girl in your grade, you know, the actress, did he look OK, do you think he's doing all right, did you drink anything, tell me the truth, Steven. And me, keeping it simple, Kelly's, everybody, OK, he was there, seemed OK, I had a beer, just one, I swear, no mom, everybody drinks now, just ask Lindsey.

Closing my bedroom door behind me, popping open my laptop to see who was on, not being able to think about anything else except the lost opportunities and how Burn, in his own way, totally ruined my big night.

Lights out and I tried to sleep, but instead completely replayed in my mind the minutes I had with Roxanne, sharing a blunt with me and supercharging me with a kind of electricity.

"It's called shotgunning, Crash."

I heard this over and over again in my brain. No way was I getting to sleep, not with my mind spinning and Roxanne, after all these years, calling me Crash, not Crashinsky, without making fun of my last name. That had to mean something.

And Christina, what was up with her? She did look good too. And smell great.

But not as great as Roxanne.

I replayed the shotgun feeling and the body contact and the mouth-to-mouth contact.

And everything she said.

"Have it your way, Crash. Call me when you're ready."

She actually did say that.

Yep, no sleep at all. After I convinced myself that I should call her, I convinced myself that she was definitely fucking with me and that I could never actually call her, so I had to stop thinking about her and put her out of my mind completely.

And besides, now I had a new goal, and I was going to be a hero on this, because I was not going to waste any more time on trying to get oral, oral is for losers, and besides, Bobby had already won that tournament, so it was time for me to go all in. If Maddy wanted to continue to go out, I would go out, but she had to put out as in *all* out, or I was moving on.

Summer was coming. A few more weeks of school, finals (ugh, I was really, really, really sucking at school), and then ten weeks, just my boys and summer ball and no more missed opportunities.

I would give Maddy until the end of the school year.

Then, there was always the summer. Point was, if I wasn't devirginized by the middle of August, I would, regardless of the consequences, call Roxanne. She did say to call, after all. Actually, it had to be the second week in August—I couldn't afford to go beyond that. Like Lindsey, Roxanne was starting college in the fall, and I had heard that she was heading out west somewhere. I couldn't risk waiting any longer than that.

With the weed wearing off, I was starting to drift into that place between alertness and sleep, absolutely optimistic, because, when I thought about it, Burn hadn't ruined my night at all. Actually, I was the one who bailed on Christina, and at the same time, Burn's sister, if she was serious, had offered me an absolute gift, when you think about it.

Point was, I was definitely going to have sex, real, actual sex, before anyone else in Club Crew or for that matter, as far as I knew, the rest of my grade.

And it was all because of the beans that my father's girlfriend, soon to be my stepmom, had given me. There was magic in those beans, after all.

Thank you, Felicia. Good night.

CHAPTER SEVENTEEN

HOW BURN AND ROXANNE DEALT

It turned out that things went a little differently than planned.

And yet. Not.

First off, Maddy did finally deliver on the oral, right after finals, in, of all places, the back of my sister's car, which was in the garage, with both of my sisters home at the time.

I know, not particularly smart on any level. But if you're a teenage boy, you gotta take what's offered when it's offered, especially the first time for anything.

What made it even stupider was that while we were super-quiet about it, sneaking out of my house into the garage and then quietly opening and shutting the door to Lindsey's car, Maddy insisted on having music, and so I boosted up the stereo enough to make Maddy happy, but hopefully not enough to call attention to the sound. It would not, of course, be very good if Lindsey caught us. I wasn't even supposed to touch Lindsey's car, much less turn it into my own personal Vista Cruiser (thank you Eric Forman).

I was not worried about Jamie, because Jamie was in the middle of watching an advance DVD of *Eight Below*, which I managed to get from Duncan because his father is in the business, being as it was Jamie's favorite movie of all time, and McClaren was just about to slide down the embankment into the water and had to be rescued by the dogs, so no way was she getting up for any reason for a while.

So it was 10:10 on the dashboard clock, and me and Maddy were making out in the car, which was all she was good for at that point, more or less, and her mom was coming to pick her up at 11:00, which gave me less than an hour if anything was going to happen, and unless *everything* happened, I was planning to dump her at, like, 10:55, figuring if I timed it right, she would be upset but wouldn't be able to argue about it for too long.

So given that she was wearing this skirt thing, which gave me easy access, I figured we could do this. I kept reaching up her leg and she kept moving my hand away and going back to the make-out thing like everything was fine until the next time my hand went up beyond her thigh. Finally she moved my hand up to her shirt, thinking that would be good enough, which was definitely not good enough, which I made clear when I reached into my pocket and pulled out a condom.

"What's that for?" she asked, and I could tell from her expression that it totally scared her. All the better, get it out in the open. This is what I'm all about now.

"You *know*."

"Not now," she answered.

"Why not?" I was doing my reaching up her leg again, which I knew was going to cause a problem, but I was not going to stop so easily. She would really have to make a choice, as in her principles or her boyfriend, she couldn't have both. I had to keep the pressure on, so I kept talking as I was massaging, looking into her eyes, all sincere and all: "We've been going out like three months, and so far all you do is make promises." And even though nothing I was saying was actually true, it sounded good. As in, we weren't actually going out for three months, not, at least in my mind, sure we hooked up in school and at a bunch of parties and because she wanted to, we held hands, and I *let* her call me her boyfriend, but all of that was, at least in my mind, part of the master plan.

"I'm not ready." She was saying this but not exactly moving my hand away.

10:25.

I was thinking this girl was too into me to make me stop. I could make it happen.

Still, I was running out of time.

"C'mon" was all I said. (I know, I know, in writing this, "C'mon" doesn't sound like all that persuasive an argument, but you should've heard the way I said it.) Also, I was getting places with my hand and I think she was getting into it. At least I thought so, until she pulled my hand back.

"OK, OK, I'll do you, OK?"

That immediately quieted me down.

She made me raise the volume on the car radio, which I was supercareful about, given the risk of Lindsey discovering us and all. And then at 10:44 P.M., Eastern Daylight Time, on June 24, during "Hips Don't Lie," which was on the radio like a billion times a day at that time, I entered one form of manhood, even though I had still not accomplished my ultimate goal.

She had definitely not done this before, this much I knew, even though I had never done it before either. Still, she was good enough to stay my girlfriend beyond the 10:55 P.M. deadline. She had no idea that she was, at one point, twenty minutes from losing her boyfriend forever.

And at precisely 11:03 P.M., every member of Club Crew knew about my accomplishments, having received my text messages. Back at you, Bobby G.

Turned out that keeping the pressure on the bigger prize made the smaller prize easy to get. As in, every time we were together, I took out a condom or suggested that we have sex, and she said she wasn't ready and then went down on me. It got to where it became automatic for her, without me saying anything, during movies, in the bathroom stalls at Pinky's, in some random room at like every party we went to. So while I didn't really feel anything for her, I was becoming addicted to getting head, so no way could I actually break it off with her. And the problem was, while we were kind of a couple before, Maddy now thought she had bragging rights to me, so I ended up having to stay with her like all night at every party in order to get my prize.

To give you an idea of the sacrifices I was making, there were these superhot girls showing up at different parties from different schools, and they all seemed into me, and just when I was doing good with one of them, Maddy would show up out of nowhere, stepping out of the shadows after spending some time with one of her girlfriends, and start hanging on to me, draping herself over my shoulder with that total "I own him" look.

By July I was going out of my mind from her when I ran into Burn, or rather, he almost ran into me. Literally. He was driving his aunt's minivan, even though he had no license or anything, and he pulled alongside me, on my bike.

"Yo, Crash, I'm going to Pinky's. You want lunch? My treat."

I told him that I was on my way to Maddy's house, and he laughed and pulled the van in front of my bike, telling me to let her wait. Easily convinced, and most definitely needing a break, I lifted the bike into the back of the van, noticing that he had this wheelchair contraption, which took up most of the space.

Then I slipped into the passenger seat and he shoved a half-burned joint at me, telling me to try it, that it's Roxanne's latest stash. "Purple haze," he muttered, referencing a particularly strong strain of weed. "This stuff has quite a kick to it."

I honestly don't know what made me get into the van, as I knew it was illegal for him to drive and never really trusted Burn in the first place. Plus I couldn't believe it was pure coincidence that he found me on my way to Maddy's, so I had to believe that he was up to something. He still seemed like the normal Burn to me, just more subdued, but again, Roxanne's purple haze was so fucking dank.

We got to Pinky's and he ordered seemingly every single thing on the menu, and then as we sit together, he starts in, first, for some reason, all about Arcade Fire, who I had never heard of, and he was telling me how great their album was, how he won't listen to anything else. They were like the new Beatles, he said, even though he knew that I knew that every time he discovered a musical group he compared them to the Beatles, like they were gods or something.

A tray of food came: a stack of Pinky burgers piled high, cheese fries, onion rings, desserts, milk shakes. I grabbed a burger and a chocolate shake before he started on the rest.

He continued to talk, stopping only to one-bite the first burger, then on to the next, and that's when I realized that he had been bulking up. His arms were twice the size they were a few weeks before. So I asked him was he doing steroids, because he was too big for his own good. And he said no, just working out a lot and taking natural supplements, which, he added, he got off the internet.

I had to wonder if he was into something dangerous without knowing it, except Burn, being Burn, never did anything without knowing every possible angle, which meant he probably knew the entire chemical makeup of whatever it was he was on.

So I asked him about the wheelchair, and he said he was working on a new invention but he didn't want to talk about it. What he wanted to talk about was my relationship with Maddy.

"How's that working out for you?"

"OK." Me, being suspicious. Did she somehow set him up to ask? What was his motive on this otherwise?

"She seems a little too into you. Like a redonkulous amount."

"Kind of" is what I said. I finished my burger and started in on his fries, still hungry, but from the look in his eyes, I was actually afraid that he might snap at me like a wild dog if I touched another burger or even another fry.

"And you still can't get her to go all the way." He laughed, demolishing another burger in another one bite. I considered lying, except that, like, everybody in town knew that if Maddy *had* gone all the way, everyone would have found out, and he would have found out the same way. Besides, he wasn't asking, he was telling. "Which means you are still a virgin. . . ."

"Like you're not?" I said, sneaking more fries under his suspicious eyes.

"Of course not," he said, confirming in my mind, at that time, that he and Christina did it. It made sense, as they had been going out for months. I didn't exactly know what to say, but what came out was "how was it?" and he answered, "which time?" and I said, "what do you mean which time?" and he said, "with which person?" So I had to ask, "how many?" and he said, "five, working on six."

Now five may not seem like a big number to a guy who was like a junior in college, but we're talking a sophomore in high school. If it was anybody else telling me this, I would have known that they were completely full of shit, especially a guy who spent most of his time hanging with one particular girl as he did. But Burn never lied. It was a known fact that he was compelled to share the truth with you, good or bad. Whenever he talked, that was just the way he was. What he said next was: "Once you get out of high school, getting laid is like no big thing at all. Older girls want it just as much as we do. And so, in my case, all I had to do was find older girls, which is easy for me because I look older than you." Which, no question, he did, as anyone walking into Pinky's that afternoon could have taken him for my older brother or cousin, given that he was taller, more developed than I was. "And which is also easy for me," he continued, "because my sister's friends are all older, and whenever my mother wants us out of the house, I go with Rox on weekends into Manhattan. When you mix older girls and alcohol and X," referring to ecstasy, which was as foreign to me, at that time, as actual intercourse, "you have a perfect recipe for a wild encounter, especially with one of Roxanne's friends, because, I don't have to tell you, Roxanne is out there, so you can imagine that her friends, well you know, birds of a feather."

I must have made a face like I didn't know birds at all. So he got more explicit. "One of her friends wanted to train tigers, spent like a year in Thailand on a tiger farm, and she said that I had tiger in me, so I let her, you know, totally train me, and I did whatever she said to do, which was pretty much everything you've seen on the internet, and a few things even *I* never saw before. And then she introduced me to one of her friends, this girl Irina, who made me do things to her you can't even imagine. Of course when they both found out I was only sixteen, it was pretty much over, which is why I'm working out . . . I need to look even older."

He demolished another burger in a second.

I cautiously took another french fry. This was too much to handle. I was still trying to figure out whether there were such things as tiger farms at all, and finally coming to grips with the fact that Burn had approached getting laid as he did everything else. He had turned it into a science.

Motherfucking genius.

"And given the fact that you got April to go out with me back in the day, in case you thought I forgot, I do kind of owe you for getting me started on the process." And I was thinking he's finally getting down to it but having no idea what process he meant.

"Follow my instructions and I can pretty much guarantee that you will get what you want."

Which made me ask the obvious, "You mean . . . ?"

He nodded. "Absolutely," as I took another fry with him staring again.

"Crash," he said, "don't fucking touch the onion rings. They're mine."

He went on to explain that the only way to get what you wanted from a high school girl who liked you was to go out with her, then after you're sure that she really, really likes you, you have to dump her unexpectedly. Then after that, call her, and get back together on your terms. This way, she'll deliver on the expectation of getting you back. He said that that was what I had to do if I wanted to get with Maddy beyond oral.

To be honest, by that point, it didn't matter if it worked or not, the concept of not having to deal with her for a few days was incentive enough. So I agreed to try his plan.

"Call her now," he said, "with me here to guide you."

Suddenly I got skittish. I mean, she was taking care of me whenever I wanted, and she wasn't all that bad as a girlfriend, just overly clingy. She was actually pretty good to me. Plus I didn't exactly have a tiger trainer in Manhattan waiting for me if his advice turned out to suck.

But he was adamant. "Trust me on this, Crash." He grabbed my phone and punched in her number without hesitation, then handed the phone back. Before I could even ask how he knew her cell number from memory, she was on.

"Steven? You were supposed to be on your way over. I was getting worried about you."

I looked at Burn. He stared back, picking up one of his precious onion rings and pointing at me with it. *Do it,* he mouthed.

"It's not working out," I said to her. "I think we need to stop seeing each other."

On the other end of the phone there was complete silence. Then, faintly . . . "Why?"

OK, I started feeling immediately terrible. I hadn't actually broken up with a girl before, and this girl didn't do anything wrong.

And there was Burn, mouthing *Just do it*.

"It's not working out is all," I said, and as I started searching for more things to say, Burn snatched the phone out of my hand and snapped it shut.

"You will thank me," he said.

The phone immediately buzzed on vibrate. I knew it was her. Burn held on to my phone, letting it dangle like one of his onion rings. "If you don't talk to her for the rest of the week, by Friday, you will get what you want."

I could not believe what I had just done. But I instantly felt something else, which was extreme relief, not to have to talk to her, even for a few days.

"One more thing," he added. "Now that you're not seeing Maddy anymore, I need you to call my sister. She's been depressed lately. I want you to fix her, like you did the last time."

This startled me. My brain processed three bits of information at the same time. (1) Was Roxanne suicidal again? (2) Why did Burn, someone who was all about logic, even consider that I could have somehow made his sister better? And (3) Did he know about the magic beans?

All of which he answered without me having to ask.

"I mean she's not going to kill herself or anything, not like that, but she doesn't laugh lately, Crash. The one thing you have to say about my sister is that she knows how to laugh, like when she does it, she totally commits herself to the utter and complete joy of laughter. I have never seen anyone do that, Crash, not like her. I have watched people laugh all my life, and it's nothing like the way Roxanne does it. To be honest, I don't even know how to try." Which was probably true, as I didn't think I ever actually saw Burn even crack a smile, much less actually laugh out loud.

"And you"—he was shaking his head up and down, all excited, like he was a jockey on a winning horse—"you, Crash, make my sister laugh."

Point was, it wasn't about the hospital or the magic beans at all, but he was making me feel like I was the only one who could snap her out of a major funk, which made me feel like a hero, so of course I agreed to call her.

I had to ask, why did he care, as he never seemed to pay that much attention to Roxanne, or so it seemed to me. He explained that he always loved his sister, but resented her for not sticking up for him when he was younger. So after she got out of the hospital, they started talking and she told him about how much she hated things, people mostly, how nothing made any sense to her. And he told her how hard it was when they sent him away, and he admitted to her that he didn't understand why nobody loved him, sending him so far from what wasn't actually home but was the only home he knew and so far from his family.

And they would go out to the garage at nights, to talk about how devastated he was about the fox, which wasn't just about the fox, but about everything in his life, even though she was the one who was supposed to be sad. And sitting in the garage, facing each other so they could only see each other by the light of the flashlights, Roxanne cried for him, because, she told him, she didn't know then, and never knew, what it felt like to be him. After all, they told her he was crazy, so she believed it.

And so, Burn explained, when Roxanne tried to commit suicide, he was sure it was his fault, because he knew how sad he made her.

"Which is why I need you to call her now," he told me.

Now, trust me on this, if you ever felt like you were the only one in the world who could do something that no one else could do, could you possibly not do it? This is exactly how I felt when I took back my cell phone. And by then of course there were already like thirty calls from Maddy, and now those were easy to ignore, because all I could think about was Roxanne and me saving her again.

So I dialed Roxanne's number, and as soon as she hears my voice, she says this:

"Crashinsky. Let me guess what you're calling for." With her voice sounding nothing at all like the depressed version that Burn was describing. In fact, she sounded like the super-sarcastic Roxanne that I was used to.

"It's not what you think," I said, genuinely concerned.

"You're still a virgin, aren't you?" she asked. "Well, are you? What's the matter, Brancato not giving it up?"

"We broke up," I said, like this was old news, even though it had happened less than five minutes ago.

"And so you figured that it was time to have me make good on my promise?"

Now Burn was scribbling a note on a napkin that was blotched with ketchup. I struggled to read it and finally made out his handwriting, which said, *Ask to take her to a movie.*

Which I did, but instead of agreeing, she starts laughing like crazy and says this:

"A movie? A frickin' movie? Crash, you stupid shit, are you out of your frickin' mind? Did you really think I was serious that night, that I was going to fuck you just because you gave me a few beans?" She is cracking herself up even if I'm not laughing.

Burn hears the echo of her laughter on the other side of my phone and actually breaks a smile, like he knows he's doing the right thing. So I repeat, "What about the movie?" because Burn was writing it out for me on the napkin again, underlining the words over and over.

And she says: "Actually, Crash, know what? I *would* rather fuck you than sit with you while you watched some stupid movie and laughed like a frickin' retard in all the inappropriate places. Besides, you would *not* like the movies I like. I only watch foreign movies. With subtitles. Do you think you can sit through a whole movie that you have to read? If you can frickin' read?"

Did I forget how frickin' crazy this family was?

I looked at Burn, who was continuing to coach me. Was he screwing with me or was this the real thing? Because the Roxanne who was on the phone wasn't interested in seeing me at all. With his prodding, I told her that yes I could sit through a movie I had to read (even though I knew I couldn't, or at least didn't much want to).

All she did was laugh when I told her this. So maybe it was working, but not the way I expected when Burn told me what he wanted. I'm about to hang up when she says, OK, but your mom will have to drive us. So I told her, yes I was sure my mom could drive us, and she tells me, "Crash, I'm fucking with you, can't you tell?" She laughed again. "As in being frickin' sarcastic. I'm not having your mommy drive us to the movies, that was my point. I have my own license. After all, I'm *your sister's* age. And oh yeah, I'm not fucking you either."

She hung up. Leaving me to stare questioningly at Burn, who was stuffing the remaining onion rings into his mouth.

"She'll go," he said, his mouth filled with onion paste, which he made no effort to hide.

He was right.

She called back a few days later and said she was sorry for being so cunty when I called, telling me that she felt bad, so she would make it up to me and take me to a regular movie. And a few hours later, we were at a theater in Connecticut, watching *The Fast and the Furious: Tokyo Drift*, not a foreign flick, because she thought I would like it better. She had driven to

Connecticut because no one in our school goes that far for a movie, and she did not want to be confronted by anyone she knew, for my sake, she said, whatever that meant. I didn't question it, as Connecticut was just fine for me, and along the way, she reached into her glove compartment and produced a perfect joint for us to share.

She even bought me popcorn and a soda, which of course made me feel like her younger brother. And even though she said that she was only seeing the movie for me, she was way more into it than I was, laughing like crazy at the speed and the noise, and she didn't seem at all depressed or suicidal or anything. Of course, I couldn't concentrate on the movie at all, given that the stakes were so high, as in based on Burn's assessment of her situation, I had to keep her laughing, so the pressure was on, and also I tried not to think of sex with her, which was all I could think about.

So sex and laughing was still all I could think about when we were sitting together at this restaurant outside the theater, having chicken wings and fries, which of course made it beyond difficult to follow her as she talked about going to college and leaving home at a particularly bad time and being concerned about how David was going to be without her to control him especially now with his mother's special needs and all and her aunt Beth (who frickin' knew that was Aunt Peesmell's real name?) was being so bitchy and not helping her mother at all when she needed it most.

I had nothing, absolutely nothing, to say.

"You're such a little boy, Crashinsky," she said, attacking the wings, sauce making her clown faced. She wiped off the sauce with one hand, munched with the other. It occurred to me that she ate with the same mannerisms as her brother. "It's a very endearing quality, honestly, Crashinsky, but I can't be your girlfriend, so get that out of your frickin' head."

"I didn't . . . I wasn't . . ." Me, all flustered. "Burn, David . . . your brother told me to call you," I stammered. "He said that I had to make you laugh, that you were depressed and all. Like last time. Well, not like last time."

This got her to laugh. "With everything going on in our lives, I didn't know that he had time for practical jokes."

"Meaning?"

"Meaning I'm supposed to let you off easy."

"Because?"

"Because you're a kid, you're the same age as my brother, younger, and even if I liked you that way, which I *don't*, I couldn't go out with you. You don't even frickin' drive, much less keep up with me on any level. Are you going to pick me up on your bicycle and make out with me at your teenage parties? You have to know that I'm beyond that at this point."

"I'm just supposed to make you laugh, is all." I was suddenly not at all hungry, and she continued to eat the rest with increasing speed.

"Look, Crashinsky, I know you like me, that you've always liked me, but get it through your head, it's not going to happen. So please, go back to your world."

I had absolutely nothing to say.

And then, after she finished the remaining wings, she drove me home and parked outside my house. Then she unbuckled her seatbelt and slid over and put her arm around my neck,

and then jolted my seat back,

and then climbed on top of me, kissed me deeper than I had ever experienced before, with her on top and me beneath her, making me totally feel like the girl.

And then she whispered in my ear: "Because I wanted to and nothing more. Now get out."

And as she said this, she flipped the door open and nudged me out of her car, wiping her mouth like she had just finished the wings again and climbing back into the driver's seat, laughing.

"Had a nice time, Crash. Maybe we'll do this again one day when you're older." And she drove off.

WTF, as in what the fuck.

For whatever else it was worth, Burn was right about Maddy, as in she never stopped calling all week, then had her friends call. She left messages that it was all her fault, that she was sorry, that she was too demanding, and if I could just call once, that would be enough.

Then by the end of the week, angry messages, like I'm a scumbag, and how could I not see her. Then, more resigned to "call me when you can."

And so a week later, I did. Even though by then, all I could think about was Roxanne. I just couldn't get it out of my head that if she was so adamant about not seeing me, then there was no reason to say good-bye the way she did.

Now comes the weird part.

When I finally call Maddy, just as Burn suggested, instead of telling me that she was ready for the full commitment, as in going all the way, she tells me that she heard I was going out with someone behind her back and she doesn't want to see me or talk to me.

WTF.

Now comes the even weirder part: The next night, I'm at a party with my boys and hanging with the Herd and in walks Maddy, with, of all people . . . get this:

David Burnett.

Like, they are totally together. So I go over to Burn and pull him aside and ask what the fuck was going on, after all I did for him, as in taking Roxanne out, and I had to tell him, as far as I was concerned, she wasn't having any issues at all, unlike what he told me, and what was he doing with Maddy? After all, banging Maddy was supposed to be my reward for taking his sister out, everything according to plan, the plan that he laid out so completely a week before over lunch at Pinky's. So what the fuck?

And he said, get this, "I told Maddy you had a new girlfriend. I figured she should know."

"Figured she should know?"

"Yeah, figured she should know that you were just out to bang her," he said. "Payback is a bitch, isn't it?"

"Payback for what?"

"Christina. I always knew we were connected in some way, and you can imagine when the girl I love more than life itself tells me that she likes me as a friend because she was always into someone else that way, that news did not make me happy. And then I figured out it was you. But it figures, doesn't it, because except for that one night when I beat you at poker, you're always benefitting from the things I do. Well, no more, Crash. I'm done."

All I could think was, Christina? How did she figure into the equation? I had nothing whatsoever to do with her since eighth grade. I asked what about April, but he dismissed the April concept. He even had Roxanne thinking that she was doing me a favor by taking me to the movies, because, he told her, Maddy had broken it off with me and I was devastated. So Roxanne was part of his plan, even though there was no way she could have even known that she was.

Then he disappeared with Maddy into another room, and I left before they emerged. When I got home and switched on the computer, there was an IM from him. What he said was:

Revenge is sweet.

* * *

Truth was, I actually didn't give a shit. Turns out I didn't miss Maddy one bit. And I realized that Roxanne was right, that she and I lived in two different worlds.

I also had what Newman called residual popularity, which he described as being considered off the market for a while, so now that I was back (even though I was never actually gone), some of the Herd Girls missed me. Plus, they all seemed to like the fact that I could commit to a relationship even though it was only for a short period, and even though no one actually liked Maddy (actually that was helpful as well, because no one felt any sympathy for her about being dumped, especially with her hooking up so quickly with Burn).

Speaking of Burn, I was happy for him. He seemed to be into Maddy. Plus, on some level, he probably felt that he beat me at another game, even though, and I can admit it now, in the immediate days after I confronted him at the party, on a purely coincidental basis, I managed to finally hook up with April Walker, who picked up where Maddy left off. OK, maybe it was wrong of me, but I was wasted at one of the junior parties and she came over and said that she heard that David Burnett had stolen my girlfriend and I was supposed to be devastated, and before I could argue the point, she was consoling me with her mouth.

So like it or not, once again, Burn somehow did all of the work for me, just like he complained about. But I had the good sense not to send him a text bragging about getting even, because truth was, I wasn't even at all. Given that April and her willing mouth was available whenever I wanted without the heavy-duty obligation of having to be a boyfriend and hold her hand and tell her how pretty she looked in her new Juicy T-shirt, I once again had a straight flush to his full house.

And, as I said, the Herd Girls were all happy to have me back, so when I wasn't secretly with April, I was hooking up with Annie Russo, who was always fun, and even though she had her limits, she was the best time I could have with a girl my own age.

And I even thought a lot about calling Christina after what Burn told me. But she was away that summer at some kind of performance camp. Besides, I didn't much care for her drama friends, so being as life was going along pretty good, my thinking was, why ruin a good thing? Besides, no matter what Burn said, he wasn't done with her, and he was crazy, so whenever my mind wandered to Christina, I called April.

And Lindsey finally had a boyfriend, some supernerd who went to MIT and was mad into computers, so he wired our house and every laptop for TV, which I don't have to tell you at this point made Jamie fall in love with him. Plus, he got me into all of the porn websites without needing a password, which made me fall in love with him too (jk, not a homo).

His name was Nick and he was the biggest Red Sox fan, and my mom liked him and apparently even Jacob approved. And what's more, to everyone's surprise, he thought I was the coolest kid he ever met. So he would spend time in my room with me arguing over the Red Sox/Yankees rivalry and playing Xbox 360 and telling me about how cool the PlayStation 3 was going to be since in effect it was a supercomputer and he had heard that they were going to use the same technology to find life in other solar systems. He was always saying stuff like that. For some odd reason he reported back to my mom that I was a genius in my own way and that he wished that he was more like me, which made Lindsey look at me a little differently (although, let's be honest, not all that much).

And Jamie was spending time out of the house, and doing real good at camp, where she started making real friends. And to prove the point, she came home drunk one afternoon, which only I knew, and we had like the best time on the deck with her laughing at every single thing I said. And she apparently took a liking to vodka, because she was coming home like every afternoon beyond loopy, which was OK to me since Jamie needed an outlet, given that Medusa had pretty much become my dog by that time and was completely attached to me, ignoring Jamie's pleas for affection.

Then, at the beginning of August, in the blazing heat of the summer, the weekend that *Talladega Nights* opened, the entire Club Crew blazed in the parking lot of the multiplex and celebrated our close bond and Evan's seventeenth birthday with a bottle of Cristal, which, even though I didn't much like champagne, tasted pretty good and got us laughing. And Annie Russo was there and she took care of me in her car.

And there were more parties after that and tremendous weed and flowing drinks and hookups. So it was a pretty fucking awesome summer, filled with good times and surprises.

And in a summer filled with surprises, Mrs. Burnett did the most surprising thing of all:

She died.

I had no idea she was even sick, but apparently she, Burn, and Roxanne were dealing with the fact that she had breast cancer for years. First it was in one breast, my mother explained to me on the night that she told us, and then she was OK for a long time, but then it came back, so the doctors were more aggressive and treated her with all kinds of chemo to keep it from spreading.

She didn't actually die of breast cancer. She ended up dying from the treatment. Apparently some kind of rare reaction to the chemo and a blood clot that traveled, don't ask me, I'm no scientist, alls I know was it was a sudden, unexpected thing.

And I had to go to the funeral. All of us, not just me, but Jamie and Lindsey and even Jacob and Felicia, as Jacob managed Mrs. Burnett's accounts and all.

So in the middle of August, on a rainy morning (not just rain, like, monsoon rain) in the middle of the week, the group of us were sitting together in a row listening to some rabbi talk about Elaine like he knew her, even though I knew and everybody else knew that Mrs. Burnett no longer considered herself Jewish and had joined some cult that believed that the world was coming to an end, which it did, for her, anyways.

More importantly to me, this was the first time I had seen Caroline Prescott and Felicia in the same room together since that fateful Thanksgiving dinner. They seemed to be ignoring each other very well, as I didn't see either woman talk to or even acknowledge the other's existence.

Burn was in a suit that didn't fit at all. Lindsey, being Lindsey, commented that he looked like a homeless guy, which might be what the future had planned for him. I went over to shake his hand and he just stared at mine, with a look like when the fuck have we ever shaken hands so why start now? So I pulled back and then he said:

"Your father's girlfriend actually got better looking. How is that even possible?"

That's when I saw Roxanne. She didn't look goth or emo or anything else at all. She had dyed her hair back to normal and was apparently wearing one of her mother's black dresses, looking real adult.

And absolutely beautiful. In fact, I couldn't take my eyes off her. She was, hate to say this, unbelievably sexy at her mother's funeral.

I went over to her, extending my hand again. She ignored it and instead hugged me for a long time and whispered, "Thanks for coming, Steven."

This completely disarmed me. I'm not going to lie, I was looking forward to seeing her, in a weird way, having not seen her since the movie date thing and knowing that I wouldn't otherwise have the opportunity again.

What I said was "Sorry for your loss," which is what Jacob told all of us we had to say and not to say anything else to avoid fucking things up (especially to me, no surprise there, thank you, Jacob, for your continued support).

And then there was the coffin. There, in the front of the room. This was my very first funeral. Call me lucky, but no one had died around me until Mrs. Burnett. So I couldn't look at it for too long, knowing that she was in there, and yet, somehow, not.

And my mom came over to me and asked how I was doing. But I was doing fine. So she asked Jamie, and Jamie thought it was cool, all of us being there together. And Felicia came over to me and asked was this my first one and I said yes. And she told me that she had been to many in her country, but not so much here and they are different. It seemed that everything was always different in her country.

A bunch of my friends were there, most of the Club Crew and a lot of Burn's friends too. Plus some of Roxanne's friends—you could tell who they were by the way they looked. Also Christina, looking superhot, and Maddy and April, two girls I had majorly hooked up with, were there, and it only made me think of how different it would have been with Roxanne, when, as if on cue, she got up to speak. She was saying the nicest things about her mom until she started to cry, and then she waved off the rest of her speech, with a "sorry, Mommy," sat back down, crying, saying, "I miss you, Mommy. I miss you."

Of course that got most of the adults crying too and me wondering what was going to happen to the two of them, her and her brother.

Then Burn got up and announced that he and Roxanne were orphans now and that God sucked and so did anyone who believed in God. "So if you do, please don't bother to talk to me ever again. That's all. Thank you."

He was all about rage. I made a mental note not to go anywhere near him.

After it was over, I watched to see if my mom and Felicia ever interacted, but except for a possible mutual nod, they never did.

Then the Burnetts left for the cemetery and we went home. But not for long, because my mom had worked it out with Burn's aunt to set up for visitors at her house, so we were quickly on our way there, despite our protests.

"Listen to me, the three of you. You are going to do the right thing if it kills you," she announced to us as she drove us over, in a very uncharacteristic shout which pretty much took the wind out of our complaining.

So there we were, the three of us, each of us on our cell phones talking or texting. I paced the rooms nervously, not feeling comfortable about being in a dead woman's house and knowing that I was going to have to make conversation with Burn and his sister, both of whom were entirely unpredictable.

Then a limo pulled up and out came the aunt, then some random relatives, and finally Roxanne. No Burn in sight. I found out soon enough that David had taken his mother's car and left the cemetery on his own.

We were there for hours while other kids came and went and Burn never showed up. Lindsey said about everything that she could possibly say to Roxanne in the first five minutes and then mostly sat with other adults. Jamie found her way into the den and was watching TV, so no problem there. And me, I was going out of my frickin' mind, watching Roxanne spend time with her friends in another room, waiting for some of my friends to show, which they didn't, and finally sneaking off to watch TV with Jamie. At least until Roxanne finally tapped me on the shoulder and asked me if I could go with her.

I followed her up the stairs, past the closed door that was her mother's bedroom, past Burn's room, to the room at the end of the hallway that was hers.

It was a mess. A huge pile of interconnected clothes covered the floor, more clothes draped on her desk and her chair, and another pile on her unmade bed.

"Turn around," she told me, making me face the wall. Ten seconds later, she said "OK," and when I turned back to her, she was out of the black dress and into sweats.

She pushed the clothes and the other stuff on the bed onto the floor and motioned to me. "I need you to lie down," she said, which of course I did, wondering what she had in mind. Was this somehow going to be it? And when I did what she asked, she followed, lying down beside me, facing away from me so that I was staring at the back of her head.

"I need you to hold me," she said. "And not say anything. Can you do that?"

I put my arms around her. She pulled them tighter, one under and around her, the other around her waist, until we were curled up in a ball.

"If you so much as get a hard-on, I swear to frickin' Christ I will sic David on you" is what she said with me holding her.

"Don't worry, I'm here for you" is what I told her, all the time wondering how in hell I was going to control my sixteen-year-old ever-ready love bone. I don't have to tell you how difficult that was, with her hair smelling like coconut and her body gently heaving because she was quietly sobbing.

But I was able to control it, and soon enough we both fell asleep, with me not feeling like the younger brother of anyone anymore, although I had never actually "slept" with a girl before.

Jamie woke us, standing over us, and I felt completely exposed even though nothing had happened. "Mom says we're going" was all she said.

Roxanne said she just wanted to stay in bed, so I asked if she wanted me to stay and she said she was OK. I invited her back to my house, told her that she could always stay with us, and she seemed to be back to being Roxanne, because she answered, "Good idea, Crash. I'll sleep in Lindsey's room."

So I told her that I could be there for her whenever she wanted, and so she hugged me again without saying anything at all.

I went back downstairs looking for my mom.

It was superlate. Apparently my mom planned to stay a little longer with Aunt Peesmell. Burn was still MIA. Not my problem, I thought. Except I was feeling terrible for Roxanne and even him. I could not imagine life without my mom. Me and Jamie and even Lindsey talked about that on the way home, Lindsey driving, me in the passenger seat, and Jamie in back, just a normal family for once.

According to Lindsey from what she heard from hanging with the adults, Burn's aunt was going to take care of them, at least for now, unless Burn became too difficult. What she had told them was that she wasn't equipped to handle the two of them. Not too big a deal where Roxanne was concerned; she was heading to college in a few weeks anyways. David, however, was a whole other problem, as he still had two years of school left and he was not exactly the most stable kid in the universe.

What she also told my mom, in front of Lindsey, was that my father, the ever-helpful Jacob, had offered his services, if she needed it. What his services consisted of, according to Lindsey, was finding a place for David if he couldn't make it work at Meadows. Finding a place meant, of course, getting Burn into some kind of appropriate school once again. Had this actually happened, I would just be another stoner kid without a book to write or a medal from the mayor or anything else that happened to me as a result of 4/21. Not to give anything away, but of course Burn did not end up going to any Jacob-recommended school.

What Burn did was drive.

Newman once joked that Burn had become like the Forrest Gump of driving, because after school started in September, Burn was hardly around. Everyone knew that he was on the road, which meant that he was on some excursion by himself to another city or another state or upstate New York or wherever his GPS took him.

That was how he dealt with his mother's death. Newman said that maybe he was looking for his mom in all those places. Kenny, who probably knew Burn best, said he just wanted the solitude of being in a car.

Whatever. All I know was Burn was all about driving during the beginning of junior year.

How Roxanne dealt was another story entirely.

CHAPTER EIGHTEEN

HOW ROXANNE TAUGHT ME HISTORY

Roxanne went retro.

That's what Aunt Peesmell told my mom, who stayed in touch with her in the weeks after the funeral. What she meant was that Roxanne had apparently decided that she wanted to be a hippie, even though there were like no hippies left. This transition took place after Roxanne was rummaging through some of her mother's boxes in Aunt Peesmell's attic and found pictures of her mom all decked out in clothes from the sixties. After searching some more, she found the actual clothes and tried them on and then decided never to take them off again. Not only that, she started shopping at vintage stores in the city, finding more vintage clothes and apparently deciding to single-handedly bring back the look.

So when I ran into her on Main Street at the end of September, I hardly recognized her. In fact I might not have recognized her at all, except for her screaming out:

"Yo, Crashinsky, why in frickin' hell haven't you called me?"

She was in a bright shirt that had peace signs all over it, making her look like one of those Grateful Dead/Phish heads that are always traveling to see some jam band or another. She also had what she called granny glasses on. Plus long hair, blond hair, and I couldn't figure out how she managed to grow it out so quickly.

"It's a frickin' wig, Crashinsky," she had to tell me, making me feel stupid when she caught me staring. "I dyed my hair to match it. You like?"

I did, actually.

Turns out she never made it to college in California, and had decided at the last minute to stay home with Burn, which meant that she enrolled in a school in Manhattan so that she could commute. Which, after all was said and done, she didn't mind, because she loved spending time in the city with her real friends and didn't want to leave them anyways. And by the way, how was Lindsey doing, she asked, but she knew and I knew that she wasn't really interested, so I said OK, even though I didn't actually know, since it had been like three weeks since school started for both of us and I hadn't actually talked to my sister since she left.

"I heard the new Jackass movie is opening this weekend—you wanna go?" she asked, and even though I had plans with the entire Club Crew for opening night, I said sure. And she said, "I'll call you," and I said, "Sure," and then she hugged me for a long time before she left, and I got to watch her continue her stroll down Main Street like she was a visitor from another time.

She never called, which didn't surprise me at that point. I didn't call her either, which I didn't think I could do, even though I kind of obsessed about it for a few days, even to the point of actually picking up the phone before giving up.

Instead, I ended up blazing and going to see *Jackass Number Two* with my boys, which was way, way better than the first one, if nothing else just for Johnny Knoxville, who was back in a big way and taking even more risks than my hero Steve-O.

And school sucked again for me, except for the social scene, which was heating up as the girls were getting more into drinking and the guys were getting into experimenting with everything, which made it more difficult to concentrate in school and virtually impossible to do any kind of homework.

This being my junior year, which was apparently considered to be the most important for purposes of getting into college, my mom was determined not to sit back and watch me do poorly again. Also, ACTs and SATs and all kinds of other college tests were coming up, and half my grade already had tutors coming to their houses to teach them how to take these tests, which meant that I was going to have to have one of those guys as well, which was scheduled for every Saturday morning at nine, and which, I don't have to mention, wasn't working at all. And just as I was starting to seriously drown in schoolwork, my mom came up with a master plan that would, if all things went well, put me on a path to success. No, not another type of drug, or after-school courses, or biofeedback, or a gluten-free diet; those were last year's solutions. This year, she found me the perfect tutor.

Roxanne Burnett.

Caroline Prescott had arranged everything without consulting me first and without having any clue as to the possible implications as far as I was concerned. Her logic was infallible. After all, Roxanne was, academically, as brilliant as Burn was. She was available, she needed the money, and she told my mom that I was a "good kid" and she seemed to think we could work well together, which, of course meant that my mom already had had direct conversations with her, so she was in on this.

In fact, it was all set. I was supposed to go over there Tuesdays and Thursdays after school, and after doing my homework with Roxanne, whose schedule coincided with mine on those days, my mom would pick me up after. For that, my mom was going to pay Roxanne twenty-five dollars an hour. Which gave her motivation to have me over. And my mom promised it would be way different from the time that Lindsey tried to tutor me.

The fifteen-second scene from *Billy Madison* flashed before my eyes, with Adam Sandler's teacher-girlfriend challenging him to learn by removing one article of clothing for every correct answer that Billy gives her. I pictured myself on a bed, with Roxanne across the room, slowly removing her jacket just like Billy's girl. Yeah, it could be way different from the time that Lindsey tried to tutor me.

Even so, when I showed up for my first tutoring session, I was beyond nervous, and not because I didn't know which Roxanne I would be dealing with, the one who wanted me to lie in bed with her when her mom died or the one who considered me to be a "good kid," words that stayed in my brain after my mom mentioned them, but because I was smart enough to know that while she knew that I wasn't the sharpest kid in high school, the truth was she didn't actually know how smart or stupid I really was. After all, there was a part of me that was always able to keep up with her sarcasm, so despite the fact that she was older than me and into entirely different things than me, somehow we connected on a certain level, because I was able to deflect her in my own way. Meaning she was fire, more fire than Burn was, and probably most people were scared of her. I mean, they had a right to be scared of her, because she saw you for who you were, not who you pretended to be. So I was pretty sure that when she actually got a chance to review my schoolwork, when she actually started to read my handwriting and my class notes, she would know, *she would totally know* that I was an idiot.

Let's face it, if I could have made things better at school, I absolutely would have. I would have listened more carefully if I could have, taken better notes if I could have, been better organized if I could have.

Except I couldn't.

I just couldn't follow the conversations of my teachers, or read a word of my notes, or keep my books in order, or prepare for tests and papers due, because my stupid motherfucking mind could not, no matter how fucking hard I tried, keep up.

And once Roxanne opened my notebook, she would know, and it would change her opinion of me forever.

Which was exactly how I was feeling standing in the hallway of Aunt Peesmell's massive Victorian house, which still smelled like urine, while Aunt Peesmell yelled up to Roxanne, who was in her bedroom down at the very end of the hall in the room where a few weeks before I lay beside her and smelled her hair.

"The Crashinsky boy is here."

No response, leaving me holding my backpack until it got heavy, not sure whether to put it down or back on my shoulders, thinking maybe it was a setup by Burn or something. Then, footsteps, and then there she was, at the top of the stairs wearing more sixties stuff, a black-and-white miniskirt dress thing, and standing in a way that I could almost, but not quite, see all the way up it.

"Time starts now," she said, looking at her watch. "You have two frickin' hours to learn something, Crashinsky."

Once in her room, she motioned for me to sit, pointing to the far corner, so I slouched into the beanbag chair on the floor. She took my backpack and sat cross-legged on her bed, brushing her hair/wig thing as she emptied the contents onto her quilt.

"Are you OK with this?" she asked.

Then I said what I thought was the most perceptive thing that I have ever said. I asked, "Are you?"

She laughed her huge Roxanne laugh. "What the frig is that supposed to mean, Crashinsky?"

I had to laugh too, as I didn't exactly know what I meant.

She sat on her bed and went through my notebook, smirk-laughing, me feeling just as stupid as Roxanne could make me feel, for like half an hour, with me staring at her looking through my work, and her making occasional random comments:

"Your handwriting sucks."

"You write like a child. We can fix that."

She studied my books for math, then earth science, which I was actually doing OK in, then English, then Spanish, which I was really super sucking at.

"First, history," she said, finally. "You have a test in two weeks."

I, of course, had no idea, but it must have been in one of the handouts. Who even thinks about a test two weeks in advance?

She tossed me the book.

"Open to page sixty-eight," she said, which I did from my corner of the room. "Read it out loud," which I did, one paragraph, then the next. "Keep going." So I read and read and read for, like, forever, and she listened as I got to words that I had never seen before and I glossed over them, trying not to make a big deal out of not knowing. But each time she stopped me and asked me if I knew the word or not, and she would tell me the meaning and then tell me, "Go on."

And when I finally finished the entire chapter, she asked me questions, some of which I knew the answers to and some I had no idea, even though I had just read the passages. And all this under the very watchful, doctorlike eye of Roxanne, staring down at me from her bed.

"Now what?" I asked.

She stood up. Walked across to me. She had these glossy boots on, called them go-go boots. I could practically see my reflection in them when she approached me. Then she stood over me, and I seemed to sink deeper into the beanbag chair.

"What's the difference between observation and inference?"

"That's from earth science, not history," I told her defensively.

"I know where it's from. What's the difference?"

I told her how observation was the direct gathering of

information using your five senses, and inference was the con- clusion based on the observations that you made, pretty much directly reciting the definitions that I remembered hearing in science class on the first day.

"See, you're not stupid, so get that out of your head now, because we can't work together if you continue to think you're stupid and use that as an excuse not to learn, which is what you do. If I didn't already know how smart you are, I never would have talked to you in the first place, because I frickin' hate stu- pid people and most people are stupid, Crashinsky."

"So how come I can't learn?" I asked meekly, which got her to nod her head and smirk at me; then she moved closer, and when she got close, she lifted her skirt slightly. Then, deftly, with her fingers on each side of her skirt, she lowered her pant- ies, pulling them down under her skirt, without even moving the skirt fabric in the slightest way. She did this so methodi- cally that even sitting there almost directly beneath her, I could not, even for a second, see a thing. Plus it happened so quickly that I didn't expect it at all.

"You can't learn because you always get what you want, so you never had to concentrate on something until you get it." She told me this as she removed the underwear one leg at a time, keeping herself covered with her free hand, with me too startled to even think about what was next, still craning my neck to peek and simply not being able to see anything.

"That's your talent, isn't it? Manifesting the things that you imagine, like magic," she said, more than asked. "I believe that everybody comes into life with at least one special talent. Yours is a really, really extraordinary one; it's what attracts other people to you, among other things. Unfortunately, it also victim- izes you, because you never learned how to work for anything. So you have decided that you don't need to concentrate on what you consider to be useless information."

She tossed her panties at me. "The kind of information that is not somehow useful to you."

I didn't know if she was insulting me or complimenting me. Or both. All while completely distracting me physically to the point of intoxication. This was just like Roxanne.

"I got my first tattoo," she said. "It's right here," using her finger to point to the area of her skirt just below her hip bone. Then she leaned forward, as if to kiss me, but instead whispered, "It's a bee . . . and I will show it to you if you answer all of the questions correctly in the next chapter."

She twirled around, heading back to the bed. "Now, read."

OK, at first I couldn't read at all, because I was thinking about what she said, and what she was offering, which was, in fact, *exactly* what I had wished for when my mom first mentioned the possibility that I would be working with Roxanne. I guess that scene from *Billy Madison* put it in my head, but it was just a fleeting fantasy, not like I really expected it. And yet, there it was, like the straight flush that I managed to pull out of nowhere against her brother. So yeah, she was totally correct, there was a part of me that, no matter what happened, expected that it would all work out, a part of me that believed that if I thought about something long and hard enough, I could make it happen.

So when I finally started to read, I stuttered, but went so slowly that I didn't miss a word, and I tried to listen to my voice, as if someone else was reading to me. Afraid that this technique wasn't good enough, I switched in my mind to other voices: Mrs. Terrigano, my history teacher, and then even Felicia, how would she sound reading the book? And as soon as my mind wandered, I stopped and reread the passage in my own voice, struggling against my wandering nature, and every time my mind strayed, I thought about the prize and started over again, taking a breath before every new paragraph.

And when I was done, she had five questions that she had written out while I was reading.

She read the first question. Easy. Andrew Jackson.

The second question, my answer, no hesitation, was, of course, correct. The third, correct. The fourth, correct. The fifth . . . the fifth . . . *I should have known.*

What a sucker I was. She wasn't going to let me see anything all along. She would let me go four questions in, then make it impossible, just to prove a point. How could I have been so stupid? The fifth question was some one-line thing from the book: What was the name of the guy who was the president of the Second National Bank, the one who was opposed by Andrew Jackson? I needed the entire name of the guy, first and last names.

OK, this was where I usually panicked on tests in school and ended up making something up. But not this time, not with so much at stake. Instead, I decided to play back, in my mind, the voices that I used to read the passage in my mind, was that passage Mrs. Terrigano, or my own voice, or Felicia's?

Second National Bank.

I recalled that I was using Felicia's voice in my head for that paragraph and she struggled with some of the words but not the name. It was . . . It was . . . I had nothing.

Then I remembered that when I was reading the passage, I was thinking that the name was similar to Tom Riddle, which I was pretty sure was Lord Voldemort's real name, the name he was born with.

Got it.

"Nicholas Biddle," I exclaimed triumphantly.

And now Roxanne was doing that smirk-laugh thing again, shaking her head, nodding in a way that I wasn't sure if I was right or wrong, and I honestly didn't know for sure until she got off her bed, stood up . . .

And lifted her skirt for me.

It was the most perfect bee that I had ever seen.

"Time's up, Crashinsky," she said, lowering her skirt almost immediately. "See you Thursday," which she had to repeat a few times because I was simply not getting up from the beanbag chair.

When I finally got the message, I grabbed my backpack off her bed, hearing the sound of my mother's car in the driveway, wishing that there was another hour, and already thinking that I wouldn't be able to last until Thursday without seeing her again.

On my way out, I had to ask.

"What's yours? Your special talent. You never said."

She smirked. "You already know my talent, Crashinsky. I laugh."

On Thursday she got into Spanish and let me touch the bee with one finger through her skirt, or at least where the bee should have been. I couldn't exactly tell because this time she wasn't offering to actually show anything, which only left me hungry for more time with her. The following Tuesday, English, and she flashed her breasts for ten seconds. Actually, one for math and the other for English. The following Tuesday, I proudly brought her the test that I had taken in history, showing off the grade: 92. The answer to the last question was, you guessed it, Nicholas Biddle. So thank you, Roxanne.

My reward: She let me sit on her bed and watch her while she changed out of her hippie outfit of the day into her sweats, getting totally naked in the process, and OK, I'll admit this, making her the first totally naked girl I had actually seen up close, because, not gonna lie, everything I did until that point I did in the dark or by receiving more than giving. And when Roxanne got naked for me, she did it in such a nonsexual way, walking across her room casually, hanging her things, going through her drawers, that I got to watch her body move, surprised that it wasn't a perfect body, not like the images and videos of the girls that I had studied so closely on websites. She didn't have the legs of a dancer or the boobs of a stripper; she had kind of droopy ones, a little uneven, I noticed, and she had a little roundness to her belly, not fat, but not solid and athletic like so many of the girls in the Herd. Also, her ass was kind of flat. If I had come across just the body on the internet or somewhere, I might have even clicked to the next girl.

But in person, with her quiet, comfortable, nonsexual nudity, she was completely arousing and somehow, yeah, perfect.

And then she was dressed, in like one quick movement, show over, like it never happened, except that she saw my expression and literally bellowed with laughter, knowing how completely sucked in I was by her performance. And then, instead of studying, we smoked some of her weed together and watched TV for that two-hour session, with her head in my lap, removing her wig and telling me to stroke her hair, which I did obediently.

As I was leaving, she said: "If you get all B's or better on your report card, I will solve your virginity problem."

Suddenly it was important to me that she did it with me because she wanted to and not because I got good grades. Call me a douchebag if you want, but suddenly it mattered to me.

Then, the next time I was there, she was all business, reading through my English paper from before we started with the tutoring, one that I got a C– on, and making me sit at her desk to rewrite it.

"You have to learn to write, Crashinsky. It's like the most important thing you can learn in school."

And me, all sarcastic, "Yeah, like when am I ever gonna need to write?"

And she said, "Trust me on this. I know what I'm talking about. If you don't learn now, you'll never get anywhere in college. You are going to need it one day. And when you do, you are going to thank me like you've never thanked anyone before." Not a trace of sarcasm in her voice, like she was absolutely sure of this.

I didn't tell her that I was thinking of maybe not going to college, although I didn't exactly think that there was any alternative. I couldn't help thinking that if high school was a suckfest for me, then how could I even describe what I imagined college to be like?

"Look at the sentence structure in your opening paragraph, it's all over the place."

"Yeah, OK."

"Not OK, what was your thesis? The point that you were trying to convey?"

I shook my head. I didn't have one. I never had any preconceived ideas when I wrote. I just put stuff down on paper and then kept going until I was done. When I explained this to her, she just laughed in her Roxanne way. "How do you know if you're done?"

I shrugged. "I don't," which of course got her belly laughing, and there was clearly going to be no nudity in this session because she was intent on teaching me this thing, so much so that when my mother came to pick me up, she went down to the car while I stayed in her room to restructure the outline that she was helping me create. And when she came back up, my mother was gone. We worked for hours, until I had a new paper to hand in, one that had all the words from the one that I did without her, only this time they were part of a much better version. She had me read it to her on the drive back to my house, clearly proud of her own efforts. And I had to admit, it sounded really good, but there was no way I could do it again without her.

Except in the following session together, she made me write another essay from scratch. Then another, then another. All this time, not even a flash of her breasts although first marking period was halfway done, so I started thinking that it was most definitely time to get the party started. Like, when was I going to see the bee again?

Except, week after week, we worked on different subjects, with her always making me write something new, and us having this great, incredibly easy time together, talking about everything. Like about all of the girls in my grade and in the senior class, which Roxanne loved because even though she didn't like anybody, she still liked to hear gossip, so I always brought her a tidbit. And she talked to me about life with her aunt, and I talked to her about living with, well, not exactly living with, but having to deal with Jacob. And she admitted that she was totally lesbo for Felicia, who she even noticed at her mom's funeral, and who, according to Roxanne, had a kind of lesbian Angelina Jolie vibe, so, she said, it wouldn't have surprised her at all if Felicia had "experimented." We talked about her a lot, and about my sisters, and then about how her mom died and how she was dealing with it. Also about her trips into the city, which created a lot of friction with her aunt Beth (Peesmell to me). And then she admitted that she was seeing someone over the summer, this girl Cassie, who broke it off when school started, and I pretended not to be completely shocked but couldn't help being disturbed by it, not because of the gay thing, well, not only because of the gay thing, but because I kind of wanted her all to myself. And while I didn't tell her that, it must have been obvious, because we became more intimate after that, more touching, more holding, and more weed smoking and watching sitcoms with my head in her lap or sometimes making out a little, but not getting beyond that. And I stopped feeling like her student and started feeling, at least in my mind, like a boyfriend, and without giving it a name or a label, it was just the two of us every Tuesday and Thursday and the rest of the world didn't matter or even exist.

Of course, none of this could have happened if Burn had even once decided to come home after school. But he was always out driving. So we were safe because he always called her to tell her where he was and when he was coming home, and she always got me out of there before he returned.

And when I asked her about him, where he went, she said she didn't know. She only knew that he had to drive, that it was his way of dealing, that he simply could not return to the house where his mother died, not unless he absolutely had to. According to her, sometimes he never made it back home at night, and while she worried about him, he always called, and besides, she knew that he was good at taking care of himself after all he'd been through. Still, I couldn't believe that after weeks of me being in his house every Tuesday and Thursday he still hadn't once ever shown up.

Then the first marking period was over, and even though I got a C in Spanish, Roxanne said that was good enough. And even though I needed to know whether it actually mattered to her or whether it was just keeping a promise, in the end, I said nothing, not wanting to ruin the opportunity. So she let me crawl into bed with her, which I did, but I was quick and sloppy, couldn't even get the condom on right, which she made me wear. After the first mishap, she had to put it on for me, and then we did it again and I finished too quickly again, and she wanted me to take care of her, so I tried, but she slowed me down and told me that I had a lot to learn and that she would teach me.

And then she showed me what worked for her and what didn't.

And every Tuesday and Thursday, I was rewarded for my excellent work. And she told me that I was getting better at pleasuring her, and then she admitted that I was pretty good at it.

And then she was all business again, because she said now that I had experience, it was time to write again, because there was one more thing about writing that she had to teach me, something that I'd be able to get now, something that she knew I was capable of.

And when I asked her what it was, she pulled out an essay that she had written and made me read it. It was about her mom, about a side of her mother that she never showed to the outside world, the stuff that only the people who are very close to you ever find out. I will admit that her writing choked me up and made me want to read more, and even now, just thinking of it, I can get choked up all over again. It was *that* good.

And then, she explained, it wasn't just her stuff, it was everywhere, all I had to do was look for it. I told her that I didn't understand, and she said that seeing this one thing, this real emotion in everything, *that* was her true special talent and that she totally lied when she told me it was laughter.

"Here's the key," she said. "Whenever you're writing about anything, find the emotion in it. Don't be afraid to express it. Even in history, like Andrew Jackson, like how the fuck was he feeling, being president in like the eighteen hundreds with all these things going on and no matter what, he acted like he was on top of the world, like when his opponents called him a jackass and he totally used that against them. The something that happened in his mind when he came up with that, that's what's pretty fucking cool if you ask me."

"I guess" is what I said, thinking, OK, that is a pretty cool way of looking at it.

"So if you have to do an essay on Andrew Jackson, then put yourself in his mind at that time, and ask how are you feeling about this, being called a jackass. Does it make you angry? If so, who are you angry at? Like that. Get it?"

And that's how Roxanne taught me history. Well, history and writing. Well, history and writing and a way of looking at things in a different light.

OK, by now, in case there were any doubts before, I was totally convinced that I was completely in love with Roxanne. I can finally admit this now, almost two years later, though I told absolutely no one at the time. Also, I didn't exactly know what it felt like to be in love with a girl. For me, what it felt like at the time was that this girl was the most fun ever and that I wanted to have more fun with her. She was way more fun than spending time with my boys in the Club Crew, if that was possible.

Plus, I couldn't stop thinking about her. So what else would you call it?

And of course, I couldn't tell anyone. I was smart enough to know that I couldn't, what with Burn being Burn and all. He would definitely catch wind of it and would definitely not approve, as he was still reeling over the fact that Christina told him that she liked me. This was his sister, after all.

In fact, I couldn't even tell my boys that I had finally had sex. So there was Bobby, bragging about how he was going to nab April, who was back with him, and how he was sure that he was going to be first in Club Crew. And I had to quietly take it, even though I knew better.

Actually, not true. I didn't just take it quietly. When I couldn't keep it to myself any longer, I confided in Newman, the one kid who I knew could keep a secret. But, because I was in so deeply with Roxanne, I felt funny telling him everything, so I minimized it, kept it short and simple, and wouldn't answer all of his questions. Newman being Newman probably figured there was more, but he respected the fact that I would end up telling him some other time (he always had a level of patience that escaped me). He did have one question that I couldn't answer, which was, "What would happen if Burn came home early one time and surprised you both?"

Honestly, call me stupid, but it never occurred to me.

As to those things I didn't share, I'm not going to share them, not even here. Because a lot of that was between me and Roxanne, and it's going to stay that way, book or not.

My grades continued to improve beyond anything I had ever accomplished before, mostly because I was writing better, which made my mom think that Roxanne was some kind of genius. So get this, she wanted to pay Roxanne for even more hours a week, maybe add a Monday or a Wednesday into the mix.

Roxanne, however, couldn't do it. In fact, she was going to have to cut back, because her own schoolwork was getting intense. And then one week she had to cancel on me entirely, which made me out-of-my mind panicky about not seeing her again. Not only panicky, but by Wednesday of that week, I was going through severe withdrawal, as in once you start having sex and expect it on a schedule, your body starts to get all twisty if things don't work out the way they are supposed to (OK, maybe not you, but most definitely me).

Plus, on an emotional level, I simply could not stop thinking about her. During classes, then after school, during baseball practice . . . truth was she made all of the girls in my grade seem like, well, like kids by comparison.

So when we finally got together again the following week, I had to tell her. After all, it shouldn't have been a surprise to her, given her special talent, and given that I was all about emotion at that point.

She was changing into her sweats, when I said it. Well, not *it*,

I was going to get to that; I started with, "I missed you."

And she stood there as naked as the first time I watched her change, and she said this in response: "Crashinsky, don't you fall in love with me. Don't frickin' do it. Do you understand me?"

And I said, "I thought you already knew."

She just nodded like she did, but she was pretty much silent for the rest of our time together, and I was silent and I couldn't even guess what I was working on that afternoon.

Then, on Wednesday night she canceled the Thursday session. She called my mom to tell her.

And after hours of deciding whether or not to call her, I broke down and did it, and when she picked up what I said was:

"I need help in history." OK, I had nothing else to say.

And what she said was "Crash, you need a frickin' girlfriend. Call me after you get one."

She hung up, and I couldn't tell if she had dumped me— which didn't seem possible as I guess we were never actually going out—or challenged me, the way she had challenged me to answer five questions correctly. She was always testing and then rewarding me. So I had to believe that if I somehow found a girlfriend, Roxanne would be back in the picture again.

But then I started thinking that maybe she told me to get one because she was cutting me off for good.

So I was depressed. Not depressed in the way that Burn was depressed when he was in Down mode, but depressed as in confused about what I needed to do to get back to with Roxanne. By the second week, I was having my mom call her, and she promised that once she finished some major school project, she would be back on track with me. It sounded like a lie to me, so I texted her and she responded:

did you get a girlfriend yet?

Clearly I had no choice. Which left me with a number of possibilities. There was Annie Russo, who had been coming on strong all year. There was Christina, who was in my history class, but although we talked and joked around a little, there was nothing to prove that what Burn said about her liking me was true, not that I would have even noticed because I was so over-the-top obsessed with Roxanne. There were a few other girls who were friendly, but they mostly hung out with other groups, so I didn't really know them and didn't have the time to invest in the possibility of establishing something just to prove it to Roxanne.

And of course there was Madelaine Brancato. The obvious choice. Sure, she might still be pissed off as hell. Except that I knew that she still liked me, so I wouldn't have to work too hard. The problem was how to get Maddy back. The solution was to call Pete, who was friendly with Nancy, who was Maddy's best friend, because Pete could tell Nancy my version of the "truth," as in my recollection was that Maddy dumped me, not the other way around, since she ended up hooking up with Burn behind my back.

Point was, in my version, I was the victim. Sure, this version had its flaws, but given that it was coming from third-party translations, and counting on some confusion between Pete and Nancy, by the time it got back to Maddy, I was sure that she would end up feeling sorry for me.

And sure enough, Maddy ended up calling me, to explain that the only reason why she went out with Burn in the first place was that she thought that I had dumped her and of course she wanted to get back at me. And I told her that what I said so many months ago was that I needed some space, not that I was breaking up with her.

We were back together by the end of the week. Good, because now I had Roxanne covered. Bad because I had forgotten how painfully annoying Maddy could be.

Now comes the weird part.

We were in her car (she got her license before me, being older and all), and she tells me she's ready. Ready, as in *ready*. Reason being, she confessed, she went all the way at summer camp. So it wasn't going to be a problem for her now.

We parked by the nature preserve and talked some more, and then we started making out, with her turning up the radio again, which to me signaled that something was going to happen. Only, get this, I didn't really want it to. I was missing the hell out of Roxanne and couldn't stop thinking about her. So when Maddy started to get it on, I actually stopped her, telling her that I had to call my mom and tell her where I was. I stepped out of the car and pretended to call, but what I actually did was text Roxanne.

OK, I have a girlfriend, now what?

Try out some of the things I taught you was the response.

So I did. I got back into the car and got busy and, using every technique that Roxanne had taught me, I did to her what no other kid my age was capable of doing to a girl her age. Not going to get into it, but when Maddy dropped me off at the end of the night, she was a changed woman.

Me, not so much. Sex with Maddy was absolutely meaningless, didn't make me happy, didn't turn me on, didn't make me feel anything at all. If anything, it was merely practice to better prepare myself for the next time I would be with Roxanne, if there was a next time.

In fact, I almost forgot to call my boys and report back and only did so because this would count to them as my first. And of course, the second I got home, I texted Roxanne.

OK, done. Can you be my tutor again?

And the following Tuesday afternoon, after school, like nothing had changed, I was back at Aunt Peesmell's Victorian house, this time having to deal with the cold damp rain of late autumn, shaking myself dry on the welcome mat while I waited nervously for Roxanne to come down the stairs.

And then, there she was, back to goth again, new piercing in her nose and apparently her tongue because when she spoke, she had a distinctive lisp. Not a trace of the hippie stuff left.

"Come on up, Thteevin. I have thomething to show you. Firtht tell me about your date."

So I told her how I did all these things to Maddy and how girls were looking at me differently in school after the weekend, because apparently Maddy was telling her friends that I was absolutely amazing and that I was her first, carefully omitting the fact that she was with some summer guy at her camp, and she was now my girlfriend again.

Which brought me to ask Roxanne why she did the tongue thing.

She closed the door to her room and turned to kiss me so I could feel the tongue, and it clinked against my teeth as I tasted metal. I was not an instant fan. But still, her actions were making me think that things were back to normal. So that was good.

Then she unbuttoned her shirt, and I thought that maybe we were just picking up where we left off, and then she took it off completely, revealing a humongous and incredibly frightening tattoo that ran the length of her arm.

"You like?" she asked.

It was an outline of images of the Twin Towers of the World Trade Center all ablaze, and an image of the devil in the smoke, intertwining snakes, then, across her shoulder, gravestones and her mother's name and the dates of her birth and death.

"Cool" is what I said.

But it wasn't cool at all. It was truly disturbing. Psycho crazy.

"I've been having it worked on, like, every day. It won't be done for a month," she told me.

I couldn't imagine how much more work was necessary or what she was planning. I also couldn't imagine why she needed to totally deface her body that way. I understood how you could get a few tats, and will probably even get one myself when I start college. But this was out of control. Then she asked if I was ready to work on history.

And I said that I was, even though the furthest thing from my mind that afternoon was history and even though all I wanted to talk about was what I was feeling and whether she was feeling anything, even though I knew that she had to be. Otherwise why was I there?

"Five quethtions," she said, and I started to read.

I got halfway through when her cell phone rang.

It was Burn. He was, she told me, somewhere in Massachusetts. He had Christina Haines with him. He wasn't coming home.

CHAPTER NINETEEN

HOW BURN WENT TOO FAR ONE DAY

"My Mom warned me that something like this was going to happen."

This from Roxanne as we pulled into Kenny's driveway. She blasted the horn until I stopped her, reaching out to grab her hands. Car horns in particular cut straight into my brain, part of my ADD I guess, but I cannot handle certain sounds and Roxanne's horn was exactly one of them.

She had this worried, severe look about her. What she was, was nervous, supernervous, and she was totally making me jumpy. I had a joint in my backpack that I had planned to smoke with her after my tutoring session. I took it out now to calm me down, and she instantly gave me a look like I had better put it the fuck away. So I did, and then Kenny came charging out of his house.

He got in, and as soon as he slammed the door, Roxanne jolted the car back into the street, just missing an oncoming Lexus. The driver blared his horn at her, and she blared back on hers, Fuck you, NO FUCK YOU without any words or hand signals. Her horn beat his horn, no contest.

My head was spinning.

This was all happening too fast for me, and I couldn't help feeling that it just wasn't fair. This was supposed to be my time with her, and I was nervous enough about it all day, but finally thinking that everything was going to be OK since she let me back into her life and resumed our sessions.

Then, after receiving Burn's call, everything changed. She calmly went to the mirror and removed her tongue ring (I didn't know it could come out that easily), then changed into one of her mother's shirts, telling me that she needed to look and sound mature if anyone stopped us along the way. She said that we had to be prepared for anything, as she applied makeup in a way that made her look much older than her actual age. As she prepared herself, she instructed me to go over to her computer and print out a map of the Berkshires in Massachusetts, concentrating on the town of Great Barrington.

When she was done, she turned to me and asked who were the best guys to bring along if we were going to talk Burn into coming home, keeping in mind that we had to get to Christina and bring her back home before her parents called the police. Because if Christina's parents called the police, they could bring charges against Burn, maybe even felony charges. She admitted that she didn't exactly know the legal terminology, but she knew that transporting a minor across state lines was like a federal crime, which, according to her, made it way worse, so we had to get to him and Christina before anyone else did.

As she switched from the shirt to a business suit, one that didn't look good on her at all, she said, "I know he's crazy, but he's not just my brother, Crash, he's all I frickin' have left."

We passed Aunt Peesmell in the hall and said nothing; without speaking, we understood each other that she should not be the wiser for anything that was going down. Aunt Peesmell eyed the business suit suspiciously, but at that point, I was pretty sure she had seen everything in that house.

As for the best guys for the trip, picking Newman was my choice. Kenny was hers, since she knew Kenny, and Kenny was exactly the kind of geek Burn related to, even though he didn't really relate to people at all.

Next up, Newman, who was at his curb, ready for us. Minutes later, we were on I-684 heading north toward Great Barrington. Newman shoots me a smiling nod like we have a secret between us, and it's all about the girl next to me and how I'm banging her. I react with immediate anger until I realize that nothing that I told him in any way let him in on my real feelings, so it wasn't his fault. After all, Newman didn't know Roxanne at all, and only knew about her from the word at school, and the word on Roxanne was never any good. He couldn't know that she was intelligent and intuitive and caring and compassionate and funny. In fact, sitting there beside her as she drove us in search of her brother, I felt like I was finally understanding this myself.

And I got it, got the reason that she tried to kill herself the year before, got the reason that she didn't like Lindsey (as if there was only one reason), got the reason that she saw something in me.

And of course, all of this only made her even more beautiful to me.

And of course, I couldn't show it.

Which was hard, because at that very moment in time, I loved Roxanne so deeply and completely that it was actually painful.

Newman pulled out a joint and began to light up, not knowing that I had tried it earlier with negative consequences.

"Are you frickin' kidding me?" she yelled at him.

He dropped the joint, still lit, into his lap, looking ashamed. I could tell that he didn't like being yelled at. Not one bit.

I turned the radio on, flipped through stations.

"How are you going to find him?" I asked her.

"I don't frickin' know," she said, then turned to Kenny, who busied himself with his laptop in the seat behind me. "Where do you think we should go?" she asked, tapping the GPS system, which had been set for Great Barrington as I handed him the maps that I had printed out. Certainly not specific enough.

Kenny was on his laptop, using a wireless card to connect to the internet, Mapquesting several possibilities, names of hotels, malls, parking lots, state parks. . . . "We have about an hour to figure that out," he told her. "Do you have any ideas?"

"Not yet," she said, pulling off the highway for gas. "I was hoping you would think of something. Aren't you two supposed to be some kind of frickin' geniuses?"

"She's got a pretty big stick up her ass for a slut," Newman whispered across the car seat when Roxanne was in the gas station with Kenny and it was just me and him. I stared back at him from the front seat. I'm not going to lie to you, that was the only time in my life that I considered hurting him, even though then, as now, Newman could have demolished me if we actually came to blows.

"Actually, she's pretty cool," I said feebly, in her defense. "And she's not a slut."

And now he was staring back at me. "Oh I get it," he said. "I thought it was totally about the sex for you, dude. I didn't realize that you are totally and completely into her, *aren't* you, *Thteeevin?* I thought it wuth all cathual, thame on me." A little of the residual tongue-ring lisp still came through when she talked.

"It's not what you think," I told him, not knowing what he thought.

"Dude, you're in *frickin'* love."

I felt exposed. This was hazardous territory, completely and utterly dangerous, because if Newman could guess that I had feelings for her, then what was going to happen when Burn saw us together? I flashed back to the Thanksgiving dinner when a younger Burn was perceptive enough to see the connection between my father and the woman who worked for him. He figured out their relationship right off, and he didn't even know them at all. Now Burn was older and considerably more experienced. There was not going to be any way to hide from him.

And when I didn't immediately deny it, Newman was all

over it, realizing that the jokes he was making were hitting a sore spot, and that the inferences from his observations were correct. "Why the hell didn't you tell me? Were you afraid that I would have reminded you how absolutely crazy it is to be in love with David Burnett's sister? Exactly how do you think he's going to react to the news? Are you out of your mind? Couldn't you have picked someone who didn't have a psychotic brother who also happened to consider himself your friend?"

They were coming back.

"One more thing, Crash," Newman said, laughing at himself. "Stay away from *my* sister." This, just as the car door opens.

Roxanne climbed back in, tossed us bags of chips, pretzels, Slim Jims, Combos, and other assorted road food junk. We circulated the bags, and I boosted up the radio when "Holiday" from *American Idiot* started to play. I thought of other days with the entire Club Crew crammed into someone's car, blazed and bouncing as we shouted the lyrics "Hear the sound of the falling rain. Coming down like an Armageddon flame . . . ," outscreaming the full-volume audio system, deaf to the sounds of the outside world. And now, not a peep from anyone.

A little over an hour later, we passed the "Entering Massachusetts" sign. It was totally winter dark by now and you could feel how cold it was outside even though the car was warm and toasty. Roxanne attempted to call her brother again. First time, no cell service for like ten minutes. Newman made a sigh like we're wasting our time, but he knew better than to say it out loud. She gave me her phone with instructions to hit send as soon as the signal bars returned, which happened, like, the very second I took it from her.

Then mostly we listened to Roxanne as she tried to get him to tell her where he was. "David, please, just tell me." Then, "I'm not going to call anyone, I swear." Silence. "Wherever you are, I can be there in an hour." More silence. "OK, two then." More silence. "I know it's been hard for you—it's been hard for me too." More silence. "You have to bring her home before her parents call the cops." More silence. "I don't know, can you put her on?" More silence. "Yes, I'm still tutoring him, and, no, he never mentioned her."

I figured this was about me, that somehow Burn got it in his paranoid mind that I was secretly seeing Christina, which must have set him off. Of course, my guess was that if that set him off, then the actual truth, as in me hooking up with his sister, was liable to *totally* melt him down.

"I don't want you driving if you've been drinking," she told him. "Just tell me where you are." More silence. "You're not in trouble yet. I'm trying to avoid that, don't you see?" More silence. "Can you put her on?"

There was a long pause. Then, "Hi, Christina."

I had forgotten that they knew each other from the year before, when the more normal Burn was spending time with Christina. "I know he seems out of control," Roxanne told her, "but he's been through a lot and he really has feelings for you."

While this was going on, my cell lit up, about to ring. My mom. Shit, I had forgotten to call her, and she was probably sitting in Aunt Peesmell's driveway waiting to pick me up. I answer as quietly as possible, telling her that I'm sorry for not calling, that I just got picked up and I'm out with friends, which in a way was true, that I probably won't be home for dinner, which I guessed, being as we were in Massachusetts, was a safe bet, and no I didn't think Roxanne was home because she had errands, and yes, I'll text Roxanne that you will have her money for her on Thursday.

And the second I get off my phone, Roxanne tosses hers to me. "Find a Barnes and Noble in the Berkshires." Kenny is already on it, because he was listening as Roxanne interrogated

Christina while I was busy keeping my mom at bay.

"There's only one. Pittsfield," he yelled from the back. "Twenty-two minutes."

It was Newman who asked the question that I never thought to ask. In all the time that I spent with Roxanne in her room, we almost never talked about Burn or his issues. It was like he didn't exist for either of us. But now, as we were heading up to the middle of nowhere to try to find him, not sure of what mental state he was in, Newman thought it was important to know.

"What exactly is wrong with your brother?"

As she drove, she swore us to secrecy (like that mattered) and explained about Burn's medical condition, as she called it. She said that he was diagnosed by different doctors with every type of emotional disorder in the book, from bipolar disorder, which we all knew about, as in Burn being Up or Burn being Down, to anxiety coupled with obsessive thoughts.

And here was the real problem, she explained: Burn would have these thoughts about something, like, for example, when he was younger, Burn couldn't get it out of his head that his father was going to die a violent death, so he became super-anxious every time his father left the house, for, like, years. Sometimes it was so bad that he would cry, just cry whenever his father left, and it didn't stop until the man came home at night, and this went on for days, weeks, months. And then of course, their father died in the World Trade Center, exactly fulfilling Burn's worst nightmare.

And, this was only one example of the problem, which was, as she phrased it, every time Burn had severe anxiety about something, whatever it was, that something always ended up coming true. Call it a self-fulfilling prophecy or whatever, it was a constant nightmare for him and his family. He'd have a thought, then the thought became all he could think about, then came the anxiety, then, oddly, came the actual event that proved he was right. And Burn, being as smart as he was, figured that somehow he had used logic, not some psychic connection to the universe, in order to come up with all these horrible thoughts. So even if he couldn't figure out the source, he knew that he would eventually have to deal with the consequences when the thought became a reality.

I was trying to follow all this, but it all got too complicated for me. Newman, however, was way into this conversation and asked, didn't everyone kind of have that feeling now and then? Not me, I said. And Roxanne said, not so much her, the world just totally sucked to her, so nothing surprised her. Kenny said that he did, maybe once.

But for Burn, it was a constant thing. This, no matter what kind of medication he was given, no matter how many pills or combinations of drugs, no matter how many assurances from his mom that there was nothing to worry about. And to make matters worse, significantly worse, ever since their mom died, Burn had taken himself off all the meds he was on, which even if they didn't help, you weren't supposed to do all at once.

And now for the kicker. According to Roxanne, there were three people who he obsessed about all the frickin' time. Wanna guess?

One . . . this one's easy. Roxanne. Especially now that everyone else in his family was gone. Burn was always worried about Roxanne, and it didn't help matters that she once tried to kill herself and that she was always disappearing for days, going off to the city, and that she was always attracted to people who were, as he phrased it, dark souls.

Two . . . Me. Ever since he moved to town as a kid. Because, according to Burn, I was in some ways the exact opposite of him, because it seemed to him that whenever I thought something positive, not negative, it came true. He also told Roxanne that I was some sort of messenger. Only he himself was the actual message and me being the messenger, I wasn't capable of knowing the message, so he had to, in some way, wake me up out of my stupor, which in some way would let him know what the message was. WTF?

OK, even Newman said, "Fucked up," when he heard this explanation.

Three . . . Now I'm willing to bet you're thinking it's Christina, because I was thinking it was Christina, had to be, who else would it be?

The actual answer was . . .

Jamie Crashinsky.

My sister?

Jamie, who had never done much except watch TV and keep to herself, was somehow on Burn's radar, because he had this idea that he had to save her. From what, Roxanne didn't know, but he was sure it was his responsibility. And get this, according to Roxanne, Burn felt that being at my house that Thanksgiving night years before, figuring out about my father's relationship with Felicia, was all about saving Jamie's life, not mine.

Go figure.

There were others on his list, ranking well below us three: Mr. Connelly, Pete, a few teachers, one of Roxanne's city friends, and of course Christina. And there was also Jacob, as in my father, who Burn hated intensely because he said that my father was a bad man without a soul.

I felt a momentary twinge of feeling for my father and almost defended him, but truth was, I couldn't argue with Burn on that one. Not then, not now. Still, according to Roxanne, if you asked David Burnett who he was most afraid of, his answer was always the same: David Burnett.

Good to know, as we were, according to the GPS, one minute from arriving at our destination.

We pulled into the shopping center, past the Walmart on one side, and followed the GPS, driving slowly along the outer rim of the parking lot to Barnes & Noble. The minivan was easy to spot because it was parked in an area where there were no other cars. Burn had backed in, and the van faced away from a row of trees behind it. I could make out two people in the front seats.

"Pull up in front of it so they can't drive off," Kenny's contribution from the bottom of his genius mind; this as Roxanne was doing exactly that. Duh.

We got out as a group, me and Kenny from the passenger side, Newman and Roxanne from the driver's side. Four car doors slam at once. Other than that, there were no sounds at all. A blast of winter air hit me, and I realized that we were all completely underdressed. It had to be like twenty degrees colder than it was when we left Westchester. The cold blast felt good and bad at the same time, definitely woke you up. Plus it was a very dark night, pitch-black, except for the amber glow of the mall lights.

I went for the passenger door of the van and saw Christina staring back from inside the passenger window, which was partially fogged up. The door was locked. I motioned for her to open it, but she wasn't moving.

At the same time, Burn got out of the van, slamming the door, way louder than our door slams, not that it was a contest, but you could tell from the sound that this was one angry motherfucker.

"Get the feeling we're in a bad western?" Kenny said. "Showdown time."

"What the fuck are you doing here?" Burn yelled at his sister. Then, turned to us, "What the fuck are *they* doing here?" he asked her.

"Taking you home," she yelled back with equal force.

Now he was moving quickly toward her, so I crossed over in front of the van, knowing that I was going to do whatever I had to in order to protect her from her brother. I moved her back, behind me, to shield her.

Apparently that simple movement was enough for him to figure everything out. "Holy fucking shit, you're banging my sister, aren't you? Please don't tell me you're banging my sister."

Well, that was quick.

Roxanne forearmed me in the chest, pushing me back, not afraid of Burn at all, and got up in his face. "This is not about Crash, David. This is about you and your stupid road trips. If you want to go on them, fine. But you can't just kidnap people and force them to go along with you."

"Who said anything about 'kidnap'?" He was talking back to her, but he never stopped looking at me. "She agreed to come along. We were just talking."

"Then why hasn't she come out the van?" Newman asked.

"Shut the fuck up, Alex." He shot Newman a look, then back to Roxanne. "Why in fuck's name did you bring all these morons with you? Did you think I was going to do something . . . ? You did, didn't you?"

"I just want you to come home, is all," Roxanne back at him. Now, Christina was finally stepping out of the passenger side. I backpedaled, basketball style with my eyes on Burn until I got to her, asked if she was OK, she said she was OK, asked if he did anything to her, she said he didn't do anything to her, this all while he was staring at me, tapping his right hand on his pants like a drumbeat from a song that only he could hear.

"Tell them, Christina," Burn demanded.

"We're fine here," she said, adding, "I just want to go home." She was shivering. Even though she was wearing a winter coat, the cold was cutting into her, making her look frail and tired. I, for one, was not feeling the cold at the moment. In fact, I was feeling oddly hot.

"Crashinsky"—Roxanne motioned over to me—"why don't you and your friends take her into the bookstore and get her some coffee or something. I need to talk with my brother."

I thought this wasn't such a great idea, given the way Burn was looking at his sister, so I suggested, "Why don't I stay here with you. Newman and Kenny can go."

"Yeah, Roxanne," Burn concurred, "Crash should stay with us, don't you think?"

"We're fine without him," she said.

"Then why did you fucking bring him in the first place?" yelling.

"I'm c-c-c-cold," said Christina interrupting, all chattering teeth, and with that, Kenny walked off with her to the bookstore. The rest of us watched. Burn turned to Newman. "Go with them," he commanded

"Fuck you, Burnett," Newman said. "I'll do whatever I want."

And then Burn just stood there, nodding, still tapping his leg with his hand, more inner music, I thought. He was watching Christina, not saying a word. I started to lose my heat and finally noticed how biting cold it was.

And then Christina and Kenny disappeared into the store.

And then Burn whipped out a gun.

And pointed it at me.

"Are you or are you *not* fucking my sister, Crash?" he said from behind the weapon. "And before you answer, bear in mind that if you admit you are, I will shoot you. Of course, if you lie, I will shoot you twice."

I will admit that at that point I had absolutely no previous experience with real weapons. Sure I had played paintball numerous times and done things like laser tag and shit like that, but facing down the barrel of an actual real gun was an entirely different experience. Especially a gun that was held by a guy who his own sister only minutes before said had like every emotional disorder in the book. To make matters worse, my options were not good. Because I *had* fucked his sister and I couldn't tell him that. Burn, being Burn, would know I was lying if I said otherwise.

Also, I was now frozen, not feeling like Crash Bandicoot at all. This was not an obstacle that I could escape from, not a boulder to outrun or a turtle to jump over. Plus, one good shot and game over.

Something else I will admit, not having admitted this before. I tasted my insides. I know that sounds weird, but my mouth went dry, and there was this metallic taste coming up on me. I never until that moment thought about dying, and now I wondered if the taste that I was tasting was like a death taste or something.

I remained absolutely still.

So, apparently, did Newman, though I didn't see him. To be honest with you, I didn't see anything except the barrel of the gun, which grew increasingly larger in my vision until I started to feel sucked into it.

"You have three seconds to answer," said the voice on the other end of the chamber. "One . . ."

"Two . . ."

My body tightened into a ball, all muscles contracted at the same time so I felt the pain before I heard the shot. Only there was no actual shot.

Because Roxanne stepped in between us. Just in time.

"What you going to do? Shoot me, David?" she yelled at him, demanding to know.

This was only a small consolation to me, because if the answer was yes, since I was directly behind her, the bullet would probably go right through me as well.

"Put the frickin' gun down, David," she said. "This kid came here to save you, you idiot. He's your goddamned friend. Is this how you repay him? And get it out of your frickin' head that he's after your girlfriend. She's not your girlfriend anyway, get that through your thick skull. And as for Steven, he doesn't even know she exists. He's been studying with me every week. I know all there is to know about him. He's in love with *me*, you idiot, and I kind of have feelings for the kid too, so leave him alone."

"Move the *fuck* away, Roxanne," Burn said, her confession only fueling his anger.

Instead, she stepped closer. "Go ahead, *do it*, David. I frickin' dare you."

It was, for an instant, as if she changed from totally responsible to totally reckless. Like she actually wanted him to do it, baiting him, and he recognized that. His face went blank.

She took another step closer.

Another step, and then she put her hand out and gently lowered the barrel, so it was facing the ground, still with the two of them holding it.

I felt absolutely no relief whatsoever.

"One condition, Roxanne," he told her. "You have to promise not to see him, or even speak to him again."

Up until that point, I was merely watching from the outside, definitely not capable of resolving anything between the two of them, in fact, not capable of even speaking, between the absolute cold and the shock of the gun pointed at me and the absolute clarity of Roxanne's revelation to her brother. And now, because of what she said, of what I now knew, it was on me.

"You can't do that" is what I mumbled to him and her at the same time.

"Fuck you, Crash. It's karma. If I can't be with Christina, you can't be with my sister," he said to me before turning back to his sister. "Is it a deal?"

She looked at me, then him, then me again. Our eyes met on the second glance, and what I felt was how much I needed this girl, no matter what her reputation was, no matter how nasty or sarcastic she could be to me, no matter how much she pretended that what we had was strictly fun or whatever it was to her. To me she was my lover, my closest friend, and, in a way, the big sister I never had. And now, for a fleeting instant, she had finally admitted it, so everything would work out.

And this is what I tried to tell her just from my staring into her eyes.

And the message I got back from her eyes was "Good-bye, Crashinsky."

"First you promise me something, David," she told him. "Promise me that you will leave him alone from now on, that you won't go near him . . . or Christina again. Ever," she insisted. "Promise me, David."

He looked at me for a long time, and the message I got back from his eyes was "It's not over."

Still, he nodded to her. Game over. I lived. Although it didn't feel like it at the moment.

"Then, I promise," she told her brother, looking away from me, took the gun, and hugged him. And now, seeing as she finally had the gun, all of my muscles released at once and I felt like a pool of Jell-O that was starting to melt from the release of all that heat and simultaneously to jell up from the freezing cold wind that snapped across the mall with a sudden whoooooooooooosh . . .

Newman grabbed me from out of nowhere. I didn't know that I was collapsing from the weight of the pressure that I had been feeling.

"Let's go home, David," Roxanne told her brother. "I know

how hard it's been for you." She tossed Newman the keys to her car and ushered Burn back to the van, signaling us to go, always looking directly at Newman, never glancing back to me. It was as if I had instantly disappeared from her mind, vision, and memory.

Then they were gone.

Newman and I watched the van drive off.

"OK," Newman said. "That was fucking amazing."

He was still holding me.

"You don't think she means it, do you?" I asked him, hoping that he saw something that I didn't.

"Crash," he said, "you better get yourself a new girlfriend. The sooner the better."

We went together, scratch that, Newman basically carried me, into the bookstore to thaw out. And while we sat with the others, neither of us said anything about what had transpired, or even mentioned the gun. I think we figured that we would be talking about it some other time. What we needed to do was get Christina home and then figure out what to do about Burn.

When we were about to leave, she pulled me back away from the others and gave me a look like I was the real hero, then said, "Thanks for coming for me, Steven."

She had no clue whatsoever as to the real reason I was there. (Sorry, Christina, if you thought it was for you.) And when I realized that she had no clue, I gave her one of my famous Crash smiles, like, of course, what did she expect, all in a day's work.

"One thing you should know," I told her. "His sister made him promise that he won't go near you again. And he agreed."

She thought for a moment. "And you believe him?"

I thought for a moment. *No way*, was what I was actually thinking. But I couldn't tell her that, so I gave her another Crash smile, and I told her, "Yeah, he's afraid of Roxanne. At the end of the day, he'll do whatever she tells him."

So we drove home.

Newman, having just gotten his license, insisted on silence so he could concentrate on driving, and then admitted that it would be the first time he had actually been on a highway without his dad. When we got back into town, I got everyone to agree that we would keep everything to ourselves, not for Burn's sake, but because I owed it to Roxanne to trust that she would take care of her brother. Besides, we had just survived another day, and being kids that age and all, by the next day, we had other things to think about. Well, this was probably true for Newman and Kenny, but Christina and I were a whole different matter. Because we both knew, we totally knew, in our own way, no matter what promises he made, no matter what kind of comfort I gave to Christina, that David Burnett was gunning for us.

Plus I had this Roxanne problem to deal with.

CHAPTER TWENTY

HOW BURN CRASHED HIS MOM'S CAR AND MY FATHER'S WEDDING

The Roxanne problem, as Newman called it, was my way of handling, or rather not handling, the aftermath of the incident in the parking lot of the Pittsfield Barnes & Noble, which he and the rest of us ended up referring to only as "Massachusetts."

It didn't hit me until the next day, being as I was so wiped out from the incident that I was basically in shock and didn't know it. I woke up with Roxanne's name in my brain like it was graffitied onto the inner walls of my skull, so that every other thought had to pass by it and somehow also become a Roxanne thought. Like, I have school today/should I text her; I have baseball practice/could we somehow still be on for Thursday; did I remember where I put my backpack/she had so much fun going through my backpack; and so on.

I honestly don't remember a single minute of being in school that day.

Or the next, which was the Thursday that I would have been scheduled to see her. I woke up with Roxanne fever, which is what I called it, because I was totally sick, as in temperature sick. Maybe it was from being outside in Massachusetts for so long without a coat or maybe because I lost my will to do anything, either way, by that afternoon, I was so sick that I wouldn't have made it to her house even if it was still on.

OK, yes I would have, temperature or not, and I know this because I snuck out of my house that night and "borrowed" Lindsey's car for the short drive over to Aunt Peesmell's (even though I didn't have a license at that point), just to see if her car was in the driveway, just to catch a glimpse of her at her window, or maybe even to talk to Burn directly.

Except the lights were off in her room and there were no cars in the driveway. I supposed that Burn was still doing his driving thing and that maybe she was in the city, but wherever she was, she had to be thinking of me. After all, she did say that she had feelings for me, and feelings don't go away on a dare or a bet or even a promise, which she only did, I understood, to keep me safe.

Only now, in the car, in the cold with my raging fever, I did not feel safe at all, so what was the point?

I stayed in bed Friday and throughout the weekend, watching/not watching television, and still all of my thoughts were Roxanne thoughts. Then the next week started, and still, all of my thoughts were Roxanne thoughts. And of course, there were no responses to my calls to her cell phone, no texts back to me, no proof that she was still alive.

Until Caroline Prescott came into my room on that Monday night to tell me that Roxanne had to move out of her aunt's house and would be staying in the city, so there would be no more tutoring sessions, which disturbed my mother because she knew that I was, as she put it, "really making progress with the Burnett girl."

Then on Wednesday, I saw him in the hall. Nothing, not even a loaded gun, could have stopped me from approaching him.

"Sorry, Crash, you know I can't talk to you. I made a deal with my sister."

"But you were the one to make it, so you can break it anytime."

"Can't do that, Crash. Now you know what it feels like to be me."

"Please."

"Revenge is sweet," he said, and I had to hold back my urge

to hit him. "Maybe you should go back to Maddy. Did she tell you that I was her first?"

Short version, it did not go well.

So I stopped texting Roxanne, or at least cut down a lot, and I continued brooding, staying in my house, sitting on the couch with Jamie, watching TV together instead of going out with my friends, ignoring their calls. And sitting with Jamie, I had the feeling that Burn was in contact with her, and I was going to tell her to watch out for him, but then I had a better idea about that, so I didn't mention anything to her.

And then one Thursday, when I would have been at Aunt Peesmell's spending time with Roxanne, I got a single text message from her. Two lines. It said:

Sorry about my brother. The gun wasn't loaded.

I was pretty sure that what it meant was "I miss you, Crashinsky. I miss us."

I quickly responded, fast as I could, asked where she was, what she was doing, could I call her, could I talk to her, was she OK, did she get another tattoo. Whatever I wrote, and I tried everything I could think of, she did not respond. Still, it was a sign.

The next day, she removed herself from my friends list on Facebook. Not a good sign, as I was going to her page every five minutes searching for clues, thinking that maybe she would have me meet her in the city, our little secret. I suggested as much in a text, which, like the others, went unanswered.

And a few days later, Newman came over, because I wasn't going anywhere with the Club Crew after school, and he decided that enough was enough and what I needed was a one-man intervention. What he said was:

"Get it through your head: She's not capable of being your girlfriend. Besides, she's in college. Do you think she'd really be interested in going out with a high school junior on a long-term basis?" Not knowing that I had heard all of this before. And continuing, "All you're feeling is the emptiness that comes from not fucking someone you've been fucking, so my advice, call Maddy immediately. In fact, I'll call her myself."

And it hit me for the first time what Burn had told me in the hall. That he was her first, not the guy in camp who she claimed was. It was Burn all along, which meant that he was banging her then so that one day he could use it against me, that's how much he hated me, and for some reason he wanted me to hate him as much.

Well, now he got his wish.

And that night, Newman and me and Maddytheslut and Jeannie Castro were out in Newman's father's car, because, after all, Newman was totally right, beyond right, that I should be out, because Roxanne could not control my life and if she wanted to call, she would.

And even though I couldn't stop thinking about her, I was busy getting busy with Maddy, so even though that sucked by comparison, it was still fucking and fucking beats mostly everything else, not going to lie to you, even fucking out of hate.

As for the possibility that Burn had connected with Jamie, I waited until Lindsey came home from Georgetown for winter break. And I waited patiently for her to unpack, listening to her tell my mom about how school was, waited until after dinner, since my mom prepared a whole Lindsey feast for her return. And finally, when she was back in her room, doing her Lindsey things, I went in and mentioned that I needed to talk with her. And she immediately slipped into total Lindsey voice, "What do *you* want, Steven?"

Keep in mind that I hadn't talked to her in three months— where was the love?—but I remembered that I wasn't there to socialize anyways, so I told her about Jamie, as in Jamie was on Burn's hit list, to which Lindsey responded:

"What do you expect me to do about it?"

And so I told her, she was Jamie's big sister, and she had an obligation to take care of her. Like it or not, we both had that responsibility, and I was willing to do my share if she was. And then she looked at me as if I had matured while she was away, maybe with a twinkle of respect. I couldn't tell for sure; you couldn't trust Lindsey for anything.

"I'll talk to her," she said.

"You have to tell her to stay away from Burn. I know him—he's dangerous."

"Maybe we should both do it," she said.

Jamie was watching TV (what a shock) when we both dropped into the family room. I watched Lindsey do her Lindsey thing, which I could tell was good enough to make her a good lawyer one day, which was what she and Jacob had decided that she was going to be.

"So Jamie, what's up with you and David Burnett?"

Jamie, surprised that her sister was actually talking to her, decided to respond without objecting when Lindsey lowered the volume.

"Nothing's up with me and David Burnett."

"Have you talked to him?"

"No."

"Have you seen him?"

"*No,* of course I haven't seen him."

"Have you IMed him?"

"No."

"Then what?"

"Facebook, OK?"

"No. Not OK," Lindsey said with her teacher voice. "Not OK at all. Here's what you are going to do. You are going to defriend him tonight and not talk to him or email or IM or contact him or respond if he contacts you. Do you understand?"

"Whatever," Jamie said, raising the volume.

Lindsey grabbed the clicker, in total control, and clicked the television off. "I'm serious," she told Jamie. "I don't want to find out that you're in contact with him, ever. Do you understand me?"

Jamie, getting up. "OK, OK, OK, OK, OK, whatever. What's the big deal if I talk to David Burnett anyways? He's not so bad. He happens to hate the same things I hate."

That was probably when I should have known better about Jamie.

Point was, I kept watching her, and Lindsey kept watching her, and we both spied on her Facebook account, but David was defriended, so she was complying, at least as far as we knew. All I could think about was how happy Burn was whenever he got to say "Revenge is sweet." I didn't want to hear him say that about Jamie.

And then one day, I was watching TV on my own, Jamie actually being out with one of her friends, and Lindsey came crashing into the family room, dropping onto the couch next to me, as close as she had ever gotten, and asked for the clicker. I was watching a rerun of *That '70s Show*, so no big, and as she flipped channels, she thanked me for watching over Jamie, actually saying, "You did the right thing, little brother" and acknowledging that it was our job together as siblings.

"You've changed since I went to college. Like you got older or something."

I wondered for a fleeting moment whether I could confide in her. Was there a part of her that changed as a result of college? Maybe a part of her that I failed to recognize before? I not only considered it, but actually started to tell her.

"Roxanne Burnett has been tutoring me. . . ."

Which had the exact opposite effect from what I expected, as

Lindsey immediately launched into one of her tirades. "There's a rumor going around that Roxanne was accepting money for sex at some club in the city, and that she was making money giving lap dances to middle-aged men in some sleazy strip joint."

I had heard these rumors before and figured that they were started by mean-spirited ex-friends or whatever. Also, Roxanne once told me that sometimes, just for sport, she spread rumors about herself, just to see how far they would go.

"I'm just telling you this, Steven," Lindsey told me, "because, from what I heard, she has like every STD in the book."

Short version, it did not go well. The second that I defended Roxanne, I was hit by various accusations about my naïveté and immaturity. It didn't matter that I was getting B's and better in all my classes, not to her.

Then winter break was over and I went back to classes and Lindsey went back to Georgetown. Jacob and Felicia announced that they had set the date for their wedding and I was still brooding.

But gradually life returned to normal for me, hanging with my boys more and more. We were into the winter Jackass thing, still trying to outdo Johnny Knoxville and company, eating dirt, or flinging darts at each other, or swallowing live frogs and stuff and vomiting them up while they were still alive. And when we weren't sliding down the steps in the back of Meadows High in a "borrowed" shopping cart, we were smoking honey blunts at our secret place in the nature preserve or playing video games at Evan's or basketball at the Y. And blazing and going to the movies, as in *Night at the Museum* like five times, and *Borat*, for, like, the tenth time. Who was funnier than Borat? The guy is *the* fucking genius of comedy.

And then there was Maddy, who I was determined to

humiliate because she committed the crime of sleeping with my now mortal enemy and lying about it, and because I continued to hate Burn for what he did to me, I decided to take my hate out on her by association, even though to her it seemed like positive attention.

And we were still going to parties, and things got more and more out of control. To show off in front of my boys, I got Maddy superdrunk and then, to prove that I could make her do whatever I said, I made her take her top off and even hook up with a genuine lesbian in the pool house in Kelly's backyard. And she agreed to do all of this, not looking very happy to tell you the truth, but saying if it makes me happy, then she would do it for me. She claimed she would do *anything* to please me, which also meant that I stopped using protection with her because I just didn't care whether Roxanne had given me an STD like Lindsey had suggested or whether there were any consequences to being unprotected. In my mind at the time, I totally figured that it didn't matter because she was a slut and that's what sluts do. So I did not, for a minute, feel guilty, because at the end of the day, I never forced her to do anything. Except I knew, all the time that I was using Maddy, that Roxanne wouldn't have approved, and so I had to wonder, was I doing it because maybe she would somehow find out from Burn that I was out of control and intervene?

Point was, by the middle of junior year, I was still suffering the aftereffects of getting too close to Roxanne and her brother and conflicted by my feelings about both of them.

And then we got word during February break that Burn had demolished his mother's car on the New York Thruway, west of Albany, and my first thought, my first hope, was that he would die from the accident, because if he did then Roxanne would be free. As it turned out, though, he didn't. Apparently he was still doing his long-distance driving thing, and he must have fallen asleep behind the wheel or something, because the mini-van veered off the road and down an embankment and all the people who saw the car could not believe that anyone survived. There was even a picture on the internet of the crumpled mini-van all accordianized on the side of the road, down in a ditch.

This, of course, was no big deal to the rest of the Club Crew, as many of us new drivers were having accidents. Pete had ruined his father's Mustang, and Evan was in, like, five accidents in a row.

But Burn's accident was different for the following reason: He needed a new car and he had no parents and the insurance apparently didn't cover everything, so Aunt Peesmell apparently was obligated to help him buy one. Only even with Aunt Peesmell's help, he still needed more money, so Aunt Peesmell apparently petitioned their financial adviser, who said that he wasn't permitted to send money under the terms of his mother's will or something. And even though even Aunt Peesmell tried her best to convince him of the necessity for some cash, at the end of the day, the financial adviser refused and said no anyways.

As you probably remember, the Burnetts' financial adviser was none other than Jacob Crashinsky, who, as I already mentioned, was, according to David Burnett, the sworn enemy of David Burnett.

Not being the type of kid who could accept no for an answer, Burn started calling my father's office and screaming at secretaries over not having access to his money. And when that didn't work, he apparently started calling Jacob's apartment at all hours of the night, threatening to come after my father.

So I decided that I had to tell Jacob, well, not *him,* but Felicia, that I was worried, because Burn had a gun and had threatened to use it in the past. I didn't exactly tell her how I knew, but I assured her that it was true.

And next thing I hear, the police showed up at Aunt

Peesmell's house and she allowed them to search the premises, but they didn't find any weapons. They tracked Burn down at the gym (he was back to working out again), and as he was leaving the gym, the cops showed up and asked if they could take a look at his car (actually Aunt Peesmell's car, at that point). He told them to go fuck themselves, so he ended up getting arrested, but Aunt Peesmell got him released.

Only now he needed even more money, not only for a new car, but now he had to hire a lawyer to defend him in a criminal case resulting from the failure to cooperate with a police investigation or something like that, plus, apparently, resisting arrest. And all this time, not a single word from or about Roxanne.

By the time the wedding rolled around, junior year was pretty much over and my grades were back to sucking again. My teachers had all conferred with Caroline Prescott, who managed to set me up with passing grades in every course as long as I could pass the finals (a challenge yet to be achieved without the benefit of a private tutor). And by then, the Club Crew boys and some of the guys from other groups had experienced our first dose of ecstasy, rolling on a Saturday night at a Kelly party, and we knew that this was a drug that could fuck with you because you felt soooooo good when you were on it and soooooo burned out the next day. But this was a drug that the girls could finally love too (as most of the girls in our town were not big into weed).

And after continuing to hook up with Maddy for a while longer, I heard that Diana Ordoñez liked me. Being as Diana was this superhot girl from Miami and was a cheerleader and all, I decided that Diana had to be the one to break up with Maddy on my behalf. And, no shit, she had no problem telling Maddy that she was hooking up with me, which might not have worked on its own, but seeing Diana draped on my arm at the next varsity game, Maddy had to realize that I was no longer part of her world. And besides, being associated with Diana got me respect in a way that I had never gotten with Maddy.

And baseball was going well, with our team going to the divisionals and me holding a record for the most RBIs in a season and solid fielding at third base. And did I mention how much school sucked?

But back to the wedding. It was set for the Sunday of Memorial Day weekend. Jacob got one of his superrich friends to lend him his house for the event, which was out in the Hamptons on a huge beach. This was no ordinary house, but an enormous block-long brown-shingled mansion that you had to drive up to through a gate.

As we got out of the limo that Jacob got for us, I noticed the valet guys parking other cars. These guys were kids my age, maybe a little older, and one of them was eyeing Jamie like she was hot. And old enough. I wanted to yell at him, let him know that he was checking out a fourteen-year-old.

Actually Jamie did look good. Me and Jamie and Lindsey were dressed in the special clothes that Felicia got for us. Me in a tux, but not my junior prom tux, no, not that tux at all, that one was not going to be good enough for my father's wedding. Felicia had found some designer who made this Italian cut version of a tuxedo that was super South Beach. We had to go into the city for special fittings, each of us, to make sure that our wedding clothes fit perfectly, which they did. Even Lindsey looked pretty good, I have to admit.

It was a perfect day, not a cloud in the sky.

We stepped along the platforms that had been set up, and Jacob was there to introduce us around. But first, the photographer.

There we were, the four of us, Jacob and his offspring, smiling as a family, as the photographer snapped away. He took another set with us standing in a row on the wooden staircase descending from the deck overlooking the beach, then another set against the background of the mansion, then another group of photos on the beach, wind blowing our hair, and there was a hairstylist to make sure that everything was in its place. And then a few pictures of me and Jacob, the two Crashinsky men, one with his arm around me, another set of him standing behind me, one hand on my shoulder.

Only as soon as the flashes went off, I could feel my father's hand slip away with a sudden shake, as if he was cringing that I was his son.

And he never said a word to me, other than to suggest that I move left and get closer to Lindsey when the cameras went off. I watched him posing for pictures with Lindsey and Jamie. He had a different smile, not the fake one that he had with me, but a real pride in his daughters, mostly for Lindsey, but you could see that there was something there.

So I had to ask myself, what the fuck did I do to make him hate me so much?

But then there was Felicia's hand on my shoulder and that felt warm and supportive, a totally different feeling.

"Cresh, you lewk like a moddle."

This, with a kiss on the forehead, and the deepest hug. I guess that was why I bothered to go in the first place.

And Felicia in her white dress looked like there was a spotlight on her, following her every move. This was definitely not a normal woman.

I had to just stare. And when I stared, I noticed that I wasn't alone. Other men, business associates of my father's, distant relatives I hadn't seen in years, even the caterers, all seemed to be doing the same thing, as in . . . just staring.

Even the women, just staring.

And she walked across the wooden platform on the beach, like a prize racehorse, with a bounce that made you anticipate the next step, made you feel that you were breathing in time with her.

"She's hot stuff," said my aunt Randi over my shoulder, breaking the spell.

It was good to see Aunt Randi; it had been a long time. She had gotten heavier and older looking. We hugged. She hugged Jamie. She introduced us to yet another one of her loser boyfriends, this one an artist who looked extremely gay to me. At least he had a full beard.

We grabbed some minifoods from the passing trays, chicken satay in peanut sauce, lobster quiches, small slices of filet mignon and on and on. Typical of Jacob's refined palate, the food was spectacular. I handed my used wooden skewers and napkins to Jamie. Jamie was always good for things like that.

Another tray came by. I quickly grabbed a glass of champagne as it passed and downed it in a single gulp, placing the empty glass on another tray, or at least trying to, because as I reached my hand out, Jacob grabbed it.

"You will not embarrass me today. Do you understand?"

I yanked my hand back. "Leave me alone."

Felicia noticed the confrontation and came over to divide us, interlocking her arm around his, and heading after the photographer, pushing Jacob forward, glancing back at me.

When they had melted into the crowd, I stepped back and happened to come across another tray of champagne glasses, so I quick-snap-grabbed another one and sucked it down. No way was I going to get through this sober, was my thinking.

And then there were more pictures, Felicia and her family, then she joined ours, just the five of us, then a few with Aunt Randi and other family members, cousins, people who I didn't even know were related to us.

Then the crowd was called to take their seats around a huge altar that had been set up on the beach. Chairs in rows, aisle down the middle leading to the stage. They brought in trees on all sides to make it look like an enclosed space. Plus there were all these flowers, hundreds of them, actually thousands of them lined against the altar, twining the top, making it look all fairy tale.

Me and Jamie and Lindsey sat together in the front row, Jamie watching the altar area with an intensity that she generally reserved for *SpongeBob*.

"Those are the most flowers I've ever seen," she told me. "I guess Dad is superrich."

She and Lindsey kept turning their necks to see who was coming down the long platform: first Jacob's mom, our grandmother, then Aunt Randi, and then some of Felicia's relatives who flew in from her country.

Then some of my father's best friends, or rather business associates, I don't think Jacob had any regular friends.

Then the violins started up, "Here Comes the Bride."

And with everybody's eyes on her, Felicia stepped out, looking even more beautiful than she did before. The music stopped. You could hear the waves crashing against the shore and a few seagulls. Other than that, it was totally silent as she stood there.

Single frozen moment in time.

Camera flashes going off in rapid succession.

Then the music started up again, and she walked between us, smiling and waving, one side, then the other, and I had to think, how was I ever going to do as good as my father? Mad money, superhot wife, big place in the city, friends with a beach mansion and a boat. He had it all.

And I could not feel one ounce of happiness for him.

Now, at the altar, my father was joined by his about-to-be wife. And two older guys, one a rabbi, the other a priest. The two of them looked like they were friends and talked to each other until the violins stopped again. Then the rabbi went first and introduced himself and made some kind of adult-type joke that all the adults laughed at. Next the priest, not as funny, all business, joining the two of them in matrimony stuff.

My mind wandered. I started fidgeting. I was looking past the stage, to the ocean: kicking-rough waves, no one was swimming. And I remembered thinking, a few more weeks of school and then summer. I couldn't wait. Too much pressure for me to do well and, not going to lie, I was not dealing. I couldn't concentrate in any class, didn't know how I was going to pass the finals. Plus I was still, even then, despite my new relationship with Diana, thinking about Roxanne a lot.

So I didn't notice that anything was going on in the back row until I heard his voice.

"Where's my money, Jack?"

David Burnett was standing exactly in the spot where Felicia had stood minutes earlier. He was dressed in a tuxedo, like he belonged there. The entire wedding party and all the guests in their chairs turned to find the source of the voice at the same time.

All of the wedding sounds stopped, and all you could hear besides Burn were the waves crashing against the shore and a few seagulls.

Another single frozen moment in time.

"All I wanted was the money that is rightfully mine," he announced as he started walking up the aisle, taking the same path as Felicia to the altar, "and instead, you had me arrested."

Not knowing, of course, that, technically, I had him arrested.

OK, now I was wondering if he had his gun. Because, here's the thing, if he had a gun, then I was going to jump in front of him to prevent him from firing at my dad and his new wife. I felt my reflexes poised to attack, against my conscious will, and in doing so, I shocked myself at the fact that I would risk my own life to save my father.

Maybe another kid in my position would have balked at this,

I mean, given that my father was a huge dick and all, but I didn't have it in me to walk away if he needed me. I could not stand aside; I would have my father's back no matter what.

I was better than that.

My father looked around, motioned to the catering staff. He seemed unsure of himself, unsteady on his feet.

Fuckme, I thought. I really was going to have to come to his rescue.

I stepped into the aisle just as David crossed my path. I grabbed his arm, which was as hard as concrete.

"Let him go, Cresh." This from behind me, at the altar.

"I want my money." Burn kept advancing. I held on, grabbing him tighter, and was actually being dragged forward slightly. I was not aware until that second how powerful he was. I felt like I was trying to hold a tiger by its tail.

Despite my absolute best efforts, he continued to move forward like a seasoned running back determined to cross into the end zone, capable of carrying a team of defenders on his shoulders if he had to. Only instead of a team of three-hundred-pound linebackers, there was me. Just me, still convincing myself that I could take him down and have him detained, maybe arrested again. Even stoked by residual anger, I was nothing compared to the solidness and single-minded determination that David Burnett had going for him.

"It's OK, it's OK." Felicia motioned to me from the altar. My father looked at her like she was out of her mind. I was not comprehending what she was trying to do, so I kept holding Burn, but he kept moving, with me attached to him, no major obstacle for him at all.

The good news was, he didn't seem to have a gun or anything. However, based on his raw strength, he might not even need one to do damage.

"Please, Steefin, let him go," Felicia commanded.

And simultaneously, I let his arm slip from my wrist. Not that I had a real choice anyways. And once I let go, he actually slowed down, still approaching the altar, but now at a more normal pace.

"Please, Davit, join us." She stretched her arms out toward him. "It was our mistake not to invite you and your sister, especially since you haf had such a divicult year. . . ."

"My money . . ." David kept moving but seemed to have lost his edge.

Meanwhile, Jacob was looking at Felicia like maybe he was having second thoughts about the whole wedding thing. Felicia did not bother to look back at him; her mind and energy was focused solely on Burn. She led him up the stage to the altar in a way so intimate that he must not have realized that like three hundred people were watching him. He actually stepped between Jacob and his new wife, looking like a wild animal that had just been tranquilized.

Still, I wasn't about to trust him and stepped up to the altar at the same time, so now I too was staring down at all those people.

Then she whispered to Burn, and I got within earshot so I could hear everything. And what she said was:

"We were wrong. We shoot have gifin you the respect that you deserf. But you don't understand that Jack as a leegal obleegation to honor the trust that your mother set up for you. There are vords in that trust that do not permit him to give you more than your mother allocated. I read it myself. Ve ver not in a poseetion to explain. But we shoot haf anyvay. In the meantime, Davit, dis is my special day, please do not ruin it for me."

And to this, Burn responded, "I'm sorry too. I didn't know."

So this was the second time in a few months that I watched two different women talk Burn off a ledge.

The problem was, how many more ledges would there be

before this guy was out of my life forever? I had to find a way to disconnect him from my family for good. He was dangerous. Supremely dangerous. And I was, like, the only one in the universe who completely understood that.

She walked off to the side with him, motioning for her guests to be patient. I followed, sticking close by her.

"Vill you stay as our guest?" Felicia asked, adding, "Ve vill vork things out together ven Jack and I return from Europe."

Burn seemed to shake off her magic for a second. "I can't wait until then. I need a car now."

"How much?" she asked.

"Seven grand," he snapped.

"Den I vill give you my personal check until den. Vill dat be helpful?"

Tears came to Burn's eyes at that very moment.

"I could probably live with five thousand," he admitted. "I mean, if you are going to write me a personal check, then that should be enough."

"Vill you stay?"

"I don't think so," he told her. "Well, maybe just for the ceremony."

So now I watched as Burn took a seat at the end of the last row in the back. The wedding continued, and the whole do you take him and do you take her thing was done in a few minutes. Then Felicia made this speech about how she was lucky enough to meet someone who understood her, who got her jokes and let her believe in trust, he was a kind man, a deep man, a caring man, and being part of his family, sharing her life with me and Lindsey and Jamie made her a better person, and that she hoped that we felt the same way about her, which of course, we did.

It was a great speech and all, but it could not have been about the very same Jacob Crashinsky who lived in my house from the time I was born until the time that Caroline Prescott kicked him out. Because nothing could make me forget that he was a total and complete prick, even though as it turns out, I learned that afternoon that I would save his life, if it came to that.

Burn kept his distance but stayed for a while after the ceremony was over. I caught him trying to talk to Jamie, but before I had to do something about it, Lindsey interrupted him and soon he was talking to some adults, making conversation like he was there as a guest. I thought about the possibility of going over and asking how his sister was doing, but I was sure that doing anything like that would just give him the satisfaction of reminding me that it was no longer my business to even ask, and whatever happened after that would most likely ruin my father's wedding.

Then Felicia went over to him and the two of them talked. And before long, Jacob approached me. I was thinking that he was going to be all about thanking me for trying to stop Burn, but Jacob, being Jacob, had this to say: "If he does anything, it's on you."

It actually made me laugh, thinking that this was the same line he delivered to me years before, at Thanksgiving dinner. And that the thing Burn did back then was the reason we were all here today. Jacob apparently had no idea, though, and took it that I was somehow laughing at *him*. Whatever.

I saw no need to argue with him on his wedding day.

I guess I was better than that.

CHAPTER TWENTY-ONE

HOT WATER, REALLY, REALLY HOT WATER

"How could you, Steven?"

When Christina showed up at her uncle's place, things were not exactly the same as when she left five days earlier. I hadn't left the house, shaved, or even showered during that time, given that I wasn't feeling good and given that I suddenly felt the need to write, like, constantly. In fact, when she called to tell me that she was coming to get me, I convinced her not to come back, because the quiet and the isolation allowed me to focus in a distinctly new way.

And I needed to focus, on account of wanting so badly to get through the chapters about my relationship with Roxanne so that I could move on.

And even though we weren't supposed to technically be there, at Christina's uncle's place, in the first place, as she never actually got permission, and even though it was inconvenient to come and get me later in the week, she worked it out, because I asked her to and because that's the kind of person she was, and remains.

So when she stepped into the house and looked around, all she said was:

"How could you, Steven?"

And I realized for the first time that I had created a complete mess in every room, clothes on the floor, pizza boxes on the counters. Her uncle's now-empty vodka bottles on the couch.

She practically pushed me into the bedroom, and right away my mind snapped into gear. I grabbed her playfully, and she said, "No way. You've got to clean yourself up, and we have to get out of here."

I didn't much see the love in her eyes at that moment.

I showered as she (A) cleaned up, (B) gathered the laundry, (C) vacuumed, (D) swept, (E) sprayed the sliding glass doors, (F) found the empty champagne bottles on the deck, (G) bagged them, (H) bagged everything else, and (I) threw everything into the car, all before I was out of the bathroom. Either I was slowing down or she was on meth or something.

"Better now?" I asked about me, looking in the mirror, all clean shaven and fresh. And naked, except for a towel, which I was about to remove when she said, "C'mon, Steven. Get your clothes on, we are out of here."

I couldn't argue that point. In fact, I couldn't actually function, as I was still having what I referred to in the chapters that I was working on as "Roxanne fever." The mix of sleeplessness, isolation, alcohol, and what remained of Jacob's Gold in combination with my vivid memories of that relationship had fucked with me big-time, had taken me to a place in my mind that was as close to crazy as you could get. And made me realize that I didn't love Christina the way that she loved me.

"Sorry" was all I said, as we were leaving. I meant it in many, many ways.

Sorry meant a lot to her. She instantly softened. "Was it worth it?"

And I had to tell her.

"No. It was too scary. No one should be by themselves for this long. Ever."

And we were out of there, back in my car, her driving this time and me in the passenger seat, my shades hiding me from the sunlight. I was feeling all vampire at the moment. My bare feet pressed against the windshield as I extended my seat all the way back to full recline and pulled a Yankees cap over my face.

"When you said over the phone that you hadn't stopped writing for a minute, I thought that you were, you know, exaggerating," she said. "Did you even sleep at all?"

. . . Which is the last thing I remember about the trip, because before we hit the Thruway, I passed out and didn't wake up until we were home (actually at Christina's house). She got out and gave me an obligatory kiss on the lips and told me that she loved me in a businesslike tone, and I wondered if she still did after our time together or was she disappointed, because maybe, along the way, she had come to the same realization that I did.

And as soon as I dropped her off at her house, my phone lit up. Claudia.

I know, I know, you're going to think I'm an idiot, and I can practically hear you saying, don't answer it, but being that I hadn't talked to her in a long time, I figured what could the harm be in just hearing her voice. So I flipped my phone open and she said two things that changed the course of the rest of my summer.

The first was: "I really, really miss you."

The second was: "My parents are out of town for a few days."

Actually, scratch that. Well, not completely as those two things totally gifted me with the spark that I hadn't had since Christina left me alone in the woods. The truth was, it wasn't just her saying those things. It wasn't even the fact that she had this slightly raspy voice that reminded me of you-know-who. It wasn't the fact that, after becoming someone totally radically different in the woods, I was craving to be just Crash again, or the fact that I knew how difficult it was going to be to get to the main event of the book and the secret and all and I just needed a real vacation.

What changed the course of my summer is that after she told me that her parents were out of town, I asked her, "Well, who's watching you then?" OK, not the best line I ever came up with, and if you take it in the abstract, it actually sounds creepy, but she didn't take it that way at all.

Instead she laughed. Really laughed. Really, really laughed.

And I was a goner.

I suspect that you don't have to be a genius to know what happened next. Shit, if I was reading this, I would totally know. And you wouldn't be wrong, but you're not going to guess all of it, so I'll have to tell you anyways.

For one, no surprises here, I didn't go straight home. After all, after my two-hour car nap, well, after the phone call, I was completely refreshed. And getting mad hungry. And having called all of my boys earlier, and none of them were around due to summer jobs, family vacations, whatever, I figured why eat alone when in like twenty minutes I could be having dinner with someone who really, really missed me and who couldn't stop laughing. So I reset my GPS to Claudia's address.

I swear that at that moment, getting it on with her was the furthest thing from my mind.

Actually, I just wanted to see her and hear that laugh in person. Plus, when I told her that I was coming over, she sounded, swear to god, just like my dog Medusa sounds when I come home after sleeping out for a few days, all whimpering with her tail wagging so hard it hits both sides of her ass. Well, Claudia made a sound just like that.

Now how could you ignore a girl who whimpers for you?

Plus, she said she would get me whatever I wanted. Did I want Chinese, sushi, Italian, whatever, and what did I want to drink, she had it all.

Not trying to be a bastard or anything, but knowing that this girl had just whimpered, I figured I would test her dedication, so get this: I ordered a few burgers, plus hot and sour soup and cold noodles, plus chicken parm with ziti, plus a slice of pizza. Which meant she would have to either go to three different restaurants or order from all of them. OK, it was just a joke to see how far she would go, I wasn't really going to make her do that. Except, I could hear her writing it all down, scrambling to get the menus on her computer, clicking away, all without asking me any questions or giving me even the slightest suggestion that I was being unreasonable.

Anyways, when I finally made it to the flag point on the GPS, I pulled up to a giant arch of a gate that separated two imposing stone walls. Through the gate was this giant brick building stretching out in both directions farther than I could see from the road. I had to get out of the car to get to the intercom, and even then, pressing down on the buttons and peering through the bars, I still couldn't see both ends of the house.

Now, I have seen rich, not gonna lie. Due to Jacob's influential sphere of high-powered friends, I had been to some pretty big houses before (each time with a familiar Jacob warning . . . don't touch anything, and *don't* embarrass me). Still, I have never been to a house this huge. This was pot-of-gold-at-the-end-of-the-rainbow rich.

"Crash, is that you?" on the intercom, even as she was buzzing me in.

It took me like a full minute to drive around the curved driveway to the front entrance. And when I arrived, the door opened, and Claudia was there, dressed like a hooker in six-inch-high heels, a tight-fitting miniskirt that practically showed everything, with this bikini top. My heart began to pound and I needed to catch my breath. This is how absolutely sexy this girl was.

She was, as Burn would have put it, porn star hot.

To be honest, if there was any chance, any momentary glimmer of hope that I was going to be strong and be faithful to the woman who loved me, it was all shot to hell the instant Claudia opened the door. Because, just seeing her, I was back to being "Crash" again, just like old times, realizing how tired I was of being "Steven" to Christina and how much the book had fucked with my mind.

And now that I was "back," I had another problem, as in how was I going to keep this to myself? I mean, this was going to be a story to tell the Club Crew, only the Club Crew would tell the Herd, and one of them would tell Christina, and the last thing I wanted was to hurt Christina.

It pained me to realize that I was going to have to keep this to myself.

I hopped out of the car, jogged up the steps, and when I got to the top, Claudia flung her arms around me and hugged me so physically, I could've popped at the door. This was the kind of hug reserved for wives of soldiers coming back from Iraq or something, that's how intense it was.

"Thank you *sooooooooooo* much for coming," this girl was saying, as she started kissing my neck, making my hair stand on end. This perfectly curved girl in the stripper outfit and the mile-long house was thanking *me*.

Well, who do I thank?

There was, however, the first order of business.

As hot as she was, as hot as she was making me, I was even hungrier. I didn't know exactly how to bring that up, with her continuing to hug me and rub against me and all. But then, as if on cue, she took me by the hand and led me into the dining room, a room the size of a hotel ballroom, with this mega table, the kind you see in the movies, where if you sit at either end, you can't even talk to each other.

Well, spread out on this massive table were plates of burgers and fries and thick shakes; then platters of Chinese food, soups, noodle dishes; plates of sushi; and then, down farther, the Italian section, two piping-hot pizzas, one plain, the other pepperoni, sausages, mushrooms, olives, and onions (in short, the Crash-perfect pie—how did she know?), and plates of pasta, fettuccini, ziti, penne vodka, and other dishes. There was enough food to feed the entire Club Crew for a week, and we eat like jackals in a frenzy.

"I wasn't sure whether you would want anything else, so I improvised, seeing as you listed your faves on your Facebook page."

And while I missed it before, there were two opened bottles of wine in the center of the table and, placed strategically between them, a single, perfectly rolled blunt.

"Crash, you are dead and this is heaven" is what my brain was telling me. "You are still in the cabin sick as a dog and the Roxanne fever is making you hallucinate. Either that or the weed you smoked all week was laced with something."

Speaking of which, she reached for the blunt. "I promise no one is here to take pictures this time," she said as she handed it to me, along with a solid gold lighter, flicking it on so I could light up.

I took a deep inhale as the tip flamed up like a torch.

Swweeeeeeeeeeeeeeeeeeeettt.

Then she went for the wine, and I had to tell her, "Not much of a wine guy," which didn't stop her from pouring me a glass.

"Ohhhhh." She laughed. "You *will* like these wines," she told me in a really knowing kind of way. And then she did it: she delivered a fully robust laugh that came from the bottom of her being.

OK, I wasn't exactly sure why she was laughing until I tasted the wine. You *cannot* believe how good this particular red wine tasted. Picture a velvet cherry, squeezed into your throat where the drip got better and better tasting until your taste buds were covered like a blanket. Got the idea? And the white wine, you could taste the sun in that, swear to fucking Christ.

"You're right, these are unbelievably good," I finally said.

"They should be," she said, laughing. "Each bottle was over a thousand dollars."

I practically coughed up the full glass when she told me this.

"There's an unexpected kick to them," she said with a smile. "But you'll know what I mean in like ten minutes."

And as promised, ten minutes later, I understood her point. Holding both bottles in one hand, she motioned for me to follow her into the next room as I dutifully trailed behind her. She pulled me down onto the couch and lay back, her head on the armrest, and chugged some of the red, a few drops dribbling down her chin, down her neck, then pulling me down onto her.

"If you like it so much," she said, "lick it off me. . . ."

We immediately got busy, we got extremely busy. This girl was totally and completely into it in a way that I haven't experienced since you know who. Plus, this girl seemed to really get off just knowing that she was exciting me, which she was most definitely doing.

And after a long time, I was done, but she apparently wasn't, so she led me to her bedroom and put on a show for me that you would simply not believe, this is all I'm saying.

And then we napped, and she started up again, and every time I was done, we laughed together, and this went on all night, or most of the night, because I kept falling asleep between the wine (we opened other bottles) and the blunt and the sex.

And then I rolled over and noticed the digital alarm clock by the side of her bed reading 3:01, which didn't make sense because how could it be 3:01 if the room was so bright with sun? Unless . . .

I bolted up, into the bathroom, noticing for the first time that I was alone in Claudia's bedroom, which, by the way, was a vast castle of a room, how did I not notice that last night?

Then the search for my cell phone downstairs with the rest of my clothes. I picked it up. 3:06. Twenty-three messages, like eight from my mom, then Newman, Christina, like five, then Lindsey, my mom, Newman, then Evan, then Kenny, then Newman again, then my mom again, then Lindsey, then Jacob. Voice mails, texts, all saying the same thing:

Where are you?

And then Sally, I totally fucking forgot Sally. I was supposed to meet her in her office at 3:00 P.M. to go over a few things. Now it was 3:12 and I was somewhere in the heart of Westchester.

I had damage control to do.

First my mom, who would be easy since I had already let her know I was staying at Christina's uncle's place, but who expected me home the day before: I'm fine, no, nothing happened. I stayed an extra day is all, no not at the cabin, I know Christina is home, I stayed at a friend's house, a new friend OK, yes, everything is fine, I'll be home in an hour, no I didn't call Dad, I called you first, yes, I will call Dad, no, I didn't mean to make everyone worried, I'll call Christina (what the fuck was I going to tell her?), I'll take care of my friends, no I'm in Westchester, I'll explain when I get home, yes, I'm sure I'm all right.

Claudia, by now, was standing beside me, in her bikini. She had apparently been tanning, as she was all oiled up. This girl was looking better and better to me every minute. I refused to look at her while I was on the phone; she was way too distracting. I had to concentrate, and I had more calls to make.

"You're in hot water, aren't you?"

"What do you mean, hot water?" I asked, preoccupied with calling Sally, pacing as the phone buzzed. I went through the dining room (where she had cleaned up expertly, not a drop of food remained on the table and it shone with a new polish), into the kitchen, this rambling open space with cooking islands and endless cabinets, then into the home theater, which had the biggest private screen I had ever seen (Jamie would have loved this), all with her following, me not realizing what I was doing, concentrating on getting through to Sally.

At least until I got to the huge glass doors that led onto the deck, overlooking a path to the most spectacular pool I had ever seen. I have been to some major hotel pools in my life, even Caribbean resort pools that circled the buildings. Nothing compared to this.

I stared suspiciously at Claudia. Was she like Trump's other daughter or something? I made a mental note to get her last name, because, thing was, if she was famous, then she would have been identified when her picture was published. Except, given that her face was blurred out, maybe her father was powerful enough to keep her out of the paper.

Or maybe her father was like in the mob or something. . . .

"What do you mean, 'hot water,' anyways?" I asked, staring, just staring at the magnificent pool.

She looked at me like she didn't believe me. "It's an expression, silly. Don't tell me you've never heard it before. I didn't mean that you were physically in hot water."

"What's it supposed to mean?"

"You're in big-time trouble, is what it means."

"Then you're right, I am in hot water," I said, stepping back into the house.

I could get used to a place like this. My mind started to spin: I could get the Club Crew guys over, get her to call her friends, have them party with us. This could be big-time.

Except there was the Christina problem, how could I forget the Christina problem? Fuckme.

I tried Sally again. This time she picked up with an angry outburst, as in, "You better have a pretty good reason for missing your appointment."

Which I did, I told her, I was up all night working. I'm into the big chapter now, isn't that what she wanted? Sorry that time slipped away, but I worked through the night and fell asleep, so sorry, but wasn't I doing OK, no, better than OK, having supplied her with like five chapters in the last week.

And immediately she backed off. She had nothing else to say. And then, "OK, send me what you've done so far." And I had to explain that it wasn't ready, that's not how we worked together, that as soon as it was, she would get it from me, but didn't I just send her five chapters and weren't they exactly what she wanted?

And she agreed. It's all good.

Now the only thing I had left to figure out was what to do with Christina.

But first a snack. No way was I going to pass the opportunity to raid the massive refrigerators in Claudia's massive kitchen.

I called Newman first. "You cannot believe . . ."

I wasn't looking just to brag to Newman about how I had just connected with the richest girl in New York, but I needed to get his creative mind working. Because Sally was easy; I could handle Sally on my own, blindfolded. But I needed his expertise to deal with the Christina problem, because no way was I going to allow her to get hurt in any way, and I wasn't capable of solving that riddle on my own. So I had to come up with a lie believable enough to cover my absence in the last twenty-four. Plus I was also going to have to come up with a separate set of excuses rolling forward. Rolling forward, because there was no way in hell I was going to be able to stay away from Claudia, I already knew that.

And, just as I anticipated, Newman had a solution regarding my whereabouts last night. He was considering the rolling forward part when we were interrupted by a call from Jacob, which I felt obliged to take, cringing as I did so.

"Steven. I will cancel your cell service if I call and you don't pick up next time, is that clear?"

Yeah, hello to you too, Dad.

OK, we were not at that chit-chat stage, as if I needed to be reminded. After all, he cut me off financially only to have Caroline Prescott force his hand to reinstate my access to my own money. My first instinct now was to fight back, but it would be pointless arguing with him. Instead I opted for my other strategy, which was to minimize my exposure. In other words, "yes" him to death, as in whatever he says, I'm OK with it.

This strategy has proven effective in the past, and this being the first actual time that we've talked since the great TV interview fiasco, I wasn't looking to engage in any further conflict.

"I understand" is what I said.

"I don't think you understand."

"Oh, I understand."

"You will understand if you suddenly find yourself without a phone."

"I understand."

"I don't need your mother calling me."

"I understand."

"You're in hot water as it is. . . ."

OK, that was freaky, hearing a phrase that I'd never heard before, now twice within the same hour. I had to wonder, were people saying that all the time and I had just missed it before?

But then Jacob suddenly switched gears and was talking in a conversational tone. "Sally tells me that you've been stepping up lately, that she's received quite a bit of the book." This threw me off completely. I was about to say "I understand" again, but instead, I just listened. Was he trying to make conversation with me? Who could tell?

"She says she has high expectations for the book," he went on. "Actually I asked her if it was appropriate for me to read it, and she suggested that I wait until it's done and edited."

That had me thinking about all the nasty shit I wrote about him. I never realized until that very minute that whenever he got around to reading it, I was probably looking at World War III between me and him. No way was he going to let Sally publish a book that contained anything critical of him. And no way was I going to change a word. I felt momentarily queasy, but then I realized that, at least for the time being, Jacob knew nothing about its contents.

"Probably better that way," I admitted.

"She says she has been working with one of the top editors at the publishing house," he said. "Very, very exciting, really."

Was that an actual compliment? If so, was he backing off the hostile-father impression that I was so familiar with?

"So then why am I still in hot water?" I asked.

"You know why you're in hot water," he said, returning to his full-on Jacob voice. I could tell from this that we were done, even though I wasn't positive what he was referring to or why he called in the first place.

Next, Christina. But first, I had to call Newman back in order to develop a foolproof alibi. Knowing my own mind, I would, on my own, create a story so full of holes that she would be able to see right through to the truth. Once again, I relied on Newman's twisted brain to anticipate every possible angle.

He immediately asked me why I thought that Christina would be suspicious that I was with someone else in the first place. He pointed out that she was probably just concerned about me and once she heard my voice, she would be relieved. And that would be it.

"But, just in case, here's what we do. . . ."

I called, dreading the moment that she answered.

Only it kept ringing.

And went straight to voice mail. Which, in its own way, was perfect, because I could deliver my story without having to deal with any questions.

"Hi, Christina. I got your message. Sorry for not calling. Right after I dropped you off, I got a call from my camp friend Nick, Nick Alamante, and he said that his parents were getting divorced and that he was going to have to live with his father in St. Louis and he was thinking of running away. So next thing I know, I'm driving to his house in New Jersey. And by the time I got there, he was messed up on acid, having a bad trip, so me and some of my camp friends had to talk him down and stay with him when he went to the hospital."

I inhaled. Amazed at the precision of the tale I had just spun, improvising by dropping a name in (there was actually no one in my camp named Nick and I never mentioned him before, so she couldn't have remembered), and then having him live far away and then getting him to trip balls so we end up in the one place that we couldn't call from.

Newman would have been proud had he witnessed my performance. By the time I was done, I had even convinced myself that this was exactly what happened, almost forgetting that it was all a total and complete lie.

And then I waited. I figured Christina was going to call back immediately and yell at me and call me a total liar and cheater.

Only she didn't call back.

Not for hours, and then when my phone finally buzzed, it was a text message:

> Got your message. Glad to hear u r alive. I'm at the movies
> with my sister. lv

Lv? Again, not the first time that this girl confused me. I tried to figure out if "lv" represented initials or some kind of French word, and finally guessed that it was short for "love," which meant that she didn't suspect anything.

When I got home, even Lindsey was happy to see me. They were all apparently worried that I had died or something. Plus it had been, like, over a week since I had seen them. My mother yelled at me, which, of course, I totally expected, and threatened me, which, of course, didn't surprise me, and then hugged me and forgave me after I convinced her I was sorry. I was quickly learning that "sorry" was a magic word, just like "please" and "thank you." So thank you, Barney the purple dinosaur, for that.

And soon enough, I was back in front of the TV with Jamie, just me and her, and she waited for a commercial to ask suspiciously, "Where'd you *really* go, Steven?"

And then around ten, I yelled up to my mom's bedroom that I was going to Evan's house. And then, of course, beelined it over to Bedford and the rich girl's mansion. She was whimpering happy to see me again, like I had been gone for weeks, not hours. And I left at two A.M. and got home at two-thirty and slept until noon.

And later in the day, Christina came over and I was Steven again, and we watched TV and talked, and when she was sure that no one was home, she followed me into my bedroom. And all the time I was with her, I couldn't help thinking how terrible it would be if she found out about Claudia and promised myself that I would stop.

And that night at ten, despite my promises, I dropped Christina off and kept driving to Bedford and the rich girl's house and I was Crash again, and she was whimpering happy to see me again, you know the drill, left at two, two-thirty, slept until noon. And Christina came over. . . .

It became easier every day. It got so that I could have gone on like that for the entire rest of summer, especially since I knew what was waiting for me the second I started writing again. So even though I was getting worn down, I wasn't about to stop, despite the fact that I wasn't writing and Sally was calling and even got Jacob to call asking for the rest.

Still, I wasn't about to stop. So it wasn't me. And it wasn't Claudia or Christina. Not on their own anyways.

The reason it came to an end was all because of the "wall."

The wall, for those of you who still don't own a computer, is the section in Facebook where you post things that you want to tell people and then they comment about it. The wall also allows people to post things that they want to tell you. Then, when you sign on, you see a list of the people who contacted you with one-liners, like "awesome pics," if you posted new photos, or "r u coming to my party," or whatever.

Well, I hadn't signed on for days, since I only use Facebook to find people or get info about what's going down in my town. So being as I was otherwise occupied all those days and nights, I didn't have any need to log on to see what else was happening.

So Pete had to tell me. Actually, there was a text message from him on my phone when I woke up that afternoon, having passed out on my couch from too much partying with Claudia the night before. The text said:

u r in hot water. Log onto Facebook.

I flipped open my MacBook, clicked Safari, and there ten seconds later was a note from Claudia: "Had a great time last night. Can u get to my house earlier 2nite?"

. . . followed by a note from Christina:

"Why don't you go now, because I'm not coming over today or ever again."

Fuckme.

So I immediately called her, as in Christina, not Claudia.

She picked up the phone and said, "How could you, Steven?"

And I said that I was sorry, that I never meant to hurt her.

And she said that "sorry" was totally meaningless in this situation.

And I asked to see her, because I still had feelings for her, and I didn't want to lose her, and OK, I screwed up, but we couldn't let that come between us, given our connection and all.

And she said that connection or not, she wasn't going to see me.

And I said please and she said:

"I need time to process this. I thought you were better than that."

Now, I distinctly remembered that when I was in Woodstock, and Felicia used those very words on me, I was supercareful not to repeat them to Christina, because, tell you the truth, I felt completely ashamed about the fact that I had disappointed Felicia. And also, I remembered how it really hurt hearing those words. So I was positive, beyond positive in fact, that I never mentioned them to Christina or even said them out loud. Which of course meant that Christina had to have come to a completely independent determination that I was not who she thought I was, and that I was *not* better than that.

What were the odds of hearing a phrase like that twice in a summer? Unless of course, it was true? So I had to pretty much accept the fact that I wasn't better than that, whatever "that" was. This time, however, the effect on me was totally different: It was a totally freeing revelation. After all, if I wasn't better than that, I didn't have to pretend to be.

Except that something from my time with Roxanne jolted

me, as in, when she explained her special talent and it had to do with Andrew Jackson and how she was able to understand exactly how he was feeling when they called him a jackass. She was trying to teach me something, which I didn't completely appreciate until that very second, not really.

I finally got what it felt like to be Felicia when I fucked her over. I finally got what it felt like to be Christina. OK, I sucked, I'll admit it.

And knowing this, I was not willing to give up on Christina, so I called her back.

Went straight to voice mail. I tried her home phone number and no one answered, even though I knew she was home.

I knew she knew I was calling.

I would need Newman on this. And he wasn't around.

So I called Claudia.

"You told me I was your only girlfriend," she said, clearly hurt. Obviously, I didn't expect that. I could hear her whimpering slightly on the phone, only this was a totally different kind of whimpering sound she was making, more like a cry-whimper than a happy-whimper. It made me instantly sad.

"I never said that" is what I said, and instantly I knew how stupid that sounded. "I never said 'only.'" Which, of course, as soon as I said it, sounded even stupider.

"You said you had feelings for me."

And of course, I did tell her that, having echoed a line to Claudia that I previously used with Christina. In fact, come to think of it, there were a lot of things that either I said to Christina, or Christina said to me, that I used on Claudia. They just seemed equally appropriate is all. Plus, at the time, it made her superhappy and got her to laugh, which she wasn't doing now at all.

"I did," I answered. "I do."

"But you have them for someone else, don't you?"

Me, thinking, *Help me, Alex. What do I do now?* What I did was not answer at all.

"Well, do you?"

"I guess" is what I said. "Not exactly" is what I said next. "They're different, is all," I told her.

"Different how?"

"It's . . . complicated."

"Are you doing her too?" she asked. And then in a voice that sounded so totally hurt and desperate, she added, "Pleeeeeeeeeeese, Crash, don't lie to me."

And so I didn't. And she said, "Maybe you better not call me until you work things out with your real girlfriend."

As they say in baseball: two away.

I waited a few hours to let her get over the initial hurt, then called her again, but now she wasn't picking up her phone either. When I told Newman, he suggested that I give her more time, that she would come around.

He was not so optimistic about Christina.

Which is why I started spending more time with my boys, going back to my early-summer routine of pregaming at the nature preserve and seeking out the party of the night, or ending up at Pinky's, passing the bong around in the back of Evan's SUV, or going to the movies, or getting blazed and playing video games until practically dawn.

And I called Christina every day and she didn't call me back. And I called Claudia every day and she didn't call me back. And I wasn't sure who I missed more, but it took me back to the fact that I had completely stopped writing (it wasn't only that, as Sally was calling, like, every day, demanding the next chapter).

And the truth was, I had completely stopped writing not because of my days with Christina or my nights with Claudia, or my exhaustion at keeping them separate, or my adrenaline kicking in because I was in high gear all the time. Not because of those things, but because of the chapter that I was avoiding writing.

And now I had no excuse.

So on a Saturday night, around midnight, I started a chapter called "How Crash Landed." The title made no sense but seemed consistent with the format I set up with Newman back when I first started writing, so I left it alone, figuring something would come to me as I wrote.

And then I waited.

But nothing happened. So I waited some more. But not a word. So I figured that maybe the chapter title wasn't right, so I spent some time thinking of other chapter titles and came up with like ten different versions, and came back to "How Crash Landed."

Two A.M.

And my mom called into my room.

"Is Jamie home yet?"

Jamie had gone out earlier that night with a group of juniors, which I didn't like since I didn't trust them, as I knew either them or their brothers and sisters. But I was sure that she had come home early, and now I ran down to the family room to check.

The television wasn't on.

I had a bad feeling, that twisty ache I get in my stomach when I think something is wrong.

I called her friend Jackie. Jackie didn't pick up. I didn't know who else to call.

I went for the school directory, looking down the list of names.

My mom came down. "She's not here?"

"Don't worry," I said, sounding very worried. Still scrounging around for the names. No one I recognized. Then a call back from Jackie. I picked up.

"They're taking Jamie to the hospital."

"Why?"

"Alcohol poisoning."

"Who?" I demanded. "Who's taking her to the hospital?"

"My parents. The ambulance is here right now."

At the same time, the house phone rang. Jackie's mom.

I was driving seventy in a forty-five zone, trying to get to my little sister. My mom was in a separate car with Lindsey somewhere behind me. I couldn't wait for them; I had to get to Jamie right away.

I hit seventy-five when I heard the siren and then saw the flash of spinning lights in my rearview mirror.

"Pull over now" from a police bullhorn.

I almost didn't but decided I had to.

I sat quietly in the driver's seat, on the side of the road, filled with anger, determined to control my temper, so I kept my hands pinned to the steering wheel at all times.

A flashlight in my eyes. A tap on my driver's side window.

I thought about Jamie, and whether she was OK, and I was sure she was OK, she had to be OK, so I made myself not think about her. Instead, I thought about what I needed to write, and it suddenly came to me how I should start the next chapter.

Which I would do the second that I knew that Jamie was all right.

"License and registration," as I rolled down the window. "You're in hot water, son. Really, really hot water."

CHAPTER TWENTY-TWO

HOW CRASH LANDED

Summer 2007.

For me, it was the almost-perfect summer.

Done with junior year, by the skin of my teeth. Not too worried about senior year even though my SAT scores sucked so bad a chimp could have taken the test and done better. Seriously. Thankfully, my ACT scores were not as painful. Still, while my mom was stressing about what schools I should apply to, I was more interested in partying.

Plus, there was always September.

It was the summer of driving, as we were all legal at that point.

It was the summer of concerts for the Club Crew, because now that we could drive, we traveled wherever the music was—down to Jones Beach, up to Albany, across to Jersey and the Meadowlands, over to Hartford—and at each concert, of course, we had the perfect music weed.

It was the summer of big-time experimentation, and we found new and more adventurous ways to get to high, like salvia, DMT, robotripping, morning glory seeds, cocaine, bombs (X), and shrooms. Oh yeah, and acid. As in LSD. This will fuck you up, kiddies. Fuck you up big-time.

It was a summer of parties, and we always managed to find one, somewhere to go almost every night.

It was the summer of movies, like *The Order of the Phoenix*, *The Simpsons Movie*, and *Superbad*.

It was the summer of relationships. Bobby discovered that he was totally into Ashley, Kenny was into an about-to-be junior girl named Britney, Evan started seeing a girl from his summer camp, and then there was me and Diana and me and Kelly and me and April Walker.

It was also the summer that Newman and Pete independently entered manhood. Newman with an incoming junior, not going to say which. Pete's, you couldn't actually count his, because it was paid for, as in his brother took him to a Brazilian hooker in Brooklyn.

But in the end, none of these things mattered, because for the rest of my life, I will remember the summer of 2007 as the summer that Roxanne Burnett killed herself.

It was my mom who told me.

School had actually started, three days into my senior year, and there was already a chill in the air, like fall was closing in. And just when you reached for a sweatshirt, it was brutally hot and humid again.

She was in the kitchen, crying uncontrollably, and when I walked in and caught her with her back to me, she made me wait in suspense, with me having to ask over and over, what's wrong, what's wrong.

So weird. When I entered the kitchen, all I could think about was having to face Connelly again, because I had him for English again and that was going to supremely suck, even more than in freshman year.

And then there was my mom, reduced to quivering, and Roxanne was gone.

And then she grabbed me and hugged me, and Roxanne was gone.

And I could feel my own mother shaking like a child as she told me again and Roxanne was gone.

And then she told me, and in my mind, I was standing again

in the middle of the winter in the middle of the strip mall, with a gun pointed at me, and this time, no one was there to stop the bullet from going right through me.

Roxanne was gone.

Forever.

And it didn't make sense, my mom crying so much. She didn't know Roxanne, not really. And she also didn't know how much I really knew Roxanne. I mean, she knew about the tutoring. But she didn't know what really happened.

Or the way Roxanne looked at me when I showed up at Aunt Peesmell's drenched from the rain.

Or the way she snorted when her sweats weren't where she left them.

Or the way she giggled when I tickled her arm while we watched *That '70s Show*, showing off her goose bumps.

Or the way she worried about how I would do on a test after she taught me everything there was to know about chapter seventeen of American history.

Or the way she smiled when I showed off my A–.

Or the way she would crane her neck when she brushed her hair when she came out of a shower.

Or the way she would laugh after we made love together.

Or the way we would share each other's thoughts.

Or the way she totally and completely changed my life.

Or the way she totally and completely let me go.

Roxanne dying wasn't about to change any of that. But I couldn't explain any of this to my mother. Because she wouldn't get it.

So after my mother told me that Roxanne killed herself, I very calmly told her that I was sorry to hear that, then went back into my room.

And put my fist through the wall.

Made a steering-wheel-size hole in the sheetrock, right by my plasma TV screen. Then swirled around and did it again on the other side of the television.

It was the only way to focus the intense heat of my total and complete anger, anger that turned my stomach and actually made me shudder, and then shiver, because everything was ice cold like it was suddenly winter again.

I wasn't angry with Roxanne. Not in the least. It wasn't her fault. It was everyone else's fault. Everyone who looked at her like she was just another goth chick or a sleazy slut whore. Or whatever. Everyone who failed to recognize her for who she was. It was my fault for not being there for her when she needed me. It was David Burnett's fault for not letting me stay in her life. I was sure that it would have been different if Massachusetts had never happened.

Lindsey heard the noise and came running into my room to see what the problem was. She stopped short when she saw me with my hand covered in blood. She wouldn't dare enter my room, because she could tell from my face that it was about Roxanne. And given that she was one of those people who wrote Roxanne off as a human being, she knew that if she said anything, I would literally tear her head off.

Instead, she stood in the hallway and yelled at the top of her lungs:

"MAAAAA!"

My mother came running up, saw me, grabbed a towel, and wiped my hand down. We were both surprised to see that the damage was mostly superficial. Still, she made me put it under freezing-cold water. It numbed the pain in my hand, but the anger-pain was spreading upward into my shoulder blades, boxing me in.

I felt like I was inside an elevator and the elevator was stuck between floors and there was no air left and the lights were dimming.

I had to go. Didn't matter where. I had to leave.

So I drove. Going all the way to Massachusetts, in search of the Barnes & Noble shopping center where Burn had his breakdown. Techno blasted through the speakers all the way, drowning out the sounds of the outside world. I hit a hundred miles an hour for a brief moment before slowing down, all the time thinking about her. How she changed so much every time I saw her, how she loved shocking me and probably everyone else who ever met her, how she shook her head all the time in great disbelief whenever I told her something, and how she turned "frickin'" into the coolest word to me.

I couldn't find the exact mall, couldn't even be sure that I was in the right area of Massachusetts. Didn't care, really. Except, tell you the truth, I was thinking that if I found it, the exact location, then somehow, she would be standing there, an echo of the past, like Obi-Wan and Yoda at the end of *Return of the Jedi*, smiling at me from the other side, letting me know that she was all right.

Except she wasn't all right at all. She was dead as stone.

After hours of driving, I stopped at a Subway, bought a foot-long, couldn't eat it, not after the first bite, which soured in my stomach. I threw the rest into the garbage on the way out and then kicked the garbage can, denting it, causing people to run out of the store as I made my way back to the car.

I parked in the back of a random Home Depot and listened to Tiesto while my car shook from the bass. And waited for a very long time.

It was no good. I was still in the elevator in between floors. No one was coming for me.

I raised the volume on the music and then I cried.

I cried like a baby because no one could see me, no one could hear me, and so I cried the way I wanted to cry when she turned away from me in Massachusetts and a part of me knew that I would never be with her again. But a part of me always believed that there would come a time when she called, when she needed me again, and I would be there for her, wherever she was, whatever time she called.

Now that day would never come.

So I cried for a long time, maybe mixed with screaming. I don't exactly remember.

Then I was done.

I drove home slower and more steadily, and when I got back to Westchester, it finally occurred to me that I understood why Burn had to drive all the time after his mother died.

Burn.

I wondered how he was taking the news. I had completely forgotten him in the equation. Putting my psychic feelers out, I pictured him on a distant highway, driving even more furiously than me, in search of his sister . . . of his entire family. None of whom he would ever see again. I actually felt . . . sorry for him.

Then I put my psychic feelers out for Roxanne and felt . . . nothing.

And I went into my house when I got home, full of gratitude that my mom and my sisters were home, together for just a little while longer before Lindsey went back to college.

Gratitude that was instantly wiped away when I walked through the door.

"Crash finally landed," Lindsey screamed up to my mom when she saw me. "You're in trouble," she told me with a smug smile that made me wish I could trade her life for Roxanne's.

And I would have, at that very moment, regardless of the fact that we shared DNA.

"Also, you got a letter." She gestured to the envelope on the hallway table.

I examined the envelope, typed out in old-fashioned typing and addressed to me. No return address, plain white envelope. I pressed it. Not flat, but slightly bubbled. I tried to guess who would have sent me a letter, but no one I knew read much or actually stopped to write anything. In fact, it had been years since those summer camp letters, and I couldn't even remember the last time that I actually had received actual mail.

I very carefully tore the edge, then notched my finger between the flap and the envelope and tried to pry it open, but couldn't, so I used more force and ripped it apart.

And beans came flying out, cascading onto the floor.

"What the fuck?" is what I said out loud, though no one was there to hear me.

It didn't register. Not until I pulled out the actual letter. It was scrunched up. I had to flatten it out and press it with my palm against the hall table, already littered with other mail, catalogs, and postcards.

And when I read the contents of the letter, I started to cry again, not out loud this time, but tears escaped my eyes and I didn't try to stop them from coming.

What the Letter said was:

> *Dear Crash,*
> *Here are your beans back.*
> *They didn't work.*
> *Please remember me.*
> *Love always,*
> *Roxanne*

I looked down at the beans scattered across the hallway tiles and I knew what I had to do.

The funeral was private, according to my mom, who had talked to Aunt Peesmell. On David's instructions, they were not opening it up to anyone other than immediate family members.

We couldn't get the location. But being as someone set up a memorial site for her on Facebook, I was able to check her wall, and tons of people were writing things about her, to her, things like "too soon" and "rest in peace." And people were expressing frustration at not being able to get information about the funeral or the cemetery where they planned to bury Roxanne.

I scrolled through the list of her friends, over 500 names. I examined the profiles and the pictures of some random people. Couldn't get too far, but from what I could tell, most of them were not from town; only a few had gone to Meadows. Many were older looking, early twenties was my guess, lots of goths covered in tats.

There was a reference to a MySpace page, where another online memorial had been set up, this one with music, some song called "Playground Love," which, tell you the truth, sounded totally depressing, but also like the stuff that Roxanne used to play during our tutoring sessions. There were postings, stories about her, and a posting by someone who claimed to have found out where Roxanne was being buried. People said they were going to show up spontaneously and have their own funeral by her graveside, even though they weren't invited.

I cut school, didn't tell anyone where I was going, and, using the directions that were posted online, traveled into the heart of New Jersey. I got to the cemetery in under an hour, which was a major accomplishment in and of itself, because it seemed like every car in the entire state was out to get me.

Even though I was early, there were already about twenty other people, seemingly stranded at the gates of the cemetery by a gladiator guy who looked like he could have been in the Russell Crowe movie. I parked on the street and told the gladiator that I was a friend of the family. He told me that he had strict instructions not to let anyone in. A goth chick, not much older than me, strolled alongside me, and asked how many family members were allowed in. Eight or nine, the gladiator told her, and they were already there. No one else gets in.

Still, people kept showing up.

The group was getting bigger, more cars pulled up. There were redheaded twins with multiple nose piercings. An Abe Lincoln–looking guy in, swear to Christ, a top hat and long beard. There was a midget with more tattoos than I had ever seen before on a normal-size person. And, coming out of a dusty brown convertible, was a tall woman in a black dress and tights that appeared to be ripped in places. Then there were a few straight-looking college students and even a middle-aged guy, round and bald.

As I looked around, I wondered whether the tiger lady who popped Burn's cherry was there. Which one could she be?

Now everyone was talking to the gladiator. First they threatened to storm the gates. Then they agreed to take their ceremony down the block to a small park. I followed the group, which was growing, becoming this impromptu festival of misfits, where most people seemed to know each other and everyone was talking but no one was talking to me.

As soon as we got to the park, someone pulled out this mini amplifier and microphone and the redheaded twins began to sing, a cappella "Amazing Grace" in harmony, and then the torn tights girl spoke, and as soon as she started to talk about Roxanne, I knew, *I totally knew* that she was the tiger lady.

And they shared memories of Roxanne.

The Abe Lincoln guy took the mic next and told the group: "The only thing we are certain of after all these years is the insufficiency of an explanation."

The crowd went wild on this one, and I figured that it must have been the lyrics to some kind of popular goth song or something.

And then someone suggested that everyone get a chance to say something, so they passed around the microphone. So the first person, this tattooed biker chick, talked about how brave Roxanne was, and that suicide was the ultimate sacrifice. Then a super goth chick called the act a "simple refusal to accept the world as it was handed down to her."

And one of the redheaded girls sat beside me, asked me my name, and when I told her, she laughed and yelled out, "Crash is here," and a few people applauded. So I asked her how she knew me, and she said that Roxanne used to talk about me. And then she got up and sang again, another song with her sister, which was the same song that was playing on the Roxanne Memorial MySpace page.

And then the microphone made its way to me, and at first, I pushed it away, but a few of the people began chanting, "Crash, Crash, Crash, Crash," so I felt compelled to say something, only I had nothing to say so instead, I simply went:

"Bzzzzzzzzzzzzzzzzzzzzzzzzzzzzzzzzzz."

OK, making a bee sound may not seem like the most brilliant idea. After all, it was personal, and mostly I didn't think anyone else would get the joke. But a bunch of people laughed and buzzed back, and then there was whispering as some people questioned the buzz, and there was more laughter and then almost everyone was buzzing.

People took turns buzzing into the microphone, changing the tone, the pitch, and the sound. And people were laughing, and then the redheaded twins sang again, and this time, people were singing along and clapping and shouting as if it was gospel music or something.

And the redheaded girl was back. She told me her name was Sonya, and told me that the song she did was from the movie *The Virgin Suicides*, did I ever see it, and did I know that people were quoting from it in their speeches, and I told her that I wasn't much into suicide or movies about it, did she see *Superbad*, which was more my type of movie, and she started asking me if I'd seen the video, so I asked what video, and she said how did I know about the bee if I didn't see the video, and I asked what video again, and she thought that I was kidding, because every one of her friends knew about the video. At first Roxanne had been ashamed of it, but then when all of her friends told her it was like performance art, Roxanne owned up to it and saw the art in it, even though it wasn't art, well, it shouldn't have been, but Roxanne made it art because she was so good and so deep and so authentic. So if I didn't see the video, how did I know about the bee? And I told her that Roxanne tutored me once, and I told her about the bee tattoo, and how seeing it was my reward for learning, which made her laugh hysterically and then call her sister over.

"You're not going to believe this," she told her sister, who she introduced to me as Mia, just Mia. With me still mystified.

And then Sonya explained. "Roxanne made a movie," she said, "an adult video. She had this scene where she took on these five guys. She was amazing."

OK, I know you know I'm no prude, far from it, but the concept that Roxanne taking on five guys on camera, I have to admit, turned my stomach. This was not what I wanted to hear at her memorial service.

Then Mia added, "Roxanne came up with the story line for the video, and in it, she's teaching these five guys French, and she tells them if they get all the vocab questions correct on the test, then, well, you know, she'll show them the bee."

"And so they do," adds Sonya, "and she goes around the room and shows each of them her bee."

"And things get out of control from there," adds Mia. "And of course, everyone in the video who sees the bee starts buzzing as she takes them on. We thought you knew."

"So after that video, she was becoming known as the Bee Girl. And was even working on a website, something with bees. She was disappointed that beegirl.com was already registered."

"See that guy over there?" Sonya pointed to the middle-aged guy in the distance who I noticed earlier and considered to be out of place there.

"He was investing in her, going to make her an internet star. Like the Suicide Girls. Roxanne was actually going to be like a celebrity. I thought you knew."

That was when I spotted Burn coming at the crowd.

He had emerged from a limo, and apparently he could not resist getting involved. I pointed him out to Sonya, and she said she knew, that Roxanne was protective of him, because he was so fragile that Roxanne was concerned that one day, her brother would find out what she did, because when he found out, he was going to hurt someone.

Except probably no one there knew as clearly as I did that Burn was fully capable of hurting someone. But I didn't have a chance to explain this to her, because Burn was suddenly there and grabbing the microphone and screaming, "You're all murderers. You're all responsible for her death. . . ."

And he was booed, but no one had the courage to take the mic from him.

"You should all be ashamed of yourselves, with your childish notions of life and death, glorifying suicide. You're no better than the fucking Islamist morons who destroyed the World Trade

Center. Well, now my sister is in paradise. Are you fucking happy?"

Burn, it seemed, was not giving up the microphone. The crowd was actually listening to him.

That is, until the police showed up, asking if the group had a permit to assemble or something. Abe Lincoln turned out to the spokesperson for the group, argued politely with the cops, telling them that they were not assembling, just enjoying nature and mourning a friend.

And there was no point in me staying, not with my own personal images of Roxanne shattered and replaced by a more repulsive image (an image, it should be said, that would have excited me no end if it had been anyone else).

Plus, I understood why Burn was so pissed off. He was right. These people were fucking nuts. And I couldn't believe that Roxanne was so into them. In my mind, at least, she was better than that. And she deserved better than to be the random hole for five goth morons.

The Roxanne I knew wouldn't have allowed herself to have been used in that way. I started to actively dislike the people around me, and maybe even, just a little, the version of Roxanne that they claimed to know, the version that brought them together. I got up to leave, wondering whether any of the guys in the crowd were a part of the video.

"Look me up on Facebook," Sonya told me. "Sonya Whiticker." She handed me a crumpled piece of paper. "Me and my sister. The suicide twins."

That word again. Like suicide was an art form or something.

Burn was right.

Still, I stuck her note in my pocket, next to the crumpled envelope that was there.

I didn't go home. I still had unfinished business.

I went back to my car and waited. The crypt keeper guy was

still standing by the gates of the cemetery. I flipped through my discs, music that Roxanne ripped onto CDs for me during our sessions together, popped a fresh one into the changer. I just waited and listened and pretended as hard as I could that I was back there, in her room in Aunt Peesmell's Victorian home, with her sitting on her bed, flipping through a *Vogue* while I struggled to write an essay on a random topic that she picked.

And for some reason, I kept going back to the day at the hospital when she held my face in her hands and, on tiptoes, kissed me so perfectly and gently that I thought I had saved her forever.

It was a while before the others returned to their cars, in groups, in pairs. Talking, laughing together, piling into their vehicles and driving off, leaving a cloud of burning oil and dust behind. And me.

I watched and waited some more. I was in no hurry. I could wait for as long as it took.

It was well after noon when they were all gone and the guard finally abandoned his position. I got out of my car, slipped past the gates, and was in.

Except that now I was facing what seemed like miles of granite tombstones, all lined up in orderly rows, one after another, after another, after another, after another, after another.

So many, many dead people.

And now Roxanne's new home. Forever.

Which brought me to my next problem. As in, there was not going to be any way for me to figure out where her grave was, not standing there totally and completely directionless in front of a sea of stone pillars.

And to make matters worse, as soon as I entered the cemetery, I noticed that the crypt keeper was like twenty feet away, and he was looking up at me from this granite bench, where he was sitting, eating a Wendy's burger, no shit, in the middle of a graveyard, enjoying lunch, like he was at a picnic, ketchup dripping between his legs.

"Hey, you." He beckoned for me to approach him. Single finger, pointing at me, then folding his finger into his fist.

In my Crash Bandicoot mind, I thought for a second that I could outrun him, and I envisioned myself hopping over gravestones, weaving through the rows, over bushes, around those big tall stone buildings. I could definitely get away.

But what was the point if I couldn't figure out where to go? Plus, if this guy caught me, it was only going to piss him off, and even sitting, he was still about my height. So I followed his instructions, and as I got closer, I noticed that his massive linebacker neck was heavily tattooed and apparently his shirt must have covered over some massive tat design.

He took another huge bite of his lunch. He was clearly the kind of guy who could do a burger in two bites, max.

And I had this other thought: Me with the magic beans in my back pocket and this monster getting up, hovering over me, that somehow I was still on my early-summer acid trip, and nothing since then actually happened, except now I had somehow made it to the top of the beanstalk and was facing the for-real giant from the story.

"Go straight down, till the end of that row there." His index finger, released from his fist, was pointing in a particular direction. "Turn right, look for M section. You'll see some guys working. If they bother you, tell them that Zach says it's OK."

"So I can go then?" Me, totally bewildered.

"Yeah, knock yourself out." He laughed. "You waited long enough." He said, "I saw you in the car, sitting there for hours." He reached down, behind the granite bench and scooped up another burger from the bag that was hidden there, popping the entire thing into his mouth. "I figured you weren't about to give up."

I nodded.

"She must have been important to you."

I nodded again.

His directions were precise enough, and there was only one fresh mound of dirt in an otherwise endless sea of grass and shrubs, so it wasn't all that hard to find. The diggers were already on their way to the next job and didn't pay much attention to me, even though I gave them a nod of authority, like, I know Zach, no problem. They didn't care one bit. My guess is, they didn't even understand English.

When I was alone, I took out a piece of paper, something I had written for myself in the days between the news of her death and the funeral. And I started reading out loud:

On Wednesday, August 29, 2007, my friend Roxanne Burnett took her own life. She was not yet twenty-one years old. It was reported in a local newspaper that the "Westchester coed overdosed on prescription medications and could not be revived, and she was pronounced dead on arrival at the hospital." The paper said that she was "despondent over the loss of her mother a year before" and that "she never got over her father's death years earlier in the World Trade Center collapse."

Roxanne Burnett never made it to legal drinking age, or graduated from college, or fell in love with the man she was going to marry, or had twins, or breastfed in the park, or took them to Disney World in their strollers. She never got to stand at the bus stop the first day of kindergarten with her camera in her hand, smiling and waving good

luck, never got to watch them throw out the first pitch of
summer ball or hit a grand slam in a Little League World
Series, or see her little girl get an A for a science fair proj-
ect, or go to Europe, or tour Italy on vacation with her
family. So now I know that there is no invisible god to
change that. I know this, because I prayed long and hard
for it not to be true and it doesn't matter.

I crumpled the piece of paper and put it into my pocket.

"I couldn't have written that without you teaching me. I couldn't have done any of the things that I'm capable of doing now because of the time that we spent together. I could have been there for you."

OK, I was pretty much gone by this point, weeping like her brother did during *West Side Story.*

"Why didn't you call me?" I blurted out, feeling lost and angry at the same time, feeling oddly like I needed to argue with her, to knock some sense into her, even now, like it still wasn't too late, like her being dead didn't matter at all. She owed me some kind of explanation, at the very least.

I probably had more to say, but suddenly I realized that I wasn't alone.

The woman in the black dress from the memorial service was suddenly there, standing beside me.

I quietly stepped back, my head down, paying my respects, careful not to look at her, trying to give her the privacy that she seemed to want.

"I didn't mean for you to stop," she said.

I wiped my eyes and tried to hide my face from her, feeling, OK, embarrassed by the crying thing if you want to know.

"She told me about you," said the woman. "She told me that if anything ever happened to her, and this kid shows up, kind of matching your description, to let him know that she was sorry, but it was for your own good. She said that you'd understand that."

I looked at her face for the first time. Lots of brightly colored makeup, pink patch in the middle of her otherwise golden hair. Very heavy, very dark makeup around her eyes, or maybe it just seemed that way from all the crying she was apparently doing. But the real thing was, she had maybe a dozen facial piercings. Under her lip, two in her nose, a bunch above her eyebrow, then all these metal spikes covering one ear, but just one ear.

"She mentioned me?"

"You're the Crashinsky kid, are you not?"

I acknowledged that I was.

"Why did she think something was going to happen to her?" I asked.

"Because when she was happy, she was very, very happy. But when she was sad, she was . . ." The woman paused, to stop herself from crying. "Very, very sad," she finally said, in an almost whisper. "And when she was sad, she sometimes talked about not being around forever. Mostly when she was drunk, she would get that way," she said, "which is why I hated when she drank." She stopped herself again. "But, of course, you couldn't tell Rox what to do. No one could tell Rox what to do."

This I knew to be accurate.

"I haven't seen her in months," I said.

"She once told me, 'Cassandra, there's this kid Crashinsky, who lives in my town. He's my frickin' brother's age, and it's strange, but this kid always makes me laugh.'"

And I had to smile, not only because this woman did a dead-on perfect impression of Roxanne, but also because it felt good to hear that she had talked about me and sometimes thought about me.

"She was right. You are frickin' cute," said the woman,

Cassandra, "but so young. Younger looking than I would have guessed."

"Yeah, whatever," I said, looking back at the grave. And staring down at what was left of Roxanne . . . this is really fucked up, but it actually occurred to me, for a fleeting moment, that maybe I should try to get with this woman, right there in the graveyard. I know it's fucked up, and I'm going straight to hell, but I was actually thinking, how cool would that be, her bent over a tombstone and me banging her in Roxanne's memory, except it was a thought that was somehow more out of anger than sexual, which probably made it even more wrong.

Also, I wondered what kinds of tattoos she had. They all seemed to be covered in tats. Which made me wonder what Roxanne ultimately did to her own body before she chose to leave it behind. How many tats did she go out with? How many piercings?

But instead, I returned to reality, a little ashamed of myself for being so preoccupied with bad feelings for the girl I came to mourn.

I reached into my pocket and pulled out the envelope.

"What's that?"

"It's complicated," I said, unfolding the envelope and dropping the magic beans into my hand.

"Lemme see," Cassandra insisted, practically grabbing the note, even as I handed it to her.

Then she read it, I watched her lip-sync the words, and I read along with her in my mind, having already committed each of the sixteen words to memory.

> *Dear Crash,*
> *Here are your beans back.*
> *They didn't work.*
> *Please remember me.*
> *Love always.*

"Roxanne," she said out loud, as if calling to her friend.

And then she wept. Loudly.

And she leaned against me, completely giving in to the grief so that her body felt limp against mine.

OK, again, I know it's even more fucked up, and now you're really really going to hate me, but there standing over the girl who devirginized me, with her friend so dependent on me for support, I had what can only be classified as the most ragingest hard-on of my life. In fairness to me, I have absolutely no control whatsoever over these kinds of things, so you can't actually blame me.

And then this woman was hugging me tighter and getting closer and closer. And all I could think about was, if she came into contact with my petrified wood, she was going to get major-league bent out of shape, because no way would she understand that it wasn't my fault.

And I could feel her hot breath on my neck and her tears on my shoulder, which made things even . . . harder. And I suspect any normal guy would have known how to console her, but I was way too busy thinking about ways to avoid having her notice my extreme arousal to be able to do the right thing. So I twisted away.

Then she was whispering something to me, but I couldn't understand it as my mind was so cluttered, but I moved away from her just enough to have her tell me again, that she knew all about the beans, that Roxanne kept them in a baby food jar on the windowsill in their apartment and sometimes she referred to them as the beans that saved her life.

"What do you mean 'your' apartment?" I asked. And she told me that she shared an apartment down in the East Village with Rox.

"Didn't you know? I guess you couldn't, since she stopped talking to you," Cassandra said. "We were together. Kind of exclusively. We were working on this website together."

This was all too confusing to me. It got me to thinking that maybe Roxanne was in over her head somehow, maybe that's what made her decide to end her life. Actually, I couldn't stop thinking about what it was that brought her over the edge and left her with the idea that suicide was the only thing left.

"I'm going to plant them," I told her, displaying the beans in my hand.

"Can I help?" she asked.

And so the two of us got down on our hands and knees, her in her tattered tights and me in my summer-job-interview khakis, and one by one, we placed the beans, in a row from where we imagined Roxanne's head was, down to her feet. I dropped them onto the dirt, and Cassandra pushed them down, one by one, with her thumb, pressing them into the dirt, and then I covered them. We worked well together. We were still on our knees when she told me something else.

"You should know," she started, and it made me smile, because Roxanne started so many thoughts that way. "You should know, she understood how much you loved her, and she couldn't handle it. She said it was too pure for her and she felt like she didn't deserve it."

I didn't exactly know what that meant.

"One other thing: Rox said that if I ever met you, I should tell you to stay away from her brother. Stay as far as possible."

OK, while it did occur to me to try and talk with Burn in the past few days, being as his sister had just died and all, I didn't think I was capable of doing so in the first place.

So it wasn't going to be a major problem for me to take this advice.

I got up, helped Cassandra up, offering my hand to hers. And then she went on:

"And she said if you have any trouble with him, any real trouble, tell him this. Tell him 'Roxanne said that you can't make a fox into a dog no matter how hard you try. A fox is always a fox. And in the end, you have to let them go.'"

I looked at this woman like, how could she be serious? Except she apparently knew about the fox and all.

"Rox seemed to think that we both had to know this," she said.

I could not, at that time, imagine any circumstance under which I would be in a position to actually tell Burn those words.

CHAPTER TWENTY-THREE

DID SHE MENTION MY NAME?

Before getting to the main event, I should probably get a few things out of the way.

First off, Jamie was fine, in case you were worrying.

If you didn't know about Roxanne before now, well, after reading the last chapter, you should totally understand why I was so out of my mind about getting to the hospital for Jamie. Because the second I heard that Jamie had been brought there, every single memory about Roxanne's suicide came flooding into my mind. Especially given that in the moments before my mom told me that Jamie wasn't home, I was busy concentrating on how to write the chapter that covered Roxanne's funeral.

And so when the cop pulled me over, it took absolutely everything I had to keep from gunning the accelerator and taking my chances that I would get away from him.

And then, it took everything I had not to snap at the officer who pointed the flashlight directly into my eyes and commanded:

"License and registration."

And, as I slowly reached into the glove compartment . . .

. . . as soon as I started, not so calmly, trying to find the stuff, got the registration, where the fuck was my license . . .

. . . Caroline Prescott pulled alongside us.

As I said earlier, if you ever need someone to come to your defense, don't bother to call a lawyer, because my mom can get you off (ewwww, that didn't sound right). Anyways, if she loves you, she will come to your rescue, no matter what you did.

And there she was, methodically explaining to the cop that we were all on our way to the hospital, and she was telling him that while there was no excuse for speeding, could he kindly hold off until after we got there.

And the cop must've been a father or something, because whatever my mom was saying totally touched a nerve, and next thing I know, we are on our way again, this time with a police escort. And you think this shit only happens in the movies.

So we get there, and Jackie's parents are already waiting for us, telling my mom, with me and Lindsey overhearing, that there was a group of kids in their basement, they didn't know how many kids, and apparently the kids were playing some kind of drinking game. And then Jamie apparently passed out and was lying in her own vomit and started shaking. So thankfully, their daughter knew enough to get them immediately, and Jamie was still passed out when they got to the basement, so an ambulance was called immediately. And please forgive them, they never allow drinking at their house and they didn't know and Jackie was sooo grounded. . . .

And then some doctors showed up. They needed my mother to sign something, one doctor with a pen, the other with a clipboard, both with their hair in surgical caps, their feet in surgical booties.

So at least in my mind, things got scarier.

And then they took my mom to another part of the hospital, with her telling us to just stay put, "I will let you know . . ." as she flew down the hall after them.

Scarier still. I could even hear Lindsey saying, under her breath, "Hope my sister's OK, hope my sister's OK."

And by the time I got to see my little sister, she was conscious, but groggy. Way too groggy to even know where she was or what had happened. Apparently, her blood alcohol content was like five times the legal limit, and given that she was so skinny, they were concerned that her effective levels were even higher.

I slept in the room on a chair next to her. I wasn't about to leave her side until we were able to take her home. There are guys, like Evan, who will not leave the TV when the Yankees are playing for fear that if they don't see every play, something bad will happen and the Yanks will lose. I'm not superstitious in that way, but when it comes to Jamie, I kind of had that same feeling.

It wasn't until the next day that she was completely back to being Jamie.

I was sleeping on the recliner beside her bed when I overheard an announcer and the first thing I saw was some infomercial about toning your abs on the hospital TV across from Jamie's bed.

She was up. I breathed a sigh of relief.

She was still groggy, but good enough to be channel surfing. Thank god that things were back to normal.

"Get me water, Steven. My throat is killing me."

So good to hear her voice. I rushed into the hall, looking for a nurse. I found my mom and Lindsey asleep in the waiting room across the hall.

"She's up," I told them, then found a nurse and followed her back into the room.

Then we were all on top of Jamie, and for her it must have been like the ending of *The Wizard of Oz*, all these eyes peering down at you in a haze, looking overly concerned.

"Where's Dad?" she asked.

"Your father's in California," my mom answered, and you could tell she was pissed.

"What about Felicia?"

OK, I'll chalk that up to Jamie being out of it, but still she should've known better than to ask Caroline Prescott about our stepmom under any circumstances, especially if she was looking not to get our mom any angrier than she already was. I gave Jamie the wide-eye signal from behind Caroline, as in "shut the fuck up." I couldn't possibly open my eyes any wider, so I hoped she understood.

"With your father" was all Caroline Prescott would say before she got into all of her mom-questions that Jamie was required to answer, and there was no doubt that Jamie was going to be held fully accountable for her actions.

The whole truth and nothing but the truth . . .

And what we learned is that Jamie apparently has the same party gene that I have, which I kind of suspected.

According to Jamie, the party got boring, so she went shot for shot for shot with anyone willing to play, thinking how bad could it be? She had tried vodka more than a few times before and it just made her relaxed, nothing more, and everybody seemed like such babies with their one redcup each, and then they were all getting giggly. She hated giggly, it was, ugh, so fake. Then someone passed around a blunt, so she took a hit, and then she went back to drinking, going shot for shot with Scott Boscovich, the only person willing to keep up the challenge with her—not a fair contest at all, given that he was over six feet tall, already a starter on the varsity basketball team and also given that Bosco's brother had previous experience drinking and smoking, as we sometimes treated him as our mascot and got him superhigh and superdrunk whenever we were at Bosco's raiding his refrigerator or hanging by his pool whenever there was nothing else going on.

I made a mental note to kick Bosco's ass for letting his brother fuck with my sister like that. (As a member of the Club Crew, he had an obligation to keep his siblings the fuck off mine. Yep, I was going to kick his ass big-time.)

Back to Jamie: She did like six shots in a row and took

another hit from the blunt because she had something to prove, given that all these people at the party were good friends with each other and she felt like an outsider, and she was tired of feeling like an outsider, and suddenly, she was feeling like the homecoming queen because everyone was rooting for her.

Until she went down.

She remembered not feeling so good. It came on in a split second and that was all she remembered. Although she kind of remembered hearing voices and seeing faces in the distance. Jackie's, Scott's, and strangely, Angelica's, as in Angelica from *Rugrats*, who, she almost seemed to remember, was at the party also, but then again, how could that be?

She stayed in the hospital for a few days while they hydrated her and pumped good chemicals back into her system.

I went home and came back, bringing my laptop with me. So as it turns out, the entire Roxanne chapter was written in the waiting room of a hospital, watching over my sister while she slept peacefully in the room across the hall.

And when she wasn't sleeping, we sat in bed together, channel surfing and playing board games, or talking, with me trying to teach her that she had to know her limits, because as long as you know your limits, no one can take advantage of you, and no one knew like me, as I was an expert on getting people to go beyond their limits.

And on the second day, I had to ask Jamie the burning question, and it took me a while to bring it up, because I didn't want to freak her out, but I had to know. And so, while we were in bed and SpongeBob and Squidward were making their plans for the day in the Krusty Krab, I casually asked:

"You weren't trying to kill yourself or anything. Were you?"

And she said, in her Jamie voice, which was so perfect, you had to relax about it, because you had to believe her. What she said was:

"What are you, fucking nuts, Steven? I was drinking is all."

"Ever?" I explored, looking at her, studying her. "Have you ever thought about it? What about the time when Burn stayed over and you talked about it?"

And she gave me this scornful look. "Don't you even know me at all? I was just trying to make him feel better. After all, he was all by himself with nobody to talk to, and his sister was in the hospital after trying to kill herself. Didn't you see how absolutely lonely he was?"

OK, this blew me away. Because I realized that I *didn't* know her at all.

"What he needed was a hug and I wasn't going to do it, but I'm glad you finally did." She smiled, giving me back what I was giving her, always shocking the hell out of me.

And so we were back watching *SpongeBob* again, no problem, man.

The next morning, Jamie was scheduled to leave. She was napping, I was working on my laptop, when Jacob walked in, looking like he had aged several years since I had last seen him. Maybe it was a new haircut, or new glasses or something, but this was summer, he was usually sporting a superdark tan, always overly fit for his age in his tight polo shirts. Now, instead, he looked pale, almost green, and a little heavy.

All in a few weeks.

I wondered if his rapid aging was a result of my television appearance outing him as a weed smoker.

He leaned over and kissed Jamie on the forehead, "How's my little girl?"

Jamie was looking past him; I could tell that she was searching for Felicia.

So was I.

We were not disappointed, because seconds later, clicking in on the highest heels that I have seen on her, was my stepmom in all her poised glory. All Dolce & Gabbana, Hermès bag, who knows what the shoes were. Beyond her, on the other side of the door, several male patients walked by, then crossed back and walked by again, checking out the hot chick. Blood pressures were, no doubt, going up. Even an intern stepped in to see what was going on. This was the same intern who Lindsey thought was mad cute, but she couldn't get his attention for anything.

Felicia, however, had no problems in that department.

I sat up, not exactly sure what to do, given that the last time we talked, it didn't go well at all. The sight of her now made me immediately nervous, and I could feel a rush of anxiety bubbles in my chest.

"Allo, baby" is what she said to Jamie, all hugs and kisses. "I broot you a present." She reached into her bag and extracted a very well wrapped gift, which Jamie instantly tore open. A pair of Prada sunglasses, which Jamie modeled for everyone, checking herself out in the hospital room mirror.

"Leesin to me, you naughty girl. We cannot stop you from drinkink, but ve can only hope that you haf learnt vot moterashin is."

Of course, I had no idea what moterashin was. But Jamie seemed happy enough in her new glasses.

"What do you think, Steven," Jamie asked.

"Those," I answered, "will be perfect for your next hangover. No one will be able to see your eyes."

OK, maybe I was crossing the line with a line like that, and clearly no one seemed to appreciate it because no one was laughing. Well, no one except Jamie, because, it was a dead-on perfect Jamie line and she knew it. I probably wouldn't have said it if I didn't absolutely need to say *something*, which probably should have been "I'm sorry," especially since I recently learned how to say it.

"I haf a present for you too, Cresh," she told me. "But you will haf to give me a hug first if you vont it." She gestured toward me with open arms. "Unless you don't luv me anymore." She said this with a smile, and of course, I was going to have to hug her, because of course, I still loved her.

OK, so I hugged her, and as I did, it made me think about the way I had hugged Cassandra at Roxanne's gravesite (after all, I had just finished writing that scene), so I was careful to keep my formal distance from Felicia as we embraced. I wouldn't want to be sent to hell twice.

"I'm sorry," I said. "I *am* better than that." Thinking that she wouldn't even understand the reference after all these weeks.

She pulled back and looked at me the way she does. "I know you are," she said. "Ant here is your rewart," handing me an equally perfect wrapped box, which contained a perfect pair of Prada sunglasses for men.

"So you look sharp for all of de collidge girls," she said, as she adjusted the glasses on my face. "Or, as you sed, perfikt for those hankover morninks." She laughed. "I guess it's already too late to teach you moterashin."

I looked into the mirror. The guy staring back at me was beyond cool. He was a total motherfucking chick magnet.

I couldn't wait to see how cool they looked in the rearview mirror of my BMW.

So that's how we got to be friends again, at least me and Felicia, because nothing else was said about the interview, and Jacob being Jacob went on about his business, admonishing Jamie for being reckless and irresponsible and making her promise not to drink ever again, which even his own wife knew was pointless.

Still, my guess was it would be a while before she downed another shot of vodka. Plus it was pretty much a guarantee that Caroline Prescott would be all over her, given that in a few weeks she was going to be the only one home. Yep, Jamie was pretty much screwed.

And then Jacob pulled me aside and told me that he appreciated how responsible I was in taking care of my sister, and that he wanted us to move forward, not backward; we all make mistakes, and god knows, he's even made a few.

Then he extended his hand to me, and I shook it with equal (and totally artificial) affection.

So with less than two weeks to go before college started, I had apparently, at least for the moment, ironed out my relationship with my father and his wife. He was giving me a second chance, and I was going to try not to hate him so constantly. Let's face it, we both knew it wasn't going to last, but for the moment, standing next to the hospital bed, him staring down at his daughter, me staring at his wife and across to my sister, we made peace, at least temporarily, which had me wondering whether there was even a remote shot at ever getting another nugg of his perfect weed again.

We took Jamie home, and Jamie went on being the Jamie I know, no worse for the experience. I was still calling Christina, not getting anywhere with her. And yes, I was still calling Claudia, and yes, I did finally convince her to answer the phone. She was cold and distant, but she was willing to listen without hanging up. So we started talking, but she was not willing to see me, not just yet. Even after I gave her my going-away-to-college line and "summer is running out" line, she still said no, not for now. And I asked when, and she said that she would know when, and when she did, she would call me. Before she hung up, she added that it would be OK if I called her whenever I wanted.

My opinion: just a matter of time before she comes around.

And I talked to Sally, because before getting to the main event, there were some things about senior year that I thought that I should be writing about.

For example, there was the time when the Club Crew got lost in the woods playing paintball and the time that Kenny's mom got arrested for DWI and the cops found cartons of open liquor bottles in her trunk (which was totally our fault, because we used her car for pregaming the night before and forgot to take the bottles out).

Also, the time that we ended up driving to West Point to catch an Army game and got too drunk as a group to drive home, no way were any of us getting into a car shitfaced with all of those soldiers staring at us.

And the time we ruined Evan's little sister's birthday by trashing the party room that his parents rented for the occasion at one of the hotels in White Plains, all because we got there early and didn't have anything to do, so we started smoking and drinking and, next thing I know, we started inviting some other kids over to join us. Well, by the time Evan's sister's friends showed up, the party was in full gear, only it wasn't a kids' party anymore.

And then Halloween. I could get into it some more, except according to Sally, it was time to get to the main event.

Except she did have two questions that she wanted me to address.

One: What did I do after Roxanne's funeral?

Two: What happened to Burn after his sister died? In the fall of senior year, what was he like, where was he, was he coming to school often, what was he doing?

As you probably know by now, I didn't take Roxanne's suicide well. For weeks after, I drove a lot, leaving school and drifting, just like Burn did. Mostly because I didn't want to go home, didn't want to see my friends, didn't want to hear anyone joking about Roxanne.

And also, I wasn't ready to deal with another round of classes where I would have to pretend to listen, only to fall behind when everyone else who was actually listening did way better than me on the tests. The stress was incredible, because I had to do better than I did junior year in order to bring my GPA to more acceptable levels, and so I decided to dedicate myself to schoolwork in her honor, because she tried so hard to make me the student that we both knew I could not be.

Then there were applications to colleges that didn't want any part of me and Caroline constantly yelling at me to write my college essay, with me trying over and over again but never getting beyond the opening paragraph (OK, here's another secret—Newman actually wrote my college essay. BFD. I think I may have already mentioned this anyways).

Then there were the college tour trips, up to Boston and Connecticut and Vermont, down to Delaware, Virginia, over to Ohio. None of the schools I visited seemed right for me at all. And with every school visit, I had to sit there in a huge auditorium listening to some boring lecture, ending with my mom raising her hand to ask the administrator, in front of a room full of genius kids:

"What services do you supply to special kids, you know, the ones with learning disabilities?"

That always seemed to get a response from the crowd, as kids turned to check out the retarded boy next to the woman who inquired about special ed in college. By the third college, I actually considered purposely drooling to better look the part.

I could've used my Prada glasses then.

And, of course, the inevitable threat whenever I didn't co-operate with her during a tour: "Maybe next time, you'll go with your father."

Like that was even a remote possibility. No way either of us would survive the first tour.

And with every college visit, I had to take off from school for a few days to travel to other cities. You would think this wouldn't be a problem, except I kept missing classes, between the trips and the impromptu parties in Pinky's parking lot where we'd sometimes go for lunch and end up having to stay, after passing around a pipe and bottle of Switched-On Pinky's Shakes (add a little vodka, you get the point).

Then there was the video.

After Roxanne's funeral, when I wasn't driving by myself, I was online, searching for it, without success. I started with the suicide twins, the two redheaded sisters, found them on Facebook, friended them, searched through their friend lists, found Cassandra and friended her, but didn't exactly know how to ask how to get to the Roxanne video.

So instead, I searched.

I went through all the possibilities for the bee girl thing, but none of my searches got me to it. Went through Cassandra's MySpace and found links to a whole underground world of goth/emo sites, but there was nothing in any of the sites there that would gave me a clue. So when I stumbled on a site that promised bee girls and the best in goth porn, I couldn't believe my luck. Because, there, on the first web page, was a picture of Roxanne smiling and seemingly inviting me to join her—if I was over eighteen.

To enter, click on the right. To exit, click on the left.

I clicked on the right.

And took a tour. The first page had images of goth girls, all looking a little like Roxanne, all with heavy-duty tattoos and multiple piercings. Then, next page of the tour, the sample video, which wasn't Roxanne. Then the offer to join for twenty-nine bucks a month and you get all of these blocks of photos of other girls and then, there was an image of Roxanne, in the center square, highlighted with a bright red border and the words "In Memoriam" underneath her image. And the promise that if you joined, you would learn all about the girl in the center square, to whom the site was dedicated.

I snuck my mom's credit card out of her wallet that night and joined (sorry, Mom, you probably wondered what the charge was). And what I saw there will stay with me for life.

Because it made absolutely no sense at all.

It started as a typical internet video, the kind you can see all over the usual free porn sites.

Just as the redheaded twins promised, Roxanne was telling these superpale white guys that she was their instructor, putting on this bogus French accent, and promising to show the guys her bee.

OK, she wasn't much of an actress.

And then, after like thirty seconds, there it was, all sex, just like any other porn site. Except, after several positions, there's Roxanne, her face thrust into the camera, practically hitting it, and while the guys behind her are going about their business, she starts to sing, losing her French accent, looking *extremely* fucked-up high, and she seems far away, cut off from the things going on behind her.

And as she leans forward, she starts singing the Dave Matthews song, only to me, it's not Dave Matthews, because what she is singing is:

"Crash into me."

Over and over again, faster and faster. "Crash into me, crash into me, crashintome. Crashintomecrashintome." And since the first word was so much louder than the others, what she was really doing is calling my name out. Over and over again.

"Crashcrashcrashcrashcrashcrash."

Well, this freaked me out. Beyond measure.

So much so that I played it over and over again, watching her facial expressions. Was she just into the song, or was she somehow trying to give me a message, because that was exactly what it felt like, a message from beyond the grave.

I'm definitely not a good enough writer to even attempt to tell you what it felt like to watch this video of a girl you were with, one who was your first and only real love, your soul mate, singing to you from another dimension. OK, I'll admit that I watched it high on herb, but stoned or sober, she was still calling out to me, and I'll admit that when I was high, I started to believe that I was chosen by some special power to receive a message from another plane of existence.

The only thing was, I wasn't smart enough to figure out what she was trying to communicate. Was she still trying to teach me something? I tried, in my mind, to connect, like she taught me and like I sometimes did with her brother, but I couldn't sort it out because my mind was twisting with revulsion at what I was watching and anger at what she was doing to herself. And frustration at not being able to tell her to stop, just STOP and come home, just COME HOME, which was, I realized, what I would have told her to do if she was still alive, and it seemed to me that that was what she wanted. More than anything, maybe that's what she was telling me.

Which only had me obsessed with understanding her message.

So I went to the oracle, the only person I knew who could absolutely predict the future and answer questions from the beyond:

Caitlin Lewis, the girl who turned her father's now-ancient iPod into a Magic Eight Ball. The way it worked was you had to press shuffle and then listen to the first song that came up, and whatever came up had some special meaning, and all you had to do was figure it out.

And so the day after I saw the video, I cornered Caitlin and asked if I could try her iPod. She said of course I could, so I put on her headphones and turned the device on and hit shuffle music and got a song.

Get this, I know you're not going to believe it, but the song was called "Did She Mention My Name?" by a guy named Gordon Lightfoot. Who ever even heard of that guy, much less the song? Seriously, check it out on the internet; it's there, on Wikipedia, it's also the name of an entire album by this guy.

Freaky shit, right? Twelve thousand songs. What are the chances?

It had to mean something, but I had no clue what. I asked Caitlin but she said that she wasn't responsible for the content, that it was up to whoever used it to figure stuff out on their own.

So I tried again and couldn't find anything else that made any sense at all, which left me with this one song which definitely meant something, but who could say what?

In the end, my mom got her credit card bill and that was the last I saw of Roxanne.

Since then, I have heard this song more than once, so I still want to know. What were the odds?

CHAPTER TWENTY-FOUR

HOW I SAVED MEADOWS HIGH

For starters, we should've seen it coming.

That was the common thread that ran through all of the newspaper articles and television reports in the days follow-ing the siege. A bunch of reporters and commentators made it a big issue about the obvious warning signs and how the staff should have been properly trained to detect behavioral changes in students and take precautionary measures. There was even an article in the *Times* or some other paper headlined "Who Was Watching David Burnett?"

But consider this: Burn was not the only one at Meadows capable of going Columbine. The truth is, there were probably at least a dozen kids at Meadows who were potentially dangerous. If you asked any of us in the senior class, we could name them all, off the top of our heads, not even straining our minds to come up with the list. Guaranteed. You ask fifty kids, and ten out of the twelve names would be identical. Sure, everyone would have named Burn, that's easy. Plus Franklin, no one ever trusted him. Then the others, I could spit the names out without thinking.

Not only Meadows, but virtually every high school in the country; you go to any school and poll the kids, and they'll come up with a list of kids who are about to boil over.

Point is, even though they blamed the administration at Meadows and even though Principal Singh was basically forced to retire, none of what happened was his fault at all. We all knew that; we all told him so at graduation.

Remember: The first time they thought something was wrong, they pulled Burn out of middle school and sent him somewhere more "appropriate" for him. So they knew about him. But what do you do when a kid loses a dad to terrorism, is forced to live with his aunt in a house that smells like urine, then is forced to go to a school for crazies, then breast cancer takes his mom, and then his sister kills herself in the same house he was living in, in the same house his mother died in?

Shit. If it was me, I would have been out of my frickin' mind (well, not so much Jacob dying, tell you the truth, but that's neither here nor there).

Plus, don't forget, the kid in question was a confirmed genius who, even if he never showed up in classes, completely aced like every single test he took, plus was normal, actually better than normal, most of the time. Well, at least half the time.

So that being the case, what do you look for? Who would even want that job?

Back to Burn. My only contact with him during the first part of senior year was a while after Roxanne died. Apparently he had taken off the first few weeks of school on doctor's orders. So no one knew where he was, or even if he was coming back to Meadows.

In the meantime, a letter was sent home to every kid in every grade (probably including Burn) disclosing the unfortunate event involving one of the graduates of the school. It started with "As you may have heard . . ."

It didn't disclose who the person was, it just mentioned suicide and the suggestion that if any student had feelings of hopelessness or depression, he or she should contact their guidance counselor or the school psychologist. (Really, who was about to do that? Like what are the chances of a kid walking into his guidance counselor and saying, "I'm fucked up, help me." No kid is actually that fucked up.)

It was probably for the best, him not being around during that time, when rumors were rampant about what Roxanne was into. No one had apparently seen the video, but it seemed like everyone knew she had made one, so there was constant talk about it. It was partially because of all the talk that I avoided after-school activities during those weeks and started taking drives. Then, just when the rumors started to circulate that Burn had dropped out or was going to another school, he showed up, looking very, very normal.

I was in the cafeteria with a few of the Club Crew when he walked over.

I immediately got to my feet and assumed a defensive position, prepared for an altercation. After all, this was the first time I saw him since his sister died, and we hadn't talked in almost a year. Plus I hated him for what he did to me and still hadn't made peace with it on any level.

So imagine my surprise when he hugged me like a brother and told me:

"Thanks for being such a good friend to my sister."

What do you say to that? Even to a guy who once pointed a gun at your head?

OK, I previously made no secret of the fact that I would have nothing to do with him and avoided him like the plague ever since that night in Massachusetts. But, at that moment at least, all I could do was hug him back, not because I felt anything for him, but out of respect, and also love for Roxanne. And because I knew that we were probably the only two people in the world who would never forget her.

Leave it to Pete to interrupt, with a typical Pete line, spoken in a mock coughing fit: "Has anyone seen *Brokeback Mountain*?"

Give some credit to Burn. He laughed. And then everyone was saying, "Sorry about your sister, man. Yeah, sorry about your sister."

And that was it. He walked away, and I watched him go, thinking maybe I should have said more to him.

As he disappeared, I realized that I couldn't, not because I didn't want to, but because I couldn't have been sure how he would have reacted.

A few weeks later, just as I predicted, virtually everyone forgot about Roxanne entirely. After all, she didn't even go to Meadows anymore, and truth was, maybe once every other year or so, some student at Meadows decides to end their life. She was not the first, and will not be the last. Sad but true.

I saw Burn in the halls on other occasions, and he seemed regular enough at the time. And of course, I was busy with the Club Crew doing whatever we did so well. He was not invited and never showed at any of our parties. No surprise there.

My mom told me that she invited him for Thanksgiving, and of course I went apeshit, but there was no reason to, because no way was he going to show.

So you could say I pretty much lost track of him before the morning of 4/21. We all pretty much did.

From what I heard, Burn apparently got into music and was all about learning to play the guitar in the winter of 2008. I heard that he got to be pretty good, spent some of his trust money, when he finally got some, on a collection of Les Paul guitars and other collectible instruments, electric and acoustic. Bobby saw his collection and was beyond envious. After all, Bobby played like Hendrix, so he knew a perfect instrument when he saw one, and he claimed that Burn had somehow acquired several perfect guitars. No surprise there, as Burn was not about to buy anything that was less than perfect, no matter how much online research it took and no matter how much of the settlement cash he spent.

Sorry that I can't shed more light on what he was doing in those months, but I just wasn't paying much attention to him, and neither was anyone else (and I talked to more than a few people, like half the senior class, so I know this to be true), because let's face it, none of us had any way of knowing at the time that he was going to totally lose it before senior year was over.

The only thing that I was able to figure out was, no one knew a fucking thing.

No one remembered seeing him in classes or not seeing him in classes, or hearing him make any kind of comment that sounded suspicious, or doing anything that drew attention to himself, or anything else that anyone would think would lead up to him showing up that morning in combat gear.

There was nothing that anyone could have pointed out at the time. So I wasn't thinking at the time, What is Burn up to and how's his state of mind?

Burn was, to all of us, plain and simple, back to being Burn.

I don't want to mislead you when I say that Burn showed up in his combat gear. What he showed up with at school that day was what seemed to me to be two guitar cases, plus his laptop bag strung over his shoulder. Plus he was wearing one of those hunting-fishing jackets, you know, the camouflage kind you get in sporting goods stores.

When I saw him that morning, I was on my way out of school actually.

I wasn't even planning to go to school that day.

My mom woke me from a dead sleep that morning to tell me that I had to drive Jamie in. I couldn't explain to her that it was the unofficial Senior Skip Day. Unofficial because Senior Skip Day, for those who call it that (we don't, we simply call it 420, either you get it or you don't. BTW, if you don't, just Google 420 and you'll understand) only happens on April 20.

But this year April 20 was a Sunday.

So we couldn't exactly leave school and get high all day on Sunday, which left us, the Club Crew, the Prime Timers, and even the drama group and the science nerds and the musicians, all of the separate but equal groups of seniors at Meadows, with a predicament. Either forget about Senior Skip Day entirely and lose out totally on the day we had all waited for for four years . . . Or:

(1) Celebrate 420 on 4/20; or,

(2) celebrate 420 on 4/21; or,

(3) celebrate 420 on 4/20 *and again* on 4/21.

Some of the groups, like drama and music and the science nerds, chose to celebrate on Sunday, then go in on Monday, being as they had some drama thing or music thing or science thing to do.

By now, you probably know enough about the Club Crew to guess exactly which option we chose (option 3, in case you, like me, have a tendency to sometimes miss things).

Which is why I was so wasted the morning of 4/21, and when my mom came in to wake me, she had to practically scream me into consciousness.

"Did you forget, Steven? You're driving Jamie today."

As you may have heard, you don't cross Caroline and expect there not to be a consequence. So that got me up and out quickly in torn basketball shorts and an even more torn heavy metal T-shirt, not bothering to shave, comb my hair, or even brush my teeth or go to the bathroom. After all, school was ten freakin' minutes away and I would be coming back. That gave me twenty, maybe twenty-five minutes before I would be able to go back to sleep and wake up in time to celebrate round two with my boys and the Herd Girls and anyone else who wanted to join us in the nature preserve to lift our redcups and pass around the blunts in honor of Senior Skip Day.

So I pulled up to school, radio blasting. I nodded for Jamie to get out, and Jamie reached into the back of the car to take her backpack.

"Steven, you have to open the trunk. My science project is in there."

Grunting a perfect big-brother grunt, I popped the trunk with the remote on the key.

"Steven, you have to get out to help me."

And grunting another big-brother grunt, I reluctantly got out to help her.

There were rolls of oaktag posters. I handed them to her, and then there was this cardboard box, and she said, "Steven, you have to help me bring my project into class."

I gave her a perfect Lindsey eye roll.

"Jamieeeee," I protested, "I can't go in there. I'm not supposed to be here at all."

"Mom said," she answered, invoking the name of Caroline Prescott to persuade me.

"Fine. I'll go as far as the front doors. Meet me there. I'm not going in."

"Fine. You better be there."

I handed her whatever she could carry and went to park in the student lot. Minutes later, I was carrying the cardboard box filled with who knows what, looking all around to make sure that none of my teachers saw me. I was still high enough, with residual grogginess from the night before, to believe I could operate in stealth mode, like you do in video games.

I made it to the front doors of the school. And waited.

And waited.

No Jamie. Where the fuck was Jamie?

And finally, like ten minutes later, she emerged. There was a boy with her, all pimpled up, one I didn't recognize, she had managed to talk into helping her.

Seemed like she was doing better with her socialization issues, I remember thinking that. I also remember thinking that hopefully she had better taste in boys.

Then I was on my way back to my car, fast as I could, to get off school grounds as quickly as possible, when I ran into Burn, who was, like I said before, carrying his guitar cases and his laptop bag, his hair rock-star long, under a Thin Lizzy cap, whoever they were. My first thought was that it figured he would be showing up to school on a day everyone else was cutting out.

"Hey, Dave." I nodded, always cautious around him.

"Crash." He nodded back.

"Going in today?"

"It's a special day for me," he said.

OK, there was no way at that moment to decipher his hieroglyphics on this. Seeing as he had his instruments, I figured that he was doing some kind of music thing.

"Good luck," I told him, and I remember how he eyed me suspiciously when I said that. I meant with whatever he was planning to perform.

"Thanks," he finally said. "See you later."

"I don't think so," I told him matter-of-factly. It was a national kid holiday, if he didn't already know.

"Well, *I* think so, Steven. I *will* see you later." OK, that was definitely weird, but to me it was just Burn being Burn and no point in arguing with him.

The last thing that I thought of at that moment, in front of the high school, at approximately 7:29 A.M. Eastern Daylight Time, was that he was about to do what he was about to do.

The first thing I thought of was sleep and returning to it.

I got home at 7:40.

By 7:50 I was already under my covers again, and the world was doing just fine, thank you very much.

At 7:53, my cell phone rang. It was Jamie.

"Now what?" Me, yelling into the cell phone.

"Steven," she said, "you need to get back here. Right away."

OK, before I continue, you should probably be prepared to spend time with this book because you're not going to want to put it down until it's finished. Keep in mind that I will be revealing the secret, as in what it was that Burn whispered to me that basically ended the siege. Don't try to skip ahead; it will ruin it for you. And if you're, like, on a train or something, and you think you'll just start it now and finish it later, well, you might want to stop now or make other plans.

If this was a movie, this would be the time to put on your 3-D glasses. Also, if you want to go to the bathroom or if you want a snack, get it now.

I'll wait.

Are you all set?

Here goes. One other thing: If you have any Nine Inch Nails, maybe "You Know What You Are?" from the *With Teeth* disc or mostly anything from *Downward Spiral*, or any Rage Against the Machine, you might want to crank it up. That's how my day got restarted. At full volume.

"Why the hell should I go *back* to school, Jamie?" I asked her.

"David Burnett locked himself in the faculty lounge with a bunch of teachers. He's holding them hostage." Jamie was screaming into the phone.

"So call the police," I told her, "and get out of there. I'll pick you up." I was already up, searching for my jeans. Found them in a pile of clothes.

"I can't," she said. "He won't let anyone leave. He said that if anyone tries to leave the school, he'll kill us all."

"Did you call Mom? Why are you calling me?"

"Because David Burnett told me that I had to," she said. "He called me on my cell and told me that I had to get you to come back to school."

"*Me?* Why?" I had the feeling that there was some kind of disconnect between us.

"Steven," she said, trying to sound calm but not sounding calm at all, "if you don't get here right away, he said he's going to hurt me." Her voice rippled with fear.

"How?" I tried to be calm enough for both of us, keeping her on the phone, as I was stumbling into my jeans, pulling my sneakers on.

"I don't know, Steven!" she shouted into the phone. "All I know is he's watching me now. He's watching all of us."

"Watching you? How? Where are you?"

"In class with Mrs. Peterson. We can't leave. There was some kind of explosion outside. Burn said it was a warning."

I flew down the stairs, grabbed my keys, and was out the door in seconds, holding only my cell phone. One last look around— what should I take with me? I ran into the garage hoping for inspiration. The only thing that caught my eye was an old Little League bat. Better than nothing, I told myself, grabbing it and tossing it into my car. Then, reverse, out of the driveway full speed, pulling into drive and flying off.

School in five minutes flat.

A record.

I zoomed into the parking lot, grabbed the bat, and got out.

I was on my way up the steps to school when I noticed the sounds of sirens for the first time.

My cell phone rang. Jamie again. "He wants you to go to the football field."

"Why?"

"I don't know, Steven," she screamed back. "He said drop the bat. He said you have sixty seconds. He said that you're one dead bandicoot if you don't make it." Another quiver in her voice. *"Why is he doing this, Steven?"*

"I don't know." Me, thinking, how did he know about the bat?

"Hold on," she said. "He's calling again." She switched away, then switched back to me seconds later.

"Forty seconds," she said in a panic. "He wants you to know."

The sirens were getting louder.

I scrambled across the lawn, around to the back of the school, and made it to the football field just as the phone rang again.

"Steven," Jamie whispered to me. "David Burnett wants you to know that there are three people in the field house. He said you have one minute to get them out."

I bolted downfield toward the field house. Coach Meyers was standing by the door. I practically flew into him. "Get everyone out," I said. "Get everyone out."

"Slow down" was all he said as I pushed beyond him.

And then the two of us were in there and there was Brian, Tyler, and some other kid I didn't know.

"EVERYBODY OUT NOW!" I screamed.

"Fuck you, Crash" is what Tyler said. Always Mister Prime Time, never willing to concede a thing to us Club Crew guys.

My phone rang. Jamie. "You have ten seconds."

"Please," I said. "David Burnett's gone crazy. He's got bombs. Trust me."

I repeated her information. "Please, we have ten seconds."

Maybe it was the way I sounded or the way I looked at them, but they moved faster than I have ever seen kids move.

Good thing too, because no more than five seconds after they were out, there was an explosion from somewhere inside the field house that shook the ground under us, knocking us off our feet.

We were on the ground when the police cars pulled up beside us. Two cops got out, guns drawn.

My phone rang.

I was not about to get up with guns pointed at me. I didn't know whether I should answer it, not with the cops approaching. I reached for my cell superslowly, expecting Jamie.

I looked at the display screen.

It was David Burnett.

"I'm going to need to answer this," I told them, sitting up slowly and very gingerly lifting my cell phone to my face.

"He's OK," said Coach Meyers. "Let him get it. He got us out of there."

"We know," said one of the officers, with his gun still drawn. "We know about the kid inside the school. David Burnett."

"This is him, on the phone," I motioned, cautiously flipping the phone open.

"Hello, Crash. Let the police know that you are talking to me."

"David, why are you doing this?"

"Do what I tell you!" he yelled back. "Remind them about our arrangement. Ask them if they need more proof that there are other incendiary devices placed strategically throughout the school, including all entrances and exits. Tell them that any attempt to breach the access points will trigger a chain reaction, and I will have no control over what happens once an access point is compromised."

I told the cops, and had one of them correct me, because I did not know exactly the pronunciation of "incendiary." He could just have said "explosive." Leave it to Burn to complicate things with perfect grammar. Still, we had to believe that if he was able to rig explosives to the field house, he could also do it inside the school.

"What arrangement?" I asked him and the cops at the same time. "Where are you now?"

"No questions. You have sixty seconds to get to the soccer field." He sounded unusually calm, almost quiet.

"Or what?" I yelled back at him.

"Jamie" was all he said.

Followed by: "Fifty-five seconds." Then he hung up.

"Gotta go. Soccer field," I told them, flying back upfield, around the back of the school, and across the street to where the soccer fields were. Police cars were lining up along the front of the school. The groggy, hazy fog that I started the day feeling was wearing off, thanks in large part to the incredible bursts of adrenaline I was experiencing. As my mind began to clear, I tried to put myself into Burn's head, thinking of that poker game when I was stoned enough to look into his mind.

My cell goes off again.

"You have fifteen seconds to get everyone off the field."

So I ran across the soccer field, screaming at the group of soccer players. "David Burnett's gone crazy. Get off the field. David Burnett's gone crazy. Get off the field."

I screamed this loudly enough that no one defied my orders and the group scattered, just as a blue Porta-Potty blew open, Jackass style, sending the roof skyward and liquid goo gushing upward like a geyser in a national park.

I heard a few kids utter, "Cool."

Then a second explosion blew apart the sides.

And the phone again, startling me.

"Now, go to the back door of the cafeteria," he said. "Someone will let you in."

"Are you out of your mind?" I asked him, actually understating the obvious. "No way I'm going into the building if you have bombs planted throughout the school."

"Of course you are," he said. "Even if I told you to stay away, you'd find a way in. You are very protective of your sister. Besides, you're hero material, Crash. Even if your sister wasn't here, you'd still come if I called you. And you know why, Crash? Because you think that you're lucky and nothing will happen to you. It's easy to be a hero if you totally believe that, isn't it?"

"David, what the fuck are you talking about? Why are you doing this?"

He ignored me and instead continued, "You have sixty seconds. Anything beyond that and the police will be there and you won't be able to get in. If you don't get there in time, I promise you this much: Someone will die. Maybe Jamie?"

I was greeted at the cafeteria door by the pimpled kid who had helped Jamie with her project. Was this a coincidence, or was Burn watching her earlier that morning? The kid looked supremely nervous. I was either too adrenalized to actually feel any fear or in fear overdrive, I couldn't tell. One part of me understood that just by entering the building, I might be sealing my fate; logic dictated that Burn was capable of virtually anything, including a massacre of mega proportions, and maybe that was what he wanted all along. Another part of me believed that whatever he was planning, I could talk him down. The cafeteria itself did not appear to be too dangerous. And Jamie was in the building.

I didn't have a choice, really.

The kid opened the door for me and I stepped inside. As I did so, I held the door open so that he could leave. He looked at me, unsure what to do.

"It's OK. Go!" I yelled, and he ran through the door to the freedom that I had just left behind.

The cafeteria was deserted, like it was Sunday morning, not like a school day at all.

I took in every corner, wondering where the cameras were. I knew that the school had a security system installed some years ago, which included cameras in the hallways, so I had to believe that Burn had somehow hijacked them. He seemed to know too much about what was going on.

The phone again.

"OK, I'm in, now can we talk?" I asked, not wanting to talk to him at all.

"Did I tell you that you could let Lorenzo out?"

Lorenzo? I thought. Who names a kid Lorenzo in the twenty-first century?

"Burn, he's just a kid. . . ."

He hung up, leaving me to wonder what the consequences were going to be.

I went to the cafeteria doors and looked out. No one was in the hall.

Phone again.

"Stay put until I tell you otherwise." Burn, sounding super-angry.

Gone again.

I called Jamie. Nothing was new on her end. I told her that I let her boyfriend out. She said that Lorenzo was definitely *not* her boyfriend. When I told her that I was in the cafeteria, this only seemed to panic her more.

"What does he want from us?" She started to cry. "Is he going to blow up the entire school, Steven?"

I was about to tell my sister that there was nothing to worry about, except I had no reason to tell her something that could easily not be true.

I waited, trying to think about what to do, wondering just how much danger was I, were we all, in?

And Burn called back.

"Why don't you stop what you're doing and let everybody go?" I started in immediately, before he could say anything.

Quiet on the other end. "It's too late for that, Steven."

More sirens now, new sounds from just beyond the cafeteria door. And beyond it, another explosion. I ran to the window. A trash bin was on fire.

He had either timed it perfectly so that I could get into the building or he was controlling the devices—it had to be some kind of remote mechanism.

"David?" I shouted into the phone. "Are you there?"

"Stay where you are. Until you hear from me."

I suspected that he was preoccupied with some other crises in the building. I looked around, already completely exhausted.

It was 8:35.

The bell went off, and of course, I jumped out of my skin when I heard it, my senses preparing for a life-ending explosion. The sound continued to rip through me even after I understood what it was. I have never been able to handle classroom buzzers, one of my things.

End of first period, minutes until the next one, or at least it would have been if this was a normal school day. I ran to the door of the cafeteria again, looked into the hall.

No one was out there. Not a single person.

Second period. I would have been in contemporary literature with Collins. Screw it, I thought, fuck Burn and his stupid plan. He's not going to do anything. This is not McAllister. He's not eight anymore.

So after peering around and seeing absolutely no one, I slipped into the hall.

No one.

I had this feeling that I was missing something, I was sure of it. If the building was full, why weren't there at least some people in the halls? What did he do to convince like a thousand people, teachers and kids, to stay in their places? Kids should be trying to escape through windows, running any way they could out of the building. Something was missing.

And behind me, something exploded in the cafeteria, swinging the door back into me, knocking me down. Once again, I was on the floor. My cell rang.

"Was there something about *stay in the cafeteria* that you did not understand?"

"Cut it out, Burn," I said.

"You're going to get people killed."

"Me?" I answered. "*I'm* going to get people killed? I'm not the one setting off bombs, dude."

"The last one was a consequence of your failure to follow instructions," he said. "Everyone seems to be able to handle instructions except you. Why am I not surprised, Crash?"

"I don't care," I told him. "I'm not listening to you anymore."

"Jamie's in Room 211. It's directly above where you are standing now. Do you want to hear another explosion? This one from upstairs?"

Fuckme. I couldn't take the risk. Apparently everyone else was feeling the same way, because no one was moving down the hallway.

"*Fine,*" I spit back. "What now?"

"Go back in the cafeteria. Use the fire extinguisher on the north wall. Remember, I'll be watching you."

I swung back through the door. There was, in fact, a small fire by the back wall. I found the fire extinguisher, unhooked it, and sprayed foam all over the remaining flames.

He called back.

"Now go into the kitchen," he said. "Go over to the aluminum table. Bend down and feel underneath. There's a rifle taped to the underside. And beside that a headset. Get the gun, put on the headset, turn it on, and wait. Did you hear me, Crash? WAIT!"

I moved quickly into the next room. It looked like there had been a point in the morning when things must have been normal. Meals were in the process of being prepared. And between that time and now, the room had been abandoned.

"Where is everyone?" I yelled out, stooping down.

I found the rifle. It was like a World War I–looking weapon. Old and beat up. Taped to the corner was a headset. I yanked it free and put it on. "Hello?"

"Did you find it?" Him, clear as a bell. I could have sworn that I heard the clatter of typing on a keyboard in the background.

It hit me that he must have been planning this event for a long time. You couldn't just wake up one morning and rig all these bombs in all these places, plus hijack the school security system.

Like everything else he did in his life, he was thorough, which meant that he had to think through the consequences of what he was doing and had to know the potential outcome.

"Yes."

"OK, take the weapon and go over to the front entrance of the school and wait until I call you. You have two minutes."

8:50.

When I got to the front entrance of the school, it was crowded with people, at least fifty students, all looking to get out. There was a uniform gasp when they saw me carrying a rifle.

"I'm not going to use it," I announced. "Burn is forcing me to carry it. But I will not use it, no matter what."

That seemed to relax absolutely no one.

The custodian, Mr. Ferguson, was standing in the archway, holding another antique-looking gun across his chest, looking really, really nervous. Like me, he also had a headset on. No one was even attempting to get past him. I moved through the crowd, over to where he was standing.

"My daughter is in there," he said, pointing to the faculty lounge. "With him."

"My sister Jamie's inside the building too. He threatened to hurt her," I told him.

"He's got ten of us stationed at different places in the building; teachers, staff, we all have guns. One of us at every exit. He made some kind of arrangement with the police, no one gets hurt if no one gets out. If we let anyone leave, he's going to blow up the place. He's somehow fused some of the exits shut, must have done this during the night. He's booby-trapped windows. The police are aware of everything. He's broadcasting all of this to them using the school's security system. He has a list of demands, which he is going to give one of us, and as soon as the police respond to him, he promised to release everyone."

"How do you know this?"

Ferguson made this sour face. "We're on live with him now," pointing to my headset. "And the police can hear us too."

"Do we know his demands?" I asked.

Ferguson shakes his head, just keeps shaking his head. He knows nothing.

"How do we get out?"

"We can't at the moment, police orders. Nothing to upset the balance. They are bringing in a hostage negotiator."

"Something's got to be done," I said.

"So now do you understand, Crash?" boomed the voice on the other end of my headset.

479

"WHAT?" I yelled back into it.

"You need to convince everyone to get away from the doors. Tell them to go, single file, to the auditorium."

"David, what do you want?"

"Tell them that they need to get to the auditorium."

I yelled this to the crowd, and absolutely no one moved.

"Fire the weapon."

"No way."

"Fire the gun, Crash, or I'll level Jamie's classroom."

"I'm not shooting anyone." As I said this, a bunch of people quickly backed off the doorway, many on their cell phones, all chattering, some screaming at the possibility of me using a weapon. The noise was cutting into my brain, draining me.

I looked outside, and there were dozens of police cars, not only from our town but from all over the county, and EMS trucks and fire trucks. The street around the school was sectioned off. Professionals only. And every last cop, every last firefighter, every last EMS technician in the county had a view of me standing there in the archway and handling a weapon.

I realized at that second that I was probably in the range of some sniper.

"Dave," I said as calmly as possible. "There are cops everywhere. If I use the gun, they will probably shoot me. You gotta stop this."

"They're listening now. They know you're just following instructions."

"I don't care. I'm not doing it." It also occurred to me that he could totally be lying to me. They may know nothing.

"You have ten seconds."

OK, with all of the fucked-up things that I did with my friends in high school, I have never fired an actual gun before. Easy enough when you're playing Xbox or PlayStation. But I was holding a real gun and an antique at that. It was heavier, thicker than I had imagined, and it felt oddly off balance, not at all like the fake arcade weapons I was familiar with. Who knew what was bound to happen if I actually fired it?

"Aim it down," Ferguson suggested.

"What if the bullet ricochets and hurts someone?" I asked.

But then, there was no point, because there was an explosion coming from the second floor.

And an announcement over the PA system.

"Will someone please tell Steven Crashinsky to be more cooperative?"

Burn's words echoed in the halls as I raced up the stairs to get to the room where my sister was. On both ends of the hall there were staff members holding rifles and wearing headsets. I wondered how Burn selected them and what he told them to convince them to do their jobs.

"For your own safety, don't take any chances if you want to live," Burn was saying over the loudspeaker. "Stay in your classrooms. This will all be over in a few hours."

I got to the hallway in the B wing. Mr. Booth was there. He waved me forward; apparently he knew that I would be coming up.

I ran down to Room 211, looking for Jamie, still carrying the rifle. I was there in seconds, and there, inside the classroom, was the entire drama group, mostly staring out the window, which was heavily wired and taped, although I did not see any sign of explosives. About thirty kids, half seniors. Including Christina. All in a panic.

"Say hello to Christina for me." Burn on my headset.

"Where's Jamie?" I shouted back.

"Don't you know?" he answered. "You're her brother. Don't you have enough interest in her life to know which classes she has, who her teachers are, when she's supposed to deliver her report . . . on the endocrine system?"

"I'm done with this, David," I said, and even as I did, I searched the room for the camera. Exactly how was he doing it?

"WRONG!" he yelled back. "We're just getting started. It's going to be a long day for both of us, because you are my messenger, Steven."

Here's the thing. At that moment, I couldn't remember where I'd heard that before, that I was his messenger. It just rang out in my brain as being important.

Instead, I thought back to the poker game again, and I knew, *I totally knew* that there was no reason that I couldn't beat him at his own game again. And "game" was a perfect choice of words, because he was making me feel like I was inside a video game that he had developed specifically for me. Was it possible that this whole setup with him rigging the school with explosives was all for the purpose of forcing me play this game with him?

I thought back to elementary school—was this some kind of unfinished-business thing for him?

That thought allowed me to think with some clarity. Christina and I hadn't talked very much since Massachusetts, in part because we were both afraid that if Burn saw us together, it would trigger something inside him. And while he very much kept his promise to Roxanne during the time she was alive, from what I heard, Christina had been recently getting random texts that she never answered. It hadn't escalated to the point of her contacting me or anything, not that I could have done anything about it. It wasn't the time now to determine whether that was true, but it got me to thinking that maybe Christina could talk him down off the ledge, like his sister and my stepmom did in the past.

Mrs. Terrigano's voice came over the PA system. "Please, children, for your safety, those of you in the front of the building, please head to the auditorium. The front of the building is not a safe place to be."

My first thought was, could sweet old Mrs. Terrigano be in on this with Burn? But then it hit me that she was in the room with him, probably being forced to speak.

I couldn't stop that feeling that I was missing something.

I thrust the headset at Christina. "You can do this," I whispered to her.

At first she pushed it away. I covered the mouthpiece, mouthing the words, "You have to talk to him." She waved me off again. Another whisper from me: "Christina. You can end this."

I must have sounded superconvincing, because not only did she take the headset, but she did so with a confidence that I don't think she knew she had, as if she were suddenly onstage, completely the performer.

"David. You've got to stop this now. You need help. This is not the way to get it. Please, I'm asking you as a friend."

Her jaw dropped. She tossed the headset at me like it was a nuclear device.

"DON'T DO THAT AGAIN!" David screamed at me as soon as I put it on.

I guess I miscalculated.

I asked Christina what he told her.

"He said, 'Christina, I'm not your friend. I have no friends. Put Crash on.'"

"That's it?"

She looked around, in search of the same camera that I had tried to locate minutes before. Then she motioned for me to step into the hall, which I did, and then she whispered, "No, that *wasn't* it. He said that maybe we weren't destined to be together at all, maybe we're just destined to die together."

Wow.

I was, no question, out of my league. This wasn't poker anymore.

"What do we do next?" she asked.

And as if on cue, actually probably on cue, though I couldn't locate the camera, Burn's voice on the headset, "Next stop, Room 219," he said. "Take Christina with you."

And of course, he was gone again, and I had to explain to Christina that she was supposed to come with me. She waved me off.

"I can't handle this."

And I slowed her down. "Look at me," I told her, taking her hand. "I won't let anything bad happen to you."

"Why should I believe you?" she asked.

"Because I came for you once already," I told her. Even though that was technically a stretch, as in little white lie, because, if you recall, I only "came for her" because of Roxanne.

"Also," I told her, "we have to follow his instructions or he'll blow something else up."

Room 219.

There was Jamie. She seemed to be expecting me.

"He just called," she explained. "He wants the three of us to go down to the cafeteria."

So there we were, the three of us, minutes later in the cafeteria.

"OK, we're here," I said into the headset. "Now what?" Again, I heard intense typing in the background.

"Now you wait for me."

Another announcement over the PA, this time Connelly: "We need to have an orderly transition from the classrooms to the gymnasium and the auditorium. There will be pizza and bathroom breaks for the kids who need it."

What the fuck was Burn doing, throwing a pizza party in the middle of his siege? And typical of Connelly having to pronounce the whole fucking word instead of just saying "gym" like a normal person.

And all I could think about was the exit, because while Ferguson said that a bunch of the exits were fused shut, I knew for sure that the one in the back of the cafeteria was still operational. Which meant if the three of us moved quickly, we could be out of there, which also didn't make any sense because he left it completely unguarded.

And as if Burn was reading my mind, his voice returned: "Don't even think about it, Crash. The door is rigged."

So we waited, with me trying to keep both Christina and Jamie as calm as possible, while my adrenaline was making me feel like my skin was cooking. I could feel the beads of sweat forming on my forehead, which I quickly wiped away for Jamie's sake, as I did not want her to know how panicked I was.

"Now what?" I asked over the headset.

"Now is where it gets complicated for you," he said in a whisper. "No one has died yet." He paused. "That's about to change."

"David, you can't . . ."

"Shut up, Steven. Here's the deal. Take three big steps to the right and look up to the camera, because you are being broadcast over the webcam to the police, so they can see you and . . . now, hear you." I heard more typing in the background.

The camera here, like the ones situated throughout school, was a blue egg-shaped device that extended down from the ceiling. Until that minute, I always thought that those things were smoke detectors.

"Wave to the camera, Crash."

I did no such thing.

"*Wave*," came the immediate command. "Because I need to show the police how serious I am. To do so, I have to decide, do I kill everyone, a group of people, or just one of you?" He sounded absolutely sincere in this question, as if he was asking my advice.

"David . . ."

"DON'T INTERRUPT!" he shouted angrily. And then, after a pause, "I got to thinking. Why should it be my choice? I've been in no-win situations my whole life. But not you, have you?"

I didn't think it would be such a bright idea to remind him about Massachusetts. But it made me think of his sister. If she was still alive, this wouldn't be happening. So I wanted to tell him, yeah I have been. Instead I chose silence.

"I want to see how you will handle a no-win situation, Steven. You have the gun. Someone has to die. You can kill your sister; you can kill Christina, who, you claim, you hardly know; or you can kill yourself. If you can do this, I will let everyone go. If you can't, if you put the gun down, I will blow the school away, every kid, every teacher, every member of the staff. Oh yeah, and me." He was suddenly quiet.

"You have fifteen seconds," he finally added. "Fair enough?"

"What'd he say, what'd he say?" Jamie, jumping nervously. Christina was looking at me as if she had heard every word and knew exactly what was going on.

I was down to ten seconds.

I looked at her, then back to Jamie.

I wasn't going to kill anyone, I wasn't capable of that, but the second I put down the gun, it was over for everyone else.

I needed to think quicker. Only I couldn't think at all.

Five seconds. I wasn't going to kill myself. I'm not going to pretend otherwise.

Four. I thought to myself, does he really expect me to kill someone?

Three. It hit me. Burn was playing a game with me, I was sure of it.

Two. I raised the gun. Lifted it and pointed it at Jamie's head.

"Steven, what are you doing?" Screaming in stereo, from Jamie and Christina behind me.

"I'm sorry, I'm sorry, I'm sorry."

"Steven, PLEEEEEEEEAZE!" Jamie, all panicked.

"IS THIS WHAT YOU WANT, BURNETT?" I screamed into the headset.

And just as I cocked the trigger, I heard him say, "Put the gun down, Crash. I didn't think you could do it. Let them go."

I reeled back from the pressure of almost firing the weapon. I mean, even though I had pointed it away from both of them, I couldn't really be sure that it wouldn't hit anyone if I actually pulled the trigger.

"Just like that?"

"Do you want me to change my mind?" he asked. "Send them out the back. But not you. If you go, I *will* blow up the exit and the school and take you and your sister and Christina and everyone else out along with it. Do you understand? You have thirty seconds."

I motioned for both of them to move quickly to the cafeteria door, both of them looking at me like *what just happened?*, and I couldn't tell them anything, because what just happened was me with a straight flush again.

I almost smiled, except for the screaming panic inside me.

"Go," I told them. "He's going to let you both leave."

"Aren't you coming?" they both asked.

"No," I said. "I have to stay."

OK, you're probably wondering, hey, Crash, what was up with that? Well, I remembered something important. I remembered how Roxanne explained to me that Burn always obsessed about three people. The first was Roxanne and how he was always worried that she wouldn't be around. And now she wasn't around. And the second person was me because I was supposed to be some kind of messenger, whatever that was supposed to mean. The whole "messenger" thing finally hit me and as soon as I realized when I had heard the term before, that got me thinking about the third person.

Because the third person was Jamie.

Because he believed that he had to save her.

So I knew that if I aimed at Jamie, he would stop me. Thank you, Roxanne, wherever you are.

I hope the police understood my intentions if they were watching us, which I had to believe, because they would now know that everyone was at risk and that no one had died yet and that Burn was willing to let some of us go.

But not others.

He was back on the headset again, reminding me that, OK, I got my sister out, but I was still there, and there were still explosives and who knows what else and he was still crazy, out of his mind.

I could not believe that I stayed.

And he knew that I would; he said as much to me before I entered the building.

"Come down to the faculty lounge. Now. Leave the gun at the door. It's time to come out of your stupor."

It was 9:55.

CHAPTER TWENTY-FIVE

HOW A FOX IS ALWAYS A FOX

Standing at the door of the faculty lounge, I waited, wondering if Burn could see me.

With Jamie safely outside the building, I finally had a second to think. And when I thought about it, I realized that I was as out of my mind as Burn was if I was voluntarily agreeing to enter the room where he was holding people hostage. Was anyone left who was so important to me that I would risk my life for them? Especially with a kid who once promised to kill me and who now built the ultimate killing machine, as in an entire school filled with explosives?

Not only that, but I wondered would they, any one of the kids left, risk their lives for me? No fucking way.

Still, one part of me still figured I could reason with him. After all, good or bad, we had history in a way that neither of us had with anyone else. Plus we had Roxanne—that had to count for something. He knew, *he must have known*, how I felt about his sister. He had to respect that on some level.

I was ready to go in. I could handle him.

Except . . .

I also started thinking about the other times, the "Revenge is sweet" times, when Burn somehow got it into his head that I was his sworn enemy, and I couldn't forgive his absolute determination to keep his sister from me. He knew, *he must have known*, how much I hated him. Also, another part of me was sure that he had gone too far and there would be no way to reach him. Didn't he live in a world that was different from the

one the rest of us inhabited, a world I couldn't possibly understand? Who the fuck was I to try to figure him out in a crisis?

That part of me, the voice in the back of my head, said:

Run, Crash. Run.

I held my breath, could feel my heart beating, not only beating but doing heavy metal drumrolls in my chest, so fast it hurt,
and I could hear the sound reverberate in my ears.

I tried not to concentrate on that and forced myself to breathe,
using the technique that I learned years ago from some therapist trying to teach me anger control to keep me from attacking
Jacob when he tried to get me to boil over. Each breath deeper
than the one before it, counting backward.

I wasn't going to get through this if I stayed panicked.

I had to release all the fear. I psyched myself up. Just another
Jackass stunt to me, that's all this was going to be. Shit, I had
been doing that all my life. I had been in worse situations than
this. I had stuck my frickin' head into a pit bull's cage, for
Christ's sake, and lived through that.

This was cake.

I was feeling better, breathing better now, but my heart was not
slowing down one bit.

I knock.

No response.

I knock again.

The door edges open. A crack, slowly widening.

"Get in." An arm comes out and pulls me.

I am inside.

It is dark. The blinds are drawn; the lights are off. My eyes
take a second to adjust.

There are tables, some adjoining each other, others separated, and other circular tables pushed into the corners, with

two chairs each. I had never been in the faculty lounge before and didn't know exactly what to expect. Now, in the gray darkness of filtered daylight, I spot about a dozen adults, all with their heads on the tables.

At first I thought they were all dead. But then I see they are moving; not very much, just enough for me to see that they are alive, like some weird adult version of recess.

Freaky. Not just freaky, horror movie freaky.

It startles me, and I counterbalance by reminding myself that it could have been worse . . . far worse. There could have been a massacre in there. At least they were all alive.

And then I feel the cold steel pressed against my temple. I can make out the outline of a pistol in his hands but can't turn my head.

"Get down on your knees." A very hoarse Burn sounding totally different in person. Completely out of reach, I remember thinking. Also, his energy is electric, like he's on fire, which makes me recoil for an instant.

He lowers the gun.

I try to look him in the eyes, searching for some element of recognition. He is having none of that. Doesn't even acknowledge that he knows me.

He is totally gone.

I squat.

He squats down with me. I look over and see that he is wearing a belt that is rigged with explosives. At least that's what it looks like to me. It's even got a metal box above the belt with a red switch on it. If I'm right, he's got enough explosives on him to take down the entire school. Even if I'm wrong, at the very least, the people in this room will be vaporized if that thing goes off. It occurs to me that I am now one of the people in the room. So if this wasn't feeling like Massachusetts before, well, I am most definitely back at the strip mall again.

"Don't try anything stupid, Crashinsky. Do you understand?"

I nod, like that wasn't going to be a problem, knowing however that given my personal history, there was no way for me to obey that particular command.

He gets back up, pulling me up by the arm, and I feel a shock of electricity when he touches me, and for an instant every single muscle in my body clenches. I wonder if he notices.

"There's a table over there," he says, motioning to me. "That's where you sit. Take it. Now."

I stand slowly and he shoves me over to give me a head start.

"Easy, David, easy," I tell him.

He pushes me again, harder. "Don'T FUCKING tell me what to do."

When we reach his chosen destination, he pushes me into the chair. "Put your head down," he tells me, "like the others."

Then he goes over to the front of the room where he has set up his base of operations. There, he has sectioned off a series of desks with three chairs and three different laptops. He starts tapping on the laptop in the center for a while in silence.

Oddly, I am not feeling any fear. However, my chest is still doing the drumroll thing, like the feeling that I used to have on the ADD medications when I was younger, only more intense, reminding me of the way my body reacted when I got the news about Roxanne. I recognize that I am picking up Burn's energy. The room is filled with it. I will not be able to take it for very much longer.

I try to sit still, but that's not going to happen. Counting to ten, then backward from ten.

Not going to happen.

I pick my head up defiantly, determined not to put up with his bullshit any longer.

"Steven, I'm fucking warning you."

I momentarily lower my head again as my eyes adjust fully

to the darkness. There are nine others in the room with me. Over there is poor Mrs. Terrigano, sixty-four years old and old-lady frail, all gray haired and frazzled. She's beyond harmless, always talking about her favorite saints and their powers, always offering to help students with their assignments. What could she possibly have done to this kid that would make her a target? I don't think anyone has heard her raise her voice above a whisper in the four years I've been a student at Meadows.

Behind her Joanne Muchnick, the health teacher, Mrs. Muchnick, all into chaperoning the dances and the school events, always checking for alcohol and never finding it because we always found ways to outsmart her. Also Mrs. Dickenson, Mr. Connelly, Grace Towers, Ms. Kaushal, and some people I don't know.

These people were not the villains of Meadows High School. Except for Connelly, they were all women, and except for Connelly, the most harmless group you could ever have met. None of this made any sense at all to me.

My eyes go back to Connelly. He is bruised up pretty bad. His face shows streaks of blood. He is staring back at me and shakes his head as if trying to beg me not to try anything or even to say anything.

I can't believe all these adults are sitting there just taking it from this psycho kid. It hits me at that moment that I'm really going to have to save them all.

I pick my head up more slowly, straining to see what Burn is doing in the front of the room with the laptops.

I also see the guitar cases, now open, and immediately figure out what they were for.

No music for us today. Instead he's got assault weapons, two of them, positioned within easy reach of each of his hands, one to his left, another to his right. As any kid who has ever played video games can tell you, one was an AK-47, the unforgiving

Russian killing machine, the other an M-16, good old-fashioned American machine-gun technology. These, however, were no video-game props. We're talking the real thing, motherfucking military weapons.

"Why are you doing this?" I yell out.

"Shut the fuck up." Him, not looking up, getting busier, working on the left-side laptop now, typing away. "Not now," he yells.

He puts on a headset and starts talking into it, saying things like, "keep them away" and "let her go" and "it is what it is" and "do you want to die?"

Then . . .

"Mr. Ferguson, there are no exceptions. I don't care if she has to go, she can wait. . . ." He shouts into the device. "Do you want to see your daughter again?"

With that, Burn comes across to one of the desks and shoves the headset at the face of a heavy woman I have never seen before. I can't tell in this light how old she is; could be twenty, could be forty. "Tell your father to do what I ask," he demands.

She does, following instructions perfectly.

I wish that I had that capability.

Then Burn runs back to his base station and hits some keys on the right-side laptop. Less than three seconds later, there is a distant explosion.

I sit there, trying my hardest to be patient, to follow along like everyone else. And it works for a while. But not long enough, because a few minutes later, my run instinct is back, full force, and when it hits, I'm suddenly not in control, feeling claustrophobic to the point of panic. I just don't understand how all of the adults are still sitting there like everything's normal, just another day at high school.

It was a mistake for me to have entered the room. A big mistake.

I had to get out. I needed to get out.

I stand up.

As soon as Burn sees me standing, he steps across to the desks, drawing the pistol on me. I get the feeling that he knows what I am thinking.

"Sit the FUCK down."

I calculate the possible paths of escape. The door, too far away, and the windows, four sets, shades drawn; another door in the back of the room, by the cabinets and the sink, and no other way out. And of course there is the gun, and the madman behind it.

Suppose it starts with me? Suppose I am the first to go down?

Only he is staring directly at me for the first time and I think that this is finally my opportunity to connect, which was what I was instinctively trying to do from the moment that I entered the room.

I breathe, determined to ignore the warning signals from my overactive pulsebeat.

"David," I said, calm as can be. "None of this makes any sense." Looking back at him. Staring into him, just like poker night.

And he knows. He *fucking* knows.

"Do you really want to do this?" he practically laughs, actually inviting me in. "Bring it on, Crash."

And the electric buzz that I felt as soon as I entered the room is back in full as he steps toward me, and I understood that if I was going to get out of this alive, if I was really going to save the school, then I had to go to a place even worse than the faculty lounge, which until that moment I thought was ground zero. But it wasn't ground zero at all, because ground zero for me was being inside the head of David Burnett. Just like the poker game, except without the benefit of weed, not only without the benefit of weed, without the benefit of my friends to support me or anyone else for that matter. Without the benefit of knowing his cards this time.

And without all those things, I was no match for David Burnett. Not the David Burnett who was staring back at me, who was, as I said, too far gone to reach, well, not exactly to reach, but I had the distinct feeling that wherever he was, whatever he was experiencing, he would, in fact he *could*, pull me into it like a whirlpool where there was no escape.

All I could feel was panic. Not his. Mine. It was too hot in there.

I looked away. I had no choice.

And he knew it.

"Sit the fuck down, Crash." He laughed almost triumphantly.

But I wasn't done yet, because there was still something else. Cassandra, Roxanne's friend from the funeral, pops into my mind. She told me that in case Burn ever came after me, to tell him something. I just couldn't remember what it was.

"Sit the fuck down, Crash."

He continues to step forward, raising the pistol again. I stumble backward, still thinking. What did Cassandra say? It was about a dog and a fox. How did it go?

"We can end this, David. It's not too late. Let me help you," I tell him, even though we all know that it probably is too late for him. Think, Crash, what did she say? A fox is not a dog.

Meantime, the gun is pointed directly at my head, and I can't look beyond it because I can't connect with him again. I just can't do it.

"It was already too late when my father was killed." He was coming closer, the gun inches from my forehead.

Now I remember.

"Roxanne said that you can't make a fox into a dog no matter how hard you try. A fox is always a fox. And in the end, you have to let them go."

Spectacular. I remember every word. It was the magic incantation that would get him to come off the ledge. I am moving forward now, confident that the words will diffuse his anger, snap him to his senses.

"What the fuck is that supposed to mean?" Burn asks.

Immediately I think, maybe I got it wrong. Even if it sounded right. No, I had it right. It was just that it didn't mean to Burn what Roxanne thought it would have meant to Burn.

And in that exact second, my cell phone goes off; only it sounds to me, and actually feels, like it's Burn's gun going off; the sound is so penetrating that we both jump back from it.

I look down at the display.

No way.

Caroline Prescott.

What am I going to tell her, "Can't talk, Mom, I'm in the middle of a siege"?

I flip it open. And all of us hear my mom in the tinniest voice ever, squawking, "Steven? I just heard from your sister. What's going on?"

David is standing behind me now.

"Mom," I rush to talk, in a hushed whisper, which wouldn't have mattered, because Burn and everyone else could hear me anyways. "I'm in the faculty lounge with nine teachers and David Burnett. He has totally lost it."

With that, Burn grabs the phone. My mom's tinny voice is still chattering away. It is almost comical, I mean, it would be, if we weren't all in such a dangerous situation. This could be sitcom funny.

As her voice fades in the distance, I hear her say, "Put him on the phone."

"Hello, Mrs. Crashinsky . . ." Then there is this pause. "Ms. Prescott," he corrects himself. She had to be kidding with the name change thing right now. "Yes. Steven is here with me." He raises the phone to his ear, and we can no longer hear her tinny, tiny mom voice. "Jamie's not in school anymore," he tells her. Then silence for like ten seconds.

"I released her," he tells Caroline, sounding as if he was trying to win brownie points with her, and I actually start believing that maybe my mom could talk him out of whatever he was planning. Christina couldn't do it, and I couldn't do it, but again, Roxanne at the strip mall, Felicia at her wedding, neither of them had anything on Caroline Prescott.

Not so much this time, however. Because after another break of silence, he now starts yelling into the phone:

"Don't FUCKING tell me about my mother and my sister." And with that, he hurls my cell phone at the far wall, where it cracks into multiple pieces.

Then he turns to me. "Tell your mother not to call again."

And me thinking, OK, brainiac, you just broke my cell, how is she going to call anyways?

"Sit down, Steven," he says, pushing me back into my chair with absolutely no resistance. I am played out. I get disapproving head nods from my fellow captives.

Then Burn goes back to his base station and starts banging on the center laptop. This goes on for a while. More orders into the headset. Feels like hours. Even though it is just after 11:00 A.M., to me it's midnight, every second a minute, every minute an hour. My heart is still pounding like a bass drum.

More time passes. The beats regulate. I notice the buzz in the room has started to fade.

So even though everything could be over in a millisecond, I have this feeling that we, he and I, are not done yet. Because despite Burn having this breakdown, he is moving in a very calculated manner, beginning to look more normal, maybe getting control of himself a little.

I get the feeling the electricity in him has subsided, so I chance it, testing my impression, finally yelling across to him,

"Why don't you give me your list of demands, and I will bring them to whoever you want?"

And he yells back, "It's not time yet." Never looking away from his laptops.

And I ask when and he says, "Later."

And I ask if I could help him, with the list, thinking I'm making progress.

At least until he slams the lid down on the center laptop.

"FUCK. FUCK. FUCKFUCK." Burn goes into a tailspin, grabs the AK-47.

I may have miscalculated again.

"Your friends," he yells across to me, "are trying to leave the building."

"Can't be," I tell him. "My friends are not at school today."

"Don't get technical with me." He goes to the door. Checking the weapon.

Opening the door, then firing multiple rounds into the hallway.

AMAZINGLY LOUD. Ear-shatteringly loud.

I am completely stunned by the power of the weapon. I have heard the controlled sounds coming from the video-game guns, even paintball guns, and Airsoft. Whatever. This was a whole new sound, loud and sharp, loud enough and sharp enough to get inside you and shake you even after the echo fades. Plus you could feel the vibration. My sound threshold has been blown to bits and my core so rattled that I feel my whole body shake in sync with the shots being fired.

Also, watching him fire the gun, it registered that he had experience with the weapon. He was totally comfortable with it and was prepared for the kickback. We all knew from video games that the AK-47 packed a wallop of a kickback as compared to the M-16, which was faster and provided less of a kick. But, watching Burn, you could see how he counterbalanced when firing. You could not be prepared for the force of the real thing just by playing video games. No doubt about it, Burn had been practicing with the weapon and knew what he was doing. If he was aiming for anything, well, he probably hit it.

Which meant that there could be dead people in the hall.

And if so, the siege had just escalated, and Burn would know that immediately. Because once the first person dies, he's a murderer, and then there's no way out for him except to ultimately hit the switch on his belt. Which, of course, will definitely dust me.

And then, after the gun blast, silence, which isn't silent at all, because our ears are ringing from the sound.

Well, silence, except that there is a uniform gasp in the faculty lounge. Actually, a gasp and multiple screams as everyone in the room simultaneously drops to the floor in reaction. I'm not sure who the screamers were, maybe Mrs. Terrigano or even Connelly. The shrieks seem to come from that part of the room, but I am not looking at that part of the room. I am looking at Burn, not anyone else.

I taste the metallic dry taste in the back of my throat that I remember tasting when Burn pointed a gun at me on that winter night in Massachusetts. I now recognize the taste as the taste of fear.

The drumroll beat in my chest is back in full force.

So yeah, I began to lose it again, if you want to know the truth, and I can admit it now, looking back on that moment. I forced out a dragon breath until there was no more air in my lungs, trying to regulate my breathing.

"Crash, get over here," he yells from the door as he's peering out into the hallway.

I am not moving at this point, not hardly breathing. And that metallic taste was beginning to annoy me.

"UP FRONT. NOW!" he yells, slamming the door and going back to the laptops.

I dutifully, but very nervously, make my way to his command central.

He pushes me down into a chair, stands behind me.

Now I am staring at the laptop screens. Three screens, each with eight sections, twenty-four video images in total. Cameras in different locations of the school, inside and out. On the top left of the left-side computer, there's the front entrance, which is empty, except for Ferguson on guard duty. Next to this video feed, another image of the front entrance, from the outside, looking down the school steps into the street, which is blanketed by police cars. And then I see the other images from the cameras, revealing all the other school entrances. And in most of the images, there are adults wearing headsets.

The bottom row of the screen shows the auditorium, and kids are filtering into it in an orderly manner, line by line, and it looks almost filled to capacity.

And then on the center laptop, I see what Burn is upset about.

The gym is filled to capacity, like the auditorium. But there is one camera that apparently is having trouble, because it keeps blinking on and off. When it blinks back on, I see that kids are quietly leaving the building through the gym entrance. And another camera shows the outside view of kids running into the street, into police barricades.

"Get on the headset," he tells me, handing me an over-the-ear device, practically shoving it into my ear canal. "Otherwise I smoke the gym and everyone in there."

He taps on the keyboard, and the gym camera rotates. At first I see the tops of heads, but then I see the top of the bleachers, and there is a sizable package there that Burn wants to make sure I see. It's got a red switch, like the red switch on Burn's belt.

I glance over to the third laptop and notice that there is an identical package in the auditorium.

"Time to get started," he tells me.

All I can think of is that I'm *still* missing something, as I stare more intensely at all of the feeds. I am looking at classrooms and exits and various places where there are small detonation devices, devices that are in no way comparable to the elaborate packages that are set up in the gym and the auditorium.

"Crash, now!" he yells at me, although I have no idea what he wants.

I keep staring at the screens. No one is in any of the halls. No one is in any of the classrooms.

And it hits me that no one is any of the classrooms now because they are all in the gym or the auditorium, the two most dangerous places in the entire school.

"What the hell do you want me to do?" I ask him without turning around. I am starting to feel that electrical buzzing feeling again. It gets in the way of my ability to concentrate. And the heat coming off his body, I can feel it. Also, the metallic taste in my throat, now I think I smell it and I can't tell if it's coming from Burn or from me.

Through the video feed, I see Mr. Liu guarding the exit to the gym, looking directly into the camera, which goes blank and then comes back on. He is wearing an identical headset.

"Are you actually letting people out? What the fuck are you thinking, William?" Burn's voice, over my headset, echoes his actual voice from behind me. I know *exactly* what Mr. Liu is thinking, because it appears that he figured out that the camera was faulty and he was carefully letting small groups escape. Burn's voice startles him.

"One more kid gets out and you DIE," Burn shouts. "They ALL DIE."

I am looking down at the keyboards, wondering which of the keys detonate the explosives, knowing that Burn is preoccupied. Concentrating, like it's a video game, there must be some on-screen clue. Is there a way for me to shut everything down? A master switch? Isn't there always a master switch?

"Don't touch the fucking laptops, Crash," Burn commands, in synchronicity with my thoughts, and I'm wondering how he could possibly know. Was there some body movement that I made, that I didn't even know that I made, that tipped him off?

Same with Mr. Liu. I watch Mr. Liu's face on-screen as Burn reaches from behind me and doubles the size of the image. He is still staring back at us, almost full screen, as Burn leans over me, almost pressing his nose to the monitor, as if he's examining Liu in person.

Yep, I realize, it's Burn. He's the one who smells like that metallic smell that I am still tasting.

"Fire your weapon," Burn shouts at Liu over the mic and into my free ear. Stereo.

I am buzzing.

"I can't," says Liu.

"Then say good-bye."

I have to do something.

"Wait" is what I scream. And I see from Mr. Liu's face that he can hear me as well. Then the camera goes blank again, and Burn's hands are swarming the left laptop and he brings up another image, of another explosive device in the gym. Bigger than the first one.

"You can't be serious" is what I say.

"Shut the fuck up, Crash."

At first, I think he might be trying to activate it and I am about to try and stop him, not knowing how, when I realize that he's attempting to get the second gym camera to rotate.

The main camera goes back on, and it looks like Liu is finally following orders. The doors behind him are closed, and even though kids are pushing against him, he is pushing back.

"This is where *you* come in," Burn tells me, tapping me on the shoulder. His finger feels like a nail gun to me, practically penetrating into my bone. I flinch.

He brings up another camera full screen, an image of the side of the building. Looking farther down the road, news trucks everywhere. This is a major fucking event. This not just Eyewitness News. This is CNN. This is "we interrupt your regularly scheduled show with this breaking news from Westchester."

And I am smack in the middle of this.

And Burn turns to me, so we are nose to nose.

"In a second I'm connecting with Officer Kenyon. Tom Kenyon. You'll be speaking to him on my behalf. Actually, just reading what I type. No more. No less. Can you handle that, Steven?" I feel the heat of his breath on my face and the heat from his body. I am still preoccupied with trying to figure out how to stop it all. "Can you *handle* that?"

"Uh-huh," I say meekly.

"If you can't, there will be consequences."

Then words on the screen, as he nudges me to repeat them.

"MY NAME IS STEVEN CRASHINSKY. I AM IN THE FACULTY LOUNGE."

I speak this into the headset, into the air, not hearing anything except silence on the other end, no response, no static; just a dead line.

And a voice finally comes back. "We know who you are. Can I speak with David?"

"IS THIS OFFICER KENYON?" I read and say.

"Yes."

"ARE YOU THE ONLY ONE ON THIS CONNECTION?"

"No," he says honestly after a brief hesitation. "Can I speak with David now?"

"I AM HIS MESSENGER," I read to myself and shake my head "no way" until there is a swift poke between my ribs. Exactly between my ribs, to a soft spot that stings like a motherfucker. "I AM HIS MESSENGER," I say, repeating the words on the screen.

"Sorry, I need to talk to David directly," he tells me.

"WHERE'S THE PIZZA?" I just glance at Burn. Is he fucking serious?

He mouths the words silently. "Just read it, Crash."

As I read his lips, I announce: "WHERE'S THE PIZZA?"

"On its way. Look, can you put David on? We need to speak."

"THAT'S NOT HOW THIS WORKS. STOP PLAYING GAMES." I hesitate before reading the second part but catch Burn ready to strike my ribs again and I flinch again, finally reading it. "That's him speaking, not me," I add, then get an immediate poke through my rib cage anyways for my extra efforts.

"I understand," said the officer, deliberately. We understood each other, which meant to me that Kenyon was trying to get me to say something else, which I wasn't about to do.

"Can you ask Mr. Burnett when he will be ready to share his demands with us so that we can start letting people go?"

"TWO P.M. YOU ALREADY KNOW THE ANSWER. AT TWO P.M. STEVEN CRASHINSKY WILL DELIVER A SPEECH ON MY BEHALF." I look up at Burn—what the fuck?

"Tell me again. Why are we waiting?" Officer Kenyon asks.

"FIRST, WHERE IS THE PIZZA? WE HAD A DEAL; I RELEASE TWO KIDS, YOU GET FIVE HUNDRED PIES. I LIVED UP TO MY END—WHAT ABOUT YOURS? WHERE'S YOUR GOOD FAITH, ISN'T THAT WHAT YOU ASKED ME?"

Now I am reading more slowly, trying not to mess up a word, which, I don't have to tell you, is almost impossible, given the pressure I was under, even as I realize that the two students Burn is referring to are Jamie and Christina and that he had planned to release them all along. He was just fucking with me all that time.

"Tell him the pizza is coming. You just don't put together five hundred pizza pies. We had to order them. Tell him we need him to release more kids as a show of good faith."

"YOU ALREADY GOT YOUR WISH. WE BOTH KNOW ABOUT THE KIDS IN THE GYM. IF ANYONE ELSE LEAVES, EVERYONE DIES." Again, I felt compelled to add that these were Burn's words, not mine, which I said and as soon as I said, I get a slap across the head and instantly more words on the screen:

"AND THE MEMORIAL. WHAT ABOUT THE MEMORIAL FOR MY SISTER? NOT JUST A PLAQUE, BUT A STATUE IN FRONT OF THE BUILDING." I recite these lines as carefully as possible, even as my mind puts the pieces together.

I somehow need to tell Kenyon what I know. And I have to figure out how to do it, because they have to know. I mean, I didn't know it with certainty, but close enough so that there's every probability that I am right about what's really going on. And if I am right about what's really going on, we're all fucked because whatever anyone thinks the siege might be about, it's not. It's not about a list of demands or anything else that Burn might claim it was about.

I need to totally concentrate. I need to know if I can trust what I'm thinking about. What I know for sure is, Burn always has a plan for everything. But in this case, there are so many variables that any one of them could go wrong, too many, and almost all the kids in the school are in the most dangerous areas in case something does go wrong, and what that means is, if something, *anything* goes wrong, it doesn't mean one kid dead, it means hundreds.

Which means Burn couldn't have been committed to this big of an act without thinking about every possible outcome. Not with his genius mind. And even in my not-so-genius mind, I understood that every possible outcome was bad, some worse than others. I hear Jacob's voice in my head, like whenever I used to present him with some incredible idea for a new business. He'd listen, then ask, "What's my exit strategy? What's my exit strategy?" And while I never had one, Burn would.

Well, Burn would ordinarily have one . . . unless there *was* no exit strategy. Unless his exit strategy was to join his sister and take everyone with him.

And there it was, the piece of the puzzle I was missing.

Fuckme. Fuck us all.

On one hand, he could blame it on the kids, if they continued to escape. Part of the deal, no one gets in, no one gets out. Yet the gym door was not sealed, and Mr. Liu, the guy he had in place there, was, at five foot four inches, the least intimidating, most accommodating adult at our school, other than Mrs. Terrigano and Ms. Kaushal, both of whom were in the faculty lounge with me.

On the other hand, there are the cops. They have to be thinking about when to make their move. Sooner or later, they would figure out a way to get everyone out, or so they would think.

I had no choice. Burn left me with no alternative.

I blurt out, as loud as can be: "It's not about the demands, don't believe him. There are explosives in the gym and the . . ."

I don't think I actually get the last word out, which would have been "auditorium," because Burn is on his feet and his gun is out and before I could turn to see what he was doing, the handle makes contact with my skull, steel against bone, feeling more like a baseball bat than a gun.

And for a second, it was no big deal. For that first second only. But then the pain rockets through me like a volcano going off in my brain. I had a concussion in eighth grade during football practice. So I know what a concussion feels like. And this bang on my head, this feels like a concussion.

"Get up." His next command, and that's when I notice that I am not in the chair anymore; I am down on the floor, not remembering how I got there.

I try to stand; I can hardly focus, much less stand, but that doesn't stop him, because he grabs my arm and starts to drag me from the front of the room. "Did you think you were helping by telling him about the explosives? Well, did you?"

And I'm not answering, trying to gather my strength, still waiting for the concussive effects to pass. Painfully dizzy. I need to vomit.

He calls over two women, Mrs. Muchnick and Ms. Kaushal, and they help me back into my seat as I stumble toward it. And I step backward, not ready to give up just yet, but my equilibrium is shot to hell.

Burn follows after them, to make absolutely sure that I am put into my seat. Connelly attempts to assist me and Burn whacks him down like he was a mole in that whack-a-mole game at the arcade. Connelly goes down. Slinks back to his chair. Head down on the table.

Good dog.

"They're fucking with us," Burn announces to the group.

Us? I don't say this out loud. But who was *us*?

"They've hacked into the security system. Well, after I hacked into the security system. They hacked back," he says. "I was giving them very limited access. Just what I wanted them to see. Now they can see everything. So I'm shutting it down now."

Ms. Kaushal goes to the back of the room, returns with a roll of paper towels, handing them to me, motioning for me to use them, which makes no sense until I see that my desk is covered in blood. She unrolls a wad and presses it against my temple, pulls my hand over hers to support it. I feel the slickness of my own blood oozing through the wad of towels.

"Do you understand what that means?" he asked us all,

but no one, including me, had any clue. "It means that Steven Crashinsky may have killed us all with his failure to comply with instructions."

How was this my fault? I'm about to ask, but I do not have the strength to argue.

What was the point anyways?

Then he turns to Muchnick and Kaushal.

"Leave him alone. Go back to your seats. Let's continue."

Continue? I am confused. Beyond confused. Disoriented.

As if on command, Joanne Muchnick chimes in. "Before you got here, Steven, David was asking us to tell him about his sister. She was my student. In fact, most of us in the room had her in our classes, or knew Roxanne very well."

Was this for real?

"She was a beautiful soul," said Ms. Terrigano. "A real free spirit and independent thinker."

I needed to close my eyes and I gave in to the feeling for a minute, but the world was spinning too much in there. I had to concentrate, get Burn to stop. So, as I listened to Ms. Muchnick talk, I closed my eyes again and concentrated like I had never concentrated before in my entire life and, in my mind, asked Roxanne, wherever she was, for help. I asked, if she could hear me wherever she was, was there a way to save her brother and the rest of us? All I asked for was a sign, if somehow she could give me one, then I would know. Not gonna lie, I have asked for signs from her before, signs that she was somehow there in some form, and there were times when I even thought she could hear me, but of course I never got any proof of any sort whatsoever. So just one sign now could change everything. Maybe she had been holding off because she knew there would be this one time when it really, really mattered.

And I opened my eyes and looked around with a completely open-minded perspective. Mrs. Muchnick was still going on about this after-school thing with Roxanne, and there was absolutely nothing to prove that I had reached her.

Because, I had to face it, there was nothing to reach. It was just me, not willing to let her go all this time.

I looked back at the clock on the wall. 12:22.

And Burn was back to his laptops again.

And Mrs. Muchnick goes back to her stories about Roxanne.

She goes on for a while, and when she's done, Burn gives Connelly the nod, and it's his turn to tell a Roxanne story. And I'm thinking, this is the way he wants to go out, hearing about his sister, which is why he chose the people he did.

Which may have been the real reason why I'm here.

"What do you remember about my sister, Ed?" Burn asks, using Connelly's first name as an expression of contempt.

"I remember a girl with a most unusual gift. She was insightful and funny and had a nasty mouth, if you want to know the truth, Mr. Burnett."

"Go on," David said, leaning back in his chair.

"We had this assignment. You may know the one, Mr. Crashinsky. Find three songs that are related in theme and do an essay comparing and contrasting the songs, considering them as poetry."

OK, we had this assignment like two weeks before, and I had no idea when it was due. Fuckme, I thought for a second, knowing that I was not getting that assignment in on time. Not that it mattered, at this point.

"Go on," Burn says, fiddling with his laptop.

"And the theme she picked was remarkably sad, break-up songs, but not just normal break-up songs, incredibly personal break-up songs. And her essay was so wonderfully constructed, so beautifully written and so deeply emotional, that I simply could not comprehend how a seventeen-year-old girl could have understood the poetry behind those songs as well as she did. I must confess that it brought a tear to my eye when I read it. Mr. Burnett, your sister was a hell of a writer."

"What songs?" Burn demands to know.

"They were fairly obscure, Mr. Burnett. You wouldn't know them."

"What songs?" Burn shouts.

"Well, there was one called 'Separate Lives,' by Phil Collins, and a Beatles song that almost no one remembers, called 'For No One.' And the third was called 'Did She Mention My Name?' by this folksinger Gordon Lightfoot. I knew of these songs before, but did not comprehend how intensely personal they were until Roxanne pointed them out to me."

If Burn had detonated all of the explosives at that very instant, I wouldn't have known, because when Connelly used the name of the song that I had heard months before on Caitlin's iPod, it was like Meadows and everything that surrounded us ceased to exist and I was somehow beyond time and space, simultaneously standing in the cold in Massachusetts, sitting on her bed, watching her naked, shotgunning with her at Kelly's, having her crash into me on the bus line at McAllister, all at once in a terrific and terrible burst of a . . . moment.

And then I was back again, and the part of me that totally *believed* was gone, because even though this had to be more than just a coincidence, it was just too motherfucking strange. It was my head, my oozing, concussive head that temporarily shut down, no other way to otherwise explain the singular moment that I experienced.

And even though I tried to make sense of it, it made no sense at all, which infuriated me.

Point is, whether or not I connected with Roxanne, and on some level, it felt like I did, I was still in a room with her psycho brother, who was smarter than me and had an arsenal of deadly weapons and bombs. So, while Connelly is still droning on, I'm watching Burn, the way a kid watches another kid when you're playing basketball, who are you going to pass to, what's your next move. Adults would miss this; they tend to look down at us, which makes it easy to live in our secret society of childhood.

Burn has moved away from his laptops, is toying with his pistol, not aiming it but holding it in a completely nonthreatening way, no longer focused on the monitors. And it hits me, if this is basketball or poker or some other game, then Burn has just taken himself out of it, on the sidelines now, because he knows it's over, because he's no longer got control over what happens outside the faculty lounge. And as soon as someone gets close enough, it really is game over. And there's only one game over in Burn's mind right now.

And I completely understand it, because I am inside his head for the first time today. Only it's not like the night of the poker game at all.

This time is different.

I'm in his head this time because I understand now what happened to him. I understand because it happened to me and I didn't realize it. In spite of everything I had in my life, in spite of my incredible ability to have everything go my way, *my gift*, as Roxanne once called it, none of that mattered because she still killed herself, and when she did, an anger that was always inside me, there in the back of my brain, *an anger that was always contained whenever I got what I wanted as soon as I wanted it*, WAS BACK. It was something that I had all my life and only went away completely during those afternoons when I was with her, even though it was something that I finally learned to control better when Jacob moved out.

So now I could connect with David Burnett, because my anger had become pure anger, not mixed with fear or any other emotional thoughts but crystal . . . clear . . . unadulterated . . .

RAGE.

And that's exactly what was going on with David Burnett. He had completely surrendered to the rage that was always inside us both, waiting there. He was fucking Darth Vader. He had always been Darth Vader, and Anakin was trying to break through sometimes, maybe Roxanne helped him keep it in check, I couldn't say, but the only thing I was sure of was Anakin was completely gone now. He was all Vader, just like that day in the janitor's office.

Which was fine by me, because this is what I was all about now.

And so I stood up, and when he saw me, he stood up, and when we connected this time, I didn't look away, but neither did he.

And I felt the same electricity as before, only this time, it was mine. Definitely mine. And then I felt my rage-thoughts randomly focus on Roxanne, on Jacob, on Connelly, then on Burn, but then mostly on myself for being such a stupid, oblivious fuck-up and for getting into this situation in the first place. The evidence was in: What the fuck was I doing there? Who the fuck did I think I was? I was a fucking moron and I deserved to be there.

I look at Burn. He is holding the gun on me. "Sit THE FUCK DOWN."

I continue to stand.

Everyone is looking at me.

"Sit down, MR. CRASHINSKY," Connelly shouted behind me.

"Please sit down." Joanne Muchnick.

"Sit down, Crash," Burn shouts over them, "or I swear I will put a cap in you and pop you to hell."

I'm thinking that I have to end it now, that I can no longer back down, and somehow I have to stop him. My head starts to hurt again. I can feel the gash on my temple bleeding again.

It's beyond painful. But that only makes the Rage somehow more . . . PURE.

And then Burn does something totally unexpected. He looks away, steps back, and flips a light on.

Everyone jolts back from the sudden change in the lighting. Suddenly daytime again.

"Time to get started. Mr. Connelly, will you please stand up."

He refuses to look at me, knowing I am still staring at him.

Connelly is in a sudden and complete panic. He is not moving.

"Ed Connelly, you are required to stand." Burn pretends to ignore me.

Connelly pushes his chair back and gets to his feet.

I don't know what he's planning with Connelly. I don't care.

I inch forward.

"Sit the FUCK down, Crash."

"How did it make you feel when you saw the video of her, David?" I ask him, actually screaming at him.

That gets him to look my way.

"Do you want to know what it made me feel like?"

"Don't, Steven. I'm warning you."

"Why not?" I answer. "You haven't asked me yet, David. You haven't asked me to share my memories about your sister."

With that, I finally have his full attention. He is moving toward me and looking at me again and we are connecting and he knows that I am prepared to let him in, because he already knows what it feels like in there and it couldn't possibly hurt any more than the hurt I was already feeling.

"I'm not interested in hearing how you fucked my sister."

"Actually, she was fucking me, as I remember it. Like she did to all those guys in the video."

That certainly gets him to come after me with everything he's got.

Across the room in a single heartbeat.

Over me in the next heartbeat.

We are face-to-face. The middle of the room is suddenly empty, teachers are on the move. Even Connelly, who was previously absolutely frozen, is all the way across the room with the rest of them.

"Do I really have to explain this mechanism?" Burn asks me, pointing to his belt and to the homemade box with the red button. "I flip it, we all die. Are you ready to die, Steven? To be as dead as my parents? As dead as my sister?"

Now there is some kind of chanting sound going on behind us, because many of the teachers are trying to tell me, "Stop it, Steven. Leave him alone." Even though Burn is the one coming after me.

"She was my fucking soul mate until you cut us off from each other!" I screamed at him, all hate now. "And I will never, ever love anyone the way I loved your sister."

Well, that stops him now, because his expression changes, and for a second, all the anger is gone, replaced by grief. I see this change flicker in his eyes, like it was poker night. And maybe this is what Roxanne, from wherever she was, would have wanted. Because we were, the two of us, finally emptied of our feelings.

In that instant, it was just me and him, Steven and David, and the rest of the world didn't matter or even exist, and I had the same feeling for him that Roxanne must have felt that night in Massachusetts when she told him, "Let's go home, David. I know how hard it's been for you."

I almost wished I could tell him that, but we both knew he was in too deep now.

"If you really loved her, then you really need to know," he whispers to me, grabbing my neck, tightening his grip around it; then he pulls my face closer to him. He was always taller than me, and his arms were like iron. I feel his hot breath against my cheek.

"Our secret," he whispers softly. "You have to promise."

I can hardly hear him. No one else can hear him. I have this incredibly sad, incredibly scared feeling that I don't *want* to hear him.

"*What's* our secret?" I struggle to break free.

Softer whisper.

"Roxanne was alive that night when I went into her room and found her. Her head was back on the pillow, and there were empty pill bottles on the floor. I knew what she did. She reached for me, and when she did, I ran out of her room and closed the door. Then I waited. I lay in bed all night and waited, and I didn't open her door until the next morning. I can't believe I did that, Crash. I can't believe that."

With that, he let go of me.

That's the secret.

"Our secret."

That's what I could not tell anyone, what I couldn't and still can't speak out loud, because it still tears away at me when I think about it.

That's what's been inside me since 1:05 P.M. on April 21, 2008.

When he told me this, he let go of me.

And he started crying, so completely that his entire body gave in to the feeling.

And the truth was that ever since she killed herself, I had kind of given in to a very quiet, very personal version of that feeling as well. Even though it never showed, even though I was able to balance it every day so no one knew.

I understood how empty my life was going to be without her, and how angry I was at her for leaving me alone forever, which is exactly what David felt, what he always felt. Like he said, it was too late after his father died and it only got worse after his mom and then his sister.

His sister fucked us both and now we are both too far gone.

But he could have saved her.

Hit with the realization that he let his sister die, that she would still be alive if not for him, the rage inside me was back full force, beyond any rage I had ever experienced before. It boiled through my insides, making me feel like I was on fire, like there was no escape, and with that powerful, horrible force building inside me, I went after him.

And I crashed into him. Completely rammed him with every ounce of my energy, with every ounce of every horrible feeling that I ever had in my life, all culminating in NOW.

But he didn't go down.

Instead, his arms wrapped around me.

And we were hugging, the most intense hug I have ever had. It was that intense for two reasons:

The first was that Burn was still crying and he felt unstable on his legs, like he was unable to stand on his own, and he needed me for support, or else he was going to crumple.

The second reason was—and get this—to all of you teachers and coaches and everyone else who sold me short, who said that I wasn't smart enough to take a foreign language or advanced bio or whatever. In the instant of that hug, in spite of my hateful rage, I became the smartest kid in the history of Westchester, maybe in the entire U.S.

Because I hugged him back.

I locked my hands together around his waist. And held him in a complete wrestler's lock.

Because as long as we were locked together, Burn could not reach the button on his belt. And he would be unable to get to his guns.

Of course, when he realized what I was doing, he tried to break free, first stepping forward as if to pin me against the wall, but I pushed back on my legs and countered his progress, using everything I had inside me, every emotion that had driven me to insanity, because if someone had entered the room at that very moment, there was no contest who was crazier. Not at that moment. No contest at all.

He tried to twist his body free, but I twisted with him. Then he tried to pry me loose with his hands, and all this time I was screaming to the others, "Get the police. Get the police, get the police."

And then he bent backward and lifted me off the ground, but I pulled myself back down, all with my fingers locked in a tight-knuckled embrace.

I stayed down.

And I stayed attached.

And I was still in such a rage that it didn't matter to me that, with my body pressing against his, I could feel the lumps of the explosives and the switch that could have detonated based on the sheer force of us clinging together so tightly. And I didn't care.

And Connelly, of all people, came in to help and grabbed one of Burn's hands to keep him from trying to separate from me.

And then the cops came charging in. And they were on top of us, but I wasn't letting go and they weren't stopping me, because they were pulling Burn's hands back, up and away, and then they managed to cuff him, with me still holding on, refusing to let go. Once they had his hands safely away from the switch, I finally released my grip.

As they got him down, his face got close to mine again, and he said, "You have to promise."

They were turning him over, and some bomb guys were all over him. I saw another flash of anger, but then he was all about weeping again, completely surrendering to it.

Some other officers pulled us apart. They wanted me out.

"You better not tell anyone what I told you," he screamed at me through his tears, as they forced him back through the door. "I'm warning you, Crash."

Thinking of what he had done to his sister and knowing what I knew, I said the only thing that I knew could hurt him any more at that point.

"I had a straight flush," I yelled back. "I let you win."

I heard him yell something that I could not understand. It sounded like "Boston hikes. Boston hikes."

Whatever.

At 1:11 on April 21, the siege was officially over.

CHAPTER TWENTY-SIX

HOW I MADE THE COVER PAGE

Two police officers accompanied me out of the building, physically holding on to me as we headed for the front entrance of Meadows High School.

On the way out, someone thrust a bottled water at me, and I chugged it down, tossing it back, empty. Someone else tossed me a T-shirt. Mine was covered in dried blood and drenched in sweat.

Quick change. I looked down at my new shirt, a police shirt. Jamie was going to love this.

I could hardly keep up with the cops, so it was a good thing they were there for me. My head was literally throbbing. I was suddenly hungry and tired and hot and cold and dizzy and calm all at the same time. My arms felt like overcooked macaroni, like my bones had melted, probably from holding on to Burn so tightly that every muscle had fused to him. Now they were having exactly the opposite reaction, all rubbery and loose. Plus I was still wobbly from the concussion I was sure I had.

I was totally unprepared for my first step outside.

There were crowds applauding for me, going wild, like I was a rock star, with me looking down from the stage at an audience. I held up my hand, trying to wave, and flashes of light went off in rapid succession. The sudden lights, the sound of applause were like lightning and thunder to me. So loud, so bright, and all I wanted to do was get home again and hug my little sister. And then lie down again.

I looked into the crowd: so many faces and I couldn't focus to recognize anyone I knew. Then individual faces started to come together. There was Christina, waving to me, and good old Caroline and Jamie. There were my boys, Evan and Bobby and Newman and Pete, with Kelly and Annie Russo and Bosco—it was even good to see Bosco at that moment. And of course, there were other kids and their parents, kids still making it out of the side entrances and the gym exit and all converging around the barricade of official vehicles and press vans.

I stepped forward and the applause grew louder.

Everyone there was going crazy over me. There were cops clapping and firemen cheering. Some people were, swear to Christ, waving flags; others were holding their cell phones high, like it was a concert.

It was the motherfucking Fourth of July and I was America.

OK, maybe that's an exaggeration, but this felt World Series good; not only World Series, but final-game, final-pitch, out-of-the-park-home-run good.

How good? Fuck you, Jacob Crashinsky, good. Your boy is a motherfucking hero after all, so maybe you should reconsider your opinions of him good.

That good.

Plus other kinds of good. Knowing that you saved every-one good, knowing that everyone was still alive because you reached into yourself and found an ability that no one else believed was there good, knowing that, except for you, many of those people, the ones coming out of the building, the ones standing on the lawn and being greeted by their moms, all of them could have died if not for you good.

* * *

And then microphones were thrust at me. Ten questions at the same time: How did you know, what made you think, what did he do, when did you realize . . . buzz, buzz, buzz, buzz buzz buzz. It was too noisy for me.

"What did he tell you?" A blond woman came at me holding her microphone like a baseball bat. "The teachers in the room said he whispered something to you. What did he tell you?"

More flashes of light and noise. My head was pounding. I was thinking I might actually pass out if I didn't get food quickly. Plus I needed another water desperately.

"What did he say?" More microphones.

"That's between me and David Burnett," I said.

But they weren't done with me. People had a right to know, I heard one reporter say. I was supposed to deliver a message. What was the reason for the siege? What was going on in Burnett's mind?

There had to be a reason, and it seemed to them that I was the only one who knew what it was. Except there was absolutely no way for me to explain what I knew, so all I could do was shake my head.

What about the message?

I could only shake my head again. There was no message, except maybe something about Boston that made no sense at all. Also, besides everything that went down, besides everything I understood, maybe Burn really had a message and somehow I had missed it. Who could say?

I couldn't. I was pretty sure that he was there to die and take all of us with him.

It was Connelly who deflected their attention. The reporters were as eager to hear from him and the rest of the Faculty Lounge Hostages, as the newspapers would later call the nine people who shared the room with Burnett that day.

Connelly was apparently all too eager to talk, and it sounded to me, from what I could hear, that he had somehow gotten it in his head that he was the real hero of the day. All I could hear was "I" did this, and "I" did that, and "I" challenged Burnett. But then, in a surprise move, he turned toward me, with all of the cameras rolling, and personally thanked me for saving his life and the lives of the teachers and my fellow students. And then, in front of the cameras and the newspeople and the mics, he called me a hero.

I was thinking, that should pretty much bring my C– up a few notches, to the A range, don'tcha think?

Then the reporters were back to me and the same questions all over again, what was the secret, and now I was getting more than annoyed.

So I made my way down through the crowd, not looking at the mics and the cameras, but focusing only on my family, and when I got there, my mom gave me a hug to rival Burn's grip and Jamie joined in. Then not only Jamie, but Christina and then my friends and it was pretty much a lovefest on the lawn of Meadows High.

And then Caroline, being Caroline, made it clear that her family was ready to go home. She had even managed a police escort, which I thought was amazing, until I realized that the police had their own questions for me, and a bunch of detectives followed us back and stayed the afternoon and interrogated me, making me go through my day, minute by minute (which is pretty much the reason that I remember things so completely, even after all these months, so thank you Officer Kenyon and the rest of your posse and all of the guys in the FBI, even though tell you the truth, you were pains in the asses that afternoon and I always got the feeling that you didn't totally trust me).

And then they made a superbig deal the next day in the

papers, calling me the "Hugging Hero" and a "Class Act" and other names like that. The *Times* ran a long story, detailing the lives of everyone involved and talking about the circumstances that led to Burn's public breakdown. There was a shorter article about me, with pictures of my family (where did they get those?), and somehow Jacob got his business into the mix and managed to get mentioned in many of the articles about the siege even though he had nothing whatsoever to do with it. Leave it to Jacob. Way to go, Dad, mooching off your son's celebrity.

And hundreds of newspapers throughout the country ran pictures of me and Burn and Meadows and anyone they could get and the headline was virtually always the same:

CRASH AND BURN

Except for the *Post*. The *Post* ran the headline "Hug of Life," with an exclusive photograph of me and Burn intertwined in the faculty lounge. I didn't remember anyone being there when it happened who could have taken that picture. Maybe it was Connelly for all I knew.

Speaking of Connelly, I received a big-deal gift basket the next morning from him and his family, with a new PlayStation 3 and all kinds of video games and a new camera. It must have cost a thousand bucks. With a card that said, "Thanks for saving us all."

With that and his story about Roxanne, I started thinking, maybe I shouldn't have been so hard on him. Naaah, he sucks.

There were other articles, a few about the guns and an investigation into how a teen had access to assault weapons. Then the inevitable comparisons to shootings in other schools. Then more on David's past, complete with pictures of Aunt Peesmell's

Victorian, looking like a haunted house, which it may have been by now. Pictures of Roxanne and David as kids, then Roxanne in full goth gear (that must have been taken off the porn site).

There were pictures of our class, the Class of 2008. There were pictures of the school and the devices that were planted throughout the campus. The police eventually confirmed that there were enough explosives to completely demolish the school if they had been detonated. No question that the auditorium and the gymnasium would have been blown away. So to anyone wondering if Burn could have really killed us, no question, he had the means, between the explosives and the assault weapons, and as a reminder, he was, in case you weren't clear about this, totally and completely gone. Did I mention that?

And there were other gifts and thank-you cards sent to me, which my mom said I would have to respond to. (Didn't she know who I was? And who writes a thank-you card for a thank-you card anyways?)

As for Meadows, it closed down for a week while the investigation continued, and after that, when school opened and I got there the first morning, there was a banner up in the lobby, by the front entrance, that read:

WE LOVE YOU, CRASH!!!!

And the mayor or whatever he said his title was, the runner of our town, had me down to town hall, where a picture was taken of the two of us, with him handing me a commemorative plaque.

And of course Jacob got involved, no surprise there. He said that I was a hot commodity at the moment and I needed to have representation. So next thing I know, I'm in the city, meeting with all these adults and being told how to dress and what to wear. And then there's Sally something or other, an agent from William Morris, and she's going to get me on television. And meanwhile I'm being interviewed one by one for the cover pages of national magazines.

And they size me and fit me in new clothes and wake me up in the middle of the night to get to a studio in time for the morning news so that they can interview me. And mostly the interviews were short, because Sally knew exactly how to run a client like a business. So more than news, it was a goodwill tour.

And almost every interviewer shook my hand, asked me the same five questions, and called me courageous. They always ended with the question, "Can you tell us what Mr. Burnett whispered to you?"

And I always ended with my answer: "That's between me and Mr. Burnett."

And Sally was out-of-her-mind pleased with my performance, especially the fact that I withheld information. This was gold to her. So she contacted the publishing companies and promised them a book written by me, a book in which I reveal the truth about what Burn told me the day of the siege.

Now, in spite of the constant search by authorities, not much had been disclosed about Burn's intent in taking the school hostage. The police went through his room, his house, his car, his computers, everything that he had ever touched, and basically came up with nothing. There was a list, and my name and Christina's name and Jamie's name, and a bunch of others were on it, but it made no sense, so they didn't tell us anything more.

Apparently, there were no other notes, no secret files, nothing to indicate what the reason was.

Which made sense to me and only confirmed what I already understood.

And because of this, the publishing companies were in a

frenzy, all wanting to know what the secret was. So with a little help from my agent, Sally, they start bidding against each other for the rights to my story.

And then, when the bidding is over, Sally calls to tell me the final dollar amount of my advance, and I hang up feeling like I just hit a home run in the bottom of the ninth, last game of the World Series, all over again.

I was not only a hero. I was now a rich-kid hero.

And a few weeks later, I'm sitting in my lawyer's office while my lawyer and my agent are giving me the drill.

And that's pretty much where the story begins, doesn't it?

THE LAST DAYS OF SUMMER

There was a party last night at Kelly's to celebrate the last days of summer. Kids are leaving for colleges tomorrow.

I go next week.

I finished the last chapters of the book just in time to be able to celebrate with the group. It took a lot out of me. If you're reading this, you'll probably understand why. Hopefully all of the stuff, past and present, ends up in there. If so, here's another secret:

The final chapters were written on the deck of Christina's uncle's house in Woodstock, overlooking the most incredible mountain you've ever seen, where the trees look like aging woodsmen and the bats fly right at your face the second it gets dark.

I snuck up there, knew where the key was, and unraveled my last nuggs of Jacob's Gold. So when you read the final chapters, just know, every word was brought to you with the help of good old-fashioned marijuana. Nothing cures ADD quite like a deep, big hit or two, no matter what the research says.

OK, I know it was illegal (not just the weed, but the house-sitting), and I could have gotten into mad trouble if anyone had caught me. But, tell you the truth, I'm pretty sure that I would have been able to talk my way out of anything. Besides, I can still count on my reputation as a hero.

Plus I promised myself that I would give them credit in the book. So here's to you, Mr. and Mrs. Christina's uncle. Thanks for your house. I couldn't have written it anywhere else.

* * *

Which brings me back to Kelly's party.

After a week of solid partying with my boys, me celebrating sending out the final chapters and getting smashed night after night after night, we all knew that Kelly's would be our last time together as a group.

And so all week long, I looked forward to the event. And all week long, no matter how fucked up I got, I snuck into Jamie's room, just to make sure that she was there, just to make sure that she was sleeping.

And she seems to be doing fine.

So was I.

Except I missed Christina and I missed Claudia, and I wanted to see them each once more before school started.

So last night, at Kelly's, I finally got my opportunity to see Christina. She showed up fashionably late, and she was with that guy Ruiz that Bosco introduced to the Club back in June.

She had her arm around him, making it clear there was no room there for me. But summer was coming to an end, and I had to talk to her.

So I asked if it would be OK to talk for a few minutes. And to my surprise, she said OK.

And I told her that I was sorry for not being who she thought I was.

And she said, "Actually, you were. It was all for the best, Steven. I couldn't get to college still a virgin, and it had to be done, so you were as good as any." She smiled as she walked away, turned and said, "But, sadly, you are not nearly as good as he is," pointing to Ruiz.

I shook my head, having, in a way, predicted that the two of them would hook up. I had to ask myself, where was the love? I wanted to stay with her for a while, to talk to her some more and to tell her that I still wanted her in my life, all of those things and more. But I couldn't. Shame on me.

To be perfectly honest, my heart broke for just a minute when she left. Of course my boys saved me with a fresh redcup filled with jungle juice and a perfectly rolled blunt, our last together as a Crew.

And so we got drunk and superhigh and we laughed and told stories, and some of us cried a little, I will admit this, and we partied until the sun showed up and then we scattered.

So thank you, Kelly, for always being a perfect hostess, and thank you Kelly's parents, for always being in Europe or some other country.

And school on Monday. College.

Which should get me pretty excited, as in new opportunities and all.

But the inevitable truth is that I know that I am leaving my home, where people consider me a hero, to go to a place where I will be just another kid with another story to tell, among thousands of kids who have been told that they are special with their own stories to tell.

So just being Crash probably isn't going to cut it there (well, maybe a little, as in some of the girls may have noticed me from TV or YouTube or seen my Facebook page and want to hook up with someone who was famous for a little while).

So yeah, I'm not gonna lie, I'm just a little scared. I'm sure that Felicia would tell me, so is everyone else. But then again, most of them will be able to listen in class and take notes that make sense and answer questions with the right answers, while mostly I have my rep, which may have worked in high school with teachers who heard from the guidance counselor who heard from the unstoppable Caroline Prescott that they were somehow required to give me special treatment.

And they did, as in give me the benefit of the doubt. Some

of them did because they loved Lindsey and knew I wasn't her, and felt sorry for me. And some of the others did because, well, probably because it was just easier, and they just wanted to get through their days without any hassles.

And then there were a few along the way who did because I could make them laugh, I could use whatever magic I had to make them break their adulthood for a minute or two. And when that happened, I could see a glint return to their eyes as they remember, just for an instant, what it was like for them when they were kids struggling against their own demons in high school.

So good luck to me.

And good luck to you if you're reading this and struggling with your own demons.

And good luck to you, David Burnett. Hopefully you will be OK one day. I can't hate you anymore. Your sister wouldn't want me to.

And every night before I go to sleep, I think of you, Roxanne Burnett, and just like your note said, I will remember you and everything about you, now and forever: every single laugh, every single kiss, every single nasty version of my last name, and every incredible moment of the short time we spent together. What you taught me saved my life and your brother's life and about a thousand other people. So even though I never got a chance to tell you how much you changed my life and to thank you for what you gave me, I know that you know. I guess that's good enough for now. And even though you aren't here to see it, this book is dedicated to you.

And every night, I say a prayer that you will find peace wherever you are.

Well, almost every night. But maybe not tonight; because tonight I'm headed back to Bedford. Claudia says she's ready to see me again, and her parents are out of town.

   Yeah, baby.

Love,

Steven Crashinsky

Crash, to you.

ACKNOWLEDGMENTS

The single thing that separates a "writer" from a lunatic who sits in his room creating a fantasy world is the confirmation of a professional that the world that he created can actually be inspiring to others.

Kirby Kim of William Morris Endeavor is a consummate professional who assured me that I was both a writer and a lunatic after reading *Crash and Burn* for the first time. How could you not love a guy like that? Kirby is my personal Joe Namath, a guy who guaranteed that he would find the perfect home for my book and then managed to very confidently make good on his promise. Thank you, Kirby. And thank you also, Ian Dalrymple, for your hard work.

Which brings me to Jordan Brown and his team at Balzer + Bray. Since I threw around a football analogy in the previous paragraph, Jordan has been my personal Lombardi. When Jordan got involved with *Crash and Burn*, I, frankly, had no idea what exactly an editor did. All I knew was that Jordan shared my vision for the book. I figured that he would cross out a few words and take out some italics. What I did not know was that he was going to send me to training camp and challenge me on every level to make every single word in Crash's world as authentic as possible. So never mind the opening paragraph, the single thing that separates a "writer" from a lunatic who sits in his room spinning a fantasy world is a really incredible editor. Thank you, Jordan.

Of course, none of these guys would have had a chance to read it and improve upon the original vision if not for the constant efforts of my brother, Rich Hassan. Thank you, Richie—sorry I ate your Scooter Pies and blamed it on the dog.

Also, this book could simply not have been written without the constant contributions made by the members of RPC: Matthew Noonan, Justin Schwartz, Peter D'Amato, Karl Quinn, Mike Mueller, Dylan Lonergen, Billy Sather, RJ Kueppers, Phil Cohen, Nigel Gordon, Alex Binder, and Sam Meyer. They are and remain the heart of the Club Crew.

There are a few others who need to be mentioned, including Lee Weiss, Bill Dowling, Kristin Rosenblum, Darren Klein, Jordan Kannon, Zach Blei, Stephanie Sugin, Jackie Magee, Jamie Shankman, Alana and Derek Hassan, Nikki Pressman, Linda Pressman, Howard Elman, Linda Cosmero, Melanie Canter, Emma Wiseman, Karen and Joel Solomon, Hazel and Aaron Baer, and Morris Missry, my attorney and superlawyer, who once told me that I had to do something to commemorate the passing of my father. In fairness, he may have been thinking of a plaque or a contribution to a nonprofit group or something along those lines. In retrospect, that might have been easier.

Also, so that no one thinks I'm an ungrateful son who forgot to put his mother's name in the book, thank you again, Lena Hassan. You are the greatest mom, and if this comes out on Mother's Day, all the better; consider this your present.

In the beginning and at the end, there would not have been a story without Adam Hassan, who inspired Crash in the first place and who dared me to write a book that a kid with ADD could actually read, and Valerie Hassan, my first critic and second favorite editor, who stayed up late, night after night, rereading chapters with her red pen and asking all the right questions before sending me back to my room.

And finally, there's Bonnie Hassan, without whom I probably would never have left the room at all. Thank you, Bonnie—you made this possible.

And thank you, Roxanne, wherever you are.